THE DREAM THIEF

'Children being *hurt*, sir. A little girl who won't wake up, children going missing, sir . . . Don't mistake me, the police would be perfectly happy to beat you to a pulp and throw your body into the river if they ever even thought you were protecting someone who *hurts children*, Mr Majestic, sir. Do you have any children, sir?'

The ringmaster gave a cry. He raised his head to the sky and his hands to his face, and his whole body seemed to wrench and shiver with an uncontrollable rage. Yet Lyle couldn't help but notice, as Mr Majestic swung the long dark end of his cane with all his strength into the side of Lyle's head, that even as his body twisted in fury, all that came from his lips was a little child-like giggle.

Even if nothing else was real, the cane felt solid enough where it smacked into Lyle's skull. And as his mother always said – you know you're onto something if they're trying to kill you.

The thought gave him little comfort, as the sky turned topsy-turvy, clowning with the earth, and then went out entirely.

By Catherine Webb

Mirror Dreams
Mirror Wakes

Waywalkers
Timekeepers

The Extraordinary and Unusual Adventures
of Horatio Lyle

The Obsidian Dagger:
Being the Further Extraordinary Adventures of Horatio Lyle

The Doomsday Machine:
Another Astounding Adventure of Horatio Lyle

The Dream Thief:
An Extraordinary Horatio Lyle Mystery

The Dream Thief

An
EXTRAORDINARY HORATIO LYLE MYSTERY

Catherine Webb

www.atombooks.co.uk

ATOM

First published in Great Britain in 2010 by Atom

A CIP catalogue record for this book
is available from the British Library.

ISBN 978-1-905654-25-3

Typeset in Fournier by M Rules
Printed and bound in Great Britain by
Clays Ltd, St Ives plc

Papers used by Atom are natural, renewable and
recyclable products sourced from well-managed forests and certified
in accordance with the rules of the Forest Stewardship Council.

Mixed Sources
Product group from well-managed
forests and other controlled sources
www.fsc.org Cert no. SGS-COC-004081
© 1996 Forest Stewardship Council

FSC

Atom
An imprint of
Little, Brown Book Group
100 Victoria Embankment
London EC4Y 0DY

An Hachette UK Company
www.hachette.co.uk

www.atombooks.co.uk

ABOUT THE AUTHOR

Catherine Webb is one of the most talented and exciting young writers in the UK. She published her extraordinary debut, *Mirror Dreams*, at the age of 14, garnering comparisons with Terry Pratchett and Philip Pullman. Subsequent books have brought Carnegie Medal longlistings, a *Guardian* Children's Book of the Week, a BBC television appearance and praise from the *Sunday Times* and the *Sunday Telegraph*, amongst many others. Catherine lives in London without a cat but plans to remedy that, soon.

CHAPTER 1

Stories

Let me tell you a story:

Once upon a time . . .

(All the best stories begin like this.)

. . . there was a princess locked in a tower by an evil witch until, one day, the handsome prince came to save her and called out, 'Fairest one, I shall pluck you down from these harsh stones!' or words to that effect. And while being saved from a witch's tower may not have been a sound basis for a prudent relationship, the princess concluded that the chances of her encountering a man of appropriate class, chivalry and, most importantly, dragon-proof armour were probably remote, and so she was plucked off her feet and whisked away to live happily ever after.

And once upon a time there was an evil dragon . . .

. . . that was slain . . .

. . . and an evil wizard . . .

. . . who drowned in his own bubbling cauldron . . .

. . . and a monster of a thousand, thousand teeth that reared its ugly head from the sea to devour the ships that passed above, as the green lightning fell and the waves crashed, and it was mighty and eternal . . .

. . . and was eventually killed . . .

. . . and all things concluded, everyone who had ever been wronged by the darkness that waits just outside the bedroom window. . .

. . . lived happily ever after.

Once upon a time.

That was then.

This is now.

Run, Sissy Smith!

Hadn't meant to see hadn't meant to hadn't meant to maybe just a peek, just a peek, just to see, hadn't meant to see what she had seen, hadn't meant, hadn't meant, please, she hadn't meant nothin'! Wouldn't tell no one, promise, honest, wouldn't tell no one please please please . . .

. . . too late . . .

. . . now run!

Once upon a time there was a marsh by a river with not much to recommend it except that it was there and so were they and

2

because no one in the vicinity was actively trying to kill them at the time. Then it became a village, made of wood and spit and a good deal of optimism; then a town that burnt down as quickly as it could be built; then what at the time passed for a city. And with the city came the cathedral and the palace and the stone walls with the gates closed against the night, and watchmen and fire buckets and bridges and the occasional cobbled road. Among the inhabitants grew a general attitude: 'What do you mean . . . *elsewhere?*' and things were generally good and happy (apart from the odd tedious outbreak of plague and rioting) and the people who lived there concluded that, really, they were onto a very good thing after all and it was only ignorance that meant the rest of the country couldn't see it. And they called their city London for reasons known only to a select handful of dead scholars, and it thrived and prospered and felt fairly pleased with itself.

And as prosperity does, it brought its friends to the party, and within a relatively short time the city of London found itself heaving under the weight of coppers, mudlarks, costermongers, lawyers, snipes, beggars, thieves, physicians, surgeons, tramps, sailors, tinkers, tailors, colliers, farriers, sweepers, blacksmiths, seamstresses, hat-makers, glove-makers, rope-makers, sail-makers, mill workers, organ-grinders, tattlers, rattlers, tracters, priests, vicars, wardens, dustmen, postmen, politicians, printers, writers, painters, actors, carpenters, bricklayers, masons, rabbis, Moors from the south, Hindoos from the east, vagrants, penny-a-day labour, cheap-johns, missionaries, secretaries, clerks, officers, soldiers, jugglers, acrobats, fire-eaters, match girls, flower-makers, flower sellers, rat-catchers, bird tamers, snake sellers, and . . . so on.

So that pretty soon the inhabitants of London were hammering on the doors of their local parish council and demanding to know just *why* the price of plum pudding had risen so high, and just why the queues to the union ward stretched round the corner of the building, and *who* had decided to put the privy house by the water pump, and why the police had beaten the strikers who had smashed the machines that had taken their jobs and, for goodness sake, where *was* Blackwall anyway and why were they supposed to live there when they'd lived eight to a room in Holborn since Grandpa's time?

And it all could have ended in another Peterloo, or with more of that damn Chartist nonsense, until some bright spark, watching the smoke rise from the chimneys of London and the once-white stones turn black with the stain of coal, raised his hand and pronounced the one magic word: progress.

Somehow, that made it all a little bit better.

Once upon a time . . .

He said, 'Once upon a time . . .'

She replied, 'Borin'!'

'Once upon a time . . .'

'Borin'!'

'Listen! Once upon a time, a long time ago, there lived a young man who didn't know his destiny . . .'

'*Urgh*,' sighed the girl. Candlelight flickered at the force of her disdain, spilling yellow shadows up the four wide walls of the untidy bedroom. 'Borin' borin' borin'! I bet as how this young man what you're talkin' 'bout goes an' finds his destiny an' he's got a magic sword an' there's this wizard what tells him what he's gotta go an' do, an' it's all *nice*, an' it ends all happy ever after an' – *borin'*.'

'Not at all! It's a . . . it's a . . .' There's a fluttering of pages, a pursing of lips. A silence. 'All right,' said the man at last. 'So there are certain salient literary traits you might have put your finger on here.'

'See! Borin'!'

'Well, what do you want me to read? This was your idea!'

The girl thought about it. 'Penny dreadful?' she asked at last.

'I am *not*—'

'Pirate story!'

'I hardly think it's approp—'

'Ohohohohoh, one of them stories 'bout them Americans in the big boots what shoot people! Then you can do the silly voice what makes you sound like there's a poker shoved up your nos—'

'No! Miss Chaste says that all children's reading material must have a moral and educational—'

'*Borin'*!'

The man sitting on the edge of the girl's bed gave its occupant a long, hard look. 'Tess,' he said at last, like a man grappling with a difficult and tiring problem. '*Tess* . . .'

'Yes, Mister Lyle?' Sugar-coated caramel couldn't have been sweeter than the angelic expression on the girl's face.

'Tess, remind me why I look after you?'

'Who said it were you what did the lookin' after, Mister Lyle?'

By the rules of the storyteller, the sentiment would be . . .

Meanwhile . . .

She thought perhaps she'd managed to lose them, down by

Tyburn, where the new white stones of Marble Arch were already turning grey from the chimneys all around. Respectable gentlemen on the way to their respectable homes mingled here with street traders hoping to make a few pennies on their pies, stockings and steaming mugs of rum. In between darted the busy travellers hurrying south to Victoria Station and thieves from the eastern darknesses of St Giles and Soho to see that, while the travellers might make it to their train, their purses never did. The crowds made it easier; no one was going to notice a girl with bleeding feet stained black with mud – no one wanted to see. So she staggered and crawled towards the east, her knees stained with dust and soot, while her head pounded and the blood in her veins turned to slow burning sludge.

Poison.

She only knew the name of one poison – arsenic – and only then because of the rats. Knowing didn't make anything better, not without knowing a cure as well.

Marble Arch met with the dignified terraces of Mayfair; then Mayfair's grand houses collided with Soho, whose busy, blackened streets melted into crooked walls and ruinous houses. Roads lost all meaning. She ran through basements knee-thick in mud and floating red slime, crawled up a flight of stairs containing two planks to each gaping void, scuttled for a few yards down a half-cobbled, wretched space that might once have been wide enough for carts, tumbled through an open doorway and across a floor where eight people slept in the space for two, crawled out of the broken wall on the other side to a square where the black iron pump had long since lost its handle and old grey shirts dripped muddy brown stains onto the churned-up ground. She should have lost them here – of all places – not even the coppers entered the rookeries without a guide, and every thief paid another a shilling for protection. She should have lost them! A ladder onto a balcony that skirted unevenly into the heaving guts of an old brewery, where ladies with empty eyes slumbered in corners held up with rope and hope, and not much of either. Down a rotting plank, scaring off the one-legged pigeon hobbling at its end, past the brewery stinking of hot yeast, down the long wall of the stained black church with its broken tombstones, under the twisted metal bridge that used to lead to the textile factory, before the supports began to snow orange rust into the street. Hot steam crawled and wormed its angry way out from between the shuttered windows of the mill, smoke twisted into the air and, from somewhere not so far off, the thud of fat new pistons mixed with the solemn tread of the costermonger's thin donkey on its way home for the night.

Anyone else would have given up by now. Just another child lost in the streets; who'd believe her anyway? But she knew – Sissy Smith *knew* – that, after what she'd seen, they weren't going to stop.

And if this were a fairytale, the word would be ...

Elsewhere ...

The woman wore a white apron, and a white hat so crisp and bright, the air seemed to move out of its way when she turned her head. Her voice, when she spoke, wanted to be firm, commanding, authoritative, but sounded like a nag, just two dribbles short of a whine.

She said, '*Another* one?'

7

'I were hungry.'

He is a child in an adult's grey coat. He is chewing the sleeve. That's all that really matters, for now.

She says, 'Yes, but that's two in—'

'I were hungry. I get hungry.'

'Well – very well. I suppose there's still space on the ward. What about this girl? You're sure she saw?'

'She ran.'

'Can you . . .?'

'She's scared. Not proper scared – not fun scared. She's so scared it makes her feel sick. She'll sleep, an' then she won't be scared no more.'

And for just a moment, the woman looks at this child in a grey coat, and she is disgusted.

Turn a page.

Look down.

Deeper.

A picture of a house in Blackfriars.

Identical to hundreds of houses in dozens of terraces thrown up in so many streets and fields across and around London. Its bricks had, once upon a time, been pale yellowish, but it had only taken a few months for the furry black soot from the city's smoke and fog to turn the walls dark grey. The front door and area railings were painted black to disguise how thick the dirt lay upon them; the sash windows were grimy, though the chimneys were clean; the front steps had never been swept.

Look deeper.

This house doesn't belong. Among the other tall, narrow

buildings on a street making its crooked way down towards the river, this house was an interloper, being scarcely older than the man who lived here, and all in all it looked . . .

. . . not quite One of Us, but certainly not One of Them.

Just like its owner.

Deeper. See it yet?

Fresh stucco lay over much of the walls, disguising, somewhere beneath, pockets of wire thick as a man's wrist, running from top to bottom, along with iron pipes that only occasionally carried water. The new indoor privy, a thing of technological wonder, sat in a cupboard that should have been twice the size, the remaining space being taken up by a tangle of cables, pipes and pistons that hummed and sang when the wind was high. If the drawing room had once possessed a floor, it was now visible only as thin patches of stained carpet under a mountainous growth of stacked-up books; if the kitchen was intended for cooking, any chef had to be careful to choose the mustard and not the sulphur which sat coyly nearby in the same lopsided cupboard. The basement, where servants should have slept according to the expectations of society, contained tables of twisted glass hiccups, of strange stands, bottles and boxes, labelled sometimes in a careful crooked hand as 'DANJERUS', or by a scrawled grinning skull and crossbones with a fake moustache and a pirate's hat. In the loft, where more servants should have slumbered in little cots between the hours of 11 p.m. and 6 a.m., were the remnants of old, forgotten projects whose combined, if entirely incidental, firepower would almost certainly be enough to blast a hole in the Great Wall of China.

It was a house big enough for a well-ordered family of four

and their servants, or – almost – an overcrowded family of eight, with theirs.

That was what it should have been.

However, truth be told, it was absolutely and entirely too small for its current inhabitants, their experiments, their bickering and their dog. The dog in question, as much a mismatch of accidental things as his owner, was now sitting, chin resting on his paws, ears trailing out like maypole ribbons on either side of his long head, watching the nightly debate between his two pet humans.

One said, 'I am *not*—'

One said, 'Please please please please please pretty please?'

'Polite young lady-persons—'

'Oh, but please pleasepleasepleaseplease . . .'

The first human to have spoken raised his hands in despair and exclaimed, 'Discipline! Duty! Patriarchal . . . things!'

There was a pause while both parties to this debate considered their own potent and powerful arguments. The second human, roughly half the first human's height and a third his age, looked up through a tangle of what a romantic would have called thick black curls, and what the man perched on the end of the bed called, 'that disreputable mess' and said, very carefully and thoughtfully, 'What's a patri-ack?'

'A patriarch,' proclaimed the man, wagging a finger the effect of which seemed so profound that his whole body quivered with the indignation of it, 'is the master of his own house! He is the fath— the dominant force within the domestic situation, the chief male, the leader, spiritual guide, moral centre, the . . . the . . . Look, he is *not* the kind of man who goes all the way downstairs to re-kindle a stove to boil a kettle to make a young lady perfectly capable of doing all this herself a cup of hot milk for bedtime!'

The girl, whose name was, according to the parish register, Teresa Hatch, considered this for a very long while. Then she said, 'An' what's he gotta do with us, Mister Lyle?'

Mister Lyle seemed to sag. 'You know,' he sighed, 'I have no idea.'

Poison poison poison poison poison oh god oh god oh god don't wanna don't wanna not poison please please not poison not poison slow too slow too young too young ain't seen nothin' didn't mean nothin' oh please not not not so scared don't wanna don't wanna don't wanna please . . .

Do you understand what's happening here, Sissy Smith?

Probably not. Probably not the part that's thinking about it with every gabbled terrified thought that scuttles across the mind's ear. Doesn't understand, and that's what makes it so frightening. Say sorry to God – pick a god, any god – just be sure to say sorry, and hope that a vicar finds the body and sees it gets a proper burial, a trip on the train to the necropolis in the north, a decent seat in the carriage with all the pauper corpses heading for a ditch where a man in robes will say sorry for you, just in case it slipped your mind. It would make sense, if you'd other things occupying you at the time.

Sissy Smith?

Are you listening?

Say sorry before it's too late . . .

. . . or keep on running . . .

. . . it's entirely up to you.

A street. As London streets go, a quiet street, in that there are only a few dozen beggars, tracters and painted ladies loitering in the gloomy puddles of darkness between the sloshes of yellow-green gaslight.

A door. A very boring door, painted black to disguise the dirt.

A door knocker. Also very boring, hammered in by someone who understood the practical applications, but couldn't be bothered to consider any further than that.

The knocker isn't quite the right height for a child to reach it.

Besides, who was to know when the world is going black? Think of it as nothing more than an extended, deep sleep without the need for a privy on a cold winter night.

. . . knock knock . . .

. . . can't reach . . .

Good night, Sissy Smith. Sweet dreams.

Horatio Lyle – scientist, inventor, special constable, and, through no fault of his own, unofficial guardian and protector of the unknown orphan by the name of Teresa Hatch, marched up a flight of cold grey stairs.

His hair was sandy-red, as if it couldn't quite decide on one colour or the other, his eyes a grey that shifted to the edges of green or blue depending on the time of year; and his accent, when he spoke, instantly placed him as being – Not One of Us. Close – but Not One of Us, regardless of whoever 'We' happened to be.

His clothes were, in principle, fine, being as they were neither eaten by rats nor blurry with fleas, but neglected chemical stains had turned the once-white of his cuffs to an off-beige smudge, that matched the discolorations across his fingers and nails. In his right hand, he was carrying a metal beaker. In the metal beaker, swishing happily to itself, was half a pint of hot milk. As he walked up the stairs, Lyle muttered to himself. 'Bloody patriarch bloody discipline head of the bloody house . . .'

As he passed through the hallway and towards the next upward flight of stairs, he half imagined he heard a sound from the front door and, glancing towards it, hesitated. But it didn't come again, and there were a hundred reasons, only some of them malign, to explain a little bump in the night. As he climbed the stairs, the dog – a creature only called a dog because no other species would claim him for their own – waddled past him downstairs. The dog's name was Tate, and, like most things in his life, Lyle could never quite work out how he'd come to be such a feature of his home, or how, with four paws and a long belly, Tate had learnt to swagger.

At the top of the stairs, Lyle nudged open a bedroom door with the end of his toe and pronounced, 'This is the *last* bloody time that I bloody get you a bloody—'

Downstairs, there was the sound of barking. The scowl on Lyle's face, which had already been trying to eat the corners of his ears, deepened. On the end of her bed, large enough to sleep ten of her and still have room to kick, Teresa Hatch did her best to look angelic. The resulting wideness of her eyes and puffiness of her cheeks resembled a suffocating hamster more than a human child. But Lyle told himself it was good that she was trying, and his scowl began to fade.

'Next time . . .' he began, slightly more meekly.

Downstairs, Tate's barking grew more urgent.

'. . . you can . . .'

Tess took the beaker from Lyle's hands.

'. . . fetch your *own* . . .'

How a dog with such little room for lung and less room for brain could produce so much sound, Lyle resolved to one day know, even – possibly especially – if it involved scalpels.

'. . . your *own* bloody mil— What the hell is the matter with the dog?'

Tess shrugged, unwilling to answer in case, by doing so, Lyle noticed her existence and returned to his previous anti-hot-milk theme. Lyle stalked to the door, pushed it open and stared down the stairs into the hall. Tate was sitting, nose two inches from the front door, tail straight out behind him, barking. As Lyle started down the stairs, Tate stopped for a moment and half turned. A pair of huge brown eyes that seemed to droop at their lowest corners gave Lyle a look that made it clear just how tiresome it was having to wait for humans and their little brains. But for a few unkind twists of nature, proclaimed Tate's face, *I'd* be taking *you* for a twice daily walk and don't you forget it.

Lyle hesitated at the bottom of the stairs. To make his point, Tate turned back to the door and started barking again, then paused to scratch one great long ear while his master edged closer, then barked a little bit more.

Lyle said, 'Don't you start either.'

Tate snuffled indignantly, and, as it came within reach, started to chew on Lyle's left trouser leg.

'Thank you, oh faithful friend.' Lyle sighed.

And then, because . . . because it was a big house, and a dark night, and because Tate rarely barked and, well . . . if you believed that dogs had animal instinct then it made sense that humans had one too, and while it may not be able to rationalise a top-heavy fraction, it still managed to bang the rocks together, yes? . . . and Tate did so rarely bark, since it required too much effort on his part . . .

. . . Horatio Lyle opened his front door.

And that is how *really* it all began . . .

Once upon a time . . .

CHAPTER 2

Thomas

Dawn crept through the alleys and lopsided streets of London with the sideways slide of a thing scared of being mugged. It rolled over the creaking ships of the eastern quays, through the warehouses of Wapping, tangled in the locomotives' steam at Liverpool Street, stretched the shadows of the early morning flower sellers shouting for business in Covent Garden. It crawled round the high, gaudy music halls of Leicester Square, and slithered through the broken bricks of St Giles'. The dirt-stained thin grass of Hyde Park shimmered at its touch, the flaps creaked across the scaffolding in Kensington, shrouding the imperious new buildings built by the Queen in memory of her dead husband until, eventually, the thin grey light of dawn slunk into the suburb of Hammersmith.

'Suburb' was a new word, and an unwelcome one. It was, the inhabitants of Hammersmith felt, a word that was entirely a result of the new railways. Their village, whose grand old country villas used to be surrounded with nothing but fields and the winding muddy banks of the Thames, now had to share space with *new* people. Busy people. Scuttling city people, who every day – and here was a new and disquieting word – *commuted* to their places of work and conducted . . . *business*. Crude, messy, paper-heavy, ink-stained, number-weighed *business*.

Of course, the more polite inhabitants of Hammersmith didn't complain. Not in public. But in the high-ceilinged rooms of mansions inhabited by such as the Elwick family, there was no doubt about it – times were changing. Too fast.

Lord Henry Edward Elwick (Order of the Meretricious Rose, Knight of the White Lily, and possessor of possibly the finest pair of whiskers in west London) had seen more of these changes than he liked to admit. Dammit, his father had died invading France with Wellington, and been buried with due honours. His own two sisters were long since married to appropriately ranked members of the Austro-Hungarian aristocracy, but it was damned lucky, *damned lucky*, that one of them hadn't lost everything in that whole dreadful 1848 business – which just proved his point. Rebellion! Rabble rousing! A loss of respect! That was the problem today and heaven help him if his son wasn't *enjoying* the fact, if his son wasn't aiming to study the very things that were causing all this trouble to begin with.

The thin grey sunlight stretched the mighty shadow of Lord Elwick across the breakfast table of his fine mansion in Hammersmith.

No one dared build on the land round Lord Elwick's mansion, but even that, even the esteemed name of Henry Edward Elwick – how long could it last?

The tall grand brass clock ticked down the hours. The sunlight stretched, taking a heavy fistful of time with it.

At the breakfast table, sat a woman with pale hair and washed-white skin, wearing a neatly starched, high-buttoned stiff dress. Opposite her sat a boy. He had pale eyes set in a pale face still young enough, perhaps, to be innocent, but heading already towards being the face of a man. The clothes he wore would suit him in time, but maybe not for thirty years.

He was reading a book.

Lord Elwick frowned, a pair of mighty grey eyebrows sagged over his wrinkled face like a bridge about to collapse.

It was a book about *science*.

Lord Elwick cleared his throat. This was a rare occurrence at the Elwick Family Breakfast. Even the four servants arrayed along the far wall stiffened in brief surprise.

He said, 'What are you reading, boy?'

Thomas Edward Elwick looked up from his book, the surprise barely hidden on his face. 'Um . . .' he mumbled, ears starting to flush bright red. Across the table, Lady Elwick's fine eyebrows almost collided with her scalp. The men in her life were talking – albeit, each word was like the agonised hatching of a chick from a particularly thick eggshell. Nevertheless, this was almost the beginning of a . . . *family conversation*.

18

'Your book, boy, your book!' flummoxed Lord Elwick.

'Uh . . . I've been reading a theoretical assessment of pressure dynamics and its possible application to chemical change in the absence of appropriately exothermically excitable sources.'

There was the sound of Lady Elwick's knife carefully smearing marmalade across a thick slice of toast.

The clock ticked.

The servants radiated immaculate disinterest. Below stairs would talk about this for weeks.

'Ah.' The word came from Lord Elwick's throat like a swallowed fly making an escape. 'And is that . . . interesting?'

'Very, sir! You see, the author suggests that we can only produce thermal reactions of so much intensity based on the chemical substances we have available, but with appropriate gearing we can exert almost any pressure you care to name upon a substance, and that with the application of pressure on a fixed volume, we can obtain extraordinary —'

'Does he really?' As he struggled to acknowledge the details of what his son was saying, Lord Elwick's face almost matched the colour of the tomatoes on his plate.

'Erm . . . yes,' replied Thomas. 'He does.'

Silence.

A servant refilled Lord Elwick's coffee cup. Another removed an ornate silver dish from which all the bacon had been consumed.

'So,' said Lord Elwick at last, 'is it . . . I mean, do you . . . I think what I wish to know is . . . is . . . is it actually of any damn use to man or does it have more . . . I mean more . . . you know . . .'

Thankfully no one ever found out what Lord Elwick wished to know. Cartiledge, the new butler, saved the Family Breakfast by his on-the-dot delivery of the morning post, laid out on a silver tray.

Lady Elwick let out a barely concealed sigh of relief.

Lord Elwick took the escape that the letters offered.

Thomas tried to think about calculus.

The door closed with an almost imperceptible click behind Cartiledge on his way out.

The clock kept on ticking.

The morning post – first of almost nine deliveries made daily to the doors of Hammersmith – was deposited, as usual, next to Lord Elwick for his scrutiny. Normally, and things were always strictly normal in the Elwick house, there were four letters. This morning there were five.

One of them was to Thomas.

It was the Note.

Lord Elwick had learnt to come to dread the Note. He could recognise it immediately by the big capital letters on the front, written by a hand that wanted so very much to become a messy scrawl but, by a conscious effort of will, had stopped itself on the edge of slurring. He could recognise it by the faint odour of chemicals, by the suspicious blotches on the edge of the paper, by the Blackfriars mark on the penny stamp. For a moment, the part of Lord Elwick that had always resented having to run for Parliament, instead of inheriting his seat as his predecessors had in the good old days, considered rebellion. Just for a morning, just this morning, he could *not* tell his son. Then he looked up, and saw . . .

. . . a pair of hopeful grey eyes, watching him. He knew what they were hoping for.

He said, whiskers trembling round his face, 'For you. That Lyle fella, by the look of it,' and without being able to look Thomas in the eye, passed his son the Note.

It was short and to the point.

Dear Thomas,

To tell a story in brief – I opened the door, a child fell through it, and Tess says she knows her. The child has been poisoned. Whatever you planned to do today, this is more important.

Best wishes,

Horatio Lyle

Below, another hand had added:

P.S. DIS IS TES MISTER LYLE IS DOIN HIS NUT COS DER IS DIS GIRL WAT I NOS AN IF SHE DIES HE WILL GO UP LIK A FIRWORK. SO SHIFT YUR BOTOM. TESS.

Lord Elwick, if he had read such a note, would probably have passed straight through scarlet fury and out the other side into snow-white convulsions. Thomas, however, was a younger man, from a newer time, and merely turned pink from the ends of his toes to the tips of his ears, folded the letter, and said, 'Father, may I be excused from the table?'

For a moment, his father considered saying no.

The moment passed, almost as quickly as Thomas left the room, the family mansion, Hammersmith, and everything else besides, behind him.

Approximately five hours before Thomas Edward Elwick ran out into the morning light to find a boatman to carry him up the river to see his friend, colleague and unofficial mentor, Horatio Lyle, the following conversation could be heard issuing from the halls of Lyle's house in Blackfriars:

'Bloody hell!'

'You went an' swore, Mister Lyle! You ain't 'posed to swear!'

'Tess get water now!'

'Wha's the matter? Oh. I see!'

'I opened the door and she just fell inside. She's unconscious. Pale skin, clammy, pupils don't change size when the light moves, bleeding feet, smell of ethyl . . . methyl . . . no, ethyl alcohol on her breath, sluggish pulse. I just opened my door and she just . . . Tess? What's the matter? Tess?'

'Mister Lyle?'

The voice of Teresa Hatch was faint and lonely in the gloom of the candlelight.

'Tess?'

'I knows her. I know that girl.'

'You do?'

'Her name's Sissy. She's called Sissy Smith.'

. . . and perhaps here, perhaps after all, is where it really all began . . .

Time flowed through Lyle's fingertips like water, running away too fast to count the drops.

He remembered carrying Sissy Smith upstairs.

He remembered writing a note to Thomas.

He remembered trying every remedy he knew, and then some he didn't, to try and rouse the girl. He even drew a sample of her blood, stared at it under the microscope in the naive hope that somewhere in it would be a big black sign saying 'Poison – come get me if you can'.

And at about 4 a.m., as the clocks began to strike their off-key, out-of-tune, out-of-time dirges across the city rooftops, he sent Tess to find a doctor for Sissy Smith, who wouldn't wake up.

His name was Risdon Barnaby, physician at the Evelina Hospital for Sick Children. He didn't usually approve of making house calls at early hours of the morning. He held that daily concentration was assisted by a smooth awakening, rather than by, for example, having a little girl break in through his prised-open bedroom window and start shouting, 'Oi, where's this quack bloke?' Such things were not conducive to vascular well-being.

The house to which he was dragged by the said girl, was owned by one Mister Lyle – very much a *Mister*, he felt, though he couldn't say exactly why. This Mister Lyle had put the patient in a bed on the second floor and clearly, in his own amateurish way, had attempted some sort of deductive reasoning with regard to the child's condition. Bottles, tubs of water, hot and cold, clean linen and soft towels had all been brought into the room and, at some part of the night, applied to the child in question, who lay like no more than white paper dragged over a few pencil bones, as close a picture of starving death as the doctor had ever seen. As she slept, her eyes,

sunk deep into her skull beneath her lowered eyelids, turned
constantly.

Mister Lyle, standing in the door said, 'Her name is Sissy
Smith.'

Behind him, the *other* child, the *reprobate* child who had so
impolitely summoned Dr Barnaby a few hours before dawn,
peeked round her master's side and said, 'She come from the
workhouse. I know her, see?'

Both Mister Lyle and the creature who, with a shudder of
familial distaste, Dr Barnaby could only assume to be his savage
daughter, looked tired, skin pale and eyes bruised, from their
night of watching the child called Sissy Smith. 'She come lookin'
for *me*,' added the girl, 'she come lookin' for *this* house, see, an'
I know her. You a good quack?'

For a moment, there was something in the girl's voice, older,
much, much older, than her little face and pouting lower lip suggested. Something that had grown old without bothering to ask
why.

Mister Lyle coughed, cleared his throat and said, 'I think the
girl – I think she's been poisoned. It's not really my field, but
when we found her she had an increased pulse, and she convulsed in the night. It looked like *actaea alba*, but her pupils were
small, and she's been asleep, unable to wake, for over ten hours,
which led me to think maybe *papaver somniferum* or a derivative . . . I need to talk to her, Doctor.'

Dr Barnaby scratched his long ginger-grey whiskers, and
said, 'Yes . . . well, *actaea alba* . . . yes . . .'

'We gave her milk,' added Lyle, 'in case it was arsenic, and we
managed to induce some vomiting.'

'You did what?!'

'To help remove whatever it was from her—'

'You made this *child*—'

'. . . so that the poison wouldn't . . .'

'Are you a qualified physician, Mister Lyle? Are you even a surgeon?'

Behind Lyle, Tess muttered something in a low voice, '. . . *blockhead*.'

Lyle smiled a knife-thin smile, and Dr Barnaby realised that the blade in question might spend its time cutting warm butter, but that didn't mean it couldn't slice through other things.

'Dr Barnaby,' said Lyle, laying a kindly hand on one arm and turning the doctor away from the glaring child by the door, 'I am not a physician, nor a surgeon. I do not believe, for example, that opium is necessarily the wisest choice of drug with which to calm a child; that amputation is the best solution to a nasty cut; nor that slicing a hole in a man's skull to relieve the pressure of humours on the brain will necessarily improve his ability to speak. You may at this point choose to say, "What do you know? All you can possibly have done is read a book," and I would say, yes, I have read books. Just like you, Dr Barnaby. And I am a great believer in the power of books to enlighten as well as entertain. So I must ask you again: what can you do for Sissy Smith that we have not already tried?'

Dr Barnaby looked at Mister Lyle and his strange . . . child, that resembled Lyle in no physical way except, perhaps, a certain shrewdness round the eyes. He said, 'The girl is in a catatonic slumber. I've seen such things before, occasionally, in the victims of the opium dens, but never in anyone so young. I see no symptoms of addiction to any narcotic substances, no aging of the skin around the nose or mouth, no discoloration of her veins; but it is hard to tell. She is underfed, and clearly came a long way to find you, Mister Lyle. And as you are candid with me, let me be candid with you. I do not think there is anything you, nor I, can do to relieve her condition.'

There was silence. Two – no, three onlookers, including a small dog at the door, with great sad brown eyes – stared at him. The child, hiding behind Lyle, looked as if she was going to explode in a jungle fury – whether from sadness or rage, he couldn't tell and didn't want to guess. The dog looked equally unimpressed. Lyle just looked down and thought for a long, clock-tock moment, then said, 'All right, Dr Barnaby, thank you for your time.'

He saw the doctor to the door and there, as he found was so often the way, Dr Barnaby did have one, final thought. He turned and, in a low voice not meant to be heard by dog or child, murmured to Lyle, 'There is a place . . . a kind place, where they tend to those who cannot tend for themselves. It is in Marylebone, a hospital. I do not think you can cure this child, Mister Lyle. I do not think you want to watch her die.'

Lyle just smiled and nodded, so distant that for a moment, Dr Barnaby wondered if he'd heard a word that had been spoken.

When Lyle returned upstairs, Tess was sitting by Sissy Smith in her thick-blanketed bed, watching the slumbering child. Lyle said, 'The physician's gone.'

Tess just grunted in reply. 'Quack.' In silence she ran a finger down the thin, yellow-white tangle of Sissy Smith's hair. 'She come 'ere, Mister Lyle,' she said at last. 'She come lookin' for me.'

Lyle sat down on the edge of the bed. 'How do you know her?'

'We was at the workhouse together. St Bartholomew's Workhouse, N. District, Farringdon,' she intoned, like an ancient mantra. 'Her mam popped it when she were born, an' my mam left me by the gate, so we was kept together, right? Sorta friends. There ain't no real friends in the workhouse, 'cos you ain't s'posed to talk, most of the time. But if there was friends, she was mine.'

'Did she leave the workhouse when you did? When you ran away?'

'Nah. She were scared.'

'Of leaving?'

' 'Course. We were in the house since we was born. You leave everythin' you ever known. You gotta be real smart or real scared to do that.'

'Which were you?' asked Lyle gently, perching beside Sissy's white-bandaged feet.

'Smart, 'course!' exclaimed Tess. 'I ain't never not been smart, Mister Lyle. But Sissy, she didn't wanna go. So I went anyway. Wanted to see what was outside, what made so much noise in the night. Sissy were scared of the sounds. There were a great fat steel mill up the street; she said it sounded like they were grinding up dead bones every day, every night. She said they'd get us. They'd bring us back, lock us up in the dark.'

'But she got out,' said Lyle. 'I mean, she came looking for you, didn't she?'

'Yep.' Tess sighed. 'I s'pose.'

There was silence, then Lyle said, 'Thomas should be here within the hour.'

Tess just shrugged.

'Even if we can't – I mean, there are still things we can do. There are questions we can ask.'

27

This time, Tess didn't even shrug.

'Teresa? Tess?' Lyle edged closer to her, uncertain, then reached out and touched her shoulder. 'Hey, lass? You all right?'

Tess seemed to sigh, her whole body curling in on itself and her eyes wandering down towards her hands. 'Yep,' she said, in a little, old tired voice. 'Ain't nothin' wrong with me, Mister Lyle.'

He smiled, turning her gently away from the bed. 'Let's have some breakfast? Then maybe we can see what can be done.'

She nodded and, without a word, walked away from the sleeping little shape of Sissy Smith.

CHAPTER 3

Workhouse

Thomas Edward Elwick was a bigwig.

It was a word he was getting used to with some difficulty. He'd never heard it before until Tess, in a moment of her usual . . . refreshing honesty, had exclaimed, 'You think the bigwig knows?' It had taken him a while to work out that 'bigwig' referred to him, and exhaustive researches before he'd concluded that 'bigwig' in Tess's own special vernacular, was a way of saying 'gentleman'.

And in that single moment of typical Tess-based revelation, the guilt had set in, and Thomas Edward Elwick had thought about all that money, all that great, ill-earned fortune spent on houses and hunting and drink and food and dresses and shoes and big hats and bigger hair, and for just a moment he'd begun to think, *What a waste*. All that history and wealth, spent on buying a really . . . *really* . . . big wig.

Approximately two and a half seconds later, he had decided what to do with his life. He was going to prove himself worthy of his wealth.

That said, he hadn't entirely anticipated that the vehicles for his worthiness, the people through whom his good deeds were to be done, would take the unlikely shape of an eccentric inventor with an interest in crime, an East End guttersnipe, and their pet dog. But, he decided, the unlikely and occasionally trying nature of his allies just made his worthiness all the more worthy.

So it was, that Thomas, beaming with righteousness and ready to Do What Had To Be Done, got out of a hansom cab in front of Lyle's house in Blackfriars, marched up the steps to the front door, hammered with the dirty knocker and unconsciously wiped his fingers on a clean white linen handkerchief from his trouser pocket. A few moments later, a loud barking announced that his arrival had been noticed and, a moment after that, the door opened. Horatio Lyle stood there with a frying pan full of sizzling bacon and a slightly bewildered expression. A hairy thing of white and brown, composed mostly of ear, waddled – Tate never ran – past Lyle's feet and started dribbling contentedly on Thomas's polished leather shoes. And at the end of the corridor. . .

. . . Thomas felt his ears turn pink . . .

. . . Tess said, 'Oi, breakfast!'

Lyle seemed to notice the frying pan in his hand for the first time. 'Oh, yes,' he muttered, and just managed to stop short of saying, 'How did that get there?' It could be hard, when most of your time was dedicated to thinking about the nature of mass in general and matter incidentally, to remember basic details like shoelaces and food. This, at least, was what Lyle told himself.

'Hello, bigwig!' Tess called out down the hallway.

Thomas carefully averted his eyes. Lyle, seeing this, frowned and said, 'You all right, lad?'

'Erm . . . yes.'

Lyle looked round him, up, down, and finally behind, and seeing no reason why Thomas's face should suddenly be turning into a baked pumpkin, said, 'Eat something dodgy?'

'No. It's just . . .'

Thomas flapped a hand in the direction of Tess. Lyle turned and carefully looked her up and down. Aware that their attention was on her, Tess looked herself over as well, tugging at her nightdress and finally proclaiming, 'If there's a hole in a silly place, then I don't wanna know.'

Realisation dawned in Lyle's eye as he looked back at Thomas. 'Don't tell me you've never seen a lady in a nightdress?'

Tess giggled.

'Well, it's not—'

'Hear that, bigwig?' asked Tess. 'I'm a *lady*. Now shift yourself, before breakfast goes an' gets cold.'

Thomas watched Tess eat.

It was always a sight that surprised him: not just the sheer quantity of food her little frame seemed capable of consuming and holding, but the speed and ferocity with which even the most boring of meals was consumed – and food, with Lyle, was never anything extraordinary. As a cook, he seemed to understand the

31

need for things to be eaten on a regular basis, and if they happened to be interesting, so much the better. Nonetheless, to Lyle any meal was just fuel, and the idea of eating for *pleasure*, when you could be, say, in a lab, just baffled him.

Only once had Thomas dared to ask Tess why she ate so . . .

'. . . so much, right? If Mister Lyle was to drop dead right *now*, see, or get possessessed by an evil faerie or shot by nasty bigwigs or all burnt up in a chemical flame or blown to squishy bits by a nasty big reaction or electrocuted, see, by electric voltage, then who do *you* know what would make me more grub?'

Thomas was obliged to concede that she had a point. He couldn't cook.

So Tess ate, and as she ate she waved a fork heavy with the next mouthful and proclaimed, 'Mmmhwwwnnh!' at Lyle as they all sat round the kitchen table.

'Well,' responded Lyle, 'it's like this.' He went on to describe his discovery of Sissy Smith, and her present mysterious state. 'So, all we know for certain is that she has been poisoned. Malnourished in the long term, and recently poisoned, most likely by an oral application. I smelt some sort of drink on her breath, something strong, maybe ethyl derived—'

'Mmmnhh!' exclaimed Tess, her mouth still full.

'Alcohol derived—' corrected Lyle.

'Mmmn!'

'Booze.' He went on without hesitating, 'And her symptoms suggest an opiate derivate with maybe a hint of an organic toxin somehow joined.'

Thomas raised a hand. 'Yes?' asked Lyle with the look of a man expecting the worst.

'Mister Lyle, what do you mean, "somehow joined"?'

Lyle looked shifty. 'Well, while naturally I enjoy organic chemistry as much as the next man, and indeed find it fascinating how nature can so readily mimic mathematics – or mathematics mimic nature, depending on your point of view – in the link between the theoretical and the practical—'

Tess swallowed enough of a mouthful of food to say, 'You don't know nothin' 'bout poisons.'

'That's not true!' blurted Lyle. 'I could poison the Prince of Wales and make it look like a bad oyster without breaking a sweat!'

Two pairs of disbelieving eyes locked on Lyle's face. He shifted in his seat, and reached uneasily for the comfort of the teapot. 'Can we please stick to the matter at hand? The fact that I don't currently know the nature of the organic compound which has, regrettably, reduced Sissy Smith to a state where she is barely able to drink, let alone talk, is an interesting fact in itself, since it implies a mind of superhuman scientific intelligence and extraordinary learning to have devised a concoction of which *I*, in my remarkably vast knowledge, am not aware.

'Added to this valuable information is the fact that Sissy Smith does not appear to have taken enough of the dosage to kill her, merely to render her currently incapacitated. Or it may be that the poison in question was never intended to kill, but merely to induce an altered state of consciousness. Either way, this information helps us.'

'Helps us do what?' asked Thomas.

'Find out who poisoned her, 'course.' Tess sighed. 'Cos I ain't goin' to do nothin' while some tuppenny parish prig hurts Sissy!'

'You mean, it's our Duty . . .?' began Thomas, brightening at the prospect.

'I mean that if you don't do right by the snipes what yor banged up with,' snapped Tess, 'then that's the end of the whatsit thing right there!'

'Social order?' hazarded Lyle.

'Like I said!'

'We could inform the police?' suggested Thomas.

'An' they'd just bang her back up in workhouse!' wailed Tess. 'Bloody bobbies!'

'*I'm* a bloody bobby,' pointed out Lyle mildly, 'on occasion. And since I do sometimes consult for Scotland Yard, let us assume that by telling me, you'll ensure that the police, in their roundabout way, will know. What's more, they will be thrilled to avoid spending their limited resources on this case when I can in fact be solving it for them. Besides, Tess has a point. Children go missing all the time from the city streets; you can pay to get rid of them. There's no reason they should care for Sissy Smith. And Tess does care. And for the sake of a peaceful life, that means I care too. Oh, yes' – he glanced at Thomas and managed not to smile, 'and it *is* very much our civic Duty.'

Thomas let out a sigh of relief. So long as that was established, he wasn't about to complain.

'Right!' exclaimed Lyle, clapping his hands together to proclaim both the conclusion of breakfast, and the hopeful expectation that afterwards he wouldn't be finding bits of fried egg in Tess's pocket. 'Tess, this workhouse where you were with Sissy Smith – where is it, exactly?'

Tess's face turned green, bacon dangling halfway to her lips. 'Oh nononono,' she said. 'Ain't nothin' as you can say or do what'll make me go back *there*.'

*

Time passed.

Tess sat in the back of a hansom cab, squashed between Thomas and Lyle, with Tate on her lap. Eyes fixed on the coffin-tight wall in front of her, she said, 'I *hate* you. Yor goin' to feel sooooo bad when this is all over.'

'What you mean,' intoned Lyle, 'is, "I hate you, Mister Lyle, sir. You are going to feel extremely put out when this affair is concluded." Decorum and grammar, Tess. Like a gentlewoman should. Unless you meant you hated Thomas?'

Tess glanced over at Thomas, who wisely studied the streets going by outside the glassless window. Her scowl deepened. 'Why we goin' to the workhouse anyway?' she wailed. 'We don't know as how Sissy might never have come from there!'

'Well,' said Lyle, drawing himself up in the manner of a man delivering a prepared speech, 'we could conclude that she had come from the workhouse by her clothes, which were a cheap-looking uniform grey, made from poor fabric, very much like most orphans are expected to wear in such places. Or, we could hypothesise from her poor diet yet recent haircut, from her bad teeth yet well-worked fingers, or maybe even from the hints of tar under her nails that this was a child used to regular work and regular living but for a very low reward indeed. Naturally, all this is speculation. But I think it's safer than saying she ran away from the circus, don't you?'

There was silence. It was a thick, volcanic seethe, in which Tess's lower lip sank ever deeper.

Lyle attempted to stretch, and found he had no room. 'Her feet are a mystery. Blisters and blood and mud – and something stranger than mud. There was *grass* between her toes, and thin

35

cuts from long grass up the sides of her legs – hardly common in this city.'

Thomas thought of the open fields of Hammersmith, but decided to say nothing in case he was accounted either a bigwig or a fool.

'The extent of recent bruising and blistering to the soles of her feet suggested she had come, without shoes, a reasonably long way to reach us, run the distance most likely, a remarkable feat considering the toxins inside her. She must have known that she had been poisoned, and the only safe place she could think to go was –' Lyle glanced sideways at Tess, and a little frown deepened between his eyes – 'to you, Teresa. How did she know where you were, I wonder?'

Tess shrugged. 'I used to run with some good area sneaks. Ain't nothin' what they couldn't know – an' all without bein' seen.'

'But you'd have seen them, wouldn't you, Teresa? Being, as you are, such an excellent professional.'

The scowl slightened on Tess's face. 'Well, yes . . .'

'So you can see,' Lyle said, his voice slipping into a kindlier tone, 'why we have to go back to the workhouse. Since even I can't just extrapolate a cure for whatever has poisoned Sissy without first seeing the poison, we need to find out what happened to her, and that's the place to start. She was looking for you, Teresa. It's not fair, and it's not nice, but that makes her *your* responsibility.'

'It does?'

'Yes.'

'Because . . . because of ethics and . . . and duty and—'

'Because you've got the means to make it right.'

To everyone's surprise, most of all his, it was Thomas who had spoken. Three pairs of eyes turned to look at him. Tate put his head on one side. Tess stared up at him as though trying to see if a pencil was lodged up his nose. And even Lyle, usually unflappable in the face of many nasty and frequently explosive things, looked startled. 'Er, yes,' Lyle managed to say at last. 'That's pretty much it.'

Even to Tess, it made a certain sense.

The St Bartholomew's Workhouse was in what the Metropolitan Police District had classified as N. Division. The 'N' made the wardens who maintained it feel especially good about their noble deeds. Not only was there the reward of Christian service and charitable works, but there was the extra benefit of feeling part of a system: ordered, efficient, authorised and generally a place where all the ink would be blotted at the bottom of the page. No one knew what the 'N' stood for, but that just added to its mystique.

The workhouse lurked by one of the railway lines that had entered the city, joining up with the new-fangled Underground line worming its way from King's Cross to Baker Street. Its brick walls, when new, had been yellowish-grey, but just a few years of looking down on the crooked rooftops and lop-sided chimney stacks of Clerkenwell, had served to turn them black. The dirt-stained windows, when rubbed clean, revealed their own greyness etched into the glass by the biting London rain. The gate had been made of black-painted ironwork, but rust had started to eat into it, so that now the letters up above the entrance proclaimed:

FAR IN DO DIST IC WO HO SE

The courtyard beyond the gate was full of tossed-out remains from the kitchen: thin, soapy water dribbled between the stones; the grey remains of vegetable peelings and tea leaves boiled their regulation half-dozen times; and a black and crusty end of a great loaf of bread, at which the rats patiently gnawed, ignoring all human traffic that didn't run at them with a carving knife. Steam rolled over the wall of the yard, tumbling out of a laundry containing huge soapy vats in which women trod, knee-deep, on the clothes floating within. From another direction came the piping of a factory whistle, and the grinding of machinery that could, in a single afternoon, produce any bolt of any number you cared to name, good sir, miracle of technology, yours for an unbeatable price.

But from the walls of the workhouse, there came almost nothing. Not a squeak, not an echo, only the tap-tap-tap of a pair of nailed soles walking down a stone corridor somewhere behind the barred windows.

The four unlikely explorers stood in front of the high walls and considered the workhouse. Tate growled at the rats, who gave him one look and went right on at their work. Lyle rubbed his chin thoughtfully, where a more respectable man might have possessed a beard and where he possessed a mixture of badly shaven skin and chemical stains. Thomas shuffled uneasily from foot to foot. Tess said, 'It seemed bigger when I was 'ere.'

'That's because you've grown, Teresa.'

' 'Pose.'

The four considered in silence a while longer. 'Well,' said Lyle finally, 'there's no point in just looking. We need to find out about Sissy. Now, I propose that you' – he pointed at Thomas – 'are the, shall we say, bad bobbie in the pack, and I'll be the sympathetic good copper, and you two' – he turned to Teresa and Tate, who looked at him with matching bewildered expressions – 'try not to steal or eat anything.'

'Like there's summat worth pinching,' muttered Tess, as the four of them trudged towards the main gate.

The gate had a warden.

His name was Willocks. He looked like an origami puppet of a man, made of bent white angles and crisp thin paper dipped in glue and coated in iron filings. He had a top hat turned almost yellow by time and decay, and when he stroked his chin, his bony fingers across the grey stubble of a once-been beard crackled like a midget's firework.

He said, 'Who are you?' in a voice that was all dribble and no teeth.

Tess looked at Lyle. Lyle looked at Thomas. Thomas looked at Tess, who shrugged, so Thomas looked down at Tate, who wagged his tail half-heartedly. Having sought enlightenment and found none, Thomas fell back to his default position; he turned to Willocks, pulled himself up to his not particularly impressive full height and announced, 'I am Master Thomas Edward Elwick Esq.'

Willocks said, 'Uh?'

'I am Thomas Edward Elwick, Knight of the Yellow Daffodil, Keeper of the Royal Hounds, Squire of the Crossbows and . . . and Master of the Suspicious Precipitates!' he repeated, in the indignant voice of a man who couldn't quite believe that this ignorant baboon hadn't already wet itself in awe. 'This *is* St Bartholomew's Workhouse for the wretched, is it not?'

'Uh,' was the reply.

'Well, then – let me in!'

Willocks looked Thomas up and down, taking note of the waistcoat designed to hold a paunch that wasn't yet there, the black frock coat with the silk lining, the long trousers, the shiny shoes from the best bootmaker in town, the top hat almost twice the height of Thomas's head and finally, the boy's face. He said, 'You wantin' relief?'

'Of course I'm not wanting relief. Do I look like a common wretch?' demanded Thomas. 'I am Thomas Edward—'

'Ain't nothin' for them 'ere as don't want relief.'

Lyle coughed politely, leant forward and opened his mouth to speak.

'*You* wantin' relief? You looks like it,' added Willocks.

Lyle's eyes widened, and he seemed to half choke on the words trying to form themselves. 'Uh, no. No relief today, thank you. I was merely going to suggest that, with your permission, *my lord,*' the words tumbled like gold coins, that clanged and bounced their way over the pavement, 'my Lord Elwick,' added Lyle for good measure, 'that you might mention to the gentleman here the charitable purpose of your visit.'

At which point, Thomas, who had after all been bred for this exact purpose, excelled himself. He threw one weary hand into the air and pinched the bridge of his nose, turning his head aside from the workhouse gate as if pained to be in proximity with anything so low, and exclaimed, 'Oh, how tiresome! When one is in a position such as mine, it is almost base to consider the mere details of *money.*'

Willocks' shadow had a hard time keeping up with its master, he was so quick to unlock the black padlock on the black gate and usher them inside.

Horatio Lyle thought about workhouses.

He had visited a few in his time as a special constable, and like all good citizens of Her Majesty's Dominions, he feared them. He feared the queues of starving men and women trailing round the high walls, bony flesh sticking through the tears in their filthy clothes; he feared the men with truncheons who stood at the gates and inspected every pair of hands that came inside to see whether you were someone who could work, who did work, who had worked, because work made you worthy of care. He feared the cripples too hideous even to beg, locked away in the darkest wing of the workhouse, who would never get out, for what could they do? He feared the anonymous cemeteries of turned grey earth, the carts that arrived weekly carrying nothing but old potatoes and leaving with bodies that were little more; feared the silence and the uniform clothes and the stubbly haircuts. It was the place for the debtors, orphans, scavengers, beggars and widows, those who couldn't look after themselves and so had to be told what to do.

Be grateful, the workhouse walls said, that society has deigned in its infinite mercy to give you a wall to hide behind. Be grateful for the gruel and grateful for the cot in the dormitory that sleeps two hundred, be grateful for the silence and the toil, because by being grateful for these things, you might, just *might* come a little bit closer to paying back the debt you owe to all these charitable, rich, superior strangers. The parish wardens deigned to let their local skeletons two breaths short of the grave *live*. And to Lyle's mind, there was no greater disdain upon the earth than casually *permitting* another member of the human race to survive.

So, like all good citizens of his generation, Horatio Lyle felt fear as they made their way into the workhouse, and prayed to all the theological uncertainties he was sure did not exist, to keep him from more than a passing visit inside those walls.

Teresa Hatch, like her sometimes employer/companion/friend/ fath— grown-up bloke what did the cookin', thought about workhouses too.

She thought, *Too quiet too quiet too quiet too quiet too quiet don't wanna see 'ere again don't wanna too quiet . . .*

They walked through functional corridors made of functional brick and stone, with little square functional windows set above big black functional doors whose very express function was to stop *them*, the unclean, the unwanted ones on the other side, getting out *here* to where the good charitable citizens might be muddied by contact with those they were here to save. Certainly, once the orphans, the beggars and the thieves within the workhouse walls had been purified by good toil and a brisk education, both in the letters of the alphabet and how to sensibly apply them for six shillings a week, then the charitable philanthropists and parish masters whose good works and kindly deeds kept the doors of the workhouse open, would be only too gratified to meet the reformed creations from within these looming walls. Until that moment, though, it was considered unhealthy for these two parts of society to mingle freely, at least without a guard for company. No one *blamed* the inmates of the workhouse, not at all! It was just . . . maybe if they'd tried harder?

Up a dull flight of stairs the sunlight seemed too shy to approach, to a dull black door, at which Willocks knocked twice with his fat protruding knuckles. A voice from the other side grunted, 'Enter!'

Behind a desk on which lay far too few papers to be taken seriously, a man sat smoking a black pipe nearly the size of the hand that held it. His feet, in hobnailed boots, rested on the desk. His face was three parts black whisker to one part red nose and blinking little eyes; his lips were lost somewhere within the fuzz of his beard; his ears, if he possessed any, had long since been consumed by an exploding mass of hair. Bits of pastry, old meats and thin ales had tangled and spilt themselves in his beard and made it their home, and when he grinned, as he did often, Lyle could see the remnants of that morning's pie lodged between his uneven front teeth. A bright blue waistcoat shimmered beneath a more respectable black jacket; a top hat sat proudly on his head, despite him being indoors. At the end of the desk was a walking cane, dented and scarred from halfway down.

Tess recognised him.

He did not recognise her.

His gaze took in the motley strangers standing in his office and at once fixed on Thomas. Thomas smiled his most condescending smile, trusting to the whiteness of his teeth and silkiness of his clothes to dazzle any onlookers so they wouldn't notice his far more scruffy companions. He barked, 'And who would you be?' and before the man had a chance to answer, had taken the only other chair, a thin wicker thing from which the cushion had long since been sold, and sat down in it as proud as a peacock on a tiger's throne.

The man behind the desk grunted. 'I am the master of this establishment; my name is Mullett. And who might you be, sir?'

'I am Thomas Edward Elwick,' snapped Thomas, all pompous impatience at even having to answer such a query. 'This is Mister Lyle, my . . . manservant.'

A smile as thin and cold as a knife through a snowstorm passed over Lyle's face, and his eyes narrowed.

'And Miss . . . Miss Hatch, who has consented to take time to advise me, with her special knowledge of such matters, on the condition of the workhouses which I am visiting.'

Tess's expression could have frozen salt water.

'You are interested in making a charitable donation?' crooned Mr Mullett, whose priorities in life were firmly fixed.

'When one has such a surplus of wealth as my family labours under,' sighed Thomas, 'one finds it most tedious seeking a suitable cause to endow! It is frustrating, the constant seeking out of lesser creatures worthy of my concern. Half are too illiterate to appreciate what to do with the large amounts of money it is my duty to dispense. This is the fourth workhouse I have visited this morning, and I hope, indeed I do, that you will show me better evidence of order and discipline than I have been forced to endure in other parishes!'

Mullett's eyes flickered from Thomas, to Lyle, to Tate and finally to Tess. For a second they seemed to hold there, as if trying to dredge up a long-submerged thought. It occurred to Thomas, with a quiver of unease, that his practised impersonation of his father, all overbearing unselfconsciousness, wasn't impressing Mr Mullett as it should. It wasn't that the man was immediately rejecting the idea, it was something worse: he was *thinking* about it.

In that moment, as Thomas's confidence blinked, he saw a great black pit open beneath his feet, from the bottom of which came nothing but the sound of mocking laughter.

Then Lyle leant forward and murmured, just loud enough for Mr Mullett to hear, 'My lord, I hate to remind you, but we have an appointment at Mansion House in less than an hour.'

The pit shimmered shut. The laughter faded. He was an Elwick. That was all that mattered. Thomas turned a gaze of pure cold Elwick onto Mr Mullett. 'Well?' he snapped. 'I trust you will show me round now.'

Mr Mullett found that he would.

Halfway through the tour that followed, Mullett did have a moment's unease when the little girl said that she needed to go to the privy, and don't you worry none, she knew right where it was. A few minutes later the manservant announced that he would just nip out to check on the horses, sir. But the inestimable well-mannered rudeness of Thomas, that somehow managed to say 'please' and 'thank you' in such a way as to make both words an insult, kept Mullett from thinking too deeply, until it was much, much too late.

Unobserved and alone in the workhouse, Horatio Lyle was good at sneaking around.

It wasn't that he was particularly quiet on his feet, or especially sly in his dealings with life; it was just that, physically at least, he was unremarkable. Everything about him was *almost* striking, from a nose that was almost large to a height that was almost tall, but it seemed that his body had, at the last minute, on the verge of transforming him into something handsome, or ugly, or distinctive, just shrugged and gone, 'Nah'. And so, when asked to describe that strange man sneaking around, people would frown and venture, 'Well, he had . . . Well, his hair was almost . . . and he was nearly . . . But I suppose not really . . .' And so on.

As well as being without obvious character, Horatio Lyle had another advantage when sneaking around. He knew that the best way not to be noticed was to have the manner of a man who didn't care if he was noticed, and who, if noticed anyway, couldn't stop and speak to you, being on his way to somewhere more important.

So it was that Lyle retraced his steps through the stone corridors of the workhouse, with the confident stride of a man who'd just forgotten his hat, to Mr Mullett's office on top of those dull stairs.

The door was locked.

Lyle liked locked doors. He liked thinking about all the incriminating things that someone didn't want him to see on the other side.

He knelt by the keyhole and fumbled in his coat pockets. He had a lot of pockets, whose contents made them bulge wide in implausible places where coats should not, by all the laws of fashion, have bulged. What he carried was rarely used, but, as he pointed out, there was always going to be that *one* circumstance when a vial of ammonia nitrate, or a pot of machine oil, or magnesium fragments in a tube, or a charged capacitor with discharge leads, or the contents of the other pockets could save the day, and you never knew when that would be. How embarrassing, Lyle would say, to find yourself facing the apocalypse, only to pat down your pockets and proclaim as the disaster struck, 'Damn, I forgot to pack any cadmium today!' Words which would, presumably, be your last.

Today, the object of Lyle's interest was a regular. Acid, Lyle believed, should never be stored or carried near anything that you valued too greatly. As a result he kept a vial of the stuff sewn into the lining of his coat around knee height, on the assumption that if it did burst, and acid did go all over the place, then his knees were his least interesting part. Thus it was that he moved gingerly as he unpicked the stitches at the bottom of his coat, pulled out a silverish vial, no thicker than his little finger, unscrewed the top, releasing a wisp of pale, vile-smelling vapour, and dribbled a few drops into the keyhole of Mr Mullett's office.

The keyhole began to smoke. Round its edges the metal started to bubble and pop like boiling water; Lyle flapped his hands ineffectually as a thick brown substance tumbled out, with the consistency of steam. Coughing, he kicked the door. It swung back with a sulky thump, the lock so much dripping metal, and, with a look of self-congratulation, Lyle sauntered in.

Teresa Hatch was very, *very* good at sneaking around. One reason she'd made such a damn good thief wasn't that she picked pockets better than any other of the thieving clys and gropuses out on the streets; it was that she always knew which pocket to pick. Let Lyle go wandering round Mr Mullett's office, Tess had a completely different agenda. She knew this place: where to hide, and where to look, and what to ask when she got there.

So, having detached herself from Thomas and the work-house master, she slipped through the empty laundry stinking of cheap soap and old pee, skirted the kitchen, where cabbage was the meal of the day, and yesterday, and tomorrow, and hurried through the widows' wing, where the old women were too bored, too mad, too blind, too weak or just too tired of life to care about a little girl wandering by. All they were now permitted to do was to clean floors and pray for salvation as soon as it could possibly come. Tess sidled past the main working halls, where there were guards on duty, and climbed the high wall between the exercise yard and the children's wing, slipping her toes into the holes worn by a hundred inmates before her and dropping into a courtyard that over-looked a schoolroom. From inside came children's voices, bored, monotonous, intoning over and over again, 'The Lord is my rock, and my fortress, and my deliverer, my God, my strength, in whom I . . .'

'Nash! Sit up!'

'Sorry, sir.'

'. . . my buckler, and the horn of my salvation . . .'

Tess risked peeking through a broken window. In a room full of benches a hundred children sat before their teacher, who stalked the classroom, cane in hand, eyeing up his charges with the look of a man who'd dreamed big dreams and couldn't cope with how they'd fallen, except to punish the world for failing him.

Sneaking on, Tess found a particular drainpipe, the one that hadn't drained anything for ten years, clogged with debris and buddleia roots, which she'd used to get down all those years ago. This time, she started to climb up towards the high windows of the children's dormitories.

Thomas's confidence was back.

It helped that he didn't have an audience. The absence of Lyle and Tess enabled him to grow into the part to its very full, so that he could now chivvy and exclaim and make a nuisance of himself to his heart's content, letting the arrogance of years of wealth and breeding sweep round him like an ermine cloak. Speed was the key, he concluded. Keep overwhelming Mr Mullett with aristocratic insufferability and he won't have time to think the obvious thought: *I am being lectured by a youngster toff, how dare he?!*

So he blurted out, 'I see you keep orphans and petty children here as well. What are your terms of admittance?'

Mr Mullett mumbled something. He was less than happy about both Thomas's companions, the shifty-looking man and worse, the even shiftier-looking child, having escaped his clutches to vanish into who knew what part of the workhouse. But if he'd wanted to voice any concerns, he simply didn't have the time against Thomas's constant barrage of—

'Speak up, man, I didn't hear!'

'Orphans,' grumbled the workhouse master, 'or beggars. Sometimes children will come to us in the winter, thieves and rats for the most part, looking for a warm fire. Naturally, we turn the worst sort directly over to the police, and they are sent mostly to the hulks. But charity, good sir, I'm sure you understand that we extend charity even to the lowest members of our society, so long as they're willing to work.'

'You are a noble man to think so kindly towards such wretches!'

'Our motto, sir, our motto,' said Mr Mullett, 'is, "Truth, Labour and the Lord". We impart Christian values to those within our walls, teach them to find themselves and the good Lord in the work they do, learn a variety of useful skills—'

'Such as?'

'Letters, sir, basic letters. The girls we send out to work in the mills, of course, sir, or as domestic labour, which is indeed the greatest advancement to be hoped for by any such creature as comes within our walls, or there's other suitable trades.'

'Suitable?'

'Some class of children, alas, are not born with sufficient good grace, and must be sent to help the night-soil men in the execution of their labours, or to the undertakers, or may be apprenticed to the chimney-sweep. To needful trades, such as better befit creatures of their capacities.'

'You do not seem greatly fond of these children,' murmured Thomas.

'Fond? My dear – my noble sir,' exclaimed the man, 'I am as fond of each of these children as if they were my own. For on their actions rests the manner in which men may judge me, and the means by which I live!'

Thomas pursed his lips. 'What of entertainments?' he asked. 'What of rest, of joy, of—'

'Entertainments?! Sir, I am a soft-hearted, indulgent man, sir. But a few days ago, these creatures of sin – dare I call them so much – these ragamuffins of the slums were given the indulgence of a lifetime! We took them to see Mr Majestic's Marvellous Electric Circus, no less, and I challenge you, sir, I challenge you to find any master of any house who would have so pampered and spoiled his wards as I did with such a treat!'

'Are there many occasions of this kind?' asked Thomas, trying to fix his face in a look of firm disapproval at the thought of that dreaded disease . . . *fun.*

For a moment, something flickered behind the master's eye,

a suggestion of that same spark that *thought*, that sat behind the gabbling of his tongue and pinched it now and then with a whisper of, *Hold up, friend, think about what needs to be done . . .* Then it was gone, and Mr Mullett was all sad smiles. 'Alas, betterment before entertainment, good sir. I'm sure you understand.'

Lyle rifled.

He rifled Mr Mullett's desk, Mr Mullett's wastepaper basket, Mr Mullett's one drooping bookshelf. He found nothing that would immediately proclaim itself to be a Clue, but that was good, that was comforting. If he'd found something that had immediately announced itself as a Clue, it would have made Lyle suspicious, since, as yet, he wasn't even sure what the crime was that had been committed. Besides, Lyle generally believed that if something was too good to be true, then it wasn't just false, it was probably dancing the polka with a bottle of nitro-glycerine shoved down its left boot.

What he did find was a leather-bound ledger of accounts, scrawled in bad handwriting. And while economics and finance bored him, mathematics was Mister Lyle's best friend, so he palmed the book into one of his many pockets, muttering as he tried to shove vials and packets of wire aside to make space for it.

Two drawers down he found a bundle of certificates. They were formal, square, written on stiff paper with black ink. They had empty spaces for signatures and names, waiting to be filled by a stiff, well-informed hand. Two were freshly signed, bound together and ready for duty.

They read:

Record of Death
That upon the date of . . . from a disease of the
lungs passed away the orphan, ward of the state
Sissy Smith.
Witnessed: *Edgar Mullet Esq.*
Witnessed by Medical Examiner: *Dr Preston.*

There was one more certificate, dated from a few days earlier. He read the name. His lips were thin and pale. He folded them both, slipped them into his jacket pocket, and closed the drawer.

The locked wooden box he found two shelves later.

Inside was money.

A lot of money.

Too much money.

Well, thought Lyle, straightening up a little and forcing his sternest expression onto his face, *thank God Tess isn't here.*

A moment, to consider Tate.

The dog – for such he was if only because all other species refused to claim him – was possibly the only creature who had a good idea of the illicit activities underway in the St Bartholomew's workhouse. From the corridors above, he smelt the chlorine of Lyle's acids; from the laundry below he sensed rats disturbed by passing feet; from the walls outside he detected the distinct odour of Teresa Hatch, on whose clothes, skin and very soul the essence of fried breakfast seemed to have stamped its imprint.

There was also something else.

Something that Tate didn't even smell in the basement laboratory of Lyle's house. Something . . . older, drier, like the rustle of falling autumn leaves . . .

. . . and then it was gone.

This is why.

A woman is watching the workhouse.

Or rather, a woman *was* watching the workhouse.

But then Lyle and his companions went inside.

And now she's watching them.

Or maybe, perhaps, just watching *him*.

Her skin smells of soap, but her soul – if souls can have a smell – carries an odour of something much older than the laughter lines round her bright green eyes.

And she's smiling.

She'll prove important to Lyle's story, in a little while, just a little, little while.

She knows it too.

And that makes her happy.

Tess slipped into the empty children's dorm. She used the same broken window through which she'd climbed out all those years ago. They hadn't bothered to fix it.

The dormitory was empty.

It contained a hundred little wooden cots, each stuffed with a little hay mattress and covered by a single little woollen blanket. In winter, half the beds were empty and the children piled in together to stop themselves freezing; in the height of summer, when the sewer stench reached up to the chimney tops, the beds were pushed to the furthest, darkest corners to be apart, and even then, you burnt in the long hot nights. Tess made her way past dirty bowls for dirty washing water, beneath rafters caked with cobwebs. Edging up to the door, she pushed it open a crack. In the empty corridor the floorboards were missing every other nail – Tess herself had taken a sizeable number to sell for her first-ever penny on the city streets. She walked along the floor, taking crooked spider-strides to avoid the boards that would creak or sing too loudly underfoot, until she came to a triangular door, barely large enough even for a child to crawl through. It was bolted and locked on the outside. She tapped on it twice; a second later, three taps came back in answer.

She hissed, 'Oi! Who's there?'

Silence.

'Oi! Don't play daft! Who's in there?'

'Edith White,' came the whispered reply. 'Who's that?'

Tess didn't answer, but pulled the bolt back and fumbled in her pockets. She didn't have as many as Lyle but then, as she liked to point out, she could get out of almost any trouble *without* having to resort to acids and explosive compounds, so there. She pulled out a small bundle of tools, wrapped in soft blue fabric, and started working at the lock.

'Hello?' came the whispered voice from the other side of the door. 'Hello?!'

'What you gone an' done?' hissed Tess.

'Ain't done nothin'!'

' 'Course you ain't.'

With a little, sullen click, the lock gave. She edged the door back. Inside, a child, curled up to the size of a small slumbering dog, knees tucked to her chin, hands wrapped across her shins, blinked, startled by the light. She was in a coal hole, with her entire skin, hair and clothes covered in black dust. She peered blearily at Tess. 'Who the hell are you?! What you playin' at?'

'I'm Tess!' came the proud reply.

'Uh?'

'Tess? Teresa Hatch? Best pinch in the house? Fastest runner, best at pretendin' to be sleepin' when I weren't, could steal anythin' an' did, never caught, climb any wall, sneak out any night? Tess? You gotta 'ave heard of me.'

The child shook her head. 'Don't know nothin' 'bout that.'

Tess's face fell. 'Fame ain't no good no more,' she grumbled. 'Look, you heard of a girl called Sissy Smith?'

Edith's eyes widened. 'Ain't s'posed to say nothin' to no one! I got in trouble for sayin' summat 'bout her!'

'Smart attitude what you got goin',' agreed Tess, 'but I wanna know 'bout Sissy, see? Cos someone gone an' *hurt* her, and that means they hurt one of us. So you tell me everything what you know 'bout Sissy toot sweet, chop chop, right?'

And Edith White, who hadn't heard of the legendary Teresa Hatch, but then again, had never seen a child who wasn't in workhouse uniform, told her.

She whispered, 'It happened at the circus . . .'

CHAPTER 4

Information

It was too good to last.

As Lyle looked at the money in the master's little lock box, wondering whether that amount of money could look back, it had simultaneously occurred to him that, yes, things had been going rather well.

Half a second after this thought had begun its progress across Lyle's brain, another, smaller thought chased after it, waving its arms and shouting indignantly, determined to point out, dammit, that if it was too good to last, odds were it wouldn't.

Two seconds after that, the door opened.

It was Mr Willocks, starting in with a cry of, 'What the bloody hell do you think . . .?' What followed had been mostly obscene. To avoid hearing any more than necessary, the some-time copper ran straight at Willocks, shoved him into the wall and belted past, down the steps outside two at a time. Lyle had always known that in any fight, he'd be the one with the bleeding nose, but when it came to the 200-yard sprint, he was unsurpassed.

Behind him, Willocks, struggling to recover breath, shouted, 'Oi! He's got the . . .'

Lyle rounded the corner, leapt down another flight of stairs, and barged past a tattered collection of beggars and tramps being turfed out of their overnight dorm onto the street to work. As he ran, he fumbled in his pockets, feeling by the marks on the cork of each vial which potion was contained within, until at last he pulled two glass containers from his coat and, reaching the end of the corridor, turned to face the furious features of Mr Willocks.

'Thief!' blurted the man.

'Special constable!' retorted Lyle, and smashed the two vials together.

If Lyle hadn't let Tess do some of his routine lab work while he was focusing on more exciting projects, there would have been a quiet, satisfactory puff of smoke. As it was, he *did* recall asking her to throw together a couple of potions in passing, please. And now he thought about it, at the time it had seemed that she was using too much lead nitrate.

The blast knocked him back off his feet and into the soft wall of shuffling beggars and excavated inmates, an elbow knocking into his side as his feet slid out from beneath him. His fingers itched and stung with the flying sparks and shattered glass from the two smashed vials. Smoke billowed down the hall, sending dark fumes into every corner; it crawled under doors and pressed its angry tumbling face against each window.

In the courtyard, Mr Mullett, halfway through describing the exercise regime for elderly inmates (ten minutes of walking round the yard twice a day), looked up, and exclaimed to see black clouds billowing through several windows.

Thomas scratched Tate quietly behind the ears, and looked for the nearest way out.

On the top floor of the building, Tess said, 'Can you smell smoke?'

Edith nodded.

From downstairs came the sounds of hacking coughs and a half-hearted attempt to shout, 'Thief!' through the darkness.

'Gettin' caught!' sighed Tess, every inch the frustrated professional. 'Amateurs!' She stood up and headed for the nearest window. A pair of blackened claws closed round her wrist; with a start she realised they were the thin, coal-stained fingers of Edith.

'There ain't no gettin' out! Greybags comes an' finds you when you dreams!'

'*Right*,' said Tess, as nicely as she felt she could, circumstances permitting. 'Course he does.'

'Children die,' whispered Edith frantically. 'I heard it, I seen it! He tells you the stories an' then . . .'

' 'Ere,' muttered Tess, glancing frantically towards the end of the corridor, where smoke was now roiling in under the door, 'not as how I ain't interested, but this ain't a good time. So, tells you what, if you gets out, I got this pal, name of Scuttle.'

From downstairs, she heard the sound of breaking glass, and Tate barking.

'Scuttle?' whispered the girl. 'I know Scuttle! He were caught! He were took to the circus!'

Tess, usually the leader of the pack when it came to rapid escape, hesitated. 'Wha'?'

'He was took! Same as Sissy was!'

Tess stared into Edith White's pale little face and saw, somewhere in the sunken eyes, a bright burning flame whose one fuel was fear, pure, smokeless, glittering fear. She pulled free of the girl's grip, and Edith seemed to shrivel away into herself. The door at the end of the corridor was thrust back, letting in a wave of smoke and the irate schoolmaster, who began, 'Who are you and what are you . . .'

Tess was at the window, crawling out and reaching for the nearby drainpipe, digging her toes into the uneven bricks and wrapping her fingers round the cold rusting iron as she began the climb towards the ground, the cobbled street and escape. Behind her, she heard Edith White start to scream empty incomprehensible words, and felt a lump of coal fly by her head as the schoolmaster, leaning out of the open window, tried to knock her from her perch. But he was already much, much too late.

An hour later, a passing packman, his bag full of old nails, printed fabrics, French chocolates and penny remedies, happened to glance aside as he waddled down the crowded, dirty byway of Exmouth Market, and saw three unusual figures eating eel pie. The youngest, a girl with a mess of dark hair, face stained with coal dust, was surreptitiously feeding fragments of pastry to a dog that had claimed her feet for its own. The next youngest, by his clothes clearly a gentleman, was wheezing from what seemed like sudden and violent exercise, one of his trouser legs torn almost to the knee, while the eldest was using his sleeve to wipe smoke stains from his face, the ends of his once red-blondish hair scorched and slightly curled by heat.

The three of them were having some sort of argument.

'Next time, *next time*,' said the man, 'when I say two parts lead nitrate to five parts calcium carbonate, I actually and really do mean—'

'You can make your own next time!' exclaimed the girl with the reckless rudeness the packman firmly believed was proof of the decline of the times.

The boy said nothing, but peered into the depths of his pie as if both fascinated and repulsed by the contents within its hard pastry crust. It was clear he found the experience unpleasant, but he screwed up his face, half closed his eyes and took a bite. A little, '*Unnnngh! Unnn unnnghh!*' noise escaped the boy's lips, and the ends of his ears started to resemble a boiled beetroot.

The packman walked on, leaving the three of them to their discussion.

A few streets on, he passed a very angry-looking workhouse master, and two baffled coppers.

Lyle said, 'All right! Regardless of the chemical consistency, let us all be grateful to have got in and out safely! I, for one, found the experience most enlightening.'

Thomas had got a piece of bone from his pie lodged between his teeth and was trying his very best to find a way to dislodge it without upsetting decorum.

Tess turned from her ritual adoration of Tate to Lyle. 'Uh?' she queried.

'Enlightening?' suggested Lyle.

'Um . . .?' said Tess helpfully, as Thomas tried to work his tongue between his teeth without catching anyone's attention.

'Educational.'

'Wha'?'

'Informative?'

Tess's face stayed blank. 'Teresa,' said Lyle, 'I know you know exactly what these words mean, and are merely trying to provoke me into saying something rude and ungrammatical. Well, it isn't going to work! According to *Mrs Bontoft's Practical Advice* . . .' he groped in his coat pockets, and produced, after great struggle, a little leather-bound book that had been lodged between a pen and a fold-up magnifying glass. 'It says . . .' he flicked through the pages, while Thomas, Tess and even Tate stared in wonder, 'a child must learn from the fathe— from the paternal figure, and will come to speak as he speaks. Thus, good grammar, an economy of language and a moral, leading to verbal fortitude in times of trouble will all illustrate by example the—'

'Wha' the hell is that?' squeaked Tess indignantly.

'Um . . . this is *Mrs Bontoft's Practical Advice on Family Life,*' stammered Lyle, his confidence waning in the triple face of Thomas's, Tess's and Tate's incredulity. 'It's . . . it's a guide to . . . well . . . to running a family . . . to . . . uh . . . to . . . Look, can we please focus on Tess's consistent refusal to conduct herself in a ladylike manner and her over-enthusiastic deployment of rapidly oxidising compounds!'

Silence.

Lyle was aware he was still holding the book. He tried to force it back into a bulging pocket, which chinked and creaked under the pressure.

Thoughtfully, a strange expression on her face, as of one not entirely listening to her own speech, Tess intoned, 'I found out that the children 'ave been goin' missin', Mister Lyle.'

'Missing? What sort of "missing"?'

'As in . . .' Tess sucked in a long breath, 'as in "absent like" or "gone" or "not in the vicinitininy no more" or "totally bugge . . ."'

'All right, thank you, I think I have the idea.'

Thomas raised a hand in polite enquiry.

'See!' exclaimed Lyle, gesturing at the boy. 'This is what well-brought-up young gentlemen do! Yes, Thomas, what is it?'

'I was wondering if Miss Teresa might clarify by what means the children in the workhouse are going missing?' suggested Thomas meekly.

'Oh. Yeah. They're troublemakers, Edith said. Children what don't do right by the master, an' then they get taken out for the day, an' then they ain't never come back. Edith were this girl what I found in the cupboard.'

There was a pause while the others considered this. 'A cupboard?' Thomas hazarded.

'Yep. Cos if you do summat bad, or summat they *think* is bad, an' if you get *caught*, see, then you get punished. Like sometimes you get beat with the cane or get no supper, or in winter, like, you 'ave to 'ave a cold bath, or if you done summat an' they can't be bothered to think of nothin' special, then you get locked in the coal cupboard for a few days.'

'A few days?' gasped Thomas.

'Yep.'

'I suppose, discipline . . .'

Tess stuck out her tongue, puffed out her cheeks and made an indecent noise that Thomas had never heard before from a female – or even a male – of his acquaintance.

Lyle coughed, in an attempt to assert authority and direction. 'All right, Teresa,' he said, 'so your time was not entirely unfruitful. Did you, by any chance, get information on Sissy Smith?'

'Yep. She were taken away yesterday mornin'. Her an' . . .' Tess hesitated, and for a moment, a creature older than a child was watching from behind her eyes. 'Mister Lyle?' Her voice was soft, serious.

'Yes, Teresa?' Lyle was suddenly still and gentle.

'Sissy Smith were taken away with Scuttle.'

'Scuttle? As in . . .'

'As in spotty little Scuttle what is really called Josiah. As in spotty Scuttle, king of the mudlarks of Wappin'. Scuttle, what took us into the sewers when we had to go an' save you from your big trouble, Mister Lyle. They caught him.'

Lyle nodded slowly, sadly, pinching the bridge of his nose. 'Well,' he said at last, 'sometimes the mudlarks need a roof over their head. Perhaps . . . perhaps he chose to go to the workhouse?'

'Scuttle ain't never chosin' that! He were my friend! He wouldn't never . . . An' he were taken with Sissy Smith, he were taken an'—'

'Taken where?'

'The circus.' It was Thomas who'd spoken, sudden, sharp, confident.

The others turned.

He shrugged uneasily, tried to smile with confidence but couldn't quite muster it. 'Mr Mullett said – he said they took the children to the circus. Mr Majestic's . . . Mr Marvellous's – something like that. A big circus. I thought how strange it was, a workhouse master taking the children, especially since Mr Mullett didn't seem a gentleman of . . . of appropriately caring disposition.'

'Well,' said Lyle at last, 'I'll admit to being a little confused by the activities at your old workhouse, Tess.'

'But none of this don't make us no closer to curin' Sissy Smith, do it?' demanded Tess with a sulky pout.

'Perhaps there's something in this?' asked Lyle, pulling out the leather account book he'd taken from the master's office.

'You pinched the accounts?' asked Tess, brightening a little. 'Mister Lyle!'

'Thievery earns me respect.' He sighed. 'I build airships in my spare time and have invented a revolutionary theory to explain the diffusion, refraction and reflection of light through the atmosphere while casually walking down Baker Street. But what earns me respect? Illegality.'

'I respect you, sir!' piped Thomas.

'Erm . . . Thank you, Thomas.'

'Toff,' whispered Tess, nudging him in the ribs.

'I think,' proclaimed Lyle, attempting to impose some sort of authority on the proceedings, 'that there may be something to investigate here after all.'

CHAPTER 5

Money

And as she sleeps, she dreams of . . .

    . . . she dreams *of* . . .

        . . . once upon a time

           . . . a long time ago . . .

  . . . there lived . . .

. . . a long way away . . .

  . . . a beautiful princess . . .

    . . . an evil witch . . .

      . . . an angry dragon . . .

a child in a coal cupboard who said to the darkness, let me tell you a story once upon a time there was a child in a coal cupboard who said to the darkness, let me tell you a story

. . . and her name was . . .

. . . her name *was* . . .

No.

Nothing.

All gone now.

Sissy Smith turns over in her bed, and sleeps a little more.

Horatio Lyle liked numbers. He liked it when they did what they were told – when you said to them, 'Now go like *that*' and they did, because with numbers either you were right or you were wrong. It worked, or it blew a hole in the laboratory roof. And when it worked – if it worked – it was beautiful.

That said, numbers relating to *money* were of almost no interest to Lyle. They were simple, dull this plus that equals that, income and expense. Any fool could count pennies into shillings, shillings into pounds and, thank you kindly, he had more interesting things to do with mathematics than worry about the grocery bill. As his financial affairs had grown, and with them their need for subtleties, rules and regulations, Horatio Lyle had fallen behind the times. One morning he'd woken up and realised that, yes, he should be able to calculate the distance to the moon based on its relative position to its background objects if only he could sort out the angle versus time of observation details . . . but ask him to name the price of a hot plum pie and he'd be in trouble. As far as Lyle was concerned, he operated on such a sublime mathematical level that stooping to consider everyday money matters would violate twenty years of intellectual training.

'You is just sayin' that, ain't you?' said Tess snottily. 'Cos of how you don't know what all the squiggly bits down the side mean.'

'I am not! I grant you that accountancy has its own particular numerical language whose fluffy, vague details elude a mind as finely trained as my own.'

'See! You don't know nothin'!'

'*This*,' growled Lyle, 'is exactly what is meant by the undermining of parental authority.'

But Tess did have a point. So they went to see a banker. Or, perhaps more usefully, they went to see a banker's wife.

They headed north.

Once a wooded countryside where royalty rode out from town to hunt deer, even Stoke Newington, Lyle noticed, was showing signs of urbanisation. Rows of identical terraced houses were springing up along new paved roads. A grand Gothic-style church now stood across the village street from its ancient, rural predecessor. By the old-fashioned Unitarian chapel on Newington Green a series of plodding, teetering omnibuses were laden twice daily, morning and night, with a never-before-seen number of City clerks in top hats.

At a tall house in a terrace by the local park, gleaming in all its proud newness, Lyle came to a door painted the same black as every other nearby, with a black iron door knocker in the same style as its neighbours. A maid answered his knock, wearing, no doubt, the identical uniform of every other maid along the street. She looked him up and down and said, 'You sellin' something?'

'You buyin'?' asked Tess quickly.

Lyle smiled with all the humour of a hungry crocodile and carefully pushed Tess back behind the more respectable shape of Thomas. 'No,' he said. 'I'm here to see the lady of the house.'

'You got a card?'

'A what?'

'A card? Gentlemen what comes to visit the lady of the house brings cards that I put on a tray, an' then give to the lady of the house.'

'I haven't got a card.'

'Oh. That ain't normal.'

Thomas leaned carefully past Lyle, smiling thinly. 'Actually, good madam,' he announced smoothly, 'the fashion for exchanging cards is one mostly indulged in by the middle-class *business* sort. When one moves in circles such as we do, one needs no introduction but is merely immediately known.'

The maid tried to translate this.

Tess kicked Thomas in the ankle. 'Ow! I was just trying to—'

'Bigwig!'

Lyle said quickly, 'Bless him for trying. He's . . . keen. Could you just tell Mrs Hobbs that Horatio Lyle is here to see her? I'm sure she'll understand.'

She did.

The lady of the house was a woman in her mid-fifties, with a head of grey hair crimped down so immaculately close to her scalp that it looked sewn on like some kind of bonnet. She wore a rustling blue dress ornamented with nearly as much lace as there was flesh to cover. As Lyle entered, she rose with a broad smile on her face. 'Horatio! I'm so glad to have you call! Oh look! You've brought some . . . some . . . individuals with you!'

Lyle half bowed. It was an old-fashioned gesture for an old-fashioned lady, one who, if she put her mind to it, could remember the battle of Waterloo, in a time when news of Britain's great victories was spread, not by the electric telegraph, but by the stagecoaches as they passed through each town. Her name was Mrs Veronica Hobbs – no relation to that dreadful philosopher fella – and she was the esteemed wife of Mr Hobbs of Scrounge and Hobbs, bankers to the comfortably rich and essentially naïve.

Lyle was comfortably rich, but far from naïve. He knew, and had known from the start, that Mrs Hobbs, before her frowned-upon marriage ('Finance is such a crude enterprise,' was her mother's assessment), had been Miss Bowen, daughter of a Mr Bowen whose knack for finding and digging up coal under innocuous looking mountains was surpassed only by his incompetence at keeping hold of the ensuing profits. Thus, for part of the first twenty-five years of her life, Miss Bowen had, politely and calmly, looked after the accounts of one of the largest and most feckless businessmen in South Wales. So it was to Mrs Hobbs, rather than her husband, that Lyle looked for guidance in all things financial. She would never take any public credit for the work she did. But it was her capacity to be more than discreet – to be, in fact, utterly unnoticed because, well, she was just the wife and that, in Lyle's experience, made her an excellent guide to the world of money.

He put down on her writing desk the ledger stolen from Mr Mullett's office. 'I pinched it from a workhouse. I had a quick read through and it's utterly unintelligible.'

She picked the ledger up and flicked through a few pages. From behind a pair of gold-rimmed spectacles balanced on the end of her needle-sharp nose, her eyes narrowed at the scrawled writing. 'In my experience,' she said, 'messy financial documents are nothing more than an attempt to disguise illegality with incompetence.'

'I also found a *lot* of money in the master's room. And no sign it was being spent on the workhouse.'

Mrs Hobbs tutted, but made no other sound. Grey midday light drifted through the wide bay window, catching the thin floating dust in the air. Tess found a seat in one corner of the room and sniffed. 'Is that . . . bakin'?' she asked quietly.

'You've just eaten, Miss Teresa!' blurted Thomas.

'Yeah . . . but proper bakin'!'

'Teresa!' growled Lyle, and tapped the pocket of his coat from which *Mrs Bontoft's Practical Advice* could just been seen peeking.

Tess scowled, and slouched deeper into her chair. Tate contentedly chewed on the end of Thomas's torn trouser leg.

After some time, Mrs Hobbs murmured, 'From a workhouse, you say?'

'Yes.'

'Interesting.'

Silence a while longer.

'And what drew your attention, Horatio dear, to this workhouse?' Lyle hesitated. Mrs Hobbs' eyes flashed up above the spectacles balanced on the end of her nose, sharp, bright. 'Or would you rather not discuss it?'

'Children.' Thomas was as surprised as everyone else to hear himself speak. 'Children have been going missing.'

'Children?'

'Yes.'

'I see. And they're not accounted for?'

'No.'

'Parish records, registers . . .'

'We were hoping you might be able to help with that,' said Lyle quickly. 'I'm more of a . . . a combustible elements man.'

'You want to know if there's something – illicit? Suggestive? In these accounts?' she asked, eyes twinkling.

'Please.'

'Children go missing from workhouses all the time, Horatio. They run away; they die. We all know this.'

'Yes. But how many workhouses do you know of that take their children to see the circus?'

'The circus? None. The idea is ridiculous.'

'Well, quite.'

Mrs Hobbs sighed, put the book to one side, pulled the glasses away from the end of her nose, carefully folded them between her fingers, and rested her fingers on her lap. 'You know these children?'

'Not personally, not well.'

'I do,' snapped Tess sharply.

'But it is the unspoken rule,' Lyle went on, 'the one that didn't have to be written down, didn't have to be said, the one the coppers don't need to tell the sneaks: you don't hurt children. Children have been hurt. Will you help me?'

'Horatio,' she said carefully, 'as a very old friend of your family, I have to ask you: are you sure you know what you're becoming involved with? The kind of people who are willing to arrange for the disappearance of children, will have no problem arranging for the disappearance of adults. We must not be naive about these things.'

Lyle sat back and shrugged. 'My reasoning is that the kind of people who let children vanish and don't ask questions, deserve everything that comes to them.'

Thomas beamed proudly.

Mrs Hobbs leant across the desk and patted Lyle on the hand.

Her mouth towards his ear, she whispered, just for him, 'That, Horatio Lyle, is why you are such a nice young man, and why, if you don't mind me saying so, you probably won't last to be a nice old gentleman.'

He smiled. 'Strangely enough, Mrs Hobbs, that thought doesn't bother me.'

She leant back. 'I need a day, maybe two, to make some suitably polite enquiries. Are there any names I should look for?'

'Two children in particular. A girl called Sissy Smith – any records relating to her – and a boy known as Scuttle. Real name Josiah. Take these.' Lyle reached into his jacket pocket and carefully passed across the two folded certificates. Tess's eyes narrowed.

'What're they?' she asked.

'Medical certificates,' replied Lyle quietly. 'One relates to Sissy Smith. It claims that she's dead when she's clearly not.'

'An' the other?'

'It . . . it claims the same for Scuttle, Tess. It says he's dead. However, the certificate for Sissy lied.'

'I see,' said Tess quietly. Lyle didn't think he'd ever seen her so still. 'I get it.'

Mrs Hobbs coughed politely. 'And these names on these certificates: Mr Mullett, Dr Preston?'

'Mr Mullett is the manager of the workhouse and a particularly dubious character. I don't know anything about Dr Preston except that he has signed a death certificate for a child who isn't dead. Anything you can find out about him would be appreciated.'

'Shall I find you at the usual place?'

'Mrs Hobbs, you are a wonder.'

'Oh, don't tell anyone,' she sighed, 'it'd take away the charm.'

The circus. The idea bothered Lyle, worried him to his core, as he sat, his feet buried in filthy straw inside a creaking omnibus heading away from Stoke Newington. An old phrase kept running round his mind, sneaking into his thoughts and stumping rational deduction.

It went: *Once upon a time . . .*

That wasn't quite right either.

He twiddled his fingers and chewed the end of his thumb, a boyish habit that still haunted him in moments of worry.

Run away to the circus . . .

He'd never understood the glamour of running away to the circus. At best, you'd end up doing dangerous or demeaning stunts, in the worst case, you'd spend the rest of your days shovelling exotic dung. But to a child in the workhouse, who had never seen electric lights and smiling faces, the idea might have some appeal.

CHAPTER 6

Circus

It wasn't hard finding Mr Majestic's Marvellous Electric Circus.

Its arrival in the city of London, with music playing, animals processing, jugglers juggling and a woman slipping rum into every third cup sold from the parade, had not been subtle. Its presence was noted in every self-respecting newspaper and news-sheet under titles ranging from 'Electric Marvel!!' to 'Vice and Bawdry Comes to London', with the praise or condemnation of the event largely proportional to the length of the editor's side whiskers.

There had been posters too, stuck up on every space on every wall and door in whichever street it was felt that the inhabitants had a respectable chance of being able to read. The main picture showed a woman passed off as a ballerina, if ballerinas could have breathed in such a corset, seeming to balance a ball on her head while prancing on the back of a pony.

On every wall, the posters had a great deal of competition from signs inviting you to visit the best barber in London to advertisements for squalid penny-gaffs where, every night, boys and girls stood on a barrel and sang out-of-tune bawdy songs for an audience more appreciative than any that could afford to sport its own top hat, for the daintiest pie shop, or to buy, for no more than five shillings and sixpence, a cure for the scourge of consumption that would not only heal you, but protect your whole family by mere proximity to the precious fumes of this concoction. Railway trips for the family were advertised, to such exotic places as Brighton or Southend-on-Sea, or to take the waters at Bath or Leamington Spa. For just half a crown, you, the lucky reader of this notice, could be the first to invest in a marvellous mechanical apparatus which will revolutionise the tallow-making industry as we know it. For you there can be real Chinese silk imported direct from India for only seven shillings two pence per yard, or music hall girls in Shoreditch and entertainments down by Crystal Palace. Every industry or enterprise whose leaders felt their audiences could be beguiled by a picture and a simple word, had plastered up their message in the London streets.

But of all these, few received such rapturous attention as the picture of the curvy lady prancing on the back of the pony, round which children and, it had to be admitted, some lonely men and envious ladies flocked to read the sign which declared:

MR MAJESTIC'S
MARVELLOUS ELECTRIC CIRCUS!!
HYDE PARK, LONDON
(ADMISSION 3D)

To every onlooker's surprise, when Lyle saw this, he started to laugh. 'Hyde Park.' He chuckled because the alternative was to cry. 'Of course it would be in Hyde Park.'

'It would?' demanded Tess.

'Sissy Smith,' he replied, 'had cuts from long grass on her feet and ankles. There are very few places in London where grass grows. Come on.'

Once upon a time, Hyde Park had been farmland, well beyond the city, with a few trees. Then some bright spark had decided that a corner of these fields would serve as an excellent place to hang people. For a few hundred years this had drawn the crowds to come and cheer the demise of their favourite apple thief. Eventually though, the judiciary had grown soft, and judges started replacing the traditional Saturday afternoon family entertainment of torture and execution with deportations to such vile places as Australia. The gallows were taken down and moved to a more convenient location, nearer the prisons, where street vendors could more easily sell their goods to the expectant crowds. Around the space where the gallows had stood, great houses grew up, often of architectural note, round the confines of the field until it was encircled, and dubbed by royal decree a park, where the nobility could take their leisure without the inconvenience of being driven in a carriage for one full day or more to places as inaccessible as Hampshire or Sussex.

And though in these days the park's great elm trees were stained with smoke from the neighbouring chimneys, for many years there had been a lake, made to look like a bend on a mighty river, on which young men might court their ladies without much fear of drowning for, while the average crinoline weighed almost as much as the creature within it, the water was mostly not a fish's fin deeper than it had to be. On Sundays there was patriotic music from a bandstand and, as if to bestow on the entire landscape a splendour nothing else could achieve, the royal family, Victoria Regina and her many progeny, were – at least theoretically – in residence no more than several hundred yards away.

Lyle, however, knew the unspoken truths about the park: the men who might haunt the place at night, cudgel in pocket, or the grown-up things that could happen in the more secluded areas. Even the carriage rides along Rotten Row were sometimes much more than an innocent-seeming jaunt with the blinds down. Which knowledge may have helped his ears turn pink when Tess, surveying the edge of the park, said, 'Is this where the marks go with their painted ladies for a bit of a swagger inna night?'

'Teresa!' he blurted out. 'Well-brought-up young women do not even *conceive* of what young men may do with their painted ladies!'

'Are we,' enquired Thomas, 'still talking about clowns?'

Tess brightened, and prepared herself to divulge the Facts of Life. 'Bigwig . . .' She looked into his face, saw optimistic eagerness hoping to be enlightened as soon as possible, the better to serve the world. 'Yes,' she sighed, 'we're talkin' 'bout clowns.'

Lyle raised his eyes to heaven. *Mrs Bontoft's Practical Advice* hadn't *anything* to say about this particular conversation.

Welcome to Mr Majestic's Marvellous Electric Circus!

Wonders you have never seen before just wait to be discovered. You, sir, may we show you creatures from the exotic Indies, strange dancing monkeys on top of the organ grinder's table cavorting for your delight? You, madam, if your heart is strong enough, come see for yourself the horrific freaks born – through no fault of their own, God's mercy on them – with faces like melted wax and stooped backs from which stubby little arms hardly deign to grow! If your child fears such things, then put them out of your mind, for here instead you may drink of fresh fruit juice (laced with a little something for only three pennies more, sir) while watching a dancing bear spin to the sound of the flute! Be careful where you put your feet, sir, the elephants are mighty in *all* their functions; but no matter, for a small army of boys waits to scrub your shoes clean again in exchange for nothing more than the three pennies they need to be allowed into the great tents of the circus. Madam, have you an eye for scientific wonders? Here we have an *electric* bulb and, yes indeed, it may seem a little smoky – that is just the carbon burning – but see how much light is made for just a little electricity. And *here* we raise two towers of metal between which we can make the lightning dance in blue fire; and here the hall of mirrors – see yourself a thousand times and wonder if you will ever escape! Have you witnessed a man eat such quantities of fire, or drive a sword – how sharp the blade! – down his own gullet? Marvel at the agility of our acrobats as they flop and dive from sky to earth with not a net in sight. Have you courage? This man can throw a knife to a spinning target and never miss his mark. Do you delight in music? Here we have every kind of exotic tune, the pipers of the east, the fiddlers of the west, a German opera singer with a great beard growing from her woman's chin, an Italian boy who sings more sweetly than the nightingale, the family favourite of Punch and his puppet adventures. Or if this is not to your taste, come visit Mysterious Mai, Mistress of Mystic Mysteries – the Veil Lifted, the Past Revealed, the Future Divined – in her tent of a Thousand Secrets. Truth can be yours for just sixpenn'orth of copper coin. Or, for a shilling, we give you technological marvels, as our very own photographer captures you and your whole family in no longer than a twenty-minute sitting before his miraculous glass!

Welcome to Mr Majestic's Marvellous Electric Circus.

Welcome, ladies and gentlemen.

Welcome, boys and girls.

Don't go anywhere too fast. Mingle with the crowds, such great, heaving crowds, pushing on every side. Come dance, come sing, come delight, come hear our stories. Who knows? Once you have feasted on our marvels, you may even want to run away to the circus!

Shoulders jostled on every side, pushing in suffocating density as our companions picked their way down a muddy causeway that might once have been grass.

'I can see,' said Lyle, 'at least two dozen ways of defrauding the public within a fifty-yard radius of where we're standing right now.'

At his side, Tess sucked loudly on a toffee. The man who'd sold it to her had cunningly taken up a position by the ticket seller at what, for want of a better word, Lyle called the gate to this tented circus city – and a city it certainly was: great, tall tents of striped red and white as far as the eye could see, from which banners and ribbons hung at every opportunity in a fanfare of colour. Some tents were purely for mundane uses, such as the purchasing of food or drink, or a place to deposit the more aged and fatigued of the visitors in reasonable isolation from the bustle and stench of the rest of it. Most offered some sort of entertainment, illustrated in great pictures and banners above the entrance flap with signs like, **EGYPTIAN SNAKE CHARMER!!!** or **REAL JAPANESE PRINCESS SAVED FROM PIRATES AT SEA BY A NAVY FRIGATE** or **STARS, SPIRITS AND THE SOUL – REVELATION!** and so on.

'Ain't so many children, is there?' said Tess casually as they shoved and bumbled their way through the crowd.

'Plenty with parents, Miss Teresa,' Thomas replied, and from his pocket, pulled out a stub of pencil and a notebook. This he opened carefully to a clean page – most of them were exactly like this – licking the ends of his fingertips delicately as he turned each thick leaf, and prepared to write.

Two pairs of eyes stared at him in confusion.

'Whatcha doin', bigwig?' asked Tess.

'Record keeping,' Thomas intoned, 'is a vital aspect of a methodologically sound approach to any investigation.'

Silence.

'Well,' said Lyle at last, feeling that it was his duty to offer some opinion on the art of investigation, 'I suppose it is. Especially if the judge is deaf in one ear.'

'Oh.' Tess sucked thoughtfully on her toffee, and at great

length, in the manner of one reaching a profound conclusion, added, 'But if we ain't actually got no methododolologic . . .'

'Right!' said Lyle, before the twisted expression of bewilderment on Tess's toffee-covered face could deepen. 'Two children have come here and two children have gone missing and we have to find out why.'

'How?'

'That is not a helpful or productive attitude. We are going to seek out suspicious things, ask cunning questions and, generally, all things considered . . .'

'Solve the mystery?' asked Thomas hopefully.

'Pinch shiny things?' added Tess, her face lighting up at the prospect.

'Knowing you two,' Lyle said deflated, 'a bit of both.'

They pushed their way deeper into the circus.

There was a show.

It happened in the biggest, brightest, largest tent of the circus and did, indeed, feature a little marvellous electricity in the form of a pair of smoky light bulbs paraded round the edge of the ring on a horse and trap, to the delight and amazement of the onlookers. Tess, Thomas, Lyle and Tate sat wedged together on benches that creaked and sagged at the back of the arena, skins sweating and stomachs twisting at the smell of so much human life compressed into so little space relative to mass. They tutted.

'Carbon bulb,' scowled Lyle. 'Messy contraption. Nothing more, really, than the induction of light as an incidental effect of heat, and I mean a lot of heat to relatively little light when you consider the amount of power you need for one of the things.'

Thomas nodded sagely.

Tess ate toffee with one hand and rubbed Tate's tummy with the other.

In the ring, a gang of clowns and acrobats mingled to the farting bursts of brass band and drum, juggling a variety of objects, ranging from knives, flaming sticks and coloured balls to, occasionally, each other, with huge great grins painted onto their faces.

'Do you believe in that smile?' Thomas asked Lyle casually, as a clown chuckled his way past the front row of the audience.

'I know this bloke what had a pair of dentures made out of teeth from a *dead person*,' said Tess gleefully. 'The quack had 'em nicked from the necro . . . necrop . . . from the big train what carries the dead out to the place in the north where the bodies gets dumped, an' he nicked teeth an' sold them for three shillin' fivepence to this fence I known.'

Lyle and Thomas contemplated this for a while.

Finally Thomas said, 'I'm not sure if that's very hygienic, Miss Teresa.'

At Thomas's feet, Tate stirred gently, bored by humanity and all its entertainments. At the edge of the ring, a pair of clowns somersaulted towards a row of . . .

. . . a row *of* . . .

'Does that front lot look right?' asked Tess, pausing to unstick her teeth from the toffee.

Lyle followed her gaze. The object of the clowns' attention appeared to be a row of ragged children, sitting cross-legged in prime position at the very edge of the ring. Their ages ranged from barely five to almost eleven, and they wore a ragbag of garments unsuited to any child, but which were more like the tattered cast-offs of grown-ups. They were thin and wild-haired, with their teeth grown yellow-brown. But, as the clowns pranced and spun before them, they laughed.

'Thing is,' mused Tess, 'they look to me like the sorta snipes wot' ain't clever enough to move from beggin' to pinchin'. An' right now they're not just not pinchin' anythin' – they're *spendin'* money, on seein' this . . .'

No one could make *spending* such a dirty word as Teresa Hatch. She waved a bewildered hand at the clowns' antics as they cavorted in time to the brass band.

'Don't you enjoy the circus, Miss Teresa?' ventured Thomas.

'If I wanna see a bloke in fancy pants fall down drunk, I could've gone to Whitechapel an' saved myself thrupence.'

'But the crowd! The lights, the colours, the collective – the general – I mean . . .'

'I seen crowds havin' a better time at a decent hangin', an' no one never said as how it was bad luck to pinch a purse from a bloke what enjoys seein' that.'

As Thomas struggled to translate this sentiment into something he understood, Lyle nudged him in the ribs and murmured, 'Trapeze.'

'What?'

'I mean, *look*.'

So Thomas looked. There was indeed a trapeze, and a woman in . . . in . . . Oh my. Well, obviously she was decently attired – obviously. But there were . . . and she had *legs* that went all the way down from her . . . Well, her . . . Thomas half closed his eyes and thought of gravity. Lots and lots of gravity doing the gravitational thing.

'Thomas!' hissed Lyle. 'You're not looking!'

'Uh, no, Mister Lyle.'

'Why aren't you looking?'

'It isn't – appropriate – sir, for a gentleman and a bastion of society, sir, if I may—'

'Stop being a nitwit and pay attention!'

So, reluctantly Thomas opened his eyes and looked at the trapeze lady. Objectively speaking, he had to admit that as trapezes went, it was not spectacularly high – in fact, it stood just a short boost up from ground level. A tall man standing on tiptoe might have wrapped himself round it. Added to this, the lady, who seemed to be the focus of the act, didn't do much more than swing gently backwards and forwards while regaling the audience with some story about her first love in the Wessex countryside and how blue the flowers grow in May, while around her two unconventionally attired ladies cavorted in a not particularly inspiring manner.

At his side, Thomas sensed Tess bristling with disdain.

'Do you see?' asked Lyle briskly.

'What?' breathed Thomas. Too much was going through his mind for him to guess what Lyle could possibly mean.

'Look at the lady on the trapeze! I want you to see what happens when she gets on and off her swing.'

So Thomas watched and waited, doing his best to show appreciation for the act, and then being amazed and in a small part alarmed by the overwhelming mixture of applause and frankly lewd suggestion that the audience emitted at its conclusion.

The woman on the trapeze smiled, and slipped from her perch. Lyle grabbed Thomas by the arm, pointed, gesturing violently, 'Look! Right there! Look, look, look!'

Thomas looked.

'Oh, yeah,' muttered Tess. 'I see.'

'You do? See what?'

'Nah. Just wanna make you feel daft, bigwig.'

'And to think my mother wanted me to have children,' growled Lyle. '*Look!* Look at where her feet touch the ground!'

They looked. Tate snuffled impatiently.

'Look at how she walks, look at the bend of her knee!'

'Uh . . .' Thomas's face was reddening with the effort of observation.

'Mister Lyle,' said Tess finally, 'I'm thinkin' maybe there's summat 'ere we can learn!'

'Are her feet actually . . .?' tried Thomas.

'Finally youth catches up with mature wisdom!' exclaimed Lyle. 'And no, they're not. Even when she's walking on it, the trapeze lady's feet don't quite touch the ground.'

They counted over fourteen other . . . Lyle called them 'disparities'. Tess called them 'Bloody strange freaky shi . . . cra . . . things what ain't natural like even for you, Mister Lyle, savin' your bigwigness an' all.'

They included the following:

The lion tamer wasn't merely able to stick his head inside the lion's mouth; the lion didn't seem capable of closing its jaws.

The clowns didn't ever stop smiling, not one, not even counting make-up, and their smiles were too wide, too frozen, never-changing.

The dancing bear danced even when there was no music.

The snake charmer's thumb seemed fused to the wood of his pipe.

The dancers on the horses' backs had the same wild round brown eyes as the beasts they rode on.

The acrobats' knees bent – just for a moment, but Lyle swore it was there – *backwards* as they made their jumps.

And then there was the ringmaster. Besides the fact that he had a moustache the like of which shouldn't have been biologically possible, and whose quivering ends tickled the insides of his ears, and ignoring the fact that he had a tremendously over-the-top, maybe-French, could-be-Italian, generic-foreigner-at-a-pinch accent ('From Bermondsey,' whispered Tess), and disregarding his outrageous purple jacket and huge black curled shoes, what really caught Lyle's attention was that at the end of the show, the ringmaster turned to the children in the very front row of the circus, and proclaimed: 'Once upon a time, there was a child who ran away to the circus . . .'

Somehow, the rest didn't matter.

'It had to be . . . unsound, didn't it?' groaned Lyle, as the audience heaved, shoved, elbowed and kicked its way out of the show to the last rattle of the brass band. 'I mean, it couldn't ever just be a simple case of children disappearing or being poisoned under mysterious and unlikely circumstances, could it? There had to be a dash of scientific fallacy thrown in, a great fat fistful of implausible, unnatural—'

'Magic?' asked Tess brightly.

'That is not a word for the objective and studious to use, Teresa! Not magic – merely things we cannot yet explain. A lady on a trapeze does not touch the ground, a bear dances with no good cause, a child is poisoned and another vanishes and the children say, "Beware the circus". These are not profound mysteries, Teresa, wrought upon this earth by anything from a . . . a "magical" creature,' Lyle spat the words contemptuously, 'up to and including a theologically fallible god. These are merely' – he gestured feebly in the air, while Tate snuffled and growled at the trouser legs pressing in around him – 'mysteries we cannot yet explain.'

'How,' asked Thomas thoughtfully, 'do other people not see it? The things that are not yet explained?'

'We were looking,' replied Lyle with a shrug. 'Remarkable, the things people will go out of their way not to notice when it wouldn't make them comfortable.'

'Bunch of marks,' muttered Tess. ' 'Sides, this is one peculiar sorta den.'

'Thank you, Teresa, for that scintillating summary of our situation.'

Tess nudged Thomas in the ribs. 'Did Mister Lyle just say summat good or bad 'bout me?'

'Erm . . . I'm not entirely sure, Miss Teresa,' he mumbled, starting to turn pink with the effort of good-mannered obscurity. 'Mister Lyle? We should – we should investigate further, yes? I mean' – he waved his notebook hopefully – 'we should deploy rigorous analysis of the available information and act based on the . . . the information, shouldn't we, Mister Lyle? I mean, we probably should, shouldn't we?'

'Probably a good idea, Thomas.' Lyle sighed. 'You can find the children, talk to them, see why they're here. Let's see if anyone else has been going missing at the circus.'

'You makes us do *all* the work, Mister Lyle,' muttered Tess.

'Privilege of being the authoritative fat— pater— patriarch, Teresa!' barked Lyle happily. 'In fact, being able to tell you two to get on with something is perhaps the only perk of what is otherwise a largely unrewarding endeavour to impart moral fibre into your youthful selves. So, to quote: go shift your bottoms!'

'What are you going to do, Mister Lyle?' asked Thomas, not very hopefully.

'Me?' murmured Lyle. 'I think I'm going to have a conversation with some dubious characters.'

Horatio Lyle was, in his spare time, a bobby – a copper, a peeler, or, to put it bluntly, a policeman. It wasn't that Lyle served the law – he just took it so much for granted that if asked why he was bothering to uphold it, he'd look startled and say, 'I beg your pardon – uphold what?' He had, however, been too *different* for the regular service. The highest echelons had found him too common, middle-ranking officers of the investigating ranks had found him too well read, and as for the constables – he bewildered all who saw him. He wasn't ex-military, nor an old affiliate of the Bow Street Runners, nor an Irish Paddy come fresh from building the railways. Neither was he poor, in debt, in need of a place to sleep, nor fleeing an unhappy marriage. Worst of all, he had *ideas*. Ideas like, 'You know, it seems to me that there are better ways to identify known criminals than by the size of their skulls. Maybe the pressure patterns on their lips, or their toes, or even their fingers? Obviously I would need to do a study, with perhaps . . . oh, a magnifying glass, a very large wall, a sizeable bottle of ink, a lot of paper and two thousand volunteers, give or take.' Naturally, the chief inspector had put a stop to that ridiculous idea fairly smartish.

The police just weren't ready for a man like Lyle. That said, they could *use* such a man, and so, with a sly expression and a wink at the accounting department, they'd made him a special constable. Not that Lyle had taken much note of this because, come what may, he knew that the law was *right* and whether he was a bobby or not he would see that right was done.

So, in the best tradition of the police force, Special Constable Horatio Lyle knew that if you wanted to get to the truth – which, in Lyle's mind, was bundled up in the same for-granted package as Law equals Right equals Truth – the best place to go looking was behind the nearest privy.

That the privy in this case happened to belong to a pair of elephants was, Lyle concluded, nothing to impede an otherwise sound investigative strategy.

The words, 'Oi, you ain't s'posed to be back 'ere,' let Lyle know that he was on the right track.

This was confirmed when an old man appeared, whose face resembled a shrunken green grape furred over with grey whiskers. He was carrying what Lyle had to concede was one mighty shovel. Brandishing it at Lyle, he exclaimed, 'Whatcha doin' 'ere? Bugger off!'

'Special Constable Horatio Lyle.' Lyle could feel his voice drift into the business-like, gruff strains of your average copper looking for trouble. 'I was just admiring, uh, the pen.'

The man's eyes narrowed in suspicion. The pen was, to Lyle's mind, barely large enough to conduct a healthy experiment into the properties of gaseous diffusion, let alone house a pair of extremely skinny elephants. Meanwhile he fumbled in his pocket, digging for something friendly to offer the untrusting man with the shovel, and came out with a test tube of golden-brown liquid.

He popped the cork, sniffed carefully, and brightened. 'Whisky?'

'What's this about?'

'Just as I said. I was admiring the elephant pen. Not often you see elephants in Hyde Park.'

'You 'avin' a laugh?'

'You see my humorous smile?'

The keeper examined Lyle's face. Tombstones had more wit. The keeper took the proffered tube of whisky, sniffed it, then shook his head. 'Nah, thanks. I never drink nor eat anythin' as how I didn't get myself.'

'Really?' asked Lyle, re-corking the tube and slipping it into his pocket. 'How's that?'

'Can't never trust the other bugger's grub.'

'I see. And your job is . . .?'

The pause hung in the air. The keeper looked from Lyle to the cage doors of the pen, from the outside of which came the sound of great elephant snorts and the 'oooohs' of an admiring crowd, then to his shovel, then back to Lyle again.

Lyle smiled stiffly. 'Never mind.'

'Toffs buy it.'

'What?'

'Toffs like to buy it. To have it put on their gardens. I mean, you'd think they'd stick with chicken or cow like the rest of us, but oh no. Elephant dung's where the money is. Damn well kills every plant it bloody touches, but it's the air of mystery, see?'

'Elephant dung has mystery?'

'Cos it come from a bloody elephant, see? It's foreign!'

Lyle thought about this, while outside a sudden burst of clapping suggested one of the elephants had done something charmingly un-elephant-like. 'But,' he began, 'the Black Death was in its time an exotically foreign disease. Cholera—'

'Foreign *is* bloody posh, an' that's that. *Interesting* muck for your *interested* bigwig.'

Having reached this absolute conclusion, the keeper nodded his head once, as if to dismiss any other thought, opinion or topic of conversation from the pen and, by implication, Lyle with it.

Lyle politely cleared his throat. 'Mr . . .'

'Lovell.'

'Mr Lovell,' chimed Lyle, 'I'm sure that you, as a man with a weighty load on the end of your shovel . . .'

Mr Lovell's eyes narrowed.

'. . . have a lot to do. But would you answer one or two brief questions?'

'What d'ya wanna know?'

'I want to know if you've seen anything . . . odd.'

'Odd? At the circus?' Contempt dribbled out of every pore.

'Yes, "odd". I'm sure you can surmise for yourself what "odd" might be. Say, clowns who can't stop smiling. Or strong men who, I have no doubt, could lift one of your lions whose jaws never seem to close. Or perhaps a trapeze-lady whose feet don't entirely touch the ground. If that doesn't excite you, how about "odd" in the sense of two children that I know of so far – a girl called Sissy and a boy called Scuttle – either vanishing off the face of the earth, or being *poisoned*, Mr Lovell, *poisoned* at your bloody circus, that kind of odd, yes?'

The keeper's face had turned, during this list, first grey, then white, and was now heading into a sickly shade of green. He mumbled, 'Don't know nothin'.'

'Of course you don't, Mr Lovell. Are you sure I can't tempt

you to some whisky? At least, I'm fairly sure it's whisky, you just never can be sure with these ethyl derivatives.'

The keeper looked as though he was going to be sick.

'Ain't sayin' nothin'.'

'Mr Lovell,' Lyle asked casually, propping himself on the edge of a foul-smelling, insect-hopping hay bale, 'just out of interest, what do you think is going to happen to you worse than the full might of the law?'

At this, the old man grinned, revealing gums possessed of no more than four yellowing teeth and a lot of pink memory. It wasn't a happy grin. It was, in fact, the grin of a man who, to Lyle's mind, had planned to die many, many moons ago, and learnt to find the continued and unlikely fact of his existence nothing more than a lewd joke told on a drunken night. 'I can't tell you nothin'.'

'Well, that's an improvement from ain't. Can't means you've got something to tell me.' Lyle was fumbling in his pockets. 'You know, I'm sure I have some more stuff for occasions like this. I don't suppose you're open to bribery? It's much easier for me to bribe you than to threaten to nail various and unusual parts of your anatomy to a brick wall for letting *children* get hurt, Mr Lovell.'

His voice was level, jovial, good-mannered, but fury burnt in Lyle's gaze and as he patted down his pockets, things clanked and jangled beneath his searching fingers.

Mr Lovell backed away, but found Lyle's foot suddenly planted very firmly on his own. 'I can't,' he whimpered. 'I can't, I can't, I can't! I can't tell you nothin'!'

'You know,' Lyle said, 'I have had, in my career, enough of people being any of the following: cryptic, lyrical, insane, delusional, possessed, ignorant or downright misleading, either through direct fibs or indirect metaphorical flourish. Now, let me make it infinitely clear that I want to know what you know right here, right now, or I swear to God that ten tons of elephant shit is going to seem like summer roses compared to the wrath of the Metropolitan Police. Now,' Lyle's face was inches from Mr Lovell's own, bright and angry, 'tell me what you know.'

And Mr Lovell, to everyone's surprise, including his own, whispered, 'Greybags is gonna get you.'

And without further ado, he started to cry.

Tess and Thomas made their way through the circus.

Tess's idea of trailing the gaggle of children they'd seen in the front row of the main tent seemed, now Thomas had a chance to observe it, very simple. The children were all bunched together, held in thrall both by a stern young man who appeared to be some sort of teacher, and by a length of string wrapped round the wrist of every child in a line running to the teacher's hand. With the young man looking harassed, they drifted past men who'd discovered that an extra shot of rum at the fair was always one too few until it proved one too many, and paused before platforms on which were displayed creatures no longer graced with the description 'man' or 'woman', so strangely was their flesh deformed. These competed for the crowd's amazement with a silk-clad dancing princess who, the sign claimed, came from southern India (and who Tess swore was from Birmingham), and a tribesman of the African plains dressed in an undignified costume mostly of feathers, stitched together by a pair of seamstress sisters down in Wapping. The children goggled and gasped at everything, while the young man tried to find something educational to say. The best he could contrive tended to be: 'And this is why it is Britain's duty to enlighten the ignorant', followed by a hasty tug on the piece of string.

Thomas, as he and Tess wandered, felt he too should say something, if only because it was uncourteous for a single gentleman to be silent in the company of an unmarried female. So he cleared his throat and asked, 'What exactly are we watching the children for?'

'To see if any gets nabbed, I s'pose,' replied Tess.

'I don't wish to criticise, Miss Teresa, but you seem more interested in that undignified pirate ballad and that rather vulgar dance.'

'Uh-huh,' she said, scoffing another toffee from her bag. 'An' that shows what rubbish you are at the whole snipin' business. A real good professional always *seems* more interested in the song what is about the bucksome girls of Portsmouth an' the things they do with their stockin's, instead of her mark, so as how her mark don't get suspicious, see?'

And though Tess did indeed seem engrossed in every tent, stage and song they came upon, yet somehow they also seemed to maintain both proximity to and careful distance from the gaggle of children, right up to the moment when, led by their teacher, they vanished into a long white tent. Tess looked up at the tent, and brightened. '*Grubs*,' she blurted out, her bag of toffees vanishing into her jacket pocket, forgotten in the face of food that just *wouldn't keep* and which it was therefore her *duty* to eat *now*. 'Grubs!'

She dragged Thomas eagerly inside.

Mr Lovell was crying.

Horatio Lyle was used to almost any criminal behaviour from

general maniacal ranting up to and including trying to throw him off high places during thunderstorms. But one eventuality for which he was not prepared was to find himself sitting beside five sacks of top-quality elephant dung, with a man thirty years his senior bawling his eyes out into Lyle's vilely blotched handkerchief.

'It was so beautiful!' sobbed Mr Lovell between great gouts of tears and snot. 'The circus! I run away when I were just a boy to join it, fifty years of shovelling the, well, you know, an' now look at it! We were beautiful, an' now it's all gone ... peculiar!' More sobbing ensued.

Lyle patted Mr Lovell on the back and wondered what Mrs Bontoft would do under these circumstances.

'I mean, it's all just gone *wrong*!' wailed Mr Lovell.

'Well, I grant you, there's something definitely iffy.' Lyle tried to soothe him as best he could, his previous rage somewhat abated in the face of this unusual behaviour. 'But if you could just clarify a few of the details?'

'I wanna my mama!'

'Really?'

'I wanna my mama *now*!'

'No – but I mean, really?' queried Lyle. 'I'm just saying, it seems a little unusual for a man of your – your advanced maturity – to wanna your mama.'

'It were ... it were ...' A sound followed like an old rusted tuba being played by a herring, as the keeper blew his nose. 'He just said that he needed to sleep an' then the children were ...'

Lyle's fingers stiffened where they had been gently patting Mr Lovell's shoulder, but the weeping man didn't seem to notice. 'What children?' he asked sharply.

'The children! He said we gotta be nice to the children. Old Greybags said it an' he gave them puddin' an' . . . an' I ate it too. An' he said my dreams they ain't beautiful enough an' then . . . an' . . . *it ain't fair!*'

'Yes, yes,' stammered Lyle quickly. 'I'm sure it ain't – isn't – but if we can just try and focus on the children. What happened to the children?'

Mr Lovell sniffed, looked up into Lyle's eyes through the watery blur of his own. 'They just go to sleep,' he said. 'Happy ever after. That's how the story ends, don't it? Happy ever after for all the children. The doctor he said that.'

'What doctor?'

'They're just sleepin', see?' whimpered Mr Lovell. 'All the children. They're just dreamin' pretty stories. That's all. No harm.'

'No harm? No bloody harm? Sissy Smith was *poisoned*, she was . . .' Lyle's voice trailed away. He leant forward. 'Wait,' he breathed, staring deep into Mr Lovell's tear-filled gaze. 'Wait.' He ran his hands a few times back and forth across Mr Lovell's vision, leant right in close to his face, sniffed his breath, reached out and felt the pulse at his neck, and Mr Lovell, too busy wiping tears away with the corner of his sleeve, didn't resist. 'Sluggish pulse, slow dilation of the eyes,' breathed Lyle, 'what did you mean, he gave them pudding and you ate it too? What do you mean . . . What do you mean, you want your mother? What did you eat, Mr Lovell? Did you eat something strange? Mr Lovell? How old are you?'

'Uh?'

'How old are you?'

'Um . . . I think . . . I . . . dunno.'

'When did you run away to the circus? What year?'

'I . . . I . . .'

'Where was the Prince Consort from?'

'Um . . . dunno. Foreignland?'

'How many apples can you get for a shilling?'

Mr Lovell's face was a tortured mountain range of ridges and troughs as he struggled to find answers, and, failing, finally gave a little, toothless shrug and a smile. 'Dunno,' he snuffled, wiping his nose with his sleeve. 'Do it matter?'

Lyle leant away, stood slowly and backed up a step, his face slowly sinking into an expression first of worry, then almost of fear. 'What did you eat?' he asked. 'What . . . what do the children eat? You said – pudding – and there's a smell on your breath of . . . Mr Lovell? How can you not know how old you are? Who is Greybags?'

For a moment on Mr Lovell's face there appeared something . . . hollow. Lyle could find no other way to explain it, no better way to name it, a void of feeling, thought, sense, just a pair of empty eyes waiting to be filled with sense. 'Greybags is comin' to get you,' he said. 'Can't stop 'im. Ain't none as can stop 'im.'

'Why not? Who is Greybags? He's not a green-eyed gentleman with an aversion to magnetic ferrous material?' asked Lyle hopefully. Since when, asked a sly little voice at the back of his mind, had green-eyed semi-demonic individuals with usually malign intent become a *good* thing?

There was oblivious confusion on Mr Lovell's face.

'Mr Lovell, it's really important. You need to answer my questions. You need to tell me about the children.'

'Mr Lovell?'

It wasn't Lyle who'd spoken. They both looked up. The ringmaster, all black hat and great curled moustache, stood in the entrance to the pen. He was smiling. In one hand he held an ivory-topped cane, with the other he had swept back his great red cloak and spun it about his arm like a bullfighter. Mr Lovell jumped to his feet, wiping his eyes and nose with a single swipe of his sleeve. 'Mr Majestic, sir.'

'Something can't be wrong, can it, Mr Lovell? Surely nothing is wrong?' asked the ringmaster, and Lyle heard only incredulity, rather than concern, in his voice.

'No, sir, no. Nothing wrong, sir.'

'And this is . . .?'

'Mister Lyle, sir, Mister Horatio Lyle, sir. Nothing wrong, sir.'

'Mister Lyle! How are you enjoying the circus?'

'Very much, Mr . . . I'm sorry, what's your name?' asked Lyle smoothly.

'Mr Majestic.'

'Mr Majestic, son of Mr and Mrs Majestic?'

This question provoked a great roar of guffawing laughter, followed by a sweep of one white-gloved hand across an utterly tearless eye and a cry of, 'What a wit! What a wit, sir!'

'No, honestly,' pressed Lyle, 'I'd be fascinated to know. Mr . . .'

'Mr Majestic, as I said.'

'With all due respect, sir, I doubt that Mr Majestic is the name in the church register. I am a policeman, you see, sir, and I have—'

'A policeman! Oh, but where is your charming hat? A man is not complete without his hat. It is a hat that distinguishes a gentleman from a blaggard.'

'Mr Majestic,' Lyle's voice was rapidly darkening, 'may I ask you an important question?'

'Of course, of course!'

'How many children do you have who ran away to the circus?'

'I don't understand.'

'Of course not. Let me try this: who is Greybags?'

Mr Majestic's face darkened. His hand trembled around his cane. Mr Lovell began to back away, sticking a fist over his mouth. A whimper crawled out from between his clenched teeth.

'You . . . you should go.'

'Hilarious and not going to happen. Who is Greybags?'

'You should go now.' Mr Majestic was shaking from the tip of his moustache to the end of his toes. In a corner of the pen, Mr Lovell had curled up, peeking out between the fingers of his hands like a frightened puppy or like . . . a child. For a moment Lyle thought of Sissy Smith in her bed, wondered if she'd cowered with her hands over her eyes. Without his voice seeming to change tone or eyes wander from Mr Majestic's face he went on, knuckles white, 'Children being *hurt*, sir. A little girl who won't wake up, children going missing, sir. Who is Greybags?'

'Leave leave leave leave leave I ORDER YOU TO—'

'Have you ever wondered how flammable the ointment must be that you use to preen your moustache? It's these sorts of considerations that largely keep me from promotion within the police – *unsound*, you see. Don't mistake me, the police would perfectly happily beat you to a pulp and throw your body into the river if they ever even thought you were protecting someone who *hurts children*, Mr Majestic, sir. They just don't approve of any higher reasoning being applied to the process. Do you have any children, sir?'

At which the ringmaster gave a cry. He raised his head to the sky and his hands to his face, and his whole body seemed to wrench and shiver with an uncontrollable rage. Yet Lyle couldn't help but notice, as Mr Majestic swung the long dark end of his cane with all his strength into the side of Lyle's head, that even as his body twisted in fury, all that came from his lips was a little child-like giggle.

Even if nothing else was real, the cane felt solid enough where it smacked into Lyle's skull. And as his mother always said – you know you're onto something if they're trying to kill you.

The thought gave him little comfort as the sky turned topsy-turvy, clowning with the earth, and then went out entirely.

CHAPTER 7

Pudding

It was a tent of wonders.

Steam was the predominant feature, rising up from a hundred copper pots and pans, from fizzling grills and hissing cauldrons, billowing out above the heat of a wall of charcoal burners. Tess's jaw was halfway to her ankles, and she tugged at Thomas's sleeve, making urgent little 'Uh! Uh!' sounds as her eyes fell across new and wonderful miracles. Steamed puddings, pastries, pies, pasties hot and cold, great cakes oozing hot bubbling plum jam, grills sagging under the weight of suspicious sausages cooked to blackened perfection, pots boiling with fat greenish potatoes, huge cauldrons of pea soup and great vats of strangely bubbling shaped vegetables. The corner most popular with the men contained a wagon-weight of beer raised up on a sacred plinth, to be poured into chipped old mugs muddier than the churned tent floor. The ladies had found their way into another area, where a matron with incongruously billowing sleeves was explaining her remarkably efficient new method of peeling an egg.

As Thomas and Tess went inside, a pair of hugely grinning clowns were ushering a furious cleric out of the tent flap, whose Bible he raised aloft with a cry of, 'Vice, bawdry, sin!' His liturgy to this effect elicited nothing but giggles from the attending children, who all secretly resolved to learn as much about vice, bawdry and sin as they possibly could, since it seemed so well fed. The young teacher, seeing all this, exhorted, 'Children! Discipline!' and had to tug several times on his battered piece of string to stop his skinny followers from climbing on the tables to get at the dishes on display.

'Mr Preston has provided you with threepence each,' he said, 'so that you may *all* enjoy a slice of cake. What do we say?'

'Thank you, Mr Preston,' intoned the children with that special droning voice reserved for prayers and tedious, unwelcome obedience.

'Cake!' exclaimed Tess, as the two eavesdropped on this ritual.

'Mr Preston?' mused Thomas, feeling he ought to contribute something more sensible to the investigative process.

'Cake!' Tess squeaked again, unable to comprehend why Thomas could not share her excitement. 'Wheresa cake?'

This question was promptly answered by another great gout of steam from the far end of the tent, a rattling of wheels and an 'oooohh' of delight from the waiting children as, perched on an old wooden trolley, the cake was brought into the tent.

Tess's face fell. The cake was a dark, sludgy brown, and looked suitable to serve as a brick in any castle wall, so long as the architect didn't mind a sag in his structure. Raisins seemed its only interesting feature, for it boasted no other source of sweetness except the solid, tough mixture itself. However, it was a *big* cake, she reflected, and perhaps that made up for some of its other defects. More importantly, it was the only cake the children on the end of their piece of string seemed to have seen in their collective lives, and they all gathered around ooh-ing and aah-ing as the young man pushing the trolley presented it to them.

The young man was . . . Tess put her head on one side, trying to work out what the young man was. He wasn't particularly tall, but seemed somehow stretched, with a long, thin, almost perfectly white face topped by prematurely grey hair which was straight, thin and dishevelled and with lines round the eyes that spoke of age far more than the softness of the rest of his skin. His hands were long and made almost entirely of bone over which pale skin had been tightly stretched as if by a manufacturer with a devout belief in economy. He wore an apron splattered with flour and more suspicious-looking stuff, and a look on his face of bright, green-eyed . . .

The word Tess wanted to use was hunger. But she couldn't quite work out why.

'Mr Preston wants you all to have a slice,' the young man said. 'It's all for you!'

Tess nudged Thomas. 'Bigwig?' she began.

'Yes, Miss Teresa?'

'*Bigwig?*'

'Yes, Miss Teresa?'

'Does it seem sorta odd to you how—'

'You! You want?'

The question startled both Thomas and Tess. They looked up into the bright green eyes – was he so young? Not old, not young, but somehow stuck in between, Tess decided – of the man with the trolley on which sat the cake. He was slicing away briskly with a long steel blade, the children barely keeping order in expectation of a slice. 'You want?' he repeated. He was nodding and speaking to Tess.

'Wha'? Me?'

'Cake's for all the children.'

'I thought it was for Mr Preston's children,' said Thomas, feeling a sudden need to put himself between this strange man and Tess.

'Mr Preston pays so the children can come to the circus an' 'ave summat to eat,' answered the other man, a slight pout beginning on his lower lip at this line of questioning. 'But we always make spare cake.'

'An' you'd give summat to me?' asked Tess.

'It's for the children.'

'An' it's *free*?' she added, her voice rising with incredulity.

'Course, if you wanna.'

Tess edged towards the trolley, the children parting before her like puppies sensing a superior beast. She leant down, sniffed the cake, looked up, peered into the face of the young man and hesitated, eyes narrowing. She looked into his bright green eyes and smiling face, then down at the steel knife in his hand, down at the cake, and pursed her lips. '*Free*?' she demanded again. 'I mean, you'd gimme summat for free?'

'You want cake or not?' snapped the man and, to Thomas's astonishment, this unlikely chef stamped his foot in indignation.

Pudding

Tess shrugged. She never said no to free cake. She reached out for a thin slice.

'Wait!' It was Thomas who'd spoken. No – not spoken. Shouted. Barked in a way that would have pleased his military forebears for its combination of sheer, heart-leaping noise and utter, immoveable clarity. It was the kind of voice that could command a cavalry charge down a Crimean valley and no one, not even the doubters among the brigade, would bother to ask about those nasty cannon at the far end. He leant forward. He sniffed the cake. He picked a few crumbs off the side with the ends of his fingertips to an indignant, 'Oi!' from the young man and several grumblings from assembled onlookers. He rolled them between his fingers. Instinctively, he reached for his pockets, but a well-respected young gentleman was not supposed to carry anything in his coat, so rather than the vast collection of chemicals Lyle always carried, Thomas found himself pulling out his notebook. He opened a page. He inserted a couple of the crumbs, pushed them around on the white paper, sniffed again.

Tess huffed indignantly. 'You gonna lemme eat cake or not, bigwig?'

Thomas looked up.

One or two of the children on their piece of string stepped back. If Thomas's voice could have commanded a cavalry charge, the look on Thomas's face said that here was a general who would show no regret when the bodies were brought in. He looked straight at the young man with the grey hair and said, 'This cake isn't right.'

'Dunno what you mean.'

'It isn't right,' he repeated firmly. 'Now, I know that the common sort are forced by the unfortunate circumstances of the time to eat debased food, but this is *not* debased.' He snatched the cake from Tess's suddenly unresisting fingers. 'This is *enriched*.'

'Bigwig?' hissed Tess, starting to turn pale, wiping her hands quickly down the front of her clothes.

'You said yourself, Miss Teresa, who gives away free food to children in a place like this? There is no indication of an organised philanthropic principal at work, this is not *charity*. This is something more. Smell it.'

Tess sniffed cautiously at the slice of cake.

'All right, bigwig,' she conceded reluctantly, 'so it smells sorta peculiar.'

'More than peculiar,' proclaimed Thomas, feeling his chest start to puff with the pride and effort of detective process. 'Ethyl alcohol, and something else. When my second cousin Cuthbert—'

'You have a cousin Cuthbert?'

'Erm . . . yes.'

'*Cuthbert*?'

'Miss Teresa, if you would be so kind as to permit the deductive process to have its course!'

'If you gotta go, you gotta go,' sighed Tess with a shrug.

'. . . When my second cousin Cuthbert came back from his duties in the cantons in – well, Canton—'

'You sure you ain't makin' this up, bigwig?'

'I insist! He brought back with him the juice of a certain herb that was sold to China from the Indian plantations in exchange for silver bullion, whose smell, if I recall, most strongly resembled the—'

The cake went flying. Cheap cutlery and small metal bowls

flew across the room, thick dough splattered across the floor, children screamed and scampered out of its way as, without a word, without looking back, the grey-haired young man threw the whole thing, trolley and all, at Thomas, turned and ran.

'After him!' shrilled Thomas, the level maturity of his voice breaking for a moment into an almost girly shriek.

Tess rolled her eyes. 'Right, sure, if you'd just said that to *begin* with.'

They ran.

So, for that matter, did the rest of the people in the tent. Not because they had anywhere to run to or anything to run from, but because it seemed the thing that everyone else was doing so there was probably a good reason for it.

In fact, the only person who didn't run, was a child, a girl by the name of Effy Hall, who had been pressed at the fall of the trolley into a corner, and who sat bewildered on the floor, licking clean the end of her cake-smeared fingertips.

Horatio Lyle lay on the ground and thought about his life so far.

He thought about his father, old Harry Lyle, nails smeared with chemicals, face with coal dust, as he tried to resist the temptation to play with his son's brand new toy wooden train on its thin bit of string.

He thought about his mother, Milly Lyle, sitting in the rocking chair by the fire, carefully embroidering a small pillow with the words: Heat and Pressure at Fixed Volume Do Not Make For a Happy Home. That had been after the incident with the coal fire, the fermenting plums, the steel vat and her husband's enthusiastic discovery of the concept of catalysation. She had only got as far as 'Heat and Pres' before running out of space. Needlework had never been Milly Lyle's strongest suit.

He thought about Miss Chaste, a vicar's daughter, proclaiming, 'You know, Horatio, if you just put down those funny little books, I know a smashing place where we could play bridge.'

At the time, he hadn't understood what she really meant.

He thought he could see Tess out of the corner of his eye. He couldn't hear what she was saying. He guessed it was rude.

He thought he could see Thomas, who said nothing at all, but just looked down at him and frowned that stern little frown of his as if to say, 'When I grow up, I will consider your current predicament one which I shall endeavour to avoid. Tut-tut, really.'

He thought he felt Tate pulling at his trouser leg.

He could feel Tate pulling at his trouser leg.

Curious, that.

Even more curious, was what he saw when he opened his eyes.

Greyness.

A lot of greyness.

But not just any ordinary greyness. Oh no. This was a very special, mud-spattered, wrinkled kind of greyness, leathery and sprouting hundreds of thick yellowish hairs at odd intervals up and down its considerable length. And it smelt. It took Lyle some time to work out what it smelt of.

It smelt of elephant.

Reality came flying back like a ringmaster's cane to the skull. He gave a muted cry somewhere between a gulp of breath and a wheeze of terror that hit each other somewhere around the vocal chords and buzzed. He threw himself back onto his hands, nearly crushing Tate beneath his flailing legs as he did so, and looked up into the thoughtful eyes of an elephant. Very, very much an elephant. Tate growled, plonking himself firmly on his haunches by his master's side and glaring up into the elephant's face as if daring it to test the maxim 'size doesn't matter'. A pair of huge yellowish-brown eyes considered Lyle for a long moment. A mouth that drooped like the edge of a cathedral gutter opened and closed behind a softly curling trunk, bright pink at the end. It reached out towards him. Lyle squeezed his eyes shut and thought, *Oh God, what a stupid stupid stupid way to die. I really hope Tess doesn't find out.*

The trunk reached past him. It fumbled in a heavy trough just behind Lyle's head and, with possibly the most obscene slurping sound Lyle had ever heard even in his acquaintance with Tess (not renowned for her good manners), it began to drink the water from the trough.

Lyle looked at Tate.

Tate looked at Lyle.

If man and beast could be said to share an understanding that transcended both language and words, the two of them experienced in that single moment a mutual comprehension that more than nine years of prior friendship had not yet produced. Carefully picking Tate up in his arms, legs and ears dangling down either side of his master's grip, Lyle moved with the slow, careful waddle of the utterly innocuous, towards the edge of the pen.

Someone had locked the gate. Outside, he could see the small patch of manure-filled earth where Mr Lovell plied his trade. There was no one there. He put Tate down on the ground. Tate considered the metal bars of the gate, considered his own width, and promptly tried to force himself between them. He got a little more than halfway before becoming stuck, front paws dangling in the realms of freedom, rear paws paddling uselessly at the world behind. Lyle felt blood running down the side of his head. The trick was to focus on the elephant. Pain, bewilderment, anger and confusion could all happen later. Later, he decided, fumbling a set of picklocks out of the inner reaches of his jacket, was any time after the point where he was *not* crushed alive by an elephant.

He carefully set to picking the lock.

From somewhere else inside the circus, there came the sound of animals in distress.

Later, Tess would never be entirely sure how it had happened.

Suddenly they were chasing a – 'young man' would have to do for now – a young man with grey hair who, according to Thomas and the herbal insights of his second cousin Cuthbert recently returned from secondment to cantons in Canton, whatever that meant, a young man who was allegedly responsible for putting perfectly nasty stuff in a perfectly good cake. As if that wasn't bad enough, it was a perfectly good *free* cake and Tess had almost eaten it, and if that didn't tell you everything you needed to know about the upper classes, then she didn't know what did, so there.

The point being that one moment they were chasing him, the next moment, the world had gone mad. It had become peculiar when a matron with flour on her apron and a pair of huge bright red arms had tried to take Thomas's head off with a saucepan. It had worsened when a dancing monkey had locked itself onto Tess's head and tried to pull her ear off. This had immediately induced panic in the members of the public who were witness to this event, who had never until that moment conceived of monkeys as anything other than fluffy little creatures about which Mr Charles Darwin had some hideously unorthodox ideas. No sooner had Tess got the monkey off her head by the lucky expedient of head-butting the side of a Punch and Judy stand, than the puppeteer for the Punch character, his face every bit as strange, warped and out of proportion as his puppet, had started shrieking and attempted to bash her over the skull with – not the wooden puppet he held, but with the tiny little cosh that the *puppet* held in its hand. Which, as she was quick to discover, was no way to stop a good thief in her tracks.

It was, however, enough to slow her down.

She could see the bobbing grey head of the strange young man vanishing into the crowd as her fingers became entangled in strings and wood. For a moment as she looked at the puppet, she could have sworn that the painted eyes looked straight back at her, and they were *angry*.

By this time, mass hysteria was beginning to take hold of the crowd. Somewhere she could hear Thomas's imperious voice barking, 'Now, I'm going to inherit a seat in the House of Commons, you know, and this is really too . . .'

She kicked the Punch puppeteer in the kneecap and tried to push her way into the crowd. Somewhere nearby, horses were screaming, a wild, terrified sound and children began to cry and tumble beneath the running feet of the indifferent public, who now ran because they were afraid, because marvellous things were suddenly frightening things, and because they didn't know – above all because they *did not know* – why it was they ran. Which just made running all the more important. Someone knocked Tess to the ground. She got up blearily and saw a space between a pipe organ on little wheels, painted in red and gold that was still happily tinkling its merry tune and a knocked-over stand selling nougats of toffee. She crawled into it, rubbing her head, hands grazed and muddy. For a moment, as the chaos ignited into panic, she thought she smelt . . .

. . . ginger biscuit . . .

. . . autumn leaves . . .

. . . trodden on grass . . .

She looked up.

A purple tent, seemingly untouched by the storm, was set a few yards back from the rest of the circus attractions. It was trimmed with silver thread, and above the closed flap, a sign declared:

**MYSTIC MAI'S MAGICAL EMPORIUM —
SECRETS EXPLORED, MYSTERIES SOLVED,
THE ETHER PARTED AND THE ASTRAL VOID
PENETRATED. SPIRITS, ANCIENT SEERS AND
FAERIE PROPHETS INVOKED — ENTRY 6D.**

Tess staggered uneasily to her feet as a donkey, its ears swept back in terror, broke free from its head collar and started bucking and furiously kicking in its narrow stall. Somewhere in the distance, coppers were swinging their rattles, signs were being torn from fences and a pair of angry lions roared. She took a cautious step towards the tent.

A hand fell on her arm.

She jumped back instinctively, and looked up into Thomas's mud-splattered face.

'Did you see him?' Thomas snapped. 'Did you see where he went?'

Tess shook her head.

'We have to find him!'

'In this lot?'

'It's our duty!'

'Ain't doin' nothin' if our necks get broke, bigwig,' grumbled Tess, quickly pulling Thomas down as a round tent hook went flying overhead. 'You may be smart at the whole deductiving thin', but let me handle the stayin' alive part.'

'We have to find him!' wailed Thomas, almost pulling at his hair in frustration. 'You saw what they did; they tried to poison the children!'

'An' we stopped 'em! Ain't that neat for us?'

'But . . . but we know so little. We don't know why or who or how or . . . or . . .' Thomas's voice trailed away. 'Or where Mister Lyle is.'

Tess rolled her eyes. 'Oh yes.' She sighed. 'That's so bloody typical. Me an' a token bigwig, goin' an' savin' Mister Lyle from all his mistakes, *again*. Cos you just know he's gonna be in the poo poo don't you? Come *on*.' So saying, she grabbed Thomas by the sleeve, and dragged him out into the sweeping, scampering crowd.

From the doorway of the dark purple tent, someone watched them go.

Her name was . . .

Concentrate . . .

Her name was Effy Hall. Yes. That was it. That was what the teacher said, and that was what it was.

The teacher had said, 'You can have a bit of cake, Effy' and the man had said, 'Here you are' and she'd eaten some of the cake and then . . . and *then* . . . Then there'd been that boy and he'd said . . . He'd *said* . . . And there was the room and the sound, always the sound, nagging in her ears since the first bite of cake, the first singing cry of it, echoing, always echoing, and it had gone: '*Once upon a time . . .*'

oh god oh god oh god run run run run

Pretty stories . . .

She'd said, knowing it to be true, 'I'm going to run away to the circus now.' And undone the string round her wrist, turned and walked away.

And her name was Effy . . . Effy . . . her name *was* . . .

Running away to the circus . . .

He'd said, 'Don't be afraid, little girl. You eat your pudding now. All children like their pudding.'

Once upon a time there was a girl who . . .

. . . never mind.

She'd sleep on it.

Everything would be clearer in the morning.

Good night, Effy Hall.

Sweet dreams.

It was a truth acknowledged really quite often that when you wanted a cab in London, you could never get one. Thomas had read books, of course he'd read books, where you could wave a hand and, lo, a hansom would appear. But that was wishful thinking, in this day and age, not least when you were trying to catch a cab from outside a smoke-filled, elephant-plagued circus with – all due respect – a pickpocket, a long-eared dirty dog and a man whose chief cause of concern at that exact moment of time was, 'How, and I mean in precisely what chemical manner, how can anything cling to a fibrous object with such persistency?!'

Horatio Lyle, his clothes covered in a mixture of mud and less salubrious things, fumed as the four companions marched down the edge of Hyde Park in search of a hansom cab. His hair stuck up tattily from his head, his clothes were torn and smeared with things that bore little polite contemplation, and blood was still drying down one side of his face. In all the fuss, he seemed to have forgotten about this last detail, proclaiming, 'Do you think it sanitary to attempt to clean it now? No! Me neither! Let the clotting process do its own business until we are in a hygienic domestic environment. This is what the human body was designed for!'

All of which Thomas took as nothing more than a sign of Lyle's intense frustration, since, by his own admission, human biology was something Lyle regarded as a basely common scientific pursuit. Or as Tess might put it, 'He gets all queasy at the sight of blood, see?'

Tess was remarkably silent. Finding Mister Lyle attempting to disentangle Tate from the bars of an elephant pen was, she felt, a subject of mirth too easy for her skills. Besides, the expression on Lyle's face, that very special expression he wore only in the face of sloppy laboratory procedure, the twice-weekly battle of the bathtubs and cold-blooded murder, suggested that now was not the time to discuss his curious predicament. Nor to mention in full detail exactly the part he, Tate, the children and a particularly bewildered elephant surprised to find its pen gate ajar, had played in reducing a large part of Mr Majestic's Marvellous

Electric Circus to a chaotic tumble of snapped ropes and tumbled tents.

'Chimney sweeps and undertakers can get hansom cabs!' pronounced Lyle furiously, 'but upright citizens, nobly injured upholding the bloody law, oh no!'

In the end, they took the omnibus.

Thomas didn't know whether to feel proud or alarmed that of the three of them, he received the most bewildered stares. One old lady in her sixties even offered him her seat.

'Gentlemen,' she explained, 'ain't s'posed to stand.'

If it was possible for Lyle's scowl to deepen, it did.

It was a place for the children to sleep.

Red bricks. Black iron bed frames and soft white beds.

The ladies in peaked white hats ran water between their lips. Sometimes, in the children's more lucid moments, they could even be persuaded to eat, slurping down soup, or munching absently on warm, soft, fresh-baked bread.

But mostly, they slept.

Sweet dreams, children.

Until now.

He said, 'They came to the circus an' they nearly ruined *everythin'* an' it ain't fair an' I only got one of them to dream an' then she didn't eat much of the cake an' they *knew* they knew 'bout the puddin' an' they tried to stop it an' one of them were a grown-up but the other two were children as *spoil the fun* an' it ain't fair it ain't it ain't fair!'

She said, a soft voice, like the whispered wind on the edge of a screaming gale, 'It's all right, it's all right. There there . . .' and stroked his thin grey hair as he pressed his head against her shoulder, and held him by the shoulder and comforted him, just like a mother would. 'It's all right. Who were these nasty people?'

'Don't know name of the boy an' girl, they didn't say nothin', they just spoilt it for the rest! But Mr Lovell what looks after the elephants he talked to the man an' he said he said his name were . . . it were . . .'

'There there,' crooned the woman again, empty words for a mind that didn't really care. 'You can tell me. You can always tell me everything.'

'His name were Horatio Lyle.'

For a moment, she stiffens. Her back is cold old steel, her fingers dead meat on a pair of limp stubby arms. But the creature with grey hair, wrapped in her arms, doesn't care. Doesn't notice. Doesn't know how.

So she whispers, like the trees bending when the rain begins to fall, 'It's all right. We'll take care of it. They won't bother you again.'

And strangely, she means it.

For the good of the children.

The sun set, a great burning golden blaze across the sky that would never quite reach the horizon, but suffocated in the brown stain of smoke that hung above the western edge of the city.

Tess struck a match to light a lamp in the downstairs parlour. As the flame caught and the yellow light grew, she looked round at the high shelves on the walls, and contemplated supper.

In what Thomas supposed had to be the master bedroom – a place whose floor was nine part books to one part floorboard, with occasional exposed places between the great paper stacks to be used as stepping stones between door and bed – he tried on one of Lyle's old shirts, to replace his own muddy, torn garment.

It floated round him like the sails of a fat merchant ship, and smelt faintly of sawdust.

In the small washroom next door, Horatio Lyle patted carefully at the side of his head with a strip of white cotton, flinching at each touch to his skull and resolving that this was the last time, repeat, the *last time* that he disdained a man based on the ridiculousness of his moustache. On the table behind him, he'd emptied out some of the stuff from his pockets. *Mrs Bontoft's Practical Advice* had fallen half open, the pages turned towards the ceiling.

> . . . the son will most easily learn his father's trade, which, if base, will serve as a reminder of the family from which he will rise, and if learned, will endow him with the necessary ambition to advance further his understanding and ability to support his family when the time comes. A daughter must naturally learn from her mother all the skills necessary for being a wife and mother in her turn . . .

Tate was in his basket under the kitchen table. It was an ideal spot for him, the perfect mixture of close to the fire, and close to those frequent cast-offs from Lyle's cooking that Tess dropped down to him from her dinner plate. He didn't even have to move his head to catch them.

Sissy Smith slept.

And dreamt.

And slept some more.

'Things were peculiar at the circus, sir,' said Thomas.

They sat round the kitchen table, the lamplight stretched up the low grey walls.

'"Peculiar"?!' squeaked Lyle indignantly. 'That is no way to describe events! I woke up in an elephant pen covered in – Half of investigation is precision, lad! Exact detail! Analysis!'

'So what is it?' asked Tess casually through a mouthful of pie.

'It's . . . Well, it's . . . there are events happening at the circus – situations – circumstances that perhaps can be best described as . . . well . . . as . . .' Lyle's voice trailed away. 'Besides,' he pronounced so suddenly Thomas jumped in his chair, 'even if we cannot clarify matters immediately, there is no need to imply any sort of semi-mystical or supernatural explanation to an event based purely on our ignorance of the entirely explicable and natural cause.'

Tess raised one hand. 'Wha'?'

'Mister Lyle, I think, wants us to assume that ignorance is not proof,' explained Thomas helpfully. 'It's an argument commonly used by these atheist sorts who claim that, while they cannot at the moment *explain* how the world came to be the thing it is, it is clearly not the creation of some theologically defined deity, as there is no proof for such an event any more than there is proof of, say, a giant spider spinning the universe out of yak hairs.'

Silence.

Then Lyle said, 'I'm not sure I *was* saying that.'

Silence again.

'Although,' he conceded, 'in principal you have a very sound philosophical point.'

Under the table, Tate scratched busily behind one of his dangling ears.

'I'm sorry – what were we talking about?'

'How there is sinister forces what is workin' at the circus an' all, an' how you don't have no answer for what them is 'cept as how it isn't a giant spider spinnin' stuff from yak hair,' Tess explained helpfully.

'Right. Yes. I thought so. For example: children going to the circus from the workhouses.'

'An' then not never comin' back,' added Tess helpfully.

'Or coming back in such a manner as the unfortunate Miss Smith,' agreed Thomas. 'In some way afflicted by a narcotic, which narcotic, Mr Lyle, I'm fairly certain I found being freely distributed in a cake served by a – a young man.'

'What young man?'

'Dunno,' said Tess. 'He were a bit odd, see? Like as how he weren't . . . all sorta . . . He had this grey hair, right, which were like an old codger, see, but then he had like this young face an' he spoke . . . odd. But I saw him hold iron fine, so he can't be one of *them*.'

'The ringmaster was "odd".' Lyle flinched at the imprecision of the word. 'Mr Majestic. Not as though he wouldn't give me his true name but as if he couldn't understand the question when I asked him for it. I asked him about children and he reacted with a distinct lack of social responsibility.'

'You mean as how he went an' clobbered you one, an' stuck you in the elephant sh—' began Tess cheerfully.

'Quite.'

'Mister Lyle, an' don't go seein' nothin' bad in this, but I can think of lotsa people as would wanna go stick you in the elephant poo.'

'Teresa, even leaving aside your attempted assassination of my good character,' said Lyle firmly, 'I am entirely confident that *Mrs Bontoft's Practical Advice on Family Life* has stern words about children who repeatedly try to find ways to work excess biological products into conversations.'

Thomas raised a helpful hand. 'Sir? About that narcotic substance.'

'What? Oh, yes. What about it?'

'I was merely going to suggest that if we could perhaps find a sample of the substance in which it had been introduced—'

'Bigwig?' Tess's voice cut through, bored.

'A sample of the substance, and then perhaps subject it to ruthless chemical analysis—'

'Bigwig!'

'Polite young ladies don't interrupt slightly more polite young gentlemen!' said Lyle briskly.

'But, *bigwig* . . .'

'Then we may be able to isolate the chemical compound responsible for the unfortunate condition of Miss Smith and perhaps determine—'

'Bigwig!' Lyle raised his eyebrows, Thomas did his best not to huff at Tess's shouted interruption. She waited until she was sure she had their complete attention, and then, smiling brightly, folded her arms, treated them to her least crooked smile and said, 'I were just goin' to say, seein' as how you two were blatherin' on 'bout narcotic stuff, as how maybe you'd need a sample of the cake thin' in which there were all this poison thin', and if either of you ever went an' treated me with a little respect as one of my professionatanism deserved, then how I might have just what you went an' needed.' She reached into her pocket, and pulled out a fistful of crumbling dark cake. 'You didn't really think as how I'd go an' leave grubs behind, now did you?'

*

The lights burnt late in Horatio Lyle's house.

They burnt in the guest bedroom, where Thomas Edward Elwick read by dim candlelight a book lifted from the great stacks of papers on Lyle's study floor, whose title had been nothing more than a mathematical code and whose contents, for all Thomas could tell, appeared to have been written by a man who spoke no language but multiples of eight.

They burnt in Tess's bedroom, where she sat huddled with her knees to her chin and read *Mrs Bontoft's Practical Advice*. Lyle would, she imagined, be a little irritated to discover that the book was missing from his jacket pocket when he next went to look for it, but he would quickly become distracted by other concerns like chemical reduction, magnetic induction and people trying to kill him, so Tess wasn't greatly worried.

Her lips moved silently as she tried to muddle through the fat plodding words.

It is a truth of our times that more often than not, a parent will die before a child has reached maturity. Mothers will die in childbirth, a risk only increased by the more children they bear; fathers engaged in manual labour will often pass away before their time. In many cases, hard though it be to bear, such a thing can be accounted a blessing as well as a grief, for there are few means to support the elderly and it is unnatural to turn out a member of the family who is too old to work – and yet this is a practice more commonly done than confessed to. A child does not need the burden of feeding its parents, let alone before that child has reached a mature age. As maturity embraces the comprehension of all things, then let the child comprehend this:

that their parents are mortal, and it is their duty to honour, support and obey in both life and death all that their fathers and mothers command and bequeath. The sooner they accept this reality, the swifter they shall learn and develop into successful citizens of the empire.

For a long while, Tess thought about these words, with the book in her lap. Then she reached down, tore out the page with a long slow *sssshhhhlllllipp!* of thick rupturing paper, touched its dangling tip to the candle, and watched it burn to ash.

In the basement of Lyle's house, Horatio Lyle Esquire, a gentleman too busy to own a hat, sat with his chin in his hands and watched liquid drip, one slow drop at a time, into the bottom of a glass funnel. He was aware that there were probably more charismatic ways to spend his time, but on the other hand, you never knew whether the *next* drip would be the one that made the entire thing catch fire, and somewhere in the boredom of waiting for chemical processes to do their thing, was the fascination of waiting to find out.

He had, in truth, never before attempted to isolate narcotic substances from cake, and wasn't entirely convinced that it could be done without causing irreparable contamination of the sample. But Horatio Lyle was not a man to run away from a challenge, and so he sat, and waited, to the sound of Tate snoring gently at his side.

Someone was watching the house.

She doesn't sleep like ordinary people do.

She doesn't do anything like ordinary people do.

This thought gives her a good deal of pride.

The fact that she was the only one in the still deadness of the night to be awake to see the carriage pull up in front of the main door, and the clown get out on the pavement side, caused her rather less delight.

The church bells struck across the city.

Once, then twice. St Paul's, St Peter's, St Anne's, St Giles', St Mark's, St Luke's, St-Andrew's-in-the-Wardrobe – although no one ever really enquired what St Andrew was doing in the wardrobe to begin with – from Westminster to Bow they struck, each in their own key, each to their own time.

And in the house of Horatio Lyle, Sissy Smith dreams of . . .

Run away to the circus!

And Thomas dreams of . . .

Father looking old.

And in the laboratory, snoozing peacefully at Lyle's feet, Tate dreams of . . .

Dinosaur bones, great big fossils from great big reptiles with huge yellow eyes that look down at little dogs and don't really care because they're big and dogs are small and who'd hurt a fluffy dog anyway? Not a dinosaur, that's for sure . . .

Horatio Lyle, his head on the table in front of his experiments, dreams of . . .

Old Harry Lyle, eyes bright with wonder, explaining, 'Water will expand when cold, a crystalline form. No snowflake is ever the same.'

In the biggest bed in the biggest room in the house ('Cos you don't understand what it is that ladies need, Mister Lyle, but I is gonna tell you – we needs the biggest room.'), Teresa Hatch dreams of . . .

Black cupboards perhaps now it is tomorrow or perhaps now or perhaps now perhaps at this moment they'll open the door or perhaps at this perhaps if I hammer and shout they'll let me out let me out! it must have been a day it must have been two and must have been for ever please let me out I'll never speak words never again, so quiet in the cupboard so quiet and LET ME OUT!

And wakes, gasping for breath, dragging the blanket up to her neck, heart beating in her brain.

And because she is the only one awake in this sleeping, dreaming house, she is the only one who hears a sound like . . . *click-thump* . . . like an almost nothing sound, so infinitely small and harmless and tiny that it shouldn't have mattered, didn't matter, didn't mean anything and yet . . .

If you were savvy, if you were smart . . .

If you were, in short, the kind of girl who knew about locks . . . it sounded a hell of a lot like someone trying to ease open the front door.

But this being the house of Horatio Lyle, a man who understood that, yes, there *were* nasty people out there and, no, sometimes they couldn't be reasoned with and, yes, when you were an eccentric inventor with a taste for irritating people with very short tempers and no sense of humour, sometimes there would be consequences – because of all this, no sooner had Tess heard the unmistakeable little *click-thump* of the pick sliding into the front door, than she heard the *thwap-pop-argh!* of a hundred volts being pumped straight into the tumblers of the door, up the lock pick and into the arms of whoever it was trying to break in. She reflected that, under normal circumstances, being mildly electrocuted while trying to open a door illegally would discourage most meddlers. It was therefore testimony to how much trouble they were in that rather than run away, as would have been the sensible reaction of the average thief, this would-be housebreaker threw aside his scorched lock picks, and set about breaking down the front door of Lyle's house by brute force.

Which was why, as the doorframe began to splinter, Tess was already halfway downstairs, heading for the laboratory, and accelerating.

CHAPTER 9

Break-In

Had anyone, other than the one person who did, paid attention to the events outside Lyle's house on that lamp-washed night, they might have been surprised to see the strangest gathering of housebreakers as had ever assembled to do wrong. A man wearing a ridiculous purple cloak, with a moustache that stuck out further than his ears, was sucking on a pair of scalded fingers; two more men, sporting old-fashioned Napoleonic side whiskers and cavalry uniform from that time, all gold braid and tight trousers, strutted imperiously up and down outside the house, while a man wearing a lion skin across one shoulder and white trousers that warped under the pressure of his straining thighs, slammed a shoulder wider even than his head against the front door. Downstairs, at the basement entrance, a man dressed like a Spanish dancer, all cloak and mane, drew a knife from a sheath on his arm, flourished it dramatically like a conductor's baton, and threw it, tip first, at the nearest window.

All the time, posted in the street like a guard, stood the organ grinder. His hair was white, his nose was round, his chin badly shaven below his pendant lips. His eyes – above all, people noticed his eyes – stared unblinking like diamonds in a corpse's skull from above a fixed smile. All the while he wound the handle on the side of his little mechanical organ, oblivious to any sort of criminal protocol regarding discretion in burglaries, while on the roof, a tiny monkey, nothing more than bones and coconut skull, danced in its little red hat to the tinkling of the circus song: *Alas my love, you do me wrong, to cast me off so discourteously* . . .

For that, right there, was what they were: the circus, who, rather than waiting for Lyle to come to them, had come to Lyle.

Tess moved at speed. It wasn't running, it wasn't scuttling, it certainly wasn't walking, but it was a frantic speed that meant the hands at least got the job done even before the mind realised that the job needed doing. In the laboratory where he slept, Tate shuffled and growled, nose twitching at the distant smashing of a window, teeth slipping out beneath the ripple of his lips as a new distant sound intruded on his senses. He smelt . . . lead and mud and dust and. . . and *grass* . . . definitely grass . . . and fabric and horse manure and . . . and other kinds of dung that he hadn't even smelt before, and Tate thought he had smelt *every* kind of manure there was to smell, and metal and oil and grease and cheap soup and something else, as well, something . . . familiar. Not quite alcohol, not quite opium, something not quite sharp, bitter and organic but in between. He growled, opened one lethargic eye, saw the half slouched slumbering shape of Lyle in the fading lamplight and noticed that, on the table in front of his pet human, a half full glass tumbler of clear white liquid was slowly filling with a milky precipitate.

Ears twitched. This took some time, since Tate was composed of a very large percentage of ear relative to the rest of him, and the ripples only died away when the tips of the white-brown stained ears reached the floor and came to rest. He heard little clanking metal notes being struck by little clanking metal handles, that he supposed were what Tess (his favourite pet human, the one with the biscuits) would have called 'music'. This strange human phenomenon, one that seemed to serve no useful purpose as far as Tate could tell, had an irritating, low-pitched rhythm and seemed to originate from outside the heavy wooden door of the lab. It was accompanied by the more traditional sounds of Lyle's house – the regular *kh-thump kh-thump* of a great human shoulder slamming against the front door and the *shicka shicka shicka* of breaking glass being pushed aside from somewhere near the kitchen. Someone was breaking in, they were breaking into *his* human's house, and the most useful pet human in these sorts of circumstances, was lying asleep in front of an experiment that was starting to bubble.

Tate considered all his options.

He reached the most viable conclusion, and firmly bit Horatio Lyle on the ankle.

Thomas woke with a start.

He thought, *Interesting. I didn't know men could scream so loudly.*

He thought, *Men screaming? What a ridiculous notion. Men don't scream. Women scream. Women scream when mice appear and other delicate womanly things like that. Men don't scream because it's – Well, it's just not the done thing.*

Consciousness after a long sleep was a slow process for Thomas Edward Elwick at the best of times.

He thought, *wait, wait, wait. Gentlemen don't scream because it's not the done thing, but common people – common people might be an entirely different matter, not bred for it, you see.*

Not bred for it? shouted that part of his brain that was already figuratively halfway up the trousers and reaching for the shirt. *Not bred for working twelve hours a day in a coal mine at constant risk of collapse, not bred for battle against native hoards angered at the civilisation of their barbaric lands, like India or China and other savage places, not bred for a life spent in the company of rats and cholera – not bred for not screaming? Besides . . .*

Besides, agreed the rest of his mind, which was finally catching up with the better part of his brain, *let's be honest, you're not exactly in the company of gentlemen here, are you?*

A moment, while Thomas shuddered towards full consciousness.

He thought, *So was that Mister Lyle who just screamed? And why can I hear the sound of an organ grinder?*

Tess was in the parlour, lit by nothing more than a trickle of lamplight through the small window above. She could hear footsteps on the floorboards above her, and as she worked she whispered under her breath, almost inaudible over the beating of her heart. 'Oxygen, oxygen, oxygen . . . where's the bloody mask?' Tess swept thick bundles of drying herbs off their shelves as she rummaged through the stores. 'Bloody mess!' she snapped in frustration. 'Oh, yes, such a bloody organised bloody scientist bloke.'

With a sudden cry of joy, Tess pulled out something from a chest of drawers that to Tate's eye looked little more than a leather sack, and smelt of all the worst by-products of amateur tanning. Even Tess's insensitive human nose wrinkled in distaste as she pulled the thing over her head, covering her entire skull so that just a pair of eyes peeped out through a pair of spectacle-like circles stitched into the fabric. Somewhere close – too close – she heard a door creak open and bit back the desire to scream for Lyle. *I ain't bloody screamin' till the bigwig does, else I won't never hear the end of it.* She pushed the drawer shut, grabbed a pair of charred work gloves from a table, dragged them onto her small hands and ran for the opposite side of the room.

Before she left, she reached up for the gas lamp, or perhaps, more exactly, for the thing that looked like a gas lamp embedded in the wall, turned it on but didn't bother to strike a light.

Thomas walked uneasily down the corridor, a candle in his hand.

He could hear sounds in the house.

Instinct said, *Run run run for God's sake. This is not a gentleman's house. Of course it's not good news. Of course it's not, why don't you run?*

But against what was essentially sound instinct, a lifetime of good breeding and upbringing said, *No no no. Surely it's a misunderstanding. I wouldn't want to seem a fool now, just a little misunderstanding. It will sort itself out soon.*

It was a testimony, therefore, to the strength of instinct that, as he rounded the end of the corridor and saw the door to Sissy Smith's bedroom open, rather than advance and demand an explanation as his father would have, he carefully blew out the candle, and wondered where the nearest steel poker was.

Inwardly, good breeding rolled its eyes and sighed at so many years of fine work undone as Thomas crept towards Sissy Smith's door.

Tess ran downstairs into the darkness below Lyle's house. There were gas lamps set in every wall. As she ran, she opened the valves in every brass pipe so that the long, slow *sssssss* of the unlit gas began to shimmer and twist on the air.

Below – a long way below, close enough to below so that she could smell the old sewers washed with tidal trickles from long-dead rivers – she looked round the darkness of the lowest room, this other room, the laboratory where even Lyle didn't like to go unless he had to, and saw the thick black pipes in the walls that supplied the house.

Sometimes Tess hated Lyle's approach to 'non-lethal'. She didn't like dead things, and didn't want to kill anyone. Of course not, not at all. She just didn't like the idea of being deaded any time soon herself, let alone by a . . . whatever it was, a whoever it was, who kept on playing, relentlessly playing that damn organ!! What kind of bloody burglar played the bloody organ on a job?! It was unprofessional, gave her whole chosen industry a bad name!

There were hidden ways out of Lyle's house, of course there were. You didn't annoy that many people with that much power and so few scruples without building ways out that others wouldn't see: down through the sewers, perhaps, or up over the rooftops. Tess knew about them, had eyed them up on the first night of her acquaintance with Mister Lyle, but then, that wasn't really the point, because if – whoever it was, whoever played the organ, while they came in through the front door – if they were looking for anything of Lyle's, it was almost certainly going to be Sissy Smith. She knew she had what Lyle would call a 'tragic lack of verifiable evidence' for this assumption, but more importantly, she knew she was right, and that meant she couldn't just run away. If no one stood up for the nobody, then who'd stand up for her?

She didn't like this place, this old abandoned cellar that Lyle had once made his main workplace. In one corner was a darker patch of empty space where formerly there'd been a machine of magnets and coils. Across the ceiling were scars where a blast had taken out chunks of ancient stone. Round the door were burn marks from twisted magnetic wires, and on the floor, a lingering dark tracery of stuff that only she, Lyle, Thomas and dead not-quite-men had known for blood. This had been the room where it had all begun – the adventures, the men with the green eyes and the fear of magnets, the dead things and the lives saved – and it occurred to her now, that the only reason she wasn't afraid of the things she'd seen was that there'd never been a moment to think about it, not in a dark place like this.

Behind her the gas went *sssssssss*, and above her the organ went, *tinkle clang tinkle*, and Tate shuffled and whined, and in her bedroom, Sissy Smith tossed and dreamt of . . .

Clowns with painted faces, dancing monkeys and white stallions, creatures with long noses and necks as tall as houses, strange spotted cats that growl from behind bars, swinging acrobats and sweet smelling delights of . . . smelling of . . . of . . .

. . . once upon a time there was a boy who ran away to the circus . . .

And at the door of Sissy Smith's bedroom a man with a smile painted in huge red lines across his face, eased back the door to look in, saw the child sleeping and, as all clowns must when they see anything that pleases, giggled. Because that's what clowns do. Behind him, the shadow of a boy dressed in a shirt ten years too big for him rose up, outlined in darkness against a shimmering oil lamp, a poker in his right hand.

Upstairs, a man, a clown, his face all smiling red laughter, giggling, dressed in a lion skin and a pair of warping white trousers looked up from the bed where Sissy Smith lay and said, 'Did you hear summat?'

The organ grinder kept on grinding his organ.

The monkey kept on dancing on his stand.

Sissy Smith kept on sleeping.

Just like it was meant to be.

In the cellar below the basement, Tess looked at the great black pipes on the wall, holding up her thin light and pressing her ear to each length of metal to listen to the rumbling of the hot gases within. She had always gone out of her way to pretend not to listen when Lyle explained the way the pipes worked, explained *why* this valve led to that joint, but even she had known, as they'd stood in the darkness of this old vault, that it was important.

To one side of the pipes, a great panel of pumps and pistons had been crudely thrown together by a man for whom 'finishing touches' were a trivial extra. The only female touch to this

ragtag assemblage of metal and levers was a note nailed into the roof above, on which Tess's rough hand proclaimed:

DANJER. SMELS.

She tore the note down and looked at another one beneath it. This said, in Lyle's most careful handwriting: 'Wear a mask.'

She felt the smelly leather thing over her face, wondered how strange it must look to anyone who could see, and then ran her hands down over the pipes and pulleys. She found a handle, turned it hard to one side, heard something heavy and metallic clunk, like a heavy railway track shifting its course, heard another clang from overhead, and then heard the *sssss* of the leaking gas from the lanterns upstairs suddenly stop, their supply cut off.

The clown eased towards Sissy Smith, reached out for the pillow on which she rested her head, smiling to think of her pretty little face all warm and sleepy beneath the feathers of the pillow.

At the back of the dark cellar that stank of things no house should ever stink of, Tess climbed up onto a chest of drawers, fumbled among the shelves, stuck her hand deep into a pile of jars and boxes. She'd heard of houses where, if you pulled out a certain book, whole shelves would swing inwards to reveal a secret compartment. Lyle hadn't liked this idea at all – too easy, he'd said, too clean, too . . . Just too eighteenth century. Therefore, in order to open the secret doorway in Lyle's laboratory, he'd gone for a solution far more likely to deter any concealed door hunters, and hidden the switch at the bottom of a jar of pickled eggs.

*

The clown looked down at Sissy Smith, smiled, said, 'Once upon a time there was a beautiful little princess, but she was sleepy and couldn't wake up until the handsome prince . . . No, wait, that's not how it goes. Um . . .'

And then, eyes focused somewhere a very long way away, as if he didn't even notice what he did, he pushed the pillow over Sissy's face, held it down tight, whistling a distant tune between his jagged smiling teeth as he did so.

A voice behind him said, 'Oh, I say . . . um . . . No, really?'

He half turned.

The poker in Thomas's hand bounced off his skull, and that was the last thing the clown saw for a while.

In the basement, Tess flicked the switch.

She tried to remember what Lyle had said. The usual refrain of 'Never, ever ever, *ever*, I mean *ever*, unless someone is actually trying to kill you and, even then, I would rather you consulted me first, circumstances allowing' was all that she could hear, repeating itself in her mind over and over again. There had been something more, as well, something like, 'It'll be big, it'll be violent, it'll be *amazing* – if it works.'

There was a little clattering of glass, as the sharpened end of something small and internal punctured the top of something heavy and overfilled. There was the uncomfortable sound of two liquids that didn't want to be friends, mingling, somewhere behind the walls. Tess hopped down off the shelf where she stood, pulled open the nearest cupboard door, tipped out a pile of stained old tea towels, until she found a pair of bellows, the nose embedded in the wall. She started to pump. Somewhere inside the walls, clear liquid met foggy liquid, the two began to change, to spin and dance around each other. Tess squatted down and pulled back the last piece of the contraption, eased open the valve, smelt the gas rise and carefully, shielding her face with one hand, struck a spark to the valve.

The gas, very gently, went *whumph*.

The flame sputtered up, greenish yellow, foul-smelling, it crawled up from the valve in the floor and was sucked up immediately towards the great black pipes. Simultaneously, a vent opened behind the two glass tubes, which were now bubbling and smoking. An iron pipe descended over them as with a little *snap!* glass broke under the pressure of liquid and air and gas within, liquid and smoke pouring out of the vials. The flames rose, encasing vials, pipes, all. Tess backed away as the heat of the fire began to burn through her thick mask, wrapping every pipe with loving flames until the metal ticked and the contents began to scream.

In Sissy Smith's bedroom, Thomas looked down uncertainly at the unconscious clown at his feet and said, 'Oh . . . um . . . well, you see . . .'

And wondered why, even asleep, the clown was still smiling.

Then a voice behind him said, 'Naughty boys go to bed without any supper.'

He spun on the spot, and looked up into the great, bearded and twirly-moustached face of a knife-thrower who was holding a knife in one hand. It was long, curved, polished steel, and didn't look like it was designed with safety in mind.

Thomas dropped the poker, backed away, half tripped over the clown and sprawled unevenly over the end of the bed, rolled off it and kept on backing as the knife-thrower advanced, a

strange, distant smile on his face, as if the man in purple could-
n't understand the boy's fear.

He blurted out, 'Now, look here,' and for a moment wondered
why he tried so hard to sound like his father, 'I am Thomas
Edward Elwick,' he added quickly. 'My family is extremely
important and if you so much as presume to . . . to . . . uh . . .'

'Naughty boys,' said the knife-thrower kindly, 'go to bed
without any stories.'

Then a moment of doubt passed across the man's face. He
half looked up, twitching the end of his nose like a startled
animal, head on one side. He said, like a bewildered child
confused by something new, 'Can you smell something
funny?'

And something fast, ginger-blond, limping from a bloody
ankle and accompanied by an enthusiastically supportive, without ever risking danger, dog, exploded through the door of the
bedroom. Thomas reflected for a moment that it was a vaguely
Horatio Lyle shaped something, and that, as it grabbed the
knife-thrower by the back of the head and kicked him hard in
the soft part of the bend of his knees, that it was very, very
angry.

A woman watches Lyle's house.

She's been doing this for a while, longer, in fact, than she
would care to admit in any sort of society, particularly that of
her peers. It is not considered healthy for one of her disposition
to take an interest in such uncivilised sorts as Mister Horatio
Lyle.

Tonight, however, her interest is paying off.

Tonight, she has witnessed a carriage full of clowns, knife

throwers, strong men, organ-grinders, bear baiters and general all-purpose figures from the entertainment industry, disembark before Lyle's front door and promptly proceed to break it down. She has observed various figures running, scuffling and being unusually and excitingly electrocuted by a number of ingenious traps and scientific devices spread round the house. She is now interested to note that along with the pungent smell of cat's piss starting to emanate from the basement, a great fat cloud of dense green smoke is pouring from every gas fixture in the ceilings and walls, pressing up against the windows and flooding through the halls of the house, pouring under doors and through cracks in the stone.

It is, she reflects, unusual behaviour for any gas fixture to pour out dense greenish-grey smoke.

But then again, perhaps not in Mister Lyle's house.

Tess fell to her knees and coughed. She coughed and choked and spluttered and tore at her throat and thought, *If it works*. Men!

She'd done pretty well, she thought, as every gas lamp in the house, everything that had ever been connected to a pipe, every hole and plug, every lantern began to pump the thick greenish-grey fog into the air. She'd managed to divert both water and gas from their usual routes and replace them with the noxious chemical compounds smashed together in their two little vials. She'd succeeded in heating the resulting compound to such an extent that, under extreme thermal pressure, every inch of the house was now flooding with the stuff. She'd even remembered to wear a mask, to cover her face in case of burning, in case of choking, in case, just in case, something went wrong.

What she'd forgotten to do, she realised, as the world began to fade to black behind the tide of rising darkness filling every stair, every room, every corner of Lyle's house, was pick up something *else* to breathe.

CHAPTER 10

Ether

Thomas wheezed.

He wheezed for a number of reasons.

Primary among the causes, he suspected, and going back to first principals, was the simple truth that gentlemen of his class and lifestyle were used to being carried across town by horses, horse-drawn vehicles or, in dire circumstances, sedan chairs drawn by muscular gentlemen paid for their physical well-being. In other words, he wasn't used to much physical exertion unless it was being conducted from on top of a horse.

His secondary concern was this: that his tactful offer of, 'I say, sir, do you need assistance?' in response to seeing what he could only describe as Horatio Lyle crossed with an angry ginger weasel single-handedly attempting to tackle a purple-caped knife-thrower in Sissy Smith's bedroom had been met with a string of obscenities followed by a loud *crack*.

The crack had been the sound of Lyle hitting the knife-thrower over the head with a frying pan.

Thomas had been rather surprised to see Lyle fight. For a start, he'd never quite known that Lyle had the berserker spirit in him, but now he reflected upon it, his father always said it was the quiet ones who were the least reliable. Moreover, he'd been more than a little shocked by some of the tactics Lyle had deployed – he swore he could see teeth going where teeth should not, and as for the ferociousness of Lyle's right knee, he didn't want to consider the anatomical consequences of some of those strikes.

Then Lyle had been by him, grabbing him by the shoulders, shaking him.

'Are you all right? Boy! Look at me! Are you all right?'

'They . . . they tried to kill Sissy Smith. The men put a pillow over her mouth and . . .'

Thomas stopped talking. There was something in Lyle's face that had passed beyond words and out the other side, that sat on a hot puddle of boiling rage and found it tepid compared to the fury inside the soul.

'The smoke . . .' whimpered Thomas as the room began to fade behind the great stinking clouds tumbling out of every fixture in the wall. 'Good God,' he breathed, as realisation hit him. 'These people are from the circus. They're all from the circus.'

'Remarkable deduction,' grunted Lyle, pulling at his sleeve and tearing the stained white fabric into long pieces that he started to wrap round his nose and mouth. 'Listen to me. The smoke coming out of the house is a chloroform derivative mixed with a lot of steam, and a nitrous compound to help deliver a concentrated effect. It's pumped out through the same pipes as the gas. Breathe it for a few seconds and you get light-headed; breathe it for a few minutes and you pass out entirely; breathe it for more than five without any protection and your skin will burn and your lips will blister and anything inhaled after that . . . Look, I've never tested it, it was just that after the last time when the Tseiqin broke into my house . . . If it's too heavily concentrated, it's also extremely flammable and extremely explosive. Only Tess and I know how to pump it into the house. You need to listen to me and do exactly what I say. The controls for the pump are downstairs in the cellar below my laboratory. That's where Tess is. I'm going to find her. The house is crawling with . . . with people that are . . . with people from the circus. But they'll be feeling the effects too, they'll pass out if they breathe too deeply. We just have to keep awake. You've got to get Sissy out and, ideally, you've got to do it without breathing. There's only a limited supply of catalyst to trigger the reaction, so the air will clear of its own accord eventually. But listen! If Tess is down there breathing it for too long she'll be hurt, and so will you. Get Sissy out and get safe, that's all that ma— That's all I want. Can you do this?'

Thomas nodded, feeling his chin bounce off the inside of his stomach as he did.

'Good. Try very, very hard not to breathe. Go!'

So here he was.

Wheezing.

In the unfortunate position of trying to (1) Carry an unconscious girl down a flight of stairs while at no point violating their respective dignities and (2) do all this while a strange and unexpected substance was flooding out of every gas fixture in the house, sending tears to his eyes and fire to his lungs.

It wasn't smoke.

It was much, much more than smoke.

Thomas put his hand against the wall and counted the steps. He couldn't see. It wasn't just that the air was too thick to see through, but that when he opened his eyes and tried to peer through the smoke and billowing darkness, they immediately filled with burning tears that blinded him as well as a moonless night.

So he walked, blind, shuffling without lifting his feet off the ground, reciting: '*Ten steps door living room five steps stair down two three five steps turn corner study down again four five six seven whoops! bottom step and . . .*'

. . . and all Thomas can hear is the *sssss* of gas and smoke tumbling out of the lanterns, out of kitchen pipes and drains, rushing out of windows and stinging, biting at his skin. How long had Lyle said you could be in this stuff without getting burnt? A few minutes? More than five? Less than five? Count steps, count seconds, don't breathe, because— His foot stumped against something soft and warm, fallen across his path and he breathed, a sharp intake through his sleeve and his thoughts were suddenly: *Oh God oh God oh God . . .*

He realised that fear was the colour blue and made of fur, that the wall his father had built at the end of the garden was just for the squirrels to play in, that the sky was falling and the earth would soon fly and once upon a time in a land where the . . .

He reached the bottom stair.

Sissy Smith was a thousand-ton weight in his arms.

His head was a saucepan in which thick soup full of lumps bubbled and boiled.

His lungs had been filled with boiling water.

His eyes were full of tears.

He could see the shattered remnants of the front door a few steps ahead.

He could hear the sound of an organ, turning, turning, turning, *Alas my love*. Somewhere someone was playing an organ. There was a man on the floor, kneeling on the floor, an old man with a scraggly beard and a pair of swollen red eyes, turning the handle of the organ strapped to his belly. No, wait, not strapped, strapped implied it was separate, but this was more, this instrument was *part* of his belly, it was part of him, the straps were part of his clothes, his clothes were part of his skin and as he turned the handle of the organ, face streaming with tears and throat crackling with every breath, he looked straight at Thomas and whispered, 'Don't leave me, Daddy.'

Thomas staggered by, ignoring him, feet tied to the floor with chains of lead. The door was just there, just there at the end of an infinite fall and there was this shape in front of him and he could smell . . . *leaves on a forest floor*.

So close.

Not quite close enough.

Before the world went out.

Lyle had fallen over the books in his sitting room the second he'd tried to cross the floor. His shin had banged against leather spines, his knees had twisted and tumbled onto the unseen floor beneath. He crawled, feeling his way to the chest of drawers by the far wall, opening it and fumbling through: gloves, notes, pens, papers, bottles of ink, old magnets and ancient tubes, pieces of singed rubber and twisted wire that he'd thought he might one day have a use for, and never had, until at the very back he found what he needed, thick and hard and made of rubber and glass. He pulled the goggles over his eyes, wheezed and coughed and spat dirty slime as he tried to blink his way back to some sort of vision.

Across his brain the random giddy thoughts of gas and drugs started to sing their little songs: *Once upon a time in a land where all the horses ride across the moor beneath kites of string lightning and the child ran away to the—*

'If I take one white pea,' moaned Lyle, clutching his head and staggering across the floor, 'and one green pea, and I attempt to pollinate the one with the other . . .' Piles of books fell before his shuffling feet: the old classics, the fairy tales that had sung him to sleep as a child, Newton and Hooke, Faraday and Galileo, the drawings of da Vinci, the musings of Copernicus. Newer things too: the strange ideas of an Austrian monk about the breeding patterns of peas; the contemplations of Darwin and his cousin Galton and his weather maps; of a young Scot with interesting ideas about temperature and pressure; of a man called Nobel who couldn't understand why mixing clay with nitro-glycerine could do anything but good.

Once upon a time . . .

'No!' moaned Lyle, leaning against the door and wheezing for breath. 'If I . . . if I have a solar object of mass "M_1" acting on a solar object of mass "M_2", at distance X where the value of G can be said to be 6.67×10^{-11} and I . . . and I . . .'

He reached the bottom of the stairs and started to climb through the gases falling down past him from every lamp. *Oh God, Tess.*

A door stood half open, a black way down, a thick smoke, fumbling, feeling step by step towards the pipe room, the place where it had all begun all that time ago, all the adventures, all the experiments, all the dangers he'd put the children in. *Please, not Tess. Please, not now. Please . . .*

He half walked, half fell into the laboratory, pulled himself up by the nearest table top, saw Tess on the floor, her eyes closed. He saw a man, a grown-up man, wearing a lion's skin and a pair of too-tight white trousers, saw him bending over her, saw his fingers open for her throat. Lyle screamed, '*Murderer!*' and was across the floor in a second, throwing himself onto the man's huge back, digging his fingers into the man's eyes, his teeth into the man's neck, all thoughts of numbers and stories and foggy gaseous sleep gone from his mind, an animal clawing at animal skin. 'Murderer, murderer, murder!'

The great man, twice the width of Lyle and about the same height, groaned like a startled bull. He reached behind him, flailed at Lyle's head and tried to grab him. But if his fingers caught anything or did harm, the furious creature on his back didn't notice or care, but slammed his elbow into the back of the other's neck and his knee into the base of his spine so that, with a groan, the strong man fell to the floor, shaking and rubbing at the blisters forming across his mouth.

But then, with a great heave, he threw Lyle off, and staggered to his feet, wheezing and groaning, swaying from the effect of the gas. Rather than attack and finish the job, he just stared at Lyle, tears rising in his eyes, lower lip trembling. Suddenly he gave a rumbling cry of, 'Didn't mean nothin'!'

Lyle didn't answer, but threw himself nails first at the man again, no grace or skill, but pure animal vengeance in his attack.

The man batted him aside like an angry puppy nipping at the heels of a lion, knocking Lyle to the floor, and causing his goggles to bounce off. He blurted out, 'Don't wanna play!'

If there was any logic in what the other man said, it vanished as, with a strange, child-like wail somewhere between a sulk and furious indignation, the giant hurled himself at Lyle. He caught him square in the chest and plucked him off his feet, then kept on moving, carrying him as lightly as a flower, and slammed him into the opposite wall. Tears were running freely down the man's flushed cheeks. But, Lyle realised, there was no anger in his face, but something . . . ignorant, confused. This reasonable thought quickly faded as, with a groan, the man drew back a fist like the jaws of a giant squid, and it occurred to Lyle that even if the punch it threatened didn't kill him, it'd certainly ruin his sense of smell.

At that moment, someone who wasn't Lyle or the man in the lion skin, whispered, '*Lambkin.*'

A look of surprise passed over the face of the other man. His fingers opened. His eyes curled upwards. And with the grace, majesty and Newtonian inevitability of a tree falling in a forest, he fell over backwards.

Lyle slid to the floor.

A few inches away, he could see the sleeping face of Tess.

He crawled towards her, felt blood running down somewhere at the back of his head. Somewhere at the top and bottom of his eyes, an invisible theatre manager was pulling the curtains shut on tonight's performance. Good night, sweet dreams, try not to think of catalysing products and dead children, these things are taboo in the polite world of modern parenting. What would Mrs Bontoft do?

'Tess?' he whimpered, fumbling across the floor towards her. 'Tess?'

And a voice, a woman's voice, soft as feathers breathed, 'Everything's going to be all right now, you lucky thing you.'

And what was left of the lights that shone in Horatio Lyle's world, went out.

CHAPTER 11

Clowns

The sun rose across London, and London wondered why it had bothered.

In the quiet suburb of Hampstead, a chubby woman with greying hair and a gentle, bewildered expression, opened the front door of her new retirement house to an unlikely sight.

This consisted of Thomas Edward Elwick, who, with the aid of a helpful policeman called Charlie, who wasn't sure if this was legal, held between the two of them a sleeping clown. Behind them, another equally puzzled constable, who wasn't sure where promotion lay, held the peacefully sleeping form of Sissy Smith. As the lady looked down, an exceptionally grumpy-looking Tate padded through her parted legs and into the house without so much as a glance in her direction, while, wearing a slightly sheepish smile, Horatio Lyle said, 'Um . . . hello, Mam.'

In his arms, Teresa Hatch lay asleep.

'Horatio, dear,' said Milly Lyle, 'am I to assume you're not just here for my mince pies?'

Thomas Edward Elwick sat with his feet in a tub of steaming hot water, a steaming hot towel across his shoulders and an icy cold towel across his forehead, eating mince pies and, all things considered, milking it. He had never been so tired. The second he'd been offered a seat in the kitchen of Milly Lyle, mother, widow, and other careers in her life that she merely described as 'Before their time, dear', he had been hit by the full force of his exhaustion.

On the other side of the kitchen table Milly Lyle dabbed at the great mauve-and-blue bruises emerging on Horatio Lyle's face.

'Ow! It bloody hur—'

'Language!'

'Sorry, Ma,' mumbled Lyle sulkily.

'Get punched by a circus strong man, did you?' Milly asked her son.

'Yes, as a matter of fact,' grumbled Lyle.

'You know,' sighed his mother, 'I would never have guessed. Unless, perhaps, I had noticed the size of the finger marks, the degree of damage, the hints of torn lion skin under your fingertips, the smell of well-oiled body odour that is very unlike yourself, may I say, and, of course, the unconscious clown in my privy.'

Underneath the table, Tate whimpered.

Thomas thought he could almost remember having found Tate. This led to another vague recollection, of . . .

. . . oh, my . . .

. . . had he really (oh, yes, here it comes) – had he *really* (yep, you bet) – had he *really, really* run through a gas-filled house, assaulted a clown with a poker, faced a man armed with a set of throwing knives, dragged an unconscious girl (yes, that would be it, another hot towel for the shoulders, please) by the armpits, crawled down the stairs half overcome with fumes, tripped over a delirious organ grinder and pulled Sissy Smith to . . .

. . . to . . .

Funny, that.

He couldn't quite recall having pulled Sissy Smith to safety.

In fact, he was fairly sure that . . .

'Tea, dear?' asked Milly.

'Um, yes please, Mrs Lyle.'

Silence descended on the kitchen, punctuated only by the occasional grumble of the recovering Tate and the whistle of a boiling kettle.

Tess hadn't been greatly impressed at her rescue, when she'd finally woken up. She'd begun with, 'Why the bloody hell do me arms feel like someone went an' tried to pull them out of me bloody shoulders?' and was about to embark on a stream of obscenities when Lyle, showing remarkable powers of recovery had burst out of his chair, crossed the space between her and him in two giant strides, grabbed her by the shoulders and said, voice trembling on the edge of that strange, ungentlemanly thing that Thomas had sometimes heard described as passion, 'Never, ever, *ever* go mixing low-pressure vapours with high-pressure airborn narcotics without asking me ever, *ever* again, you understand?'

Thomas couldn't help but feel there was a context to this remark that perhaps he was missing.

Milly Lyle sent the children to bed.

'But it's mornin'!' wailed Tess.

'It's morning and you haven't had any sleep,' confirmed Milly Lyle. 'Good grief, but if I were your mother I would be ashamed of myself, letting two children of your age run around all night playing with noxious substances and murderous types!'

In his corner, Lyle hung his head.

'But I wanna—'

'Teresa Hatch!' Milly's voice rang with imperious authority. 'You know that you are not being sensible about this, and if there is one thing I have little patience with, it is a child that is being wilfully immature!'

And to Thomas's amazement, that was that.

Horatio and Milly Lyle sat alone in the kitchen.

Milly said, 'More tea?'

'Ta, Ma.'

'Long night.'

'Yes.'

'The burns on the child – Sissy Smith? – the burns round her lips suggest some sort of ether-derived compound. Probably mixed with a form of nitrous gas to get the right concentration. Am I right?'

Lyle didn't answer, but tenderly touched his swollen face.

'The bruising round her throat and jaw suggest that someone attempted to throttle her,' added Milly. 'And of course, someone is *always* out to punch you, aren't they, dearest?'

'Suffocate,' corrected Lyle. 'Someone tried to suffocate Sissy

Smith. With a *pillow*. A grown man – a man from the circus, took a pillow to a sleeping child and tried to kill her. And someone else tried to poison her, and someone else again tried to make it look as though she were dead, right down to the doctor's certificate. And . . .' His voice trailed off.

Milly waited.

'They nearly killed Tess.'

Silence.

'They could have killed her, Ma.'

'I know.'

'Children! They . . . Who hurts . . .? I . . . I was there and I couldn't . . . What if I hadn't been able to . . .? They could have killed her.'

'I know.'

'I'm not sure,' added Lyle with a scowl, 'if *Mrs Bontoft's Practical Advice* has anything to say on this.'

(Somewhere in the smoke-filled, stinking rooms of Lyle's house, a draught from a chimney turned the pages of a book fallen on the floor, to reveal . . . *A parent cannot protect a child for ever* . . .)

'It all leads back to the circus,' added Lyle wretchedly. 'About as subtly, may I add, as a bottle of nitro-glycerin and a sudden fall.'

Milly hesitated, then said, 'How did you get out?'

Lyle glanced up. 'My . . .'

'Your pupils were slow, yes,' she said easily. 'Which means you were unconscious when the bobbies found you in the street.'

Lyle sighed and leant back in his chair. 'I don't know,' he said finally. 'This . . . this man was trying to punch me, and there was smoke everywhere, and someone said, "lambkin". And then it all went . . . peculiar, and the next thing I know, I'm lying in the street and there's Tess, Thomas, Tate and Sissy all laid out next to me – Oh, and an unconscious clown – and I promise you, I did not get *any* of them there.'

'"Lambkin". Well, at least she has a sense of humour.'

'She?' asked Lyle quickly.

'She,' replied his mother. 'Find me a man who walks into a house of gas, smoke and, not to put too fine a point on it, murderous clowns and remarks in the face of all this, "lambkin", and I shall show you Disraeli's maternity gown. And you've just had an idea.'

'What? No!' spluttered Lyle.

'Yes, you have, dearest,' said Milly, patting him on the shoulder. 'You're thinking about a woman who might say "lambkin" and, may I say, you are turning the colour of dissolved iodine while doing it. Never mind. I long since gave up on you having a traditional relationship with any creature that wasn't at least three parts hydrogen, so why don't you have a mince pie, and tell me everything that's happened?'

Lyle, however, was silent.

Milly pushed the plate of pies across the table, and still he said nothing.

'Oh,' she sighed, 'maybe you had better tell me about *her* first.'

Lyle smiled. It was a small, tired smile, that found its pleasure from something far away, and fading. 'There was a woman.'

'Who said, "lambkin"?'

'I don't know. Maybe. I don't know. I met her a few months ago, when there was . . . in this business with . . .'

'It is traditional for sons not to tell their mothers everything,' intoned Milly wearily. 'I don't even need to read a book to know that. Who was she, this gentlewoman?'

'Her name is Lin Zi.'

'Chinese, perhaps?'

'That begins to cover it, yes. A group of scientists and ill-inclined individuals were attempting to hurt her people. I'm sure you can imagine the kind of thing – explosives, magnetic waves, some *really*, really big capacitors, guns, chases, sewers, prison breaks, the whole works. We helped her. She helped us.'

'And what is she like, this Lin Zi?'

Lyle let out a long, distracted breath. 'She's a knife-wielding demon-lady from the darkest reaches of lore, who bleeds white blood, is allergic to magnetism in all its forms and can manipulate the minds of mortals with a single glance from her bright green eyes. We danced one night on Westminster Bridge, and then she said she had to go and told me there were things that were not allowed, even for her. She pinched two bottles of potassium iodide from my coat pocket as well, and went away.'

Milly was silent. Then she said, 'You know, while, naturally, I have contemplated the possibility that my one and only son might one day meet a woman worthy of his woolly socks, I never quite pictured the circumstances you describe.'

Lyle shrugged. 'I wouldn't worry about it, Ma. She's gone now.'

'But she might have said, "lambkin"?'

'It'd be the kind of thing she'd do, yes.'

'And she might have saved your life?'

'That too is a possibility.'

'Can she cook?'

'I can't imagine so.'

'Did you like her?'

'Ma! She was a demon-lady! She threatened to cut off my little finger when we first met and refers to most humans as "cranially confined monkeys". She can't tell the difference between oxidisation and reduction, between endothermic and exothermic. She just asks, "Will it blow stuff up?" as if that was all that mattered, why on earth should I— Oh God, I really liked her.' Lyle buried his head in his hands. 'What am I going to do now?'

Milly Lyle sighed, threaded her fingers together on the table top and smiled the smile of the eternally patient mother at her wayward son. 'Why don't you begin at the beginning,' she said. 'Tell me *everything*.'

Time passed.

In Drury Lane, the crowds began to push and shove for the theatres and the music halls. Down in Bermondsey a warehouse was burning, to the great joy of most passers-by with time to spare. In Wapping the whistle blew for the change of shift; at Mile End the church bells began to toll across the newly-dug foundations of homes for working men. Sails and rigging creaked in the over-crowded quays. The city's great sewer-pumping stations groaned under the weight of their never-ending task.

In her kitchen in Hampstead, Milly Lyle, a woman for whom the world would never be big enough, finally heard Lyle's description of events in full. Then she said; 'And on top of all this, you have a circus clown tied up in my privy. You know, Horatio, dear, this is why you're never invited to visit the cousins. Is there anything else I should know?'

Lyle was silent. Then he said, 'The organ-grinder. When Tess released the gas into the house, he was caught in it too. It knocked him unconscious. By the time I came round, he'd vanished, along with all the others from the circus. But he kept playing the organ, all the time. Round and round and round, just – playing. And he was unconscious.'

'You're not making the best of—'

'He was unconscious, Ma. Even when knocked out by the gas, he kept on playing the organ. I looked at his hand and . . . and his skin was fused to the handle as though it had been burnt there. Like in a fire. I could see it sticking to the handle. All bloody. He kept on grinding the organ, winding the handle round and round even when he was asleep.'

'Well,' said Milly at length. 'I've heard enough of the cases you take, to find this a possibility. The question is how. Perhaps some kind of hypnotic—'

'And the strong man? He was like a child. A numb child. And he said something, something that Tess says when she's in trouble. "Didn't mean nothin'!" And the poison that's knocked out Sissy Smith – I don't know what it is! I *always* know what the poison is, but this . . . She's going to die, Ma. I was doing an experiment on a piece of cake Tess stole from the circus, trying to find the toxic substance, then Tate bit me and I woke up and . . .' he hesitated, 'and there was a reaction. I remember. I was a bit occupied at the time, what with a bleeding ankle and people trying to kill me, but I remember looking at the beaker on the way out and there was some sort of precipitate. Something in the glass. Something in the cake. After all, what child would say no to pudding? And then there's the clown.'

'The one tied up in my privy?'

'Yes. Have you looked at his face?'

'In detail? No.'

'I had a quick gander. I think you should see this.'

'What will the neighbours say?' Milly Lyle sighed.

The two Lyles, mother and son, stood in front of the little privy shed in Milly's back garden. Lyle was holding a poker, just in case.

They eased back the door.

Inside, the clown giggled.

Because that's what clowns do.

Milly Lyle would be the first to admit that tying a clown up in her privy was not the ideal arrangement. On the other hand – where else was he to go in a civilised home?

She said, 'The clown just giggled.'

'Yep.'

'That's an unusual and extraordinary reaction to my privy.'

'Do you know, according to *Mrs Bontoft's Practical Advice*, the maintenance of a privy should actually be the man's work, so that the woman doesn't become sullied by contact with—'

'Why on earth are you reading that absurd book?'

'Well, you know . . .' Lyle made a random gesture unconnected with any kind of appropriate answer. '*Look*.' He leant forward, until his nose was a few inches from the clown's face. The clown's fake wig was gone, fallen off and trampled underfoot in the chaotic interior of Lyle's house. He looked older and sadder, a little bald smiling man in a silly shirt, grinning despite his captivity. Lyle said, 'My name is Horatio Lyle. What's your name?'

Another giggle. 'Billy the Button!'

'What's your real name, Billy the Button?' The clown hesitated.

A look of confusion flickered in his eyes, though his lips stayed stretched into a wide smile. 'Me Horatio,' intoned Lyle. 'That's my ma.'

A giggle, less sure of itself than before. 'Would you like to hear a joke?' asked Billy.

'No.'

'Once upon a time, a long time ago, there was a child who ran away to the circus . . .'

'What's your name?'

'Billy the Bu—'

'What's your real name? Listen, mister, you're in trouble. Children missing, poisoned, attacked, people hurt, my front door *inconveniently* smashed in, my house full of smoke and noxious compounds that are going to make everything smell, and I'm talking cats' piss smelly. I mean, you are in serious trouble. What's going on at the circus?'

'Once upon a time . . .'

Lyle reached into his trouser pocket and pulled out a stained and rumpled handkerchief. He spat into it and vigorously set to, cleaning Billy the Button's face. The clown grunted and grumbled as Lyle rubbed at his make-up for nearly a minute, before standing back to admire his handiwork.

The clown's face was unchanged: white skin with a painted smile.

Milly leant in, sniffing. 'Curious,' she said at last. 'Maybe a white lead derivative, injected straight into the skin?'

She reached out and carefully prodded and tugged at the clown's face. He giggled. 'Ticklish!' he said.

She pulled and poked, pushed up his chin and examined the perfect whiteness of his neck and hands, and rubbed at the giant red smile on his face. Then with a murmur of disbelief she pulled down the soft white collar of his shirt, and said, 'Horatio?'

He followed her gaze.

The painted whiteness of the clown's skin extended below his neck, across his chest and shoulders, up his arms and beyond his wrists. It covered, without failure or pause, every inch of his body.

Lyle said, 'We need a bigger bath.'

They tried the bath.

Hot water and soap didn't remove it.

They tried water and ethyl alcohol soaked in cotton, and that didn't shift it. The cotton wasn't even stained. Then Lyle got out his magnifying glass and leant right in close to the clown's skin, under the white burning light of a magnesium glow, and sniffed and hummed and hemmed and finally announced, 'It's his skin.'

'Interesting,' murmured Milly Lyle.

'I mean, his skin really is that colour.'

'Yes, I thought that's what you meant.'

'And the painted smile is also his skin. And the painted eyes. It's all . . . natural.'

'Well, dear, I feel that might depend on your semantic definition of "natural".'

Billy the Button giggled. 'Three children visit the circus—'

'Shut up!' snapped Lyle.

'Shutting up, guv'nor. Like a *clam*.'

'How long have you been like this?'

'Like what, guv'nor?'

'A clown?'

'You gotta be born a clown, to be a clown. Gotta be born to be funny.'

'How long have you been at the circus?'

'Seen lotsa circuses, guv'nor.'

'How long have you been at Mr Majestic's Marvellous Electric Circus?'

Billy hesitated, then he giggled. 'Once upon a time . . .'

'How long?'

'Don't know nothin', guv'nor.'

'Tell me!' snapped Lyle, and then felt a soft hand fall on his arm.

Milly smiled and stepped forward. She knelt down in front of Billy the Button, put her hand over his and murmured, very gently, 'Lad, I'm Mother Lyle. You may call me Milly.'

'Hello, Mo . . . Mo . . . Hello.'

And then, because Mrs Lyle knew a thing or two about eccentrics, she made a breakthrough. 'Tell me, Billy,' she said softly, 'have you been a good boy?'

Later, Lyle would blame it on a mother's instinct, something no amount of *Practical Advice* could supply him with.

Billy the Button whimpered, 'I . . . I fink so, m'm.'

And suddenly, though he was still grinning, it was a little, childish voice that crept out from his painted mouth, and he framed each word as if it were a new, uncomfortable thing.

'And do you love your mother?' asked Milly.

'Ma—' began Lyle.

'Shush! My son Horatio, now, he's not always a good boy,' crooned Milly, and Billy held her gaze, hypnotised by a pair of kindly grey eyes. 'You would not believe the efforts he went to as a child to avoid eating cauliflower; and, as for girls, oh, you would not believe the trouble it's been, trying to find him a suitable woman. I've quite given up on grandchildren, you know. At least those who aren't descended from green-eyed, knife-wielding demon-people.'

'Ma!' growled Lyle.

'I thought maybe Miss Chaste, a vicar's daughter, kind and loyal – but what did Horatio say? "She thinks ammonia and ammonium are the same thing." As if a man who finds the height of entertainment in applying pressure to carbonated products can be picky about his prospects. Where's your mother, Billy?'

'Dunno,' said the clown.

'Where's your father?'

'Dunno.'

'Do you have any brothers?'

'Dunno.'

'Where were you born?'

'Dunno. Ran away to the circus.'

'Did *you* run away to the circus, Billy?' Milly's face was a picture of slow-witted innocence, blazoned with kindness.

'Course. You gotta run away to the circus.'

'Why?'

'Because . . . because . . . *because* . . . Once upon a time there was—'

'Why do you have to run away to the circus?'

'Once upon a time there was . . .'

'Billy? Why did you try to kill Sissy Smith?'

Sweat started to rise up from the unnatural white of Billy's skin. 'Once upon a time there was . . .'

'You tried to kill a child.'

'. . . a lovely little girl who was beaten by an evil schoolmaster . . .'

'You tried to kill a child, Billy. What would your father say to that?'

'. . . an' . . . an' . . . an' they said that . . . an' . . .'

'Didn't your mother tell you to be nice to girls?'

Billy's eyes widened. His mouth opened into a perfect 'O' of surprise and then, to Lyle's bewilderment and horror, he raised his face to the low privy ceiling and wailed, 'Mama! I want my mama!'

Night settled across London, slipping into its old familiar corners where it knew that, even during the day, the sun would never get a look in. It nestled among its favourite shadows in the deep dark tunnels below the city, oozed through the old memories of the covered Fleet Ditch, slid down into the crypt beneath the ancient church of St Bartholomew-the-Great, smothered the lamps burning in the veterans' hospital and the factory wards, shrivelled down the sounds of the music halls, silenced the bleating sheep waiting for the Smithfield slaughterman, and turned out the reflected glow in the dead eyes of the fish heads strewn across the market floor of Billingsgate.

It stretched the shadows over Sissy Smith's bed, and over the huddled shape of Tess, slumbering on the floor at her feet. Tess guards Sissy, Tate guards Tess, and secretly, at the door, wrapped up in Lyle's father's old dressing gown smelling of dust and care, Thomas guards them all, because it is his duty, as the oldest of them, and the man to boot, to keep the nightmares from knocking on their door.

Lyle sits in his father's old chair and does not sleep.

Open on the floor of his still-smoky house, down towards the river, the *Practical Advice* declares, unread and unloved:

Story-telling to children is for the most part a frivolous and unnecessary activity that encourages nothing better than

Catherine Webb

the idling of thoughts, the distraction of unreasonable imaginings and a separation of mind from reality. He who coined the phrase 'once upon a time' was a jestering rogue who knew that, when all reckonings are made, fantastical tales of princes and princesses are nothing more than fictitious lies to comfort away the very natural and sensible concerns of this world. A child is deceived in pictures of 'heroes', of 'good' doing battle with 'evil', and should have no greater need to find such a figure than in the hero that is his father.

Horatio Lyle thinks of old Harry Lyle, and wishes he'd had a chance to show him some of the things he's done.

And on the other side of the city, where the buzz of urban life begins to decay into the mish-mash of the ever-growing suburbs, the lights are still shining in one special place, which even now, is humming and tinkling with activity and life. After all, the lights never really go out at Mr Majestic's Marvellous Electric Circus. As the ringmaster loves to say, 'If the lights go out, how will the children know where to find us?'

CHAPTER 12

Hospital

Next morning began at the breakfast table, where Tess learnt, without much surprise, that Horatio Lyle had developed his weak appreciation of cooking from a mother who regarded breakfast as nothing more than an excuse to eat oats.

'Oats?!' she wailed. 'What am I s'posed to do with oats?'

'You're supposed to eat them, dear,' explained Milly. 'They're very good for all sorts of things.'

'Name one!'

'A glossy mane,' muttered Lyle sourly from his corner of the table.

'Horatio!' exclaimed Milly. 'I heard that!'

Thomas felt it was his duty to show that, despite being used to having his breakfast served by two butlers and an under-chef, he could still eat the food of . . . well, *ordinary* people. Carefully, he took a mouthful of porridge. His body, which had spent most of the night in distress being a frame not used to exercise, nearly convulsed at this new outrage, and he could feel his stomach clench as if to say, 'Try eating another mouthful – go on, just you try it, if you dare. I'll show you what peristalsis is *really* all about.'

He put down his spoon and took a sip of something that Milly claimed to be tea. He could feel both Lyle and Tess studying him, waiting for something spectacular and digestive to happen. At his feet, Tate pawed a trouser leg plaintively. He did not appreciate Milly Lyle's breakfasts either.

When his mother's back was turned, Lyle made a flurry of gestures. They seemed to indicate, in so many convulsions of his elbows, that he entirely understood if his young companions didn't want to eat their breakfast and that frankly he could think of few worse fates and that if they looked under the table they might find a convenient ledge where he had once hidden many an ancient piece of cauliflower. His eyes met Tess's. Her face was bright and her eyes beamed with excitement at this new, semi-larcenous streak manifesting itself in Lyle's nature. His hands stopped waving about, and with a deep voice that he would have liked to call 'booming and firm' but which to Thomas's ears sounded like the beginning of a long yawn, he proclaimed, 'Eat your food, children!'

'Dr Morris is calling by later,' said Milly brightly, seemingly oblivious to the culinary debate going on behind her, 'to pick up Billy the Button. He's clearly not in a correct frame of mind, but perhaps, with the right remedies . . .'

'Ohohohoh!' Tess bounced in her seat. 'They gonna drill holes in his head? Or zap him with zapping electric voltage or . . . or stick him in *ice baths*?'

'Well, no. Dr Morris's approach to mental instability is rather different.'

Tess's face fell. 'Oh. What's he do?'

'He seems to favour talking to the patient.'

'He what?'

'Talks to them.'

'Whatsa pointa that?' demanded Tess. 'They're cracked – what's talkin' gonna do?'

'Billy might have been drugged,' suggested Lyle. 'There was a smell on his breath, similar to that we found with Sissy. It is conceivable that he too has been poisoned with the exact same concoction that has affected Sissy and which was most likely in the cake being served at the circus. Perhaps in the adult frame it induces a reduction to a child-like state as we can observe in Billy and some of the other denizens of the circus; perhaps in children it induces something worse. It needs more study, we need to gather more information, we need to go back to the . . .'

Lyle's voice trailed off.

Silence at the breakfast table, except for the low struggling gurgle of Tate's stomach.

Milly coughed. 'You know, I could do with some help round the house today.'

Tess looked up sharply. 'We gotta go back to the circus!'

Milly looked at Lyle.

Lyle looked at the floor. He found it largely inhabited by Tate, who merely returned his look with the expression of an animal which, if it could lament operatically, would already be into the second aria of its woes.

Lyle muttered, 'Thomas, Tess, there's —'

'No,' snapped Tess, and her voice was suddenly older, harder, a thing that surprised everyone to hear. 'Don't try an' pull this whole deductin' thin' on me. It's the circus. That's where it's at, whatever it is.'

'But—'

'An' I know where this is goin'. You say "There's danger' an' I say "Don't care, goin' with you" an' you say "But you is just a child" an' I say – I can't remember what I usually says, but it ain't important. Sissy Smith were *my* mate, an' it was *me* what was s'posed to look after her. That's just how it is, see?'

Lyle looked up to meet two pairs of bright, determined eyes. 'Very well,' he groaned, 'you can both come to the bloo—'

'Horatio!'

'To the . . . the crimson-coloured, biologically-important liquid substance which bears scarcely a passing metaphorical relevance. You can come back to the circus. But this time no messing with elephants!'

There was a general shuffling round the table, as of three people whose mission, sadly yet urgently, required them to stop eating their oats and make a hasty departure.

'Before you go,' said Milly, 'there's one thing you – all of you – should know.'

Lyle and the children looked up, questioning.

'The child, Sissy Smith – is not waking up,' said Milly flatly. 'She's barely eating, hardly drinking, doesn't seem consciously capable of either, and responds like a sleepwalker if at all. I do know of a hospital where they may be able to help in such a case.

I sometimes donate to it, and the woman who runs it is, well, an old family friend. But you can't wait much longer to find out what happened to Sissy. That's the simple way of it.'

Lyle said, 'Which hospital?'

Mrs Hobbs, of Stoke Newington parish, was a banker's wife. The wife of a banker. It was the sum of her definition, the totality of what people thought. The baker would ask the butcher: 'Do you know Mrs Hobbs?' And the answer would always come back: 'Oh, yes, she's the banker's wife.' She had no other title, no other description, no other definition, no other merit. And that was exactly how she wanted it. It made what needed to be done so much easier to do.

Which might have been why, that same overcast cool morning in London, when Lyle was seeking help for Sissy Smith from a hospital, Mrs Hobbs walked into the offices of Messrs Scroop and Blunt, bankers to the not especially privileged but well-enough-to-do to need a bank, with a stolen ledger under her arm and a guileless look upon her face, and said, 'I would like to talk to a man about a fund for the well-being of the children.'

Horatio Lyle was lucky to have an acquaintance like Mrs Hobbs.

On the edge of Marylebone, the city-builders of London had been busy: new terraced buildings and freshly cobbled roads; old canals covered with new bridges; and on the edge of it all, a new high-domed station, sending new, steam-venting trains to new, smoky cities, sat like a great red beetle trying to take wing. Nearby, to complete the picture, was a brand shining new and utterly unpleasant little hospital. The precepts of its foundation were as simple as its flat grey floors and high dark walls, as clean as its regular tall windows and orderly as its white-turned beds: this was a hospital for disadvantaged children, who, being disadvantaged, would naturally be grateful for any kind of hospital at all and didn't care too much about the presentation.

Not just any disadvantaged children, of course. Announce on the streets of London that there's anywhere outside the prison or workhouse which will give free bed and board to any creature under four foot five inches tall, and not only would the bricks burst from the inside out from the pressure of invading street rats, but said bricks would swiftly be pinched and flogged for a ha'penny a go. The hospital had to have standards. In this case, each sick child admitted had to be sponsored and vouched for by an upstanding member of the community –either a parish warden, a vicar or simply a lady or gentleman of good repute and standing – who would certify that the diseased creature in question had not, in fact, eaten a bar of soap and rubbed their skins with old wet oats to create the appearance of disease in order to nab a quick pad for the night.

There was one ward, just one, where a special exception was made.

She was the Matron.

There was no question that when addressed, it was as 'Matron', and you'd better pronounce the capital letters or else.

Lyle tried to imagine Matron wearing anything other than her Matron's uniform, but couldn't bend his usually flexible brain to the challenge.

Thomas tried to imagine Matron wearing anything other than a disapproving frown. In vain.

Tess tried to imagine Matron being somewhere else, and likewise failed. Matron was reality at its square-shouldered, unadjustable starkest.

What Tate imagined, as his stomach growled from a cruel morning without breakfast, was a secret no human would ever have the power to explore.

Matron looked at Lyle, then at Tess, then at Thomas and finally proclaimed, 'None of these children are sick. What do you want?'

'There's a child – sick – in the cab,' explained Lyle, bracing himself in the face of this woman, not a molecule of whose being didn't loom like an ancient castle-crowned cliff. 'She's been poisoned. She's sleeping. She won't wake up.'

Lyle said all this, expecting little more than a haughty twitch of disbelief. Instead, Matron almost sighed. 'Oh,' she muttered, waving a broad-fingered hand in the direction of the street outside, '*another* one.'

This is the place where the patients go to sleep.

They are not dead – not really, not quite.

Nor can it be said that they are really alive.

Except, just perhaps, when in a moment of sleepy distraction, someone whispers . . .

. . . something like . . .

. . . *once upon a time* . . .

There are many of them.

And they are all children.

Lyle stood in the doorway of the ward and stared.

Neat white beds, dozens of them, lined every wall, sheets tidily tucked into their metal frames.

On the walls someone had hung a few neat white embroidered samplers offering sentiments like: *I AM THE LORD THY GOD* or *BLESSED ARE THE MEEK* or *OH SAVE ME FOR THY MERCY'S SAKE*, each neatly edged with a sparse garland of cross-stitched flowers. Long faint slants of daylight illuminated the ward, at whose far end – the most distant, furthest end – a nurse in a stiff white cap mopped the floor, while another pushed a trolley containing bowls of water and fresh towels with which she would clean the faces of the . . . *things* . . . sitting each in their bed.

They *were* children.

Were, thought Lyle, in the strictly biological sense, all children, the oldest no more than twelve years old, the youngest barely six or seven. Each sat, one to a bed, propped up against white pillows, staring at nothing. There were toys on the floor: little red soldiers carved from wood; little railway engines on pieces of string; a rocking horse in one corner, silent and still, white pony hair sewn into its mane. But if these interested – if anything interested – the children in their beds, they showed no sign of it, but sat utterly still, staring one at the other only by the accident of where their beds were placed.

Tess went up to one, a boy her own age, said, 'Hello!' and waved her hands in front of his open eyes, but the child just blinked and made no reply. Thomas walked over to another child and looked into her face, wondering if he was supposed to wear the judicious expression of an educated man who knew what to look for in a case this strange. Lyle made his way down the middle of the ward, Tate at his heels, ears trailing on the ground, while behind them Matron gave orders and nurses obeyed, slipping Sissy Smith into an empty bed, already made as if she were expected.

Silent faces and empty eyes stared because that was all they knew how to do. It reminded Lyle of the old grey beggars on the docks, the ones who were drowning in drink and opium and who had realised that at the bottom of these, there was still no God waiting to offer redemption. It was the same hollow void, that could no longer feel anything to justify its human shape.

And it was in the children.

Lyle thought of circus strong men, smothering pillows, of Sissy Smith fallen at the door, her blistered and bloody feet, of Tess and . . .

Not of Tess!

Tess and Thomas empty shells sitting in a . . .

No!

Of Milly Lyle's mince pies and Harry Lyle's old armchair, of Tess and Thomas and . . .

And . . .

Oh, God . . .

'There are so many,' he breathed. 'How long have they been here?'

'The longest, maybe four months,' replied Matron, turning from her work of laying the mute Sissy Smith into her bed. 'The latest – excluding this new child – two days.'

'Her name is Sissy,' replied Lyle sharply. 'Not the "new child". Where do they come from?'

'They just appear. Sometimes they're wandering the streets; sometimes the police bring them here, for want of somewhere better. They can eat, but only if you spoon-feed them. Sometimes they are found too late. Children often die in this city, Mister Lyle. I am sure you understand the way of it.'

'Is there no remedy?' asked Lyle incredulously. 'Is there no cure for this?'

'None that we know of. Some doctors have tried: drugs, cold, heat, smell, taste, electricity.'

'On the children?'

'You asked if there was a remedy,' chided Matron. 'I'm merely informing you of our attempts to find one.'

'And what about their parents?'

'None have made themselves known.'

'Not one parent for all these children? Has *no one* come to ask?'

'Not under my supervision,' replied Matron. 'And, as I supervise everything – no, not one.'

'And that doesn't strike you as strange?'

'Mister Lyle,' Matron brought herself up to her fullest width and height, 'I have seen parents pay ten pounds for the removal of an unwanted child to women who are as clearly tricksters as ever a thief who was born. The streets are rife with such feral offspring. So permit me to say, I am not surprised that no parents have come looking for these vacant creatures. They are not children, Mister Lyle. They are flesh with eyes. Nothing more. Forgive me for being so blunt. But I see some of this condition in the child you have brought here. The sooner you can resign yourself to the truth of this the easier it will be for you and your children.'

'They're not—' began Lyle, then cut himself short. 'Thomas has a mother, and a father, who would damn well invade Russia if it would save their son. Because that's how thick-headed, ignorant and caring they bloody well are. Tess has me, and while I'm not about to start a land war for her sake, I would burn all Moscow to the ground if it kept her safe. Sissy Smith has nothing, except perhaps the memory of Tess and the workhouse. So for that reason alone, she can have me. I want to know *everything* about these children: who they are, what happened, how long, why, who, where, when – everything. Can you help me?'

Matron folded her hands in front of her and cast her gaze downward. 'Not I,' she said finally, 'but there is someone who could.'

And a voice from the end of the ward exclaimed, in surprise and wonder and . . .

. . . and just a little bit of something else . . .

'Horatio?!'

Milly Lyle had said: 'a vicar's daughter, kind and loyal'. But if she'd ever considered Miss Chaste as more than a neighbour to her son, she had probably not done so with much hope. True, in terms of age and gentle upbringing, Lyle and Mercy Victoria Chaste (the 'Victoria' added hastily at the font as it became evident who the new monarch was likely to be) were theoretically a perfect match. But Milly Lyle had always known, from the first outbreak of needlework in Mercy Chaste's parlour to her exclamation of 'Calculus, how dull!' that this was not destined to be more than a cordial friendship. Miss Chaste had tried, so had her parents, and all had reflected that were this a more seemly time, as described in the works of Miss Chaste's beloved Jane Austen ('Far more appropriate than those crude Brontë creatures!'), Mercy Chaste and Horatio Lyle would have married, had children and lived ever after in well-meant respectability.

All this would have been news to Lyle, who didn't merely

regard marriage as a distraction, but managed most of the time not to consider it at all. But to Mercy Chaste, whose sisters were all suitably wed, Lyle would always be the man she'd never had a chance to mould, with her mothering ways, into a suitable husband.

'Horatio!'

Surprise, wonder, delight, perhaps, and . . .

. . . and what else was in her voice, at the shrill tip of the climbing top note as Mercy Chaste, in a nurse's stiff, starched white, billowed down the ward? That something else that made Tate curl up behind Lyle's legs and Tess's eyes narrow in suspicion?

'Horatio, what are you doing here?'

A voice as contrary as the woman who owned it. Her skin was almost the colour of melting snow, her hair pale-washed blonde, her eyes a faded blue. She looked like a clownish ghost, and her voice was high and shrill to match her appearance. Then again, no ghost could muster such a pair of well-worked hands as Miss Chaste or such hard-walked feet. Nor did it seem likely to Horatio Lyle that any ghost could produce so much sound from such a little pale throat.

'Well,' he began, as Tate whimpered and pawed at his ankle.

Tess, as Miss Chaste approached, first leant forward in surprise, then back in dismay, then tried to duck behind the nearest bed, hissing, 'Oi! Bigwig! I ain't 'ere!'

'But,' ventured Thomas, trying to understand a great and taxing problem, 'you *are* here, Miss Teresa.'

'She were this mark what I were gonna filch when I first met Lyle!' hissed Tess, while Thomas sweated with the effort of translation. 'Don't look at me, just smile, bigwig-like!'

To the relief of them both, Mercy Chaste's full attention was fixed on Horatio Lyle, with a bright smile on her face and something more than brightness shining from her eyes. 'Are you, at last, Horatio, doing your Christian duty for the needy?'

'Uh, I suppose you could say that,' replied Lyle.

'I always knew you would! Are you here to donate money or to work?'

'What? No, the reason I'm here is—'

'He's been asking about the children,' interjected Matron. 'He found a child, brought it here.'

'Ah – the children.' Mercy Chaste's eyes fell, but her face still seemed to glow with the contemplative brightness of any church icon. 'Naturally, we tend them as best we may. Where did you find yours?'

'Her name is Sissy Smith,' said Lyle. 'She came looking for Tess.'

'I see.'

'You do? She's been *poisoned*, Miss Chaste. Someone tried to poison her. And all this!' He gestured at the silent children in their silent beds on the silent ward, his voice echoing off the cold white walls. 'Look! How many have been hurt?'

'They're not in pain, Horatio,' said Miss Chaste softly. 'I know how all this must appear to you. But if you work here long enough . . . The children are peaceful, in their way.'

'Peaceful?! They are empty! Look what's been done to them!'

'They do not go hungry, or thirsty, or cold. Their feet aren't bloody, their lives aren't lived in fear. No parents have come looking for them, no family. They have nothing. But here at least they are safe.'

Lyle's face hardened. 'I'm not going to accept that. I'm sorry,

Mercy, but if you had ch— Where's the latest child who was brought here?'

'A boy,' answered Miss Chaste. 'Brought here two days ago. He was found at Paddington Station, just watching the trains, not moving.'

'Show me,' grunted Lyle.

As Miss Chaste did so, Tess and Thomas slunk into Lyle's shadow, avoiding the empty gazes of the children in their beds. When Lyle saw the face of the boy, he drew in a sharp breath.

Tess peeked past him, also saw the child and turned white.

'Bloody hell!' she hissed.

Lyle gave a little sigh of agreement that seemed to drain his strength from shoulders to toes.

'Scuttle?' breathed Thomas, staring at the empty-eyed creature in the bed. The child was a boy of barely ten years old. His hair was cropped back to his scalp in the manner of a workhouse child suspected of nits; his skin was pale; his wrists were bony; his face was cratered with red acne scars.

'You know him?' asked Miss Chaste.

'He's a mudlark,' breathed Lyle, running his hands through his hair. 'He's called Scuttle – or Josiah, depending on how you feel. We met him a few months ago, when we needed a guide in – or more importantly, out – of the sewers. Edith White at the workhouse said he'd been caught. Taken to the circus.'

'The circus?'

'That's where all these bad things happen, innit, Mister Lyle?' hissed Tess. Her face had started to turn red with anger. She went to Scuttle, grabbed him by the shoulders and shook him, shouting, 'Oi! Scuttle! Oi, you got spots, you little ha'penny crab!

No good two-bit gropus. Oi! Stupid sewer snipe! Scuttle! It's me! It's Tess! It's *me*! Wake up!'

Lyle carefully pulled Tess away from the bed, and held her. Her eyes were red. She hid her face in his side and bunched her fingers into fists.

'Horatio, how do you know these children?' asked Miss Chaste, after a while. 'You never showed any sign of philan-throp—'

'It's the law,' he snapped back. 'It's the one that didn't need writing down. Don't murder, don't steal, don't lie, don't cheat, don't hit strangers – it's the one that doesn't need spelling out. Don't you dare, don't you even *dare*, don't you even *think* about daring – you just do not, even if the rest is words, you *do not* hurt children. Thomas, Tess!'

The two stood to some sort of attention.

'We're going back to the circus.'

CHAPTER 13

Circus

There's a . . .

. . . not a child, not at the moment – but that can be fixed – watching the circus, chewing the end of a well-fitting grey sleeve. And if he thinks anything at all, if the ideas in his mind can be graced with the definition of 'thought', he thinks this:

Hungry hungry hungry hungry hungry hungry WANNIT NOW!!

Ladies and gentlemen, boys and girls – especially you boys and girls! – welcome back to Mr Majestic's Marvellous Electric Circus. Stay a while. Leaving may be harder than you think.

'Right!' said Lyle, as the four companions, adult, children and dog, stood before the bright lights of the gate to the circus, ears full of the sound of music, gossip and the rattling of falling pennies. 'Plan of action!'

He waited.

So did the others.

Tess broke first. 'Yes? An' it is . . .?'

'Teresa,' Lyle sighed, deflating a little bit, 'we must discuss one day the subtle nature of my pauses. That pause was quite clearly an invitation for productive and useful feedback, a request for input.'

'Oh,' said Tess easily, 'cos to me it sounded a lot like as how you didn't have no idea what to do next, Mister Lyle. But now I knows it were in fact a pause what you wanted us to give you useful ideas in, I can go an' help, can't I?'

They waited.

'Yes?' prompted Lyle. 'And your contribution is . . .?'

Tess smiled the smile of the infinitely wise, turned slowly, and fixed Thomas with her warmest stare. 'Bigwig?'

Thomas was aware of his ears turning pink, but on the other hand, this was the kind of thing he'd been bred for: forming a plan and executing it with dignity, even if that plan involved a narrow valley, a troop of light cavalry and a lot of cannon at the far end. 'Perhaps we could summon the police?'

'Because a cry of "A clown and an organ grinder tried to throttle me in my own home and a couple of gutter snipes have gone missing" always goes down well with figures of authority.'

'But *you're* a policeman,' wailed Thomas. 'Surely if you stand up for the law and justice . . .'

'Mister Lyle is for law and justice?' echoed Tess, looking bewildered. This was not the kind of acquaintance she had ever considered herself having.

'. . . then others will too!'

Lyle patted Thomas on the shoulder.

'It's a nice thought, lad.'

Thomas looked crestfallen. 'But if no one in authority will help us, how are we supposed to help the children?'

'You know,' said Lyle thoughtfully, 'the remarkable thing about law and justice, is that it only rarely considers blowing up the tents of its opponents a valuable use of its time.'

Tess brightened. 'Blowin' stuff up?'

'Naturally,' added Lyle quickly, 'we shall *not* be blowing anything up in the foreseeable future, as this would be an act of gross irresponsibility and a wasteful use of interesting and expensive compound products. But that's not to say we can't cause a little . . . inconvenience . . . around the place. I think our plan should be something like this: go into the circus, doing our very, very best not to be throttled by any semi-possessed individuals with considerable strength in their thumbs. Find, in whichever order seems most plausible at the time, any of the following: children in catatonic states, potions liable to induce catatonic states, individuals liable to want to induce catatonic states, cures for said catatonic states, and, ideally, return samples of all of the above to a suitable laboratory for analysis.'

Thomas raised an uncertain hand. 'How do we return samples of individuals who want to cause catatonic states, sir?'

'I'm sure you'll think of something, lad.'

'What if someone recognises us?'

'Remember what I said about the irresponsibility of blowing things up?'

'Yes, sir.'

'Amazing how the memory lapses at times of stress. Also, if you find . . . no.'

Tess, never one to let a sentence wind away peacefully, said, 'If we find wha', if we find wha', if we find wha', Mister Lyle?'

Lyle sighed. 'If you happen to run into an oriental gentlewoman with a fondness for sharpened knives and a dislike of magnetism who may or may not have intervened at a previous point in our affairs, tell her . . . tell her . . .' Lyle's face crinkled in the effort of finding something suitable to say. 'Oh, just say hello nicely, will you?'

Three pairs of disbelieving eyes stared back at him. Tess's mouth worked slowly with the effort of concentration. 'You don't mean . . . you don't think as how . . . You don't *like* Lin do—'

'Come on!' barked Lyle, drawing himself quickly up to his full, not particularly remarkable height, and pushing out what was, at the end of the day, a none-too-impressive chest in a slightly stained white shirt. 'Let's finish it.'

They headed into the circus.

Welcome to Mr Majestic's Marvellous Electric Circus!

Wonders you have never seen before just wait to be discovered. You, sir, may we show you creatures from the exotic Indies, strange dancing monkeys on top of the organ grinder's table cavorting for your delight? They never stop dancing, not even when the sun has set, but dance for ever and ever and ever until they drop dead, the bodies buried by the sides of the roads the circus travels along from place to place. So hard to find a replacement monkey in the provinces, enjoy it while you may. You, madam, if your heart is strong enough, come see for yourself the horrific freaks born – through no fault of their own, God's mercy on them – with faces like melted wax and stooped backs from which stubby little arms hardly deign to grow! If your child fears such things, then put them out of your mind, for just one slice of cake, just one bite, just one sip, just one sniff of this potion I have in my pocket, and your child need never fear again. Need never be angry or afraid, lonely or lost, but will for ever sleep and dream of distant stories, and be at perfect peace. Is this not better than the pain of growing old? Is this not paradise eternal? It is yours, if you just take a taste.

Have you witnessed a man eat such quantities of fire, or drive a sword – how sharp the blade! – down his own gullet? You shall never know if they bleed inside; these are not secrets to be whispered outside the circus. Marvel at the agility of our acrobats as they flop and dive from sky to earth with not a net in sight and look! Their knees seem to bend the wrong ways, their necks turn too fast, their arms twist too roundly and perhaps, perhaps if you were the kind who did not believe in magic, you might call it horrifying the things that you can see at this circus.

Welcome to Mr Majestic's Marvellous Electric Circus.

Welcome, ladies and gentlemen.

Welcome, boys and girls.

We forgot to put up the 'exit' signs.

Tess mingled.

She was very good at mingling.

It helped that she was small, even for her age, and could duck behind many pairs of legs whenever she felt unsuitably observed. It helped further that even now, even in the cool rising night, with the lights blazing and the torches lit, after that unfortunate business with the elephant, even now the crowds flock to Mr Majestic's Electric Circus, providing a thick cover for her passage as she moves between the brightly coloured, music-spinning tents.

But even were all these things not the case, Teresa Hatch still had the art of mingling. Everything about her, from face to ambling walk, suggested that here was someone of no interest whatsoever, completely immersed in her own thoughts, of no threat, no danger, no nothing that might lead the watchful eye to consider alarm. She could have waltzed through a graveyard and still, somehow, impossibly, been considered in her place.

Thomas, on the other hand, was not good at mingling.

This was largely owing to the fact that, whenever he accidentally trod on a person's toes, as frequently happened in the press of bodies, he would exclaim, 'Oh, I am so sorry!' – a politeness that immediately marked him out as *other*. As not welcome at the circus.

As for Lyle . . .

. . . he wasn't even trying.

But his eyes were everywhere.

'Thomas, Tess?' he murmured after a while.

'Yes, Mister Lyle?'

'I'm thinking of causing a spot of bother.'

'Oh dear!' exclaimed Thomas.

' 'Bout time,' grumbled Tess.

'I'm going to the central tent to continue the conversation I had with Mr Majestic.'

'The one what ended with you in the elephant – *pen*?' suggested Tess, sweetness and light.

'That's the one.'

'But, an' I know as how you're a wise old bloke an' that, but ain't the fact as how it ended up with you in the elephant pen last time a bad thin'? Like ten spoonfuls of catalyst when you were only lookin' for one bad?'

'Teresa!' Lyle beamed with delight. 'You just used a scientific metaphor in your daily speech!'

'Simile,' corrected Thomas automatically.

'What?'

'Simile. Miss Teresa used a scientific simile, not a metaphor.'

Three pairs of eyes stared blankly into his face. Thomas opened his mouth to explain, and felt the tiny tug of a little inner voice, the voice that might one day be big enough to wear his father's coat, whisper, *Uh-uh*.

'Well,' said Lyle at last, 'I must admit that's slightly under-mined the delight of the moment, but never mind. The point is, Mr Majestic's attempted assault on me is a sure indicator that we're onto something positive.'

'It is?'

'Yes!'

'It's your skull, Mister Lyle,' said Tess with a shrug. 'Ain't my business where you go an' put it.'

'Besides,' added Lyle, getting increasingly flustered, 'this time, you two will be there to keep an eye on me.'

'We will?'

'Yes.'

'An' what we're s'posed to do if you're dumped in the ele-phant poo again?'

Lyle leant down until his face was just a few inches from Tess's. She felt him press something glassy and cold into her hand. She looked down. It was a glass tube with a cork. Inside was a clear thick liquid, that dribbled very slowly down the insides. 'Come and rescue me, of course.'

Tess started to smile.

His name is . . .

His name *is* . . .

Now, think about this.

His name is . . .

Mister Martin Michael Morris Maurice Mister . . .

No, not quite right.

His name is . . .

(Sweat stands out on his face. Was this always such hard work?)

His name is . . .

Oh yes.

What a relief.

Mr Majestic.

He is Mr Majestic of Mr Majestic's Marvellous Electric Circus.

See how easy that was, once you didn't think about it any more?

All he wanted to do was to entertain the children. So! Pull the moustache tight, stretch the waistcoat, sweep back the hair, stand up straight and prepare to inspire! Turn from the mirror to the door of the tent, smile, always there has to be a smile, because you are the ringmaster of the circus and you cannot not smile, you cannot not smile, haven't not smiled, for so many years, so, so many years, until the smile was locked in place, but that's fine, Mr Majestic always smiles and . . .

'Hello, Mr Majestic,' said Lyle.

'Why, good evening, sir. How . . .'

And Mr Majestic sees, halfway through his merry greeting, to whom his greeting is addressed, and the smile that was locked in place, locks a little tighter over the sparkling brightness of his teeth, and his fingers tighten round the cane and stay tight as Horatio Lyle leans forward until his face is barely an inch from Mr Majestic's own, and says, 'Now, we were talking about Greybags.'

Tess and Thomas sat opposite the ringmaster's tent and ate.

Thomas wasn't entirely sure what it was they ate. He knew it involved sugar in some manner that had been burnt and stewed and moulded and cast, but quite how the sugar had become the colour of old soot or acquired the taste of fish, he didn't know. Tess promised him that this was a fairly common thing for food to do that weren't brought up on a fancy silver plate, see, but as how he shouldn't worry 'bout nothin' cos of – No, wait. How he shouldn't concern himself because of her presence as his protector.

Thomas frowned.

He knew, in his heart of hearts, he knew that it was only a matter of time before some of Tess's language slipped into his own, largely because of how much of it she used relative to how little he spoke in return. Mister Lyle wasn't much help in terms of maintaining appropriate grammatical standards either, for while he was a great believer in scientific precision, he, like Tess, tended to resort to base crudities and common slang in the face of exotic yet remarkably regular danger. Thomas half closed his eyes and tried to imagine how his father would react to being called 'guv'nor'. He couldn't see it going down well.

Somewhere in his soul, two hundred and twenty years' of aristocratic breeding glowered at barely two or three years' worth of emerging social consciousness across an uneven battlefield. Next to his right shoulder, Tess said, 'You havin' yours or wha'?'

Thomas considered the sad package of fish-flavoured sugar in his hand, and wordlessly passed it over. Even his social consciousness had a limit. Tess got gobbling. Tate waited expectantly for his fill at her feet, and was promptly rewarded for his patience.

'Miss Teresa?' asked Thomas at last.

A mumbled reply that he imagined was some sort of acknowledgement forced its way out through a set of sugar-covered teeth.

'Miss Teresa,' tried Thomas again, feeling that perhaps his conversation partner wasn't fully engaged on the debate, 'do you think it's . . . well . . . *appropriate* for Mister Lyle to put you in danger?'

'Me? In danger?'

'Yes.'

'I ain't in danger, bigwig. Mister Lyle, case you ain't gone an' spied, is the bloke wha' went walkin' into the tent with the bloke with the big moustache thin' an' the heavy stick. If anythin', I feel as how Mister Lyle is doin' the whole coddlin' thin' too far.'

'But . . . but you're a *lady*, Miss Teresa.'

'I ain't never!'

'I'm fairly confident you are, Miss Teresa.'

'You take it back!'

'Mere biology, Miss Teresa, informs against you.'

'But a *lady*,' groaned Tess, 'a *lady* is this thin' what as to go an' sit at home an' do the sewin' an' tend the garden, or summat, or them thin's what proper ladies do an' all. Like . . . like prayin' or drinkin' tea. But blokes! Blokes get to go an' kill thin's an' conquer the Empire an' they get . . . they get . . .' Tess's eyes filled with misty longing, 'they get to use *swords*. You know, I ain't 'posed to know this, bigwig, but I seen, I knows. Underneath those really tight waistcoats what the men wear all the time, underneath the suit an' all, they're really wearing floppy white shirts.'

Thomas made a guttural 'Oh really how interesting' noise somewhere at the back of his throat. Tess radiated satisfaction. 'My fence down at Mile End used to say as how there weren't nothin' quite like a floppy white shirt for turnin' the head of a dolly mop down in—'

'Excuse me?'

Thomas nearly wept with relief at not having to find out any more of Tess's fence's opinion on the subject of floppy white shirts, and his attention leapt to the man who had spoken. Looking up, he saw, standing in a manner of polite interjection before him, a beard. A monumental beard. A beard so massive that the rest of his features seemed to have sunk into its dark, curly greying depths, as if eyes, nose and lips had all given up on trying to compete with their hairy surround. The man's accent was weighted with the sharp, biting tang of somewhere in the German principalities. His eyes too were dark; his face was sombre. His suit had, once upon a time, been purchased from a respectable tailor but had long since become worn at the cuffs and elbows. However, he wore this slightly battered outfit with an attitude of such defiance that Thomas half wondered if he hadn't gone and rubbed at the fabric with iron filings just to achieve the impoverished scholarly effect. He held a notebook in one hand, and a stub of heavily chewed pencil in the other.

'Forgive me for interjecting,' he said quickly, 'but I was completely fascinated to see such as the pair of you in each other's company.'

Tess looked at Thomas, Thomas looked at Tess. Tess spoke for them both. 'Wha'?'

'To see, if I may be so bold, a scrawny, scum-of-the-gutter street urchin whose merest presence exudes unwholesome odours of both the physical and moral variety, in the company of a gentleman of clearly ignobly high birth thrust by this accident of fortune into a wealth that he—'

Tess's brain had finally caught up with the previous half of the gentleman's sentence, and she suddenly sat up straight and said, 'Oi! That were me you were callin' smelly, weren't it!'

'He clearly does not deserve based on any merit of his own, but which has been . . .'

'Um . . . what?' mumbled Thomas, starting to flush red.

'. . . thrust upon him. As I said, his wealth, his breeding, his social graces all the symptoms of an over-glutted, over-fed decadent system which alas was not thrust away by the forces of revolution . . .'

'Bigwig,' hissed Tess, nudging Thomas in the ribs, 'tell me what he means in little words.'

'. . . such as those of the lost ideals of 1848.'

The man, having thus pronounced, beamed expectantly at the two of them.

Thomas said, 'Essentially, he is very interested to see a gentlewoman of . . . um . . . of apparently more practical class origins than my own in the company of a gentleman of distinguished breeding.' Then he added, just in case, 'And I'm the gentleman of breeding.'

Tess nodded sagely, feeling that asking for a translation into even smaller words might perhaps undermine her reputation for intellect. Thankfully, by now, the rest of Thomas's brain had also caught up and he suddenly exclaimed, '1848?! I'll have you know my third cousin Roderick was nearly beheaded in 1848 by a bunch of ignorant Bavarian peasants full of ideas about this democracy business and had to flee to stay with Aunty Isabel in Austria until the whole nonsense calmed down!'

'You have a third cousin Roderick?' asked Tess.

'Marvellous!' exclaimed the owner of the beard. 'You see, this is precisely what I mean! The mingling of the upper orders and the lower classes cannot take place without an immediate explosion of violence! This scrawny, scruffy, and clearly despicable and despised child . . .'

'He mean me?' hissed Tess.

'. . . will one day rise up and see that those such as yourself, who have won by no greater merit than chance the riches of your birth, are the oppressing few holding back the great mass of downtrodden labour who every day must sweat and starve for their . . .'

'I say . . .' began Thomas feebly.

'. . . for their enrichment, for their livelihood, for their freedom from the upper classes and their accomplices in the emerging bourgeoisie.'

'Now look here,' he tried again.

'And I say, excellent! Recall this moment, sir, of apparent harmony between upper and lower classes, for in the near future revolution such as we have not seen since 1789 will sweep upon the wallowing decadent aristocrats of the upper echelons and you two will be set in the bitterest of conflicts, as, indeed, through economics, you already are!'

'Are we?' asked Thomas.

'Indeed you are. For before you know it, your repressed companion here,' a nod at Tess, 'will acquire her social conscience and crush you and all your kin in a tidal wave of vengeance and economic turbulence the like of which the world has never seen!'

Thomas looked at Tess. He tried to imagine her rising up against the aristocracy. She licked dirty sugar off the ends of her fingertips and, sensing Thomas's stare, said through a mouthful of sticky goo, 'Dunno what he said, dunno what he wants, dunno if I care.'

Thomas felt a degree of comfort at this, and turned his attention back to the man with the beard. He seemed to have finished. His face was lit up with glowing pride and such a smug expectation of reprisal that Thomas half imagined it would be to this gentleman's credit to spend several days in prison, just so he could spin it into an anecdote for the rest of his life. It dawned upon him that here was someone of clearly middling class, who lacking the credentials of a lower-class labourer who had struggled for his good, nor having the casual confidence of the upper classes, had clearly turned to that foul instrument economics, for a little social salvation.

This now realised, Thomas put on the *smile*. It was something he had once seen Queen Victoria do, on one of the few, highly unpleasant occasions when she had been forced to meet the lower classes or, heaven help her, colonial natives, those savage creatures. It was the smile of the extremely wealthy preparing to indulge the extremely meek: all humility, grace and goodwill, with just a hint of tooth in between.

'I'm sorry, Mr . . .' he began.

'Mr Marx! Mr Karl Marx, sir! May I ask you about your feelings on the economic inevitability of mechanisation and the enfranchisement of the majority of the industrial classes in—'

Thomas raised a hand, commanding silence. 'Forgive me, Mr Marx,' he said smoothly, 'but as I am a thoroughly inbred aristocrat with no further interest in life than hunting and the condition of my dogs, I have neither the time nor the inclination to talk to you, and even if I did talk to you, I would find your tedious theories on such base matters as *economics* so intellectual as to be beneath my consideration.'

And again, he gave the smile, and this time, it was all teeth and nothing else.

Anyone else might have hit him.

But for Mr Karl Marx, Thomas was for just a moment, the living vindication of all that his theories were, and all they could become, and he beamed in pure academic bliss.

'Sir,' he said, 'may I shake you by the hand, while you still have a hand to shake?'

'Sir,' replied Thomas courteously. They shook hands. Mr Marx smiled again the smug smile of a man who knows the battle, whatever it is, is already won, turned and walked away.

They watched him go.

Finally Tess said, 'I didn't get not nearly nothin' of what he went an' said there.'

'Oh, revolution and uprising and the fall of the upper classes,' sighed Thomas. 'It'll never catch on.'

*

Mr Majestic found himself in an interesting situation.

He found himself with his own cane across his throat, his feet stuck out in an ungainly manner over the edge of his dressing table (not that he ever needed to put on his costume, since he never undressed) and, here was perhaps where it became surreal, a man called Horatio Lyle was patiently explaining to him the long-term effects of narcotic addiction.

'. . . then there's the question of what it does to the internal organs,' went on Lyle cheerfully. 'I mean, clearly there's some effect to the circulatory system, since the addict's responses are slow, their veins are protruding and their heartbeat struggles like the beat of the rusty grandfather clock. But I've always wondered, what about the kidneys? What about the liver? If only we had a more reliable way to study the internal composition of these organs we could do more than speculate on the consequence of illicit and dangerous substances in the blood stream, but as it is, we have barely scratched the surface of these save to say that they are in some way connected to some other place.'

'Sir?' squeaked Mr Majestic, raising one white-gloved hand.

'Yes?' asked Lyle nicely.

'Sir, why are you telling me this?'

Lyle sighed, and shifted his weight ever so slightly. The cane across Mr Majestic's throat tightened, his eyes bulged. 'No one these days appreciates the value of knowledge for knowledge's sake. "Study the stars, Galileo? Why bother? They're just points of light in a blackness overhead?" But think from that study what wonders, what mathematical wonders, what intellectual wonders have come. We have redefined humanity, placed the sun at the centre of the universe and spun ourselves giddily round its hub, seen other worlds and marvelled at their beauty, finally become less than men made in God's image and so much more than human. I'm sorry – what was the question?'

'You're hurting me!'

'Am I?'

'Yes!'

'Not so much as the gentleman who seems to have you in his thrall,' replied Lyle cheerfully. 'You see, I can't help but notice, now I look for it, that the gloves on your hands don't appear to come off, nor the buttons on your waistcoat undo. Nor, may I add, do the pupils in your eyes shrink and grow as they should when turned to and from the light. Your breath smells of some narcotic stuff, your conversation is childish and, let's face it,' Lyle leant in until his face nearly bumped Mr Majestic's own, 'I really don't like being dumped in the elephant pen. You are, in short, as is, it seems, every single member of this circus, adult and child, poisoned. Only this poison turns adults to dribbling children, and children to unconscious puppets. Fascinating stuff, isn't it? Now. We can continue this discussion about the philosophical nature of study, or you can answer me a few questions, quietly, quickly and with no silly buggers. Who is Greybags?'

Mr Majestic whimpered.

'Greybags.' Lyle didn't raise his voice, but the look in his eye assured Mr Majestic that his interest in narcotics was more than purely philosophical.

'He'll be so angry, he'll be so angry, he'll be so angry—'

'Just imagine,' growled Lyle, 'how little I care right now. Who is Greybags?'

'He likes the ones who play.'

'No silly buggers!'

'He likes to tell stories.'

'Really? What kind of stories?'

'Once upon a time . . .'

'A long time ago,' added Lyle. 'Yes? What then?'

Mr Majestic's eyebrows tightened, as if trying to remember something he'd heard a long time ago. 'Once upon a time, a long time ago, there was a child who ran away to the circus. He was a lonely child, he was small and he was scared, but the circus was big and bright and full of magic and in it all the children were happy and all the children laughed and dreamed and told stories and the child was happy too because he could hear the stories and steal the dreams and eat the dreams and never have to grow old and—'

'Eat the dreams?' murmured Lyle. 'What do you mean, eat the dreams?'

'It's just a story.'

'And a windpipe is just a muscular tube protected by a little cartilage,' replied Lyle sharply. 'It's amazing how the small things matter. This child who ran away to the circus – did he eat something he shouldn't have?'

'No.'

'Cake?'

'Children love cake. All children want to have pudding.'

'And what's in the pudding?'

'It's just to help them dream.'

'What's in it?'

'You're a grown-up. You wouldn't understand.'

'You're in your fifties you stupid little—' Lyle froze, biting down so hard on his words his teeth clattered. 'How old are you?'

'Me?'

'Yes, you.'

'Dunno.'

'How can you not know?'

'Don't matter. Grown-up too, therefore no fun.'

'You're a grown-up.'

'Of course I am!'

'And how does that make you feel?'

'Feel sad.'

'Why?'

'He won't let me play no more.'

'Who won't let you play?'

'Him!'

'Who him!'

'*Him!*' wailed Mr Majestic. 'Him, him, him, who tells the stories! Him who ran away to the circus! Him who won't never grow up! I didn't want to grow up neither!'

'Greybags.' Lyle sighed.

Mr Majestic half nodded, tears welling in his eyes.

'Greybags. The adults become children, but they stay awake. The adults become part of the circus, living, breathing parts of the circus: gloves that won't come off, an organ that never stops playing, clowns that never stop smiling.' Lyle's face wrinkled in concentration. 'The adults become *entertainment*, the way they *ought* to be to entertain the children. But Sissy Smith, Scuttle, all the sleeping children in the hospital have been poisoned and now they won't wake up. Something . . . something has been taken from them, something stolen. Does Greybags steal something from them? What does he take? Why won't they wake up?'

'They're dreaming,' replied Mr Majestic with a whimper.

'They eat the cake and it makes them dream. Adults can't dream like children can.'

'Children have imagination,' replied Lyle sharply, 'I understand that. Adults have perhaps seen things that . . . Why don't the children wake up?'

'He likes their dreams.' Mr Majestic's head tilted slightly beneath the vice of the cane pressed across his throat. 'He says that only the children are really alive.'

Lyle's eyes narrowed. 'Greybags steals children's dreams? *Needs* children's dreams, am I right? Sissy Smith is taken to the circus and they feed her cake and she eats the cake and then she sleeps and won't wake up and something was stolen from her. Not *dreams* as in that which happens when you're asleep, something . . . alive. Living breathing *awake* dreams. That's what was taken from her, am I right? Dreams of tomorrow, of what she will be, of all the things you dream of when you're a child, of mother and father and kindness and what you will become, *that's* what's stolen from her, because she can't wake up. Those are what the children have that grown-ups don't. Greybags *eats* children's dreams. Why? Am I right? Mr Majestic? Hey! Am I right?'

Mr Majestic nodded, tears running down his face, dripping off the end of his nose and mixing with his moustache.

'And what about the circus? Why . . .? Oh, I see. A circus. A moving circus. All the children come to the circus and sometimes they *do* run away, don't they? A child that runs away to the circus, who'd notice, who'd look, who'd care? Perfect place to hide. And no one asks about the children from the workhouse, no one at all. In fact, it's really very useful if they vanish, one less mouth for the parish to feed. They come to the circus and then they eat the cake and never wake up again. How could you let it happen?' Lyle shook Mr Majestic, his face filling with anger. 'How could you?!'

'He . . . he saw my dreams.'

'Who?'

'Greybags.'

'I thought he only ate the dreams of children, was only interested in the children.'

'He made us part of the circus. He knew what we were scared of an' he said "drink this" and I drank it, do you see? I drank it and . . . and then he . . . he . . .'

'What did he do?'

'I drank it and then it was all better, all all right I look after the circus that's what I do I'm the ringmaster have to look after the circus so I drank it and then he . . . he said he would . . . that he would . . .'

'What did Greybags do?'

Mr Majestic looked into Lyle's eyes, and for a moment, just a moment, a little fat man in his fifties with receding hair and a ridiculous moustache was looking out through a face full of pain. 'He gave my children cake!'

Lyle stepped back.

Mr Majestic dropped to the floor, hugging his knees, shaking like a feather in a gale, now weeping uncontrollably. 'He gave them cake and made them sleep. My two children. He said their dreams were so bright and beautiful just like the circus and I did nothing I did nothing because the circus is all that matters all that matters just part of the circus so I did nothing for my children don't have any children no mother no father no mother no father no mother no . . .'

Lyle sank to his knees by the man, held him unevenly by the shoulder as he shook and cried. 'Greybags made your children sleep,' he said softly. 'And drugged you. And did this to you, whatever it is, however it was done. Did this to the whole circus. That's what you wouldn't tell me before. Where is he? Where is Greybags?'

Mr Majestic unfurled one shaking finger, pointed behind Lyle's shoulder to the door of the tent and whimpered, 'There.'

Lyle spun round.

Standing in the door was a boy. His hair was grey, his shirt covered in flour, his skin so white as to be almost translucent, like a field of reflective snow seen at first light, his eyes were bright green, his long twitchy fingers little more than bone. He couldn't have been more than eight or nine years old, and in his eyes, bright green eyes, and that smile, was the glee of a boy who has pulled the wings off flies for many, many years. His clothes were too big for him, and when he spoke, it was in the little voice of a child.

He said, 'Hello. You must be Mister Lyle.'

Lyle stood slowly, looking down at the creature in front of him. 'Hello,' he said. 'How do you feel about magnetic materials, little boy?'

The creature giggled. 'Would you like me to tell you your dreams, Mister Lyle?' he asked. 'Would you like me to tell you your nightmares? I think, the bigger you get, the more nightmares you have and the fewer dreams. I don't think you have many exciting dreams. I think your mind is full of scary things. Spiders crawling down the insides of the walls.'

Lyle smiled, looked down at the ground, looked up at the roof of the tent, looked back at the boy. 'Eats their dreams,' he murmured. 'And what was the next part – never grew old? How old are you, little boy? You don't mind if I call you a little boy, do you? You don't find it too patronising?'

The boy giggled. 'You're funny.'

'My best jokes are all about pi,' replied Lyle with a sigh. 'Tell me, child – do *you* want *your* mother?'

The boy's face darkened, and for a moment, there was something old and cracked in those bright green eyes. 'I know your nightmares, Mister Lyle,' he said softly. 'I seen your dreams. If they were brighter, I'd eat them so as how I'd never get old. But you already dream of borin' adult thin's. No good.'

'That's a "no" on the desire for matriarchal affection, then? Not sure what *Mrs Bontoft's Practical Advice* has to say on that. I'm sorry – I feel I ought to be somehow afraid of you, child, considering what cruelties you've unleashed on this circus. You *are* Greybags, aren't you? Who poisons children? Who corrupts grown men, who sends killers in the night? Who "eats dreams" whatever that means and sends the children to sleep, who hands out poisoned cake and is generally, I mean, clearly, of an other-worldly disposition. This is *you*, isn't it? Old Greybags the grey, who feasts on children's dreams. I'm sorry, I find it hard to be afraid of a child. Even one as old as you.'

'No,' sighed the boy, 'you ain't afraid of me, Mister Lyle. You're scared of the little girl bein' dead, of the boy's blood on your hands, and it's your fault, all alone, all runnin' through the night alone, because you couldn't stop it, even though it weren't your fault. But you should have stopped it, should've kept them safe, all of them safe because someone has to.' He stuck his tongue out. 'What a borin' nightmare. What an *adult* nightmare. So grown-up to be scared of thin's as how it ain't your fault. Children don't get scared of these thin's, see? They don't

understand as how it's possible. I don't want to be scared neither, Mister Lyle, which is why I ain't goin' to eat your dreams;
they are too old for me. I want glory an' colour an' you ain't got
that no more. So you see, I know you ain't scared of me. But
you might be scared of my friends a little bit.'

The child, whose name was Greybags, looked behind him.
The lion tamer, all muscle and bulging skin, stepped round the
side of the tent. Alone, that would have been a bad start, but
looking down to his side, Lyle couldn't help but notice that the
lion tamer had brought a lion.

'Yep,' he sighed, 'you may just be on to something there.'

Tess said, 'Oh look. A lion.'

Thomas said, 'What?'

'A lion. There. Going into the tent.'

Thomas tried not to look panic-stricken. In his current part-
nership with Tess and Tate, he knew that he was both the Man
and the Elder. Consequently it was his Duty to demonstrate
Leadership even if, as now, he wasn't entirely sure what to do.

'That's where Mister Lyle is!' he cried.

'Yep.'

'What's that child doing?'

'The little snotty one?'

'The one with grey hair.'

'Dunno. Hey! Look! There's Mister Lyle!'

'He's being dragged around by the lion tamer! He hit him!
That man hit Mister Lyle! Ignobly! I say! That was not fair play!'

'If I were goin' to be beat by anyone, I'd probably want it to
be someone with a pet lion. I mean, you ain't goin' to lose no station down the street after if you say, "Yep, I were beat up by this

bloke, but he had this pet lion, so it's fine, see!" In fact, you'll probably get respect from the floor.'

'We have to help him.'

'I've just got one last thin' to finish eatin'.'

'They're dragging him away!'

'Everyone drags Mister Lyle away sooner or later; he's used to it.'

'But we're his rescue!'

'Don't tell me,' huffed Tess. 'You've got this third cousin Sir Bigwig Bottoms the Third or summat wha' has killed many lions in his time an' told you a few pointers—'

'As a matter of fact, my sister's sister-in-law's husband's nephew is in the colonial office and did give some excellent pointers on how to handle lion problems, which he picked up during one of his campaigns against the native sorts.'

'An' wha' advice did he have?'

'Um . . . use a very big gun.'

There was the long slow sucking sound of Teresa downing another fish-smelling sugar sweet.

'Look,' Thomas said at last, 'we can't just stand here and let uncouth sorts cannibalise Mister Lyle. Who, now who, Miss Teresa, would be quite so amenable to your continual demands for food?!'

Tess's eyes narrowed. 'Bigwig! You just tried to play me there!'

'I did not!'

'You did!'

'I did not! I would never stoop to such base tactics as to—'

'You tried to make me a mark with your bigwig words an' all. An' 'sides I ain't never said as how we weren't savin' Mister Lyle,

I were just a bit thrown by the huge bloody lion what is gonna be a basta—'

There was a polite cough.

Tess and Thomas looked round.

A woman in tasteless purple silk was standing behind them.

Her hair was black, her skin was deep almond.

Her eyes were bright, emerald green.

Tess pointed. She said, 'You! I know you! Mister Lyle said to keep an eye out for you!'

The lady raised a pair of delicate thin dark eyebrows. 'Did he indeed? Did he add anything to this instruction?'

Tess thought about it. She said, 'He said to say "hello".' A wan smile spread over her bewildered features. 'So I s'pose . . . Hello, Miss Lin. You ain't knowin' nothin' 'bout lions, is you?'

The woman smiled. She said, 'I have a few ideas.'

CHAPTER 14

Unravelling

Lyle opened his eyes.

Later, when considering the tally of his failures and triumphs in this particular case, he'd chalk this one up as an error.

The lion purred.

Lyle had never heard a lion purr – mainly, he reasoned, because it wasn't a creature commonly found between Cheapside and the Royal Academy. He had an idea that it made sense for a lion to purr – cats purred, and this was just a very big – a *very* big – cat. The sound rolled over him like a great mothy carpet being turned out to air. A pair of bright amber eyes set in a golden-yellow head stared unblinking into Lyle's own. He thought, *What an unlikely way to die*, and felt almost relieved that, of the many ways in which he had imagined his own death, this would at least be something improbable. He felt a certain pride that, when his body was dissected for medical science and a bit of highbrow public entertainment, the novel manner of his death would attract a decent audience.

Lyle risked looking round. He was in a tent. With a lion. Very much with a lion.

What else was going on here? There were makeshift shelves laden with toy soldiers, toy horses, little wooden trains, brightly coloured toy shields and little wooden swords, with clown hats and comic wigs, with grinning masks, miniature castles and carved roaring dragons. There was a rocking horse in one corner, a tiny delicate theatre in the other in which puppets on thin pieces of thread could be persuaded to dance, the limp performers now lying in a pile beside the stage. There were stitched animals stuffed with cotton and hay, fabric blooms stitched together by the flower-makers of Covent Garden, recorders and tin pipes, ceramic flying ducks and, suspended from the ceiling, a spinning mobile of dancing princes and princesses turning slowly in the draught from the burning oil lamps. The tent was a child's paradise, a huge playroom, and it was entirely empty except for Lyle and, oh yes, of course, oh yes, the lion.

Lyle got on his hands and knees, one agonised limb at a time. The lion leant forward, sniffing at him with a huge pair of brown nostrils; a great flat tongue rolled across the wide space of his bottom jaw.

'Nice moggy,' whispered Lyle, slipping his hands towards his pockets. 'Nice moggy.'

He heard the sound of a teaspoon rattling against glass. He

looked round. The child – or not child, or half child, or whatever it was that he – it – was, was stirring something in a glass. He grinned at Lyle. 'Pretty dreams,' he said cheerfully. 'Beautiful, pretty dreams.' Next to him, the lion tamer stood with his arms folded. In one corner of the room, Mr Majestic was hunched, arms wrapped round his knees, head hanging, make-up streaked with tears.

Make-up streaked . . .

. . . though Billy the Button's hadn't come off at all.

Lyle said, 'Just so you know, there's a daring and exothermic rescue headed in my direction any second now.'

The child shrugged. 'Big words don't make you less scared, grown-up man. All grown-ups think cos they talk big, their hearts ain't smaller than ours.'

'You're not a child,' snapped Lyle.

'I got children's dreams.'

'And you're not a child. You're something else. It's fine. I've been attacked by living statues, assaulted by enchanting demons with an allergy for iron and helped blow up enough capacitor banks to light a city for a year. I can accept that you look like a child, you talk like a child, you giggle irritatingly like a child, but you are not a child. What are you, Greybags? May I call you Greybags? That is your name, isn't it? Old Greybags who'll come for you. But you don't look that old, do you?'

Greybags – if that could even be called a name – sighed, put the teaspoon down, walked over to where Mr Majestic sat huddled on the floor and said, 'You must drink your medicine, Mr Majestic. Then everythin' will be all right.'

Mr Majestic took the glass in trembling hands, raised it to his lips, swallowed. The glass was passed back to Greybags, who, looking satisfied, went to refill it. Mr Majestic didn't move for a long while. His head lolled. He started to snore. Lyle watched, fascinated. Finally he said, 'Is he all right?'

'You all right, sir?' asked Greybags, head on one side, barely glancing at Mr Majestic.

Mr Majestic jerked awake with a shock. 'All right?' replied the ringmaster cheerfully. 'Of course I'm all right! Absolutely fine! I . . . uh . . . there was something that I . . . I . . .'

'Your children,' breathed Lyle.

'What?'

'Your children.'

'The children! Of course! I must go and entertain the children!' He turned towards the door.

'Wait! *Your* children, the children that you had!' Lyle started to get to his feet, but was swatted back down by the lion tamer. 'What about *your* children?'

'What a funny man,' said Mr Majestic. 'You should be careful of the stories you tell.'

And so he left.

'Interesting,' said Lyle at last, 'and a little bit disturbing.'

The sound of the teaspoon rattling on the glass again snapped his attention back to Greybags. More liquid was being stirred in the same cup. Lyle could guess who the cup was for. He could feel the lion's breath tickling the back of his neck. 'So, I'm next? A little drink, a little sleep, and then – oblivion? No. More than oblivion. Um . . . part of the circus? What will that drink do to me, Greybags?'

'Take away your dreams, Mister Lyle. Take away your nightmares.'

'Oh.' Lyle sighed. 'I see.'

Greybags hesitated. 'An'?'

'And . . . what?'

'You're 'posed to do silly stuff now! You're 'posed to say you don't understand an' you're scared, you're 'posed to cry like a little girl an' . . .' Greybags giggled. ' 'Ave you noticed how all the big people cry like little girls when stuff happens as how they don't like? They just start cryin'. Like being grown-up ain't being grown-up at all. It's just bein' used to thin's bein' the way they are.'

'Yes,' said Lyle slowly, one suck of breath at a time. 'Yes, that's what being grown-up is – that, and the ability to spell "psychotic" in a hurry.' He eyed up the lion again. The lion seemed no more impressed by Lyle than it had been a few minutes ago. Glass tinkled. Greybags chuckled merrily at the pretty little sound. Lyle licked his lips. To his discomfort, the lion did the same, mimicking his actions with a tongue the size of an outstretched hand, over teeth longer than the distance between the knuckle and joint of Lyle's thumb. 'Well,' said Lyle carefully, 'let's see if I've got this straight. You, Greybags, poison people. You poison the children and it sends them to sleep, an endless, deep, endless sleep. Haven't quite put my finger on the methodology there, but I'm basically right. I know I'm basically right. You poison the adults and they become part of *your* dream. The ringmaster's nightmare – his children. You poisoned his children and took them away. You take away our dreams, our nightmares – more than that – you take away our hopes and our fears. Make us . . . what's the word? Functional? An organ grinder who just grinds and grinds for ever. Oh my God,' he sat up straight. 'I'm going to be serving fry-ups to Tess for the rest of my life, aren't I? That or perpetually trying to determine whether light is a wave or a particle, which, while a fascinating debate in and of itself, is one I feel the evidence of which is . . . is . . .' His voice trailed away.

Greybags put the spoon down, took a step towards Lyle. Lyle crawled back, bumped into the nose of the lion, cringed away. 'Now,' he stammered, 'I really feel I ought to warn you, when I said *exothermic*, what I meant in little words was very, very, very hot. I mean a very hot explosion, that's what's going to happen if you hurt me.'

'No one comes for you, Mister Lyle. You gotta save everyone *else*, that's what you think. *Borin'*! Your thoughts is *borin'*! All this *oughta* do an *shoulda* do an' all these things what you don't wanna do! You ain't good for nothin', Mister Lyle, 'cept borin' stories an' dead dreams.'

'Are you Tseiqin?' asked Lyle breathlessly.

The boy's green eyes flashed. 'What you know 'bout them?'

'Green eyes, hypnotic gaze, allergy to iron, strange and mystic intentions?'

'Borin' people ain't 'posed to know 'bout them.'

'Just because my personality may be about as exciting as watching bromine diffuse, doesn't mean I haven't picked up some fascinating insights in my life. Are you Tseiqin?' He put his head on one side, babbling fast. 'You know what they are, you've clearly had some contact, there is something in what you do – playing with minds – that is similar to what they do, but then Tess said she saw you handle iron and—'

Greybags stamped his foot and moaned, 'They don't understand me. Ain't no one understands me.'

'What are you? An . . . an adaption? Some sort of albino, some variety, as if that's what the world needed now?'

'They loved me when I were young.'

'Who? The Tseiqin?'

'They said I were beautiful when I were young. But I didn't grow old like they did, I didn't think like they did, I didn't do like they did. They didn't understand! I got so scared because I weren't like them. They said I were a freak. Outcast.'

'So you're not quite Tseiqin, but an adaptation. I'm guessing you're fine with iron, but can't enchant like they can. You somehow feed on the thoughts of children, use them to keep you young. That's why you're outcast? Why the Tseiqin wouldn't accept you? How old are you, Greybags?'

For a moment, Greybags became absolutely still, eyes focused on something far away. 'I remember . . . how angry the men in the big wigs were when the men in Boston refused to pay their taxes. I remember the red coats marchin' off to fight Napoleon. I remember when the cities were small an' the land were big, so big you could go for ever from village to village an' all the little children would come and clap an' their eyes were so wide an' so big an' it didn't smell of smoke none, an' I remember . . . I remember . . . when they opened the theatres again. I remember when they killed the king.'

'That was centuries ago,' breathed Lyle.

'An' it were *borin'!* Don't wannit, don't wannit. They said you gotta get old an' get borin' an' serious an' go an' fight an' bleed an' die cos that's what the grown-ups do. An' you gotta protect, an' do *should* an' do *ought* an' do *care* an' do *fear*. So much fear. So much fear as how the children can't understand, an' I were so scared of the adult fear, of the *should* an' the *ought* an' the *must* an' the fight so I decided to make it stop. I made it stop, Mister Lyle. Don't you wish you were as clever as me?'

'Right now, maybe,' replied Lyle, eyeing up the glass in Greybags' hand.

'You ain't gonna be scared no more, Mister Lyle,' said Greybags. 'If you was a child I'd eat your dreams; but you ain't. You ain't got no dreams good enough for me to eat. But you don't 'ave to be scared. I'll *make* you a child again, Mister Lyle. Then there won't be no knowin', no thinkin', no dreamin', no rememberin'. Just games an' stories.'

Lyle closed his mouth tightly, but the lion tamer, clearly wanting to contribute something to the conversation himself, stepped sharply round Greybags and grabbed Lyle by the hair and shook him. Lyle closed his eyes to stop them rattling out of his head, felt strange liquids slosh round somewhere just behind his eardrums and made a mental note to investigate that quality in more detail, in the unlikely event that he survived long enough or had enough brain left for scientific study.

The lion tamer pushed him down towards the smelly glass. Lyle clamped his lips tight shut, and smelt something sharp, biting and foggy all at once, a smell that rammed straight to the back of his nose and then proceeded to feather-duster its way down into his lungs. He'd smelt it on Billy the Button's breath, and something like it, something almost the same, on the breath of Sissy Smith, just after she fell at his feet. Greybags calmly reached out and pinched Lyle's nose, like a mother controlling a mutinous child, and waited as Lyle's face slowly turned red, then purple, then blue. Lyle kicked at where he hoped the lion tamer's shins were with all the success of a flea against a cathedral, and heard the lion growl, felt the heat of its breath. Greybags said, 'Ain't no fun, not breathin', Mister Lyle. Yor goin' a silly colour an' all!'

Lyle's eyes were half closed, his arms sagged at his sides as his strength faded against the burning heat of suffocation in his blood. And, because there was no point in fighting, and because the human body was too clever not to breathe, even when to breathe was to die, he opened his mouth, just for one breath, just one.

And Greybags tipped in the potion.

Her name was Mystic Mai.

Actually, her name wasn't Mystic Mai, but that was what the punters called her, and frankly, they couldn't pronounce that right.

She knew things were bad.

They'd been bad since she'd had to haul the unconscious Lyle out of his own smoke-filled house without so much as a 'thank you' for her pains and a chaste peck on the cheek. It had got worse when Lyle and his funny little pets had come blundering into the circus without a clue as to what trouble they were getting into.

Now she was going to have to set things right.

She slipped a few spare knives into the sheaths in her sleeves. They were thin and bronze. She sighed. 'Now, children,' she said, 'when Mister Lyle said *exothermic*, did he mention a blast radius?'

CHAPTER 15

Mystics

Horatio Lyle hit the floor, the floor hit him, and the floor came out the winner. It was times like these, he told himself, when Newton's Second Law really made its point.

On the floor in front of him there stood a pair of feet.

The feet shuffled back to allow an upside-down head to rotate into view and a smiling voice to proclaim, 'Taste good, Mister Lyle?'

Lyle coughed, turned his head to one side, and spat, tasting all the smells of the bottle increased to maximum dosage. A hot, sticky, burning ache ran down the length of his throat and into his belly. Worse, much worse, there was a fog in his mind, a squelching inside his skull, a mixture of so many sensations, sharp and dull, all at once trying to crawl across his senses, like the final burst of adrenaline before sleep after a day far, far too long.

Poison. Lyle could name a thousand poisons, and most of their effects. But he could name a very small number indeed which had a cure. He crawled onto his hands and knees and every part of him ached, just wanted to sleep, just sleep, go to sleep, just . . .

Poison poison poison poison poison oh god oh god oh god not poison not poison please please not poison slow too slow too young haven't seen anything oh please not not not so scared don't wanna don't wanna don't wanna please Tess . . .

Lyle understood death. Not fluffy, angelic-washed death, not the death that led to heaven or hell or to long-lost loves. He understood death as being a very decisive full stop.

Please please please please . . .

Greybags giggled as Lyle tried to stand but slumped straight back onto his belly. 'Ain't no good, Mister Lyle! You go to sleep an' it'll be *alllll* better in the mornin'.'

'What was in that drink?' hissed Lyle.

'You won't never understand, Mister Lyle. It ain't the sorta thing what children like you an' me oughta know.'

'I'm not a child!'

'You're gonna be, Mister Lyle. Just like a child, 'cept a little bit older. Won't that be nice?'

'Why are you doing this?'

'It's a gift, this what I give you. I could've killed you, picked you apart limb by limb. But the grown-up lady wanted me to be kind, an' I thought I'd make her proud. So just go to sleep, an' everythin' will be all right.'

Lyle grabbed Greybags by the ankle and held on. It was the only part of Greybags he could reach from the floor; getting up seemed an impossibility.

The face of a youth stared at Lyle in surprise from out of an adult's clothes. 'Aren't you asleep yet?' he demanded.

Lyle blinked back gum and heat from across his eyes. Black and white spots were swimming across his vision like bathers in a heaving sea, taking their time as they drifted down his vision and back up, propelled there by each agonising blink.

'You feed on children,' he hissed. 'You bastard, you *feed* on *children*.'

Greybags tried to tug his ankle free, but Lyle's fingers were locked in place. He stamped, he kicked, he caught Lyle in the shoulder, but the older man just grinned, his body so lost to the potion running through his veins that the pain barely registered. 'You bastard, you *bastard*!' He didn't seem to be talking to Greybags any more. His eyes were unfocused, and all that mattered were his fingers round that thin, boy's ankle in its adult's trousers, to which he clung like an obstinate child to its teddy bear.

No no no no nonononono please no . . .

There was a sound from outside the tent.

It sounded like someone politely clearing their throat.

'I have a pint of nitro-glycerin you . . .'

There was a hurried murmur. Lyle half raised his head through a fog of bewilderment and pain, and saw, just below the flap of the tent, a pair of ridiculously bright and absurdly sparkling gold and purple slippers. The voice seemed familiar, but it was already far, far away.

The murmuring stopped.

The voice cleared its throat again and announced in a slightly irritated voice: 'Very well. I have a pint of nitro-glycerin derivative . . .'

Murmur murmur . . .

'Fine! I have two pints of chemicals that, when put together, mimic the effects of a pint of nitro-glycerin in a highly effective way and, more to the point, they're here for *you*.'

Somewhere, in a land far, far away, Lyle felt the lion tense at his side. The curtain was swept back across the front of the tent, the lion flexed its muscles, it had a lot of muscles to flex, and leapt. Somewhere halfway between ground and target, something happened to it. Its every muscle locked, its head seemed to snap into place, the roar that had been escaping from between its teeth turned into a strange sort of mewl and, as if gravity had suddenly decided to catch up, having been caught by surprise, it flopped, belly-first, onto the ground at the stranger's feet.

Lyle was half aware of a pair of bright green eyes, but now, right now, he just wanted to sleep.

'Hello, Greybags,' said a soft voice, like the brush of silk in wind. 'Your species—'

'Genus,' corrected a little voice helpfully.

'Thomas, has Mister Lyle ever informed you that you hinder a certain charismatic atmosphere? Your *genus*, Mr Greybags, wants a word with you.'

There was a whimper from Greybags as he slunk into a corner. 'You ain't 'posed to be here,' he whined. 'Not you, not one of you.' He grabbed the lion tamer by the hem of his spotted loincloth and shrieked, 'Kill her!'

In the door, flanked by the rather uncertain-looking shapes of Tess, Tate and Thomas, Mystic Mai drew herself up to her full, rather petite height. In either hand she held thin bottles, each one carefully corked and labelled. The children at her sides seemed intensely focused on these, with more than a little apprehension in their eyes.

The lion tamer hesitated. 'But she is a lady, an' it ain't nice to—'

'I don't care! Kill her, kill her, kill her now!'

He gave an uneasy shrug and lumbered towards the woman in the door. 'Sorry, miss,' he grumbled, drawing back a fist the size of Mai's little, dainty head.

Mystic Mai sighed. 'What would *your* mama say?'

The lion tamer found himself looking into Mai's deep, green eyes.

He couldn't remember the last time he'd . . . remembered . . . anything. But for a second, as he looked into her eyes, he was a child playing in an autumn forest of thick-limbed trees. She eased his fist down to his side, smiled and said, 'Now tell me, Eric . . .'

. . . and once upon a time, there had been a young man with the name of Eric, who had eaten the cake the old grey man gave him as the circus travelled east, and then Eric had been gone.

'. . . why don't you go to your room?'

The lion tamer hesitated, locked in her gaze, then giggled and said, 'Sorry, miss. I'll be in my room, miss,' turned, and lumbered off.

Greybags whimpered as the woman advanced towards him, and he sidled into a corner. 'This circus is mine,' he hissed. 'I made it! I fed it! They ate my cake, they drink my drink, this is *my* circus! My game, my story, my playhouse! *Mine!* It was given me!'

'And now I'm going to take it back,' she replied, 'because you've gone too far. You've hurt all those children. You've hurt *Lyle* and, strangely enough, I like the socially inept little man. He did the right thing by us Tseiqin when he had no reason to, and that is novel in any species – genus – whichever – on this earth.'

'My circus! Mine! I found it an' made it good! Mine!'

'Now now,' she said patiently. 'I really think you're being very childish about all this. I really hate to say something so tedious to a man of your extreme years, but the time has come to grow up and move on.'

In reply to which, and knowing no better, Greybags raised his head and screamed like a child.

'Lady-demon' was perhaps an unfair title to be so liberally applied to Mystic Mai, although she would be the first to point out that it did have a certain cultural irony. After all, her native land habitually described anyone from outside its borders as a 'foreign demon'. It was entirely fair that here, on the other side of the world, the natives should do likewise. Not that this counted as abuse, on Tess's part. 'Demon' was admittedly a nick-name got from dealings with others of Mystic Mai's uniquely green-eyed, iron-allergic, generally maniacal tribe. In her case, though, it was little other than a biological descriptor, acknowledging that while she could, yes, hypnotise a human at the merest touch of her emerald eyes, in this rare case that would-n't cause a dilemma.

Thus Mystic Mai had earned Tess's lifelong grudging respect for two reasons: 1. she had never, unlike most of her kin, attempted to kill anyone who didn't deserve it, and 2. she really did make excellent chow mein. Whatever that was.

Her real name, for anyone who bothered to ask, was Lin Zi.
And she'd always thought that Lyle had lovely eyes.

The lion, which up to this point had seemed too bewildered to
do anything other than try and swat its own nose with one leaden
paw, looked up at the sound of Greybags's scream. Its tail
twitched. Its lips drew back. Tess tugged at Lyle's sleeve. 'Mister
Lyle,' she began in her best, low voice.

The reply was somewhere between a grunt and a gurgle.
Fingers closed over Tess's own and through a pair of watering
red eyes some semblance of sanity peeked from Mister Lyle's
face. 'Poison,' he whispered. 'Tess! Poison!'

Lin was saying, 'We could settle this like adults, you know.'

' 'Bout the lion,' added Tess helpfully.

Muscles stretched and drew across the creature's back like tec-
tonic plates drifting at very high speed. A tongue the size of the
lower part of Tess's arm rolled across its teeth. Lin didn't seem
to notice or care.

'Miss!' wailed Tess. 'The huge bloody lion thing . . .'

Lin half turned. Greybags ran. The lion leapt. Beaming like
a lighthouse, if lighthouses were painted purple, had a pair of
curled slippers to wear and had a certain unnatural greenish
something to their light, Lin Zi shrugged off Thomas's tactful
scientific complaints, and threw the bottles straight at the lion's
paws.

And, in accordance with all expectation, the bottles smashed,
the chemicals within mixed, and science happened.

This is the ward where the children go.

Not dead, not asleep.

Not exactly alive either.

They sit upright in their beds in Marylebone, while the nurses slip mulched-up food between their lips. They do not move, and do not speak, and do not do anything that might make them human. Except, perhaps in the quietest part of the night, when the moon is lost behind the fog and the sounds of the trains are muffled in the nearby cutting . . . perhaps then the children lying in their beds, finally, truly sleep. And when they do, perhaps they dream.

And if they dream, what they dream is this:

Once upon a time . . .

On the floor of Horatio Lyle's house, a page billowed in an unregarded book.

Words flickered as the pages turned.

. . . to raise children . . .

. . . parent's gift . . .

. . . responsibility . . .

. . . duty . . .

. . . show no weakness . . .

. . . tell no lies . . .

. . . a child that screams is contrary and difficult . . .

. . . stories . . .

In his empty tent, Mr Majestic drifted through a world of green forests and endless eyes, and for a moment, remembered a time when he wasn't a child in a man's body, when he had a name, a real name, just for a moment. Once upon a time . . .

Sissy Smith twitched on the edge of her bed and for a moment she dreamed of. . .

. . . of . . .
. . . *run away* . . .
. . . *run away* . . .
. . . *run away* . . . *to* . . . *to* . . .
No.
Nothing there . . .
. . . not any more . . .

CHAPTER 16

Poisoned

Fire had happened.

Thomas was vaguely aware of running, screaming, angry animals and the usual and largely predictable consequences of unpredictable exothermic reactions, particularly, he couldn't help feel, particularly when they were being caused by someone quite so gleeful about such uncivilised notions as 'blast radius' as Lin Zi. But there was more.

He remembered looking into the bright green eyes of Greybags and seeing a child, just a child, a snotty little boy with sleeves far too long for him, and knowing, in that instant, that this child had been the young man who had served poisoned cake to the children in the tent, and more, that this child was *wrong*.

He was a broken limb bent backwards on itself, the general who drank tea while his men were massacred on the field, the moon rising in the wrong place against a background of foreign stars, he was just . . . *wrong*.

And then there was Mister Lyle.

Thomas didn't think he'd ever seen Tess move so fast, catching her would-be mentor as he slid towards the earth, eyes too wide, skin too pale, the word 'poison' on his breath and the smell of something untoward on his lips.

Greybags had run. He'd taken one look at Lin Zi, all tastelessly dressed furious vengeance, taken one look into her bright green eyes and seen her fingers moving for the bronze blades hidden, most literally, up her sleeves, and run. At his feet, chemicals had mixed and fire had happened but Greybags was already running, hair smoking, clothes in tatty shreds on his back, thin white blood trickling down from a tear across his shoulder. Thomas had known, sensed, felt, that Lin wanted to follow him, that it was her duty, her responsibility. That was somehow why she was here, hiding in this circus. But then she too had seen Lyle and heard the word 'poison', and for the first time, for the very first time, Thomas had seen a look on a Tseiqin's face that hadn't been derived directly from the 100 Snooty Noses catalogue of the House of Lords. But she'd already broken the bottles together, the circus was already starting to blaze, Greybags was running, Tess was crying and Horatio Lyle was in no fit state to do anything about any of it.

Lin had for a moment, just a moment, hesitated. Thomas had seen that too in her face, as the lion screamed and flames spat across the carpet and the circus had broken out into that very special kind of confusion and chaos that only a really interested

London mob with not enough to keep it occupied could manage. Thomas had seen the *look* in her eye. She'd looked at Lyle, she'd looked at the retreating back of Greybags, and for a moment, just a moment, she'd considered leaving them there.

Then the moment had passed, and Lin was grabbing Lyle by the crook of his arm and hauling upright and, somehow, despite being both a *woman* and, worse, *not one of us*, Lin Zi had taken charge.

Park Lane was a freshly cobbled road up and down which rich carriages progressed for largely illicit purposes. Occasionally reckless young men out to impress even more reckless young women would race their open-top carriages round the edges of the road and onto the grasses of Hyde Park, but usually, traffic was sedate, owing in part to congestion, and in part to the thick quantities of the inevitable waste product of having a transportation system entirely dependent on well-fed horses.

On the side of this road, the most and least glamorous in all London, stood a lady-demon in tasteless, so-called oriental trousers, a child pickpocket, an extravagantly tatty dog, a boy in fine but torn trousers, and a deranged, gabbling scientist.

Maybe not deranged. Not when all Lyle had to say was, 'Poison . . . pudding . . . poison . . .'

They'd leant him against a lamp-post, while Lin stamped her foot and raged.

'Five hundred years ago,' she shrilled, 'this was what Beijing was like! Ignorant Western barbarians and their ineffective transport solutions!'

Thomas, sensing, without knowing, that Lin was casting

aspersions on Victoria Regina and all works made in her name, suggested, 'Maybe we could find an omnibus?'

'Miss Lin!' Tess's voice was full of fear. 'Mister Lyle's falling asleep!'

In a second Lin was at Lyle's side. She grabbed him by the chin, pulled back a drooping eyelid, peered deep inside. Businesslike, she slapped him across the jaw. He jerked, half opened his eyes, and mumbled, 'Please don't do that.'

'Mister Lyle!'

His eyes drifted into focus on Lin's face. A frantic, bewildered grin spread across his features. 'Lin? What the hell are you . . .?'

'What did Greybags give you? Did you eat anything, drink anything?'

He nodded.

Lin hissed, '*Sai jai!*' the meaning of which Thomas was grateful not to know. Then, 'Mister Lyle, do you trust me?'

Lyle hesitated, then nodded again.

'Sort of,' muttered Tess.

'I need you to look straight into my eyes.'

A pause. Another nod. Lyle looked. He'd been told before, so many times, *don't look at the eyes*, not the eyes of the Tseiqin. To look was to drown, to fall for ever. But this was Lin. And Lin was different, in her way. In every way that mattered.

'You are not going to close your eyes, do you understand?' she murmured, taking his hand and pressing it between her fingers. 'You are not going to fall asleep unless I permit you. You are going to obey everything I say. Do you understand me, Horatio Lyle?'

'Bigwig,' hissed Tess at Thomas, 'are you sure we should go an' let Mister Lyle be ensorcelled like this?'

'If he sleeps, he won't wake up!' snapped Lin, half turning her head from Lyle's wide-eyed stare. 'Not as you know him. Everything that was Mister Lyle will be gone and all that stays will be a mewling, distorted infant. Like the people you saw at the circus.'

'Poisoned,' whispered Lyle. 'In the pudding. Poisoned.'

'Is there an antidote?' demanded Thomas. 'He can't just not sleep for ever!'

Lin hissed in frustration, turned back to the thronging street, searching the gloom for a cab. A hand fell on her sleeve and pulled her back. Surprised, she looked straight into Lyle's wide eyes. 'I need . . .' He groaned, his other hand pressed against his head as if it were going to explode. 'I need . . . I *need* salt water, a lot, and I need it fast. I need . . . *Mama* . . . I . . . I need . . . Oh, God . . .'

'This is good,' muttered Lin, 'this is good! What else do you need, Mister Lyle. Tell me!'

'Charcoal tablets, milk, a needle, a microscope, uh . . .'

'We have these things!' exclaimed Thomas. Then his heart sank a little. 'At least, we had them in Lyle's house.'

'Wanna play, wanna . . . wanna . . . Tess, you mustn't eat the . . . God . . .'

'Lyle!' barked Lin. 'You are not going to fall asleep! You are going to be a good English scientist, chop chop, what ho, dammit! Tell us everything you need!'

'Salt water. Sugar water, sodium bicarbonate, charcoal, uh . . . belladonna, in case it gets too slow, opiates if it gets too fast. Potassium to counteract the sodium, and as many coffee beans as you can find.'

And then, perhaps because overall it had been a trying day,

Horatio Lyle raised his head to the darkening sky and wailed, 'I want my mama!'

The sun set over London.

It set across the semi-rural village of Hampstead, and spilt its last rays into the bedroom at the top of Milly Lyle's house, where a mother, whose son had long since left home, turned down the sheets on an empty bed and remembered nights when she had told stories to her child, back when you were allowed to begin with *once upon a time*. Before an excess of time, learning and, above all, the desire to be free of all childish things, even the good ones, had taken Horatio Lyle away from home and the fairytales of youth.

The sun set over the crowded streets of Mayfair, where street vendors yelled abuse at coppers trying to organise the mess of carts and carriages. It dribbled into the thieves' alleys of Soho, told of rising darkness, and rich pickings for nimble fingers, promised close brick walls and long thick fogs in the narrow alleys of Whitechapel, warned the factory master to light his lamps and draw his shutters, summoned fishermen back from the sludge-filled Thames estuary, whispered children asleep.

In the hospital in Marylebone, Miss Chaste sits alone in the middle of the ward, opens her book as she does every night, clears her throat and breathes, 'Once upon a time . . .' Because this, as she sees it, is one of her many motherly duties, to be kindly done.

Horatio Lyle's house was a blackened, shabby hulk of its former self. Pipes had burst free from their brackets inside the walls, sticking out like broken bones from torn skin where they'd been burst by the pressure of the gas that Tess had pumped through the guts of the house the day before. Walls had been turned brownish-black by sticky substances in the filthy noxious air. Windows had been smashed, doors hung crookedly from their frames. Even the local thieves, usually quick to pick over the remains of any injured building in the city, and for whom the price of the smallest silver fork might feed a family for a day, had kept away, frightened of the stench and the hulking shadows. Anything that had stood on a table, had now fallen on the floor. Anything that had been upright on a shelf, now inclined against its neighbour. Thomas had never seen a house so abused, and felt his heart twist in his throat at the pity of the sight.

Need pushed them into the gloomy carcass of the place. Tess rummaged in Lyle's pockets until she found a box of smelly yellow matches and a ball of tinted white glass. The flame from one ignited the powder in the other, and gave off a bright hot white light that illuminated the twisted remains of the stairs. Lyle's face, in the unforgiving glare, was a sickly shade of green. With Lin's arm round his waist supporting him, his eyes flickered erratically from side to side, like someone already half lost in a dream.

They got him as far as the blackened stairs before he slipped from Lin's grasp and dropped to the floor. As he breathed, his lungs seemed to rattle and wheeze. 'Salt water,' he hissed. 'Salt water, quick, salt water.'

Thomas was already running, stumbling through the dark, down towards the kitchen. He pulled open drawer after drawer and tripped over buckets and chairs in search of what he needed. At Lyle's feet, Tate whined. By Lyle's side, Tess's face was almost as pale as his. Lin looked like a cheap iron etching, all angles and frozen poise.

In the kitchen, Thomas found a bucket of water, old, drawn yesterday from the pump, and, at the back of a cupboard, a bag of salt. He seized one in each hand and carried them upstairs.

On the stairs Tess poked Lyle in the arm. He half jerked, slowly turned his head, seemed to see her and gave the weedy smile of a tired old man relieved at the thought of an ending. '*Pickpocket*,' he said gently.

'Bigwig aristo pinchpenny,' she retorted, feigning, without much effect, sharpness in her voice.

Thomas reached the head of the stairs. 'How much salt to how much water?' he asked. But Lyle had already grabbed the whole bag of salt, tipped it to the last grain into the bucket, stirred it with one hand and then, without a sound or word of apology, buried his head like a dog into its bowl, straight down below the water's surface to drink. He drank like a desert wanderer saved from the sun, seeming to breathe the water as much as drink it. He gulped down so much, Tess thought his stomach would burst. Then lifting up his head, swallowing a last gulp, he took in a great heave of air and, staggering to his feet, ran towards the door.

He nearly reached it, got to within a foot of the dark outside world before, dropping to his knees, Horatio Lyle was violently, unforgivably and unforgivingly sick.

When Mrs Hobbs, the banker's wife, went to find Mister Lyle on a cold, dark London evening, a bundle of papers tucked into her bag and an umbrella raised ineffectually against the rain, she was perhaps a little bit surprised to discover that her destination was missing its door. Or rather, its door was still attached to the house, but by a single screw whose hinge hung off the frame with the slouch of a thing too tired to care.

Neither, for that matter, did the cutting smell of vomit and the occasional stain of blood on the floor of the front hall, fill her with a resounding confidence about the genteel qualities of this gentleman's abode. But Mrs Hobbs was not one to question the habits of her clientele, so long as her clientele demonstrated financial prudence while indulging said habits, and so she drew her shoulders back, stuck her chin out and marched determinedly into the house in the happy thought that if anything bad did happen to her, then the full force of the fiscal system would be at her back, and pity anyone who got in the way of money.

There was a glimmer of candlelight coming from downstairs, from where there also issued a series of unlikely and unusual sounds.

The sounds went as follows:

'You wanna do what with it?'

'Try injecting directly into the vein.'

'That's 'orrid!'

'Miss Teresa, I think we may have to resign ourselves to the thought that medicine *is* 'orrid.'

'You can do it. I ain't sticking *nothin'* nowhere where it weren't meant.'

Mrs Hobbs crept down the stairs, which, in defiance of all the care she took, creaked like the cracked old bones of a hanged man suspended in a gale. She reached the bottom of the stairs, eased back the kitchen door, and felt a tiny shiver of movement by her side. A brass knife, old-fashioned and slightly curved, appeared in the vicinity of her left eye; behind it, a voice hummed like a weary panther, 'Now why would a lady of your nature be in a house of such ill-repose?'

The dagger filled Mrs Hobbs' world. She gabbled, 'I . . . I'm looking for Mister Horatio Lyle, and how dare you accost me with—'

If it were possible for the dagger's point to move any closer without actually shaving off her thin grey eyelashes, it managed it. A pair of green eyes blinked calmly behind the hand that held the blade, and that voice, soft, female, foreign, breathed, 'Mister Lyle is indisposed at the moment.'

From beyond the voice a younger one, that of a child, said, 'Oi! Miss Lin! I think he's fallin' asleep again!'

The green-eyed woman let out a weary sigh. 'I am tormented,' she complained, 'by evolutionarily inhibited companions who fail to appreciate the concept of "lingering menace". I don't suppose you'd mind quivering in fear at my inexpressible and quaintly charismatic presence while I just deal with this?'

'Um . . . I suppose not,' whispered Mrs Hobbs.

'You are most understanding,' breathed the female voice, and without a sound, the dagger and the woman who held it were gone, vanished into the candlelit glow of the kitchen beyond.

Mrs Hobbs, her heart fit to burst from her throat, eased the door further back and beheld, strewn across every surface, a scene of chemical chaos. Containers of liquids or slimes, samples of flowers, finely ground powders, old dried mushrooms, strange blackened twigs, peculiar pink glands from long-dead foreign animals, needles tipped with she dared not think what, smears and stains of every colour preserved in every form, covered the floor so densely that its four inhabitants – a woman with green eyes and a terrible fancy-dress jacket and trousers, two children and a dog – had to pick their way on tiptoe to avoid knocking over the throng of bottles.

Yet if that was enough to alarm the usually unflappable Mrs Hobbs, the sight in the middle of the room shocked her to her very bones for, stretched out across the kitchen table, his feet dangling off the edge, was Mister Horatio Lyle. His eyes were red, his skin as pale as new snow, and his head lolled and his eyelids sagged as if he were falling asleep – only to be woken by a sharp slap from the green-eyed woman and a cry of, 'No sleeping, Mister Lyle! No sleeping yet!'

Mrs Hobbs had seen human creatures look so pallid, and shake so feebly, back when, as a young lady of charitable bent, she had helped tend the victims of a cholera outbreak. This was not cholera; but it might as well have been for the way Lyle looked.

'What're you doing here?' demanded the girl with wild frizzy hair. She was furiously grinding two powders together with a pestle and mortar, and only half glanced up as she spoke.

Mrs Hobbs stammered out her name. 'I've been investigating the financial records of the St Bartholomew's Workhouse. What happened here?'

'Poisoned,' said the green-eyed woman. 'It is really rather imperative that we keep Mister Lyle conscious throughout this experience.'

A boy, who had said nothing so far, now straightened up with a needle in his hand and a determined expression on his face. Carefully he lowered the point towards the crook of Mister Lyle's exposed arm. 'What are you doing?' gasped Mrs Hobbs. 'You're just a child!'

The boy hesitated, looked at her, then looked at Lyle. For a moment, there was something infinitely small and frightened in his eyes, before it was replaced by an expression of immovable stubbornness. 'Yes,' he said firmly. 'I am just a child, ma'am. But if you have a better grasp of organic chemistry and its medical applications, then kindly speak up.'

Mrs Hobbs' jaw sagged. She turned to the green-eyed woman. 'Do you permit this?' she demanded.

To which the other woman just smiled and said, 'Mrs Hobbs, was it? Ma'am, may I be so bold as to tell you, the world is never as it seems. I am not just a woman in a socially inappropriate costume; Miss Teresa is not just a petty thief with a reprehensible attitude towards personal hygiene; and Master Elwick' – Thomas slid the needle under Lyle's skin and pressed the plunger – 'is not just an aristocratic bigwig with an intellect equal to that of one of his hounds.'

On the table, Thomas drew back the needle, and they all watched in silence for Lyle's reaction. For a moment, he was lay unmoving, his breathing low and steady. Then his eyes opened wide, and he half raised his head and stuttered from between trembling teeth, 'Uh . . . uhm . . . heart faster breathing faster head hurting exploding. Uhm . . . hands shaking arms shaking legs shaking. Thomas, did you just give me purified caffeine directly into an artery?'

'Yes?' said the boy, a note of uneasy hope in his voice, seeking approval.

'I hope you're taking notes,' muttered Lyle. 'Hello, Mrs Hobbs,' he added, half turning his head as if his mind had only just registered the events of the last thirty seconds. 'Sorry about this, but I think I'm about to . . .'

However, Horatio Lyle never managed to explain what was about to happen or, more importantly, why. With a gasp his head fell back and, with his fingers clenching into claws and legs tightening into corkscrew stiffness, every muscle in his body started to shake like a butterfly in a hurricane. His eyes bulged from his face, his face turned red. Mrs Hobbs couldn't shake off the feeling that if he had enough breath, he would have screamed. As it was, every breath came in a tortured wheeze as if nothing more than the presence of air around him, rather than any action of his lungs, kept his body alive. One flailing hand fell round Thomas's wrist, locking so hard that she heard the young man gasp. Through gritted teeth Lyle wheezed, 'Pudding . . . poisoned . . . *pudding . . .*'

Thomas nodded, his mouth twisting with pain and his eyes filling with a look so frightened and young that Mrs Hobbs wanted to hold the boy to her and whisper, 'It's all right, it'll be all right'. Then Lyle's hand fell away from Thomas's wrist and he seemed to jerk like a frog trying to swim on dry land. His nails scrabbled at the table top and he beat his head against its surface. 'Lin!' he half screamed. 'Talk to her! She knows . . . she knows . . . poison . . .' Mrs Hobbs covered her mouth with her hands, waiting in vain for it to end.

'Maybe we should—' began the girl Teresa. Her eyes were filling with tears that she was too stubborn to acknowledge by wiping away.

'Caffeine will keep him awake.'

'Breaking all his bloody bones will keep him awake!' snapped Tess. Under the table Tate covered his head with his paws and whimpered in response to his master's groans.

'Then he must break his bones,' replied Thomas firmly, putting the needle to one side, 'so long as he does not sleep.'

Mrs Hobbs backed away, feeling for the stairs. Then a hand brushed hers and, with a start, she found her gaze locked into those strange green eyes. She smelt old leaves rustling in the forest, the clean smell after rain, and heard the woman called Lin say, 'So tell me, Mrs Hobbs, what do *you* know?'

Lin took Mrs Hobbs to the drawing room. The walls were scarred by burnt chemicals, the floors strewn with books and broken glass. She sat her down on the edge of a gutted armchair, and struck a light to a single candle. As she stood opposite Mrs Hobbs, her bright green eyes were almost light enough to illuminate the room without the tiny flame.

She said, 'You are a banker's wife?'

'Yes,' said Mrs Hobbs. 'What has happened to Horatio? And where's the doctor?'

'I doubt this is a poison within your average doctor's remit,' sighed Lin patiently. 'All things considered, I would say he is receiving the very best of care. They were already investigating the substance concerned and I have every hope of them achieving a cure at . . . at some point. Why did he come to you, banker's wife?'

Something in the way Lin spoke sent a shudder through Mrs Hobbs. She had a coldness, a weary hardness in her voice, as if she had walked across the world, seen every ocean and continent and been impressed by none of them. This young woman standing before her, Mrs Hobbs knew, *knew* with that implacable certainty that didn't bother to ask for proof, was old. Older, maybe, than she. Not knowing whether to try to hold the other's remarkable gaze, she recounted how Lyle had brought her the irregular-seeming workhouse accounts.

'You? Why? Why not to a banker?'

Mrs Hobbs looked up sharply. 'Because bankers' wives know all the other bankers' wives, Miss . . .'

'Lin. My name is Lin Zi. Don't try to get the pronunciation right; you'll only embarrass yourself. And you know banking?'

'I ran my father's estate for six years,' retorted Mrs Hobbs. 'I kept exact records of every farthing that went in and out, handled mortgages, brokers, lenders, buyers, sellers, tradesmen of every account, fraudsters and embezzling serving men. It is true that when my husband conducts business with his fellows, I am sent into the neighbouring room while the men drink port and discuss their arrangements; but do not think that being banished, a door away, I cannot hear every word. I can find you the destination of every shilling you may ever spend, young . . . my lady. So do me the courtesy to be honest and respectful, and I shall be with you.'

To her surprise, the green-eyed woman smiled. 'Yes,' she said at last, 'I can see why Mister Lyle went to you. I might be able to manage courtesy, but honesty? There are dangers that would come and find you in the night if you knew even a fragment of what I know. But I will try my best.'

Mrs Hobbs shifted on her uncomfortable seat. 'Does Horatio – Mister Lyle – trust you?'

Lin's gaze seemed to fill the room, a receding infinity of emerald green. 'A complicated question,' she replied softly, and for a moment, the laughing woman was gone, leaving something old and still in its place. 'But, yes, despite his better judgement, I'd say he does. I'd say he has no choice but to.'

'Who *are* you?'

Lin sighed, and for a moment, her voice was the tumbling

sound of old fallen leaves across bare stones, 'When your people scrambled naked over the rocks and found for the first time the secrets of fire, mine were already teeming in the trees and the fields, spilling across the earth like the sea across sand. When you first raised the pyramids, we sent you golden treasures, like children to be indulged. When Alexander the Great sent to the kings of the world for tribute, he was sure in turn to give us our due.

'We made the legends from which the ancient gods are derived, we are the ones behind the myths and stories, we were the spirits to whom you sacrificed your children on the altar stone, back in the days before iron and guns. We thought you just weak children, when first you began to build across this world. But you humans are so industrious, so inventive, so cunning in all that you do. You made things that not the wisest sage or greatest dreamer could foretell: a world of iron and machines. And now we scuttle in the dark, and watch, and fear, and wait. This is who I am, Mrs Hobbs. And you should know that, being all that I am, I would stop at nothing to protect this human, Horatio Lyle, and keep him safe from all this perilous world. He knows so much and so little.

'So tell *me* all you know.'

Mrs Hobbs nodded slowly. 'Very well.'

And she did.

Thomas sat alone in the basement by Lyle's side.

Too still.

After everything, after the raving, Lyle was now far, far too still. Eyes still open, still aware, but aware of what? Thomas didn't wish to speculate.

He'd read a book once – *Mr Westwood's Basic Introduction to Surgical Principles* – which had described with horrible precision all the nasty things that could happen to a body under strain. It hadn't mentioned what to do when nothing happened at all.

Thomas couldn't remember when exactly he'd read *Mr Westwood's Basic Introduction*; maybe last Christmas when the family had been inflicted with a deluge of aunts from Northumbria, cousins from Devon and, worst of all, endless in-laws returned fresh from the colonies, and full of complaint about how the Old Country had gone to the dogs in their absence. Not even Mr Dickens' latest literary achievement could keep the time from dragging.

He'd had to send Tess away.

She was crying, like a child but, like a child, refusing to let it show, glaring at him and snapping, 'No, I ain't!' even as the tears dripped off her chin. She said she wanted to stay, that it was the grown-up thing to do. And he'd said, 'No, leave. I'll stay with Lyle.'

Now Thomas sat alone, watching his . . .

. . . pick a title: teacher, friend, co-inventor, colleague, companion, fath— no, not quite that, not a father. That was a role Lyle reserved for someone else. He was a distant uncle, perhaps. A funny uncle, whom Thomas was entitled to love nonetheless.

Whatever Lyle was, he was in pain.

So much pain that every muscle seemed to have locked so that now he was still, frozen in position like a metal sculpture of a man turned to rust.

And then he spoke.

'Thomas!'

Thomas leant forwards, and saw the sweat running down Lyle's neck, in pale rivers across the dried blood. 'Mister Lyle?'

'A cure,' he gasped. 'Mustn't . . .'

'I've been trying to analyse the poison we found in the cake they were giving at the circus,' whispered Thomas, 'but it's slow, we don't have time to—'

'Listen!' hissed Lyle. 'Listen to me! You have to look after her! You have to! She'll have no one, nothing! My ma will take her in, if I . . . But you're her only friend! You're the only one who can keep her safe! Tess will be . . . she'll . . . Please, please. I'm so sorry. Please promise me, I'm . . .'

'Don't talk,' whispered Thomas. 'We'll try to keep you comfortable.'

'Promise! Please, for God's sake, please!'

'I promise. Mister Lyle, I will always look after her. I promise.'

Lyle managed a smile, then nearly choked on the effort. 'Sorry!' he murmured.

'There's nothing . . .'

'For getting in the way!'

'What?'

'Your father . . . *He's* your father, I should never have got in the way. I'm sorry.'

'You didn't. Mister Lyle? You didn't. It was just the way things were.'

Lyle smiled, then groaned and half closed his eyes. 'Course they are,' he wheezed, as his smile turned to a grimace of distress. 'Course they are. Don't ever accept it. Don't ever accept . . .'

His eyes began to flicker shut.

Thomas shook him, and though his eyes drifted open again, and seemed to see him, Thomas couldn't help but feel they were seeing without understanding what it was they saw.

CHAPTER 17

Accounts

Mrs Hobbs said, 'Would you like to hear a story? I concede now may not be the time, but . . .'

'I *love* stories,' replied Lin firmly.

'This is a story about money.'

'Oh. Bankers. One of the less charming innovations of your species.'

Mrs Hobbs avoided Lin's gaze, intent on not perceiving anything she couldn't cope seeing. 'The handling of money,' she insisted, 'is too important to leave to ordinary people, and far too dangerous. In matters such as the transfer of funds, society needs men too unimaginative to consider all the possibilities that money may present. Offer anyone with any initiative the chance to take a great sum of money, and I guarantee you that sooner or later, they will be tempted to take just a nibble – even a tiny nibble – of the prize.'

'You mean humanity is naturally inclined to embezzle?'

'Of course. Which, by the by, the master of this – St Bartholomew's – Workhouse,' Mrs Hobbs brandished her notes, 'was doing in great quantities. But what engaged my interest, far more than his crude attempts at plunder, were the regular payments from an unknown contributor which seemed to go directly, with no attempt at disguise, into the master's pocket.'

Lin folded her arms. 'I suppose there's no harm in learning even about the most tedious of mankind's creations,' she muttered. 'So what was the source of this strange finance?'

'A charitable foundation, Miss Lin.' Mrs Hobbs spoke with emphasis, having begun to feel her companion didn't fully appreciate the situation's gravity. 'A foundation by the name of the Fund for Orphaned and Unfortunate Children was making fortnightly payments of thirty pounds. In exchange for which, the master of the workhouse was expending twelve shillings ten pence one day later on taking children to the circus.'

'One day later?'

'Yes. As a matter of fact, the St Bartholomew's Workhouse isn't the only one in London to be receiving regular payments. In total, nine workhouses, one asylum and two hospices for orphaned children are regularly paid between five and twenty-five pounds, all with the stipulation that . . .' She rummaged in her papers. 'Ah-ha! That they "endeavour to improve the conditions, spiritual and physical of the children in their care, and bring the light of entertainment, education and childish joys to all their wards between the ages of five and thirteen".'

'And?' Lin looked alert as ever, but quite uncomprehending.

'Miss Lin, children are not put on this earth to be *entertained*! Youth is a time to learn, to study, to mature and grow, not to be *indulged* with . . . *pretty* things. Such an idea is anathema to the whole provision of the state!'

'Oh,' said Lin, uncertainly rubbing the end of her nose. 'But surely if you're a *child*, you should enjoy being a child for as long as is possible, and only when you get old—'

'Have you seen this city, Miss Lin?' interrupted Mrs Hobbs. 'Look around you. Count the beggars, the infirm, the dying, the dead, the starving, the crippled, the lost, the lonely. And tell me that in a time like this, most children can truly be indulged.'

'Ma'am, in a time like this,' replied Lin, 'being a child seems an infinitely superior prospect than being an adult burdened with care. But go on, please.'

'Regular payments,' continued Mrs Hobbs, spreading papers across her lap, their numbers running up and down like a frantic goldfish in a narrow tank, 'made by the fund to a dozen different institutions, all designed to improve the life of the children in their care, all of which result in some . . . excursion: a trip to the circus or to the music hall or to the theatre or to the fair, from which—'

Lin's eyes lit up. 'So this charity is *paying* to give the children to Greybags?' she breathed.

'What's Greybags?'

'He's a troublesome cousin,' replied Lin. 'A creature spawned by – but not altogether of – my kind. Genus rather than species. Or was it the other way round? Please, tell me more. The charity enables the master of each workhouse to pocket a very large profit. So the money is buying silence as well as complicity?'

'Quite so.'

'Fascinating,' breathed Lin. 'In the past, Greybags just preyed on beggars and travellers, lost half-dead creatures. I would never have thought he had the capacity to set up an arrangement such as this.'

'Curiously enough,' Mrs Hobbs brightened, warming to her theme, 'the commissioning board of this charity have gone to great lengths to keep themselves anonymous. A mountain of paperwork and some extremely difficult members of the banking trade stand between them and any form of easy discovery, and I assure you, no one can be as difficult as a banker. But . . .'

'I love it when people go "but" in telling a story,' exclaimed Lin brightly, 'please tell me that the next few sentences you are going to utter involve white floppy shirts and fencing.'

'Fencing? As in the enclosure of sheep or the . . .?'

'Swords, of course!' Lin flapped with the quavering excitement of a woman who'd read about the adventures of men with white floppy shirts and quick flashing blades, and had been disappointed to find, upon her arrival in Western Europe, a definite lack of all of the above.

'Alas, no swords,' chided Mrs Hobbs. 'Indeed, it took a great deal of fiscal adventure, including some extremely complicated yet highly interesting workings involving the subclauses of the legal framework for the actuarial examination of the—'

'Yes yes yes yes yes,' interrupted Lin. 'I know all this, and then the potassium reacted with the air and something exothermic happened to the bullion being transferred between the vaults and inflation was blown up and all that. I've heard it from Lyle. What did you actually discover?'

Mrs Hobbs managed to look only a little disconcerted at having her adventures so sharply curtailed. 'I discovered,' she said primly, 'the names and occupations of the commissioning members of the charity that has been paying the workhouses to send their children to the circus. I have traced the doctor who has been signing the death certificates of dozens of children, who have, in fact, not died; who declared this girl Sissy Smith to be dead when she was, in fact, alive, and who has been signing those same certificates across dozens of workhouses throughout London for children who may not, in fact, be dead, but whose official death on paper permits them to vanish, to what could be a far worse fate.'

'And?' demanded Lin. 'Come on, chop chop, time flies.'

'The doctor is highly respected in London circles; a do-gooder of charitable bent. His signature on every death certificate has been Mr Preston, but it is my belief, having fol-lowed the money trail between the charity and his private funds, that Mr Preston is in fact a doctor by the name of Dr Risdon Barnaby.'

Lin sucked in breath between her teeth, scratched her chin, rubbed the back of her head, examined the ends of her finger-tips, then said, 'No, never heard of him. Anyone else?'

Mrs Hobbs sighed. 'There is also a gentlewoman who is widely regarded for her charitable work in London; a compas-sionate lady, a liberal giver of family money to worthy causes. She serves as secretary to the charity and has authorised every single payment made to every workhouse, hospice and asylum from which children have then vanished. I've met her myself, and though I find her conversation highly tedious, I would never have considered her the . . .' she hesitated for a deep long breath '. . . I would never have considered her truly *intelligent* enough to practise such malignancy.'

'A name, already, a name!' Lin was nearly glowing with frustration.

'Her name,' replied Mrs Hobbs firmly, 'is Miss Mercy Chaste.'

CHAPTER 18

Charity

This is the place where the children sleep.

This is the dreamless sleep in which they spend their hours drifting through empty nothingness.

Except, perhaps, scrambling away at the very edges of their minds, a whisper of . . .

my name is . . .

. . . my name is . . .

. . . once upon a time . . .

. . . ran away to the circus . . .

Effy Hall slumbers in the bed next to sleeping Sissy Smith, who was told by teacher that it was all right to eat the cake, and who woke and ran, as sometimes, very rarely, a child will do, and who now dreams of . . .

Once upon a time, there was a child called . . .

. . . called . . .

A shadow falls across the head of her bed.

A hand reaches out and smoothes back the hair that has fallen across Sissy's face. A voice, somewhere on the edge of a high-pitched scream that has not yet found the strength to be anything more than a sigh, whispers, 'Sleep well, children. Sleep well.'

And alone in the night, Mercy Chaste walks the ward of the empty sleeping children to keep them safe in their sleep. Because that is what a mother must do.

Lyle lay on the floor of his own smelly, stained old parlour and thought about chemistry. Very, very deliberately thought about chemistry. Because the second he didn't then in crept . . .

Once upon a time . . .

. . . all the children . . .

. . . I wanna my mama! . . .

. . . in a land far far away . . .

He tried to blink. Couldn't. Every bone seemed to have been replaced with a dead weight that pressed him to the floor. Even breathing was an effort; but if that hurt, if every nerve throughout the rest of him throbbed with pain and sickness, it was nothing to the unnatural agony of his eyes.

Lin had said, 'You will not close your eyes.' It hadn't just been the command of a friend, it had been a Tseiqin, a creature whose voice was authority and whose eyes . . . *don't look at the eyes*. And he hadn't closed his eyes. His eyeballs were two sand-dry bubbles of blurred sense; they felt three times too large for the skull that held them.

He heard a footstep on the stair, half turned his head, smelt for a moment a hint of autumnal leaves. Lin sat down on the floor next to him, pulling her knees up to her chin and wrapping her arms round her legs, head on one side. 'Hello, Mister Lyle,' she said finally.

'Hello, Miss Lin.'

'How are you?'

'Poisoned.'

'And what may we do to cure you? Thomas seemed quite involved with his medical undertakings.'

Lyle half shook his head. 'Treating symptoms. Not cure. Poison to cure the poison. Raw coffee beans to make the heart beat faster, belladonna to make it beat even faster still, to dilate the eyes, to . . .'

'Belladonna, in my experience, kills people,' said Lin gently.

'Not *much* belladonna.'

'And causes hallucinations.'

'Right now, I wouldn't know. Valium in case everything gets too fast and to prevent me injuring myself from spasms, salt water to induce vomiting to remove any undigested poison from my stomach, charcoal to hinder any interactions.'

'Symptoms, not a cure?'

'Yes.'

'You can still talk. You sound like an adult.'

'I haven't slept. When I sleep . . .'

'You will dream of beautiful stories, of amazing adventures, of castles and princesses and childish things.' Lin sighed. 'Yes, I know. And when you wake . . . you won't ever really wake. My people aren't entirely irresponsible. We did try to remove Greybags long before you stumbled in. He ran from us. A Tseiqin but not a Tseiqin. We were protecting *you*, little homo sapiens with your monkey brains, we were protecting *you* from *him*.'

'Why were you at the circus?' asked Lyle softly.

'To find him.'

'He wasn't hard to find.'

'He knows how to hide from my people. And I had to find out who was helping him.'

'Helping?'

Lin sighed again, hugged her knees a little tighter, looked, for a moment, small and frail. 'Greybags is old; much older than he pretends. He chooses to be a child because, in his adult life, all he ever experienced was rejection and contempt. That is our fault, I admit it. As a child, you need never know these things. You are forgiven, you are loved, your food is brought to you on a plate. He was one of us, once. A Tseiqin, but not one of us: born differently. My people do not treat those who are different with much kindness. As a child, he wasn't aware of this. As an adult, he was. As an adult, he was shunned, hurt, discarded by my people. And more. Worse. He could not accept what we had done to him. His mind was not strong enough, his . . . his soul, if you'll pardon the theologically unsound sentiment, wasn't strong enough. He swore to become a child again, to be as innocent and free as a child. It is a result of his unusual heritage that he can do so. He lulls the children to sleep and steals their dreams, feeds on them, sucks them dry. He has no interest in the dreams of adults – too slow, too dull – but the same poison turns the adults to puppets in his fantasy, to childish mockeries of what they *should* be, the circus master with his moustache, the organ grinder for ever grinding, the clown eternally laughing, the . . .'

Lin saw Lyle's face and stopped. Smiled. Shrugged. 'But on the bright side, you are going to be dramatically and implausibly rescued, Mister Lyle! What a happy thought!'

Lyle managed a thin whimper of a smile, and winced, as if the movement of his face was too much for his nerves to take. 'You're sweetness and light underneath, aren't you, Lin Zi?'

'Greybags is not capable of organising all this by himself – of having children smuggled to his tent, of buying poisons, of mixing drugs, of arranging secret movements of money, of stealing beggars and mudlarks from the gutters of the streets; he just doesn't have the intellectual maturity to get all this done. He had to have help.'

'Who?'

'Your Mrs Hobbs, curiously enough, provided the answer. Money! Your culture does so prize its money!'

'Miss Lin, since I may not be conscious for much longer, save me the graces and tell me!'

'I am sorry, Mister Lyle.'

'Tell me!'

'Do you know a vicar's daughter by the name of Miss Mercy Chaste?'

'I . . . she runs a hospital.'

'For all the children who have lost their dreams. Greybags sucks them dry, eats up everything they are, all their hopes and innocence, and then they go to sleep and never wake again. And all, strangely, seem to find their way to a ward in Marylebone. Do you believe this to be . . . good charity?'

'Mercy Chaste doesn't have a malicious bone in her body.'

'Does she have kind bones?'

'Yes! Extremely kind bones, very, very kind, so kind that . . .' Lyle's voice trailed off.

'Yes, I thought that might be the case.'

Silence. Then Lyle said, 'I can't believe that she . . . that she would . . .'

'I think, Mr Lyle, that you can.'

'If there's no cure . . .'

'There'll be a cure,' Lin assured him patiently. 'Miss Chaste is assisted by a medical man, a doctor who signs fake death certificates – a Dr Barnaby.'

'I know him!'

'You do?'

'We had him examine Sissy Smith. He said there was . . . he . . .' Lyle squeezed his eyes tight shut. 'Damn,' he whispered. 'Damn damn damn wanna my mama! If there isn't any cure then . . .'

'I'll make sure no one laughs at you when you start picking your nose in the street,' said Lin kindly.

'Keep them safe,' he whispered.

'Who?'

'The bloody children!'

'Oh, *them*, yes, of course. Sorry, I thought you were about to impart some excitingly romantic secret. But, yes, of course, the children, how silly of me.'

'Miss Lin?' he wheezed.

'Yes, Mister Lyle?'

'Why do you seem to be so . . . childish all the time? So ignorant? You are much more than you pretend.'

She thought about this for a long time. 'I think you just asked me a foolish question. I shall attribute it merely to the heightened emotional and decreased intellectual capacity brought upon you by your present state. But, since you ask, I suppose if I have learnt one thing from my considerably elongated existence, it is that there is nothing more joyous than a childish joy. Which is, given our current circumstances, a little ironic.'

'Miss Lin—'

'Mister Lyle,' she interrupted briskly 'I would guess that at this moment you are filled with an overwhelming desire to kiss me. And may I say, while completely willing to experiment with an explosion of passionate longing on your part, the fact that you have vomited quite recently leads me to suggest we put the encounter off until a later time.'

There was a long, stunned silence.

Lyle said, 'Uh . . .'

'You *were* about to kiss me, weren't you?' demanded Lin in a tone which suggested there was only one correct answer.

'Um . . .'

'Excellent! Well then,' Lin declared, standing up quickly, her cheeks turning a faint shade of pink despite her stern gaze, 'that's something to look forward to, isn't it? Just as soon as you're cured we can even discuss whether or not you get to see my ankles before committing to a legally satisfactory mutual relationship.'

'Well, I . . .'

'This is a stressful time for you,' she added helpfully. 'I entirely understand.'

'Stop Greybags. Children—'

'It is something I was planning on, you know,' she chided him. 'Except this tedious human I occasionally run into decided to allow himself to be poisoned while pursuing a line of enquiry with good manners instead of, as was far more sensible, mystic powers and a very sharp knife.'

'I remember a nitro-glycerin derivative going off somewhere near my left ear,' mumbled Lyle.

'But a sharp knife and an offensive word could easily have achieved the same effect!'

'Find Greybags. Make him stop.'

'I'm not going to leave you, Mister Lyle. Good grief, you know I've had tea with dowager empresses, and look at me now? Staying by the side of a *human* in the face of serious danger. What would Marie Antoinette say?'

'Lin,' said Lyle firmly, 'do you understand advanced organic chemistry?'

'I can't say it's one of my main interests.'

'How about medical science?'

'I have an *excellent* grasp of anatomy.'

'Can you cure me by sitting here?'

Silence.

Then, 'You know, Mister Lyle, you are dashing any romantic overtones in our relationship before we really get a chance to explore them.'

'Madam,' he replied, dry lips shaking with the effort of coherent speech, 'while the legal system frowns on it, I promise you, nothing right now would be as romantic as you, personally, hunting down Greybags and passing him to the relevant authorities. For me.'

'He'll have fled the circus.'

'But he'll need help.'

Lin sighed, stood, stretched, tucking a rogue strand of hair back behind a little ear. 'Busy busy busy. Very well. Evolutionary alternatives!' She clapped her hands together in firm summoning at the empty air. 'Thomas, Tess, little dog thing.' She looked Lyle in the eye, and smiled, and, for a minute, there was something old and wise and true in her face. 'Let's finish this messy affair.'

CHAPTER 19

Mercy

Time passed.

Not much time at all.

And here they are, two children, a demon-lady and a dog, in a hansom cab, racing through the streets of London. Or at least, attempting to race, if the milkman's empty cart will move, if the sheep going to Smithfield will clear the way for the iceman driving to Billingsgate, if the sweeper can move aside from his crossing, if the hay wagons will shift their loads, if the old donkey will just do its business, if the omnibus can make the corner and if the damned costermongers, hawkers and pedestrians will just *get out* of the damn way!

Things, Thomas reflected grimly, always seemed easier in stories.

The bells are ringing out the hour, proclaiming that all good children should have gone to bed, thumping out ancient copper notes from high in the dome of St Paul's cathedral to St James's tucked away by Piccadilly, from St Giles' where the beggars sleep in the crypt to St Andrew's-in-the-Wardrobe which houses St Anne, however she came to be there. They strike ponderous echoes in the ancient red-brick church of the Middle Temple, resound across the creaking ships all moored up against each other in the crowded Thames, call out above the engine whistles from St Pancras station and the proud bonging of Big Ben. Ten of the clock, little children, and all's not well, go to bed, little children, go to bed, what dreams you shall dream tonight.

And here's Billy the Button shut up in Mrs Lyle's privy. He's dreaming of: *children children children make them laugh make them laugh make them laugh all the laughing children*! And he cackles in the night, though he doesn't understand what is quite so funny.

And here's Lyle.

Nowhere left to run. You can out-run knives and fists and mobs and, if you're lucky, bullets and rapid uncontained exother-mic, high-energy combustion but not this. Strange, that it took so long, so many years, so much time, to realise that sometimes there are some things you really can't out-run.

Don't close your eyes don't close your eyes don't close your eyes don't close your eyes don't don't don't *don't don't DON'T DON'T NO DON'T CLOSE YOUR EYES!!*

Just a moment.

Just a little, little moment.

(*What's that in the corner?*)
No one need ever know.
So tired.
(*A thing knocked over in the dark.*)
Just a moment . . .
. . . not sleep . . . just . . . closing his . . .
(*A remnant of cake. There was cake they took from the circus. Poisoned cake.*)
eyes . . .

And here is the place where the children sleep.

Mercy Chaste sits by the door, to keep them safe from all nightmares. And if there's nothing left in them that's capable of such a thought, then isn't the absence of a nightmare always for the best?

Then a voice said, coming out of the darkness where there shouldn't have been any voice, 'Miss Chaste? Miss Mercy Chaste?'

And that, right there, was the end of Miss Chaste's dream.

'Miss Chaste? Miss Mercy Chaste?'

Tess had silently opened the door to the hospital ward. She'd also removed the padlock from the outer gate, picked the lock between the main door and the upstairs ward, and purloined half a dozen silver spoons that the maid had left on the downstairs table ready to administer the morning dose of medicine to the slumbering patients in the other wing. Old habits died as hard as old skills in Teresa Hatch; she'd barely noticed she was doing any thieving, even as she did it.

Now Tess, Thomas and Lin stood in the door of the silent

ward, lit by little more than the thin moonlight falling through the tall windows, and the lingering greenish-yellow glow of the gas lamps hissing smelly sulky light down in the streets below.

Miss Chaste, vicar's daughter, spinster at an unfashionable age, as thin as the shawl wrapped across her bony shoulders, looked up sleepily from the great rocking chair by the door, blinked distant thoughts from her eyes and breathed, 'Hush, the children are sleeping,' in the distracted half-gone manner of someone who hasn't yet realised that this is more than just a dream.

'You're Miss Mercy Chaste,' replied Thomas. His voice was cold and level with the full wrath of aristocratic over-containment. 'A charitable,' the word dripped bitterly off his tongue, 'a *charitable* and *philanthropic* lady.'

Miss Chaste, becoming aware that this was something more than a dream, sat up in her chair, smoothed her skirts and raised the dim lantern by her side from floor to face. She said, 'I remember you. You're Horat— you're Mister Lyle's friends. Are you here to see the child Sissy Smith?'

Then her eyes fell on Lin, and her expression faltered at the sight of this strange, bright-eyed, angry-looking foreigner. But since Miss Chaste was, more than anything else, a lady of good breeding, she hid her consternation at seeing a creature so very un-English entering her tidy ward. She rose to her feet and said, 'Master . . . Elwick, is it not? How can I help you?'

'You run a charity,' replied Thomas coldly, and now Miss Chaste noticed the girl by his side, whose eyes were red with exhaustion and whose face was flushed in response to something more than mere fatigue.

'Yes, of course,' she breathed in quick reply. 'It is our duty as members of the upper orders to give charity to those who are—'

'You visit workhouses,' barked Thomas, and the armies of both Wellington and Bonaparte would have trembled at the bubbling rage rising in his too polite, far too polite, cold voice. 'You visit workhouses, pay money to the masters, the masters take their children to the circus, to be poisoned! They are given free food, free cake, free pudding. What child, what hungry child who lives on workhouse nothing, what such child says no to pudding, ma'am? Can you show me that child who would say no?'

'The tragedy of our times is the ineffective provision for the poor,' lamented Miss Chaste automatically.

'That don't sound like nothin' to me,' hissed Tess. 'Big words what mean nothin'! What 'bout Mister Lyle!'

Her voice echoed down the ward. In their beds, the children shifted and turned over in their empty sleep.

Thomas gestured at her to be silent. 'Miss Chaste,' he went on, implacable as the progress of a glacier, 'someone pays for children to vanish. The money is supplied by a charitable foundation, on whose board sit many no doubt kindly and noble donors. And *you*.'

Lin stepped forward. She had been moving down the ward, examining each sleeping child in turn. Now she wore a look in her eye as if she had never been able to imagine such a thing. 'Women,' she sighed, 'can't vote, can't work for the wages of a man, are secondary in the laws of inheritance or divorce, cannot preach from the pulpit. And *yet*,' her smile was a flash of moon-reflecting whiteness in the gloom, 'those ladies with both money and time may, at the very least, make great inroads into the world of local governance and exclaim that is all that woman should desire, and you, Miss Chaste, you, I think, are one of these women. You know, I begin to question whether the female revolution will ever throw off its corset in my life time.'

Miss Chaste smiled. It was the nervous, slightly disbelieving smile of an innocent prisoner who wants above everything else to please the executioner at the gallows, just in case it was a misunderstanding after all.

She said, 'I really don't know what it is you're talking about. Of course I have interests in charitable affairs, what gentlewoman could do otherwise? But all this talk of missing children – I do not know what you mean. Really, this is all most strange to me. Perhaps you could be kind enough to explain?'

When she finished gabbling, there was silence. Lin's shoes creaked on the hard stone floor. Thomas scratched his chin where one day – soon, surely, please God – a beard would grow. Tess, who usually had much to say about very little, was as silent and still as a carved cemetery angel.

'You and Greybags,' breathed Thomas. 'You give out the money so that children are sent to him. You use charities to hide your work, to keep suspicion away from you, but we've seen the records. We know where the money comes from, and where it goes. You didn't even bother to hide it.'

'Hide what?' asked Miss Chaste breathlessly. 'I really don't—'

'You thought as how no one would look.' Tess's voice rang through the long room, no longer angry, just flat and tired and old. 'You didn't bother to go coverin' up the money, cos you thought no one would look. No one would care nothin' about the children what vanishes from the workhouse. No one would care for the orphans what goes from the streets, 'bout the beggars an' their sons, 'bout the ones what live in the hospices on rags an' a boiled potato. You just didn't think no one would care.'

She looked up slowly from the point on the floor where her eyes had locked as if to burn it, and her gaze was on fire. 'I *hate* you,' she whispered. 'You as think you know best, think you can talk 'bout the bigger good. You, as visit the workhouses an' pat each child on the head, an' say, "There there now, it's not your fault as how you're small an' ignorant an' poor an' stupid an' ain't goin' to be nothin'. What a pity as how your parents couldn't treat you right, but then they were stupid an' poor an' weren't goin' to be nothin' neither. But it's all right cos we're 'ere now to *save* you. We're goin' to make you better than what your parents could, teach you to be proud to be so humble. An' though you be humble, proud 'cos you ain't dead, or thievin' or beggin' an' wastin' our big people's coppers an' our time." An' that'd be all well and good so long as you went an' gave us the extra copper, an' let us learn to be what we were gonna be, but you don't. Cos you can't make everythin' better, can you, bigwig? So you gotta choose. You sit down an' you say, "Let's make *these* children better. Such a shame, but *those* 'ave got to starve." An' in all that choosin' who to save an' who to let die, you ain't never lifted no finger to save me. You let me an' mine go an' starve, an' felt *good* 'bout yourself for bein' so *kind* to others.'

'An' that ain't even before what you gone an' done to Sissy Smith. That ain't even before what you gone an' done to Mister Lyle. You just didn't think as how anyone would look at that money. I *hate* you.'

'Why do you help Greybags?'

Lin's voice cut across the shuddering breath that Tess was letting slowly out. It seemed to slice into Miss Chaste like a knife. She jerked at the sound of it.

'I help the children,' breathed Miss Chaste.

'You supply him with children. Then you help fake their death certificates and hide what's left of each child in your hospital!'

'I . . . I . . . the circus is such a pretty place.'

'Greybags doesn't have the intellect,' snapped Lin, taking a step towards Miss Chaste, who flinched. 'He isn't *grown-up* enough to think of a scheme like this. Which means that you,' stabbing a finger at Miss Chaste's face, 'must have helped him, given him children who won't be traced. And unlike the clowns who drank the poison and forget their names, unlike the men and women of the circus who were made part of the circus by Greybags' trickery, you are alert, you are aware, you remember your name. *You* are a conscious participant!'

'I . . . you'll wake the children!'

'*They're* not wakin' up!' shrieked Tess. 'They ain't never wakin' up! *I hate you!*'

'Tell me why you did these things!' snarled Lin. Miss Chaste cringed from the sight of her.

'The children are . . . They are peaceful like this.'

Silence, except for the harsh rush of Tess's breath.

'Peaceful?' echoed Lin, drawing back a little. 'Are you using this word in a fascinatingly English way whose semantic meaning I don't understand? What do you mean, *peaceful*?'

'They are peaceful,' repeated Miss Chaste, gesturing futilely at the room of slumbering children.

'They are empty shells,' snapped Thomas.

'They *are* peaceful!' she repeated. 'I only looked at the work-

267

houses first, at the children, at how they ate, how they lived, how they were. And do you know how many children from the workhouse are hanged, or sent to the hulks, or deported, or go to prison?

'We can't save every one. But if we save a few? The children who would have had so much trouble, been so unhappy, destined for the gallows, the daughters of impure women, fathered by thieves and beggars! The sons of criminals. Of debtors who couldn't pay their debts.' Miss Chaste's voice had a frantic, questioning lilt. The faces about her darkened.

'They were nothing!' she wailed. 'The children were nothing, the lowest of the low, the scu— the bottom of the . . . It's not their fault, they didn't choose it, I understand that. It's not their fault that they will amount to so little. But true philanthropists don't naively dream. They accept. And I saw that this was a way to save them by . . .

'When I found Greybags, he was a dying old man! A harmless dying old man. And then I found a child, and then . . . the child was at peace and Greybags was young again – a miracle. I saw my father die when I was just a child, but this child need never see that. I said sorry, Pa, so sorry, so sorry. You should have had a son. If you'd had a son he could have carried on the name. But you don't understand, these children never see sorrow or pain or any of the things that wait on the other side of maturity. They need never understand that things end and fathers must die.

'He gives them peace! They eat cake and see the wonders of the circus and then they sleep and dream beautiful stories for ever, and need never, *ever*, see their father die!'

Her voice, almost risen to a scream, faded away.

Lin said, 'Lyle is dying.'

Miss Chaste blinked, like someone stepping into a dark cave after being dazzled by too much sun. 'What?' she murmured.

'Lyle is dying,' repeated Lin. 'Tell me, Miss Chaste, does this excite feelings?'

Miss Chaste shook her head, mostly in numbed incomprehension.

'Now that I meet you,' breathed Lin, 'I see that, though I myself can choose to indulge in childish, simple pleasures, you are nothing but a child in an adult woman's tasteless tight bodice. It's not your fault you were born an idiot, or a human, for that matter. Now, you may be so lost in this fairyland you have created that you cannot understand what I'm about to say. But I shall say it anyway. Is there a cure?'

'What?'

'A cure,' repeated Lin. 'An antidote for the poison that turns adults to children. The poison which is, may I add, currently killing a man whom I find, despite my infinitely superior nature and his lack of social graces, rather charming. Is there an antidote?'

'I . . . don't know.'

'I think you do, Miss Chaste. I think you're going to tell me.'

Miss Chaste looked at Lin, shuddered as she suspected the truth of what she saw, looked away, then slowly looked straight back at her. 'No,' she said. 'Greybags uses the poisons to make the children easier to . . . to calm. To make the adults more . . . open minded. There is no antidote.'

'And Lyle?'

'He . . .' This time Miss Chaste's voice almost caught in her throat. 'He is old enough to understand.'

Miss Lin smiled, looked away and then said, 'Miss Chaste, I feel that at this point it would be appropriate for me to show moderation. However . . .'

Her fingers bent into a fist. Drawing her arm back, she swung it upwards, twisting at the elbow, the whole weight of her body going into the punch. Miss Chaste didn't scream or cry out – didn't have the breath. She just fell to the floor, gasping in amazement and pain.

'I am not, so I am informed,' sighed Lin, 'a proper lady. Where is Greybags?'

'Why do you—'

'Greybags is what you might describe as an adaptation of my kind. He has some of our gifts, to a limited degree, and some benefits too. But he relies on chemicals to further his capabilities, hence the poisons. My tedious task is to deal with him. We lost him in the circus, at which time I had other things on my mind. Where is he?'

'I don't know.'

'Miss Chaste.'

'I don't know,' repeated the woman, her jaw hardening in defiance. 'I wouldn't tell you if I did.'

Lin stepped forward, raising her fist again, when Thomas spoke calmly from behind her.

'Excuse me?' he said. 'Might I be allowed to talk to Miss Chaste in private?'

Coooo-eeeey – Mister Lyle?

Cooey?

Mister Lyle?

A finger twitches on the floor.

A breath shudders hard and harsh.

Oi! You!

Lyle blinked back thick yellow gum from his eyes.

He'd crawled across the floor, ten thousand years ago, and now, beyond the reach of all mortal compass, just at the end of his nose, lay a small glass vial. It contained some thin liquid, just a few drops at the bottom. It smelt familiar. It smelt of the stuff Thomas had been extracting from a slice of poisoned cake, just before that trouble at the circus.

Lyle closed his fingers round it. They seemed too big; it too small.

There was something about . . .

. . . poisons.

Just had to stay awake.

Just a little bit longer.

On the table, higher and further away than the smallest star on a blackened night, he caught a glimpse of another vial. Belladonna, distilled into its nastiest elements: inducing rapid heart beat, hallucinations and, eventually, death. But not before it caused a serious case of insomnia.

He thought he could hear his mother's voice.

He thought he could hear children singing.

He sang in reply, humming under his breath, 'Two by two is four, four by four is sixteen, sixteen by sixteen is two hundred and fifty-six, two hundred and fifty-six is . . . is – hold on – sixty thousand, sixty-five thousand, sixty-five thousand five hundred and thirty-six . . .'

He started the ten-thousand-mile climb towards the bottle. All he needed was a little time.

*

Thomas sits alone with Miss Chaste, in the gloomy lamplight of the hospital.

The trains from Coventry rumble by outside, under a weight of coal and steel. In the other direction, the wagons from London are heavy with clothes, with bales of cloth and with manufactured trinkets, to be shipped to the hungry Empire's inhabitants, waiting beyond the seas. The city staggers on, like a drunkard pushed from the music hall, warmth in his belly, bottle in his hand and the sound of music ringing in his ears, as shadows stretch thin beneath the gas lamps.

Thomas said, 'Your father had no other child?'

Miss Chaste looked surprised, then said, 'Why do you ask, sir?'

'You said, no child should see the loss of a father.'

'I give them peace,' she hissed in reply.

He smiled, nodded and said, 'I am sure you do, in your way. The others, they are poorer than you and I. They do not understand the guilt, one might say, that can sometimes accompany wealth. They do not understand the responsibility, the difficulty of having to decide what is for the greater good. When my father dies, I will be in charge of over eight hundred people: tenants, servants, maids, stewards. I will even inherit an MP or two from boroughs where my patronage will decide the direction of government. I can't wait. It will be the most important duty of my life.'

'My father wanted a son,' said Miss Chaste sadly. 'A son could have continued the honour, the name, could have inherited, could have . . . And I could have had a son, too. Perhaps that would have saved the name but I didn't. And now it's too . . . People of our status don't discuss such things,' she concluded.

'No,' agreed Thomas, every bit his father in pomp and steel.

'But you see, Miss Chaste, if you don't tell me where Greybags is, if we don't find him, if we don't make things right, then Mister Lyle will be dead for nothing, and Miss Teresa will be alone with even less. So you *are* going to tell me where Greybags is, because, if you don't, I will buy this hospital ward. I will buy it and I will declare the children insane, and I will buy every newspaper in town and have them preach about how pointless it is to help people who can't even help themselves.

'And I'll open *workhouses*.' Thomas's eyes gleamed with simulated malice. 'I'll open workhouses and skim three shillings off every four that the parish gives me to run them, and I'll teach the children to pick oakum and nothing more. You see, these are things that money lets me do. Don't think, because I'm young, I don't know this. I have already seen remarkable things. And when I am older, I, in my turn, will do things that make the deeds of now seem . . . child's play.

'So, Miss Chaste, tell me – where is Greybags?'

Lyle.

Mister Lyle?

Horatio Lyle!

A glass bottle in one hand. A needle in another.

Overhead, the cracked tumbler of some liquid stuff, has been knocked from the table top. Across the floor, herbs, vials, jars, jugs, boxes of powdered stuff, scattered and spilt in every direction.

Someone has been busy.

Someone took belladonna to stay that way.

You don't have to put your ear to the chest to hear the heartbeat.

A shadow in the darkness. Tate shuffles across the floor, picking his way around the more dangerous chemical substances that a pair of blindly scrambling hands have knocked out of their way. He puts his nose into Lyle's ear and very loudly, very deliberately, sneezes.

Mister Lyle?

Nothing.

Tate whimpers and whines, chews on the end of Lyle's sleeve, slobbers on the side of his face, paws at his head, and finally, with nothing else to do, sniffs the empty glass vial in Lyle's hand. It smells of a whole host of things, thrown together in a terrible hurry and not properly integrated into one whole packet. The remnants of the smell are also on Lyle's lips.

Interesting.

Tate settles down by Lyle's side, and listens to the rushed beating of his master's heart.

Nothing else stirs.

Not a sound.

Tate imagines, for a moment, he can smell mince pies.

Curious.

And not entirely unwelcome.

But you shouldn't have fallen asleep, Mister Lyle.

It's not like you hadn't been warned.

The rising fog billowed through the hospital yard in Marylebone, greenish-yellow through the haze of the gas light and stench of coal dust floating in the air. The hansom cabby Lin had flagged down on Fleet Street sat with his feet up on his stand mentally ticking off the minutes that went by, adding an outrageous number of farthings for every moment he reckoned had passed in the dead night. Lin and Tess waited, leaning against the side of the cab, which creaked unevenly at even this lightest of weights. A door opened somewhere in the gloom; there was a momentary dull spill of orangish light, half obscured by a shadow. Footsteps on the cobbles, getting nearer approached the little red glass shades hanging over the cabby's driving lamps. Thomas appeared in the fog, his face sombre.

Tess nearly shrieked with impatience. 'Did you find 'im? Did you, did you, did you?!'

Thomas's face was grim. 'Miss Chaste was cooperative.'

'An' an' an' an' an'? Oh, come on, bigwig. We ain't got all night.'

'He's going to run,' replied Thomas. 'He's like a child. He's scared – he's going to run away.'

'It took me four months to find him!' exclaimed Lin angrily. 'If he runs, I'll have to start all over again! We have to stop him leaving the city!'

Thomas nodded. 'Miss Chaste has arranged tickets for him on the last train from Paddington Station. Tonight.'

It was, the cabby reflected as they spun away again into the night, turning into one of his more interesting fares.

CHAPTER 20

Paddington

Miss Chaste had said: Greybags will run.

He's scared of *them*.

Miss Chaste didn't know who *they* were. But when she had looked into Lin's eyes, and seen an endless emerald forest stretching away behind that ageless, laughing gaze, she had perhaps started to guess.

Greybags was scared of *them*.

He was going to run, because he wasn't clever enough for anything else; run to find more children and another place and start again. And perhaps, yes, he might have to get old while doing it. His hair might thin and his skin might sag, his knees might creak and his back might bend; within days, just a few days without feeding, he would be an old man. But that didn't matter. He'd find a way to feed. All he had to do was get out of the city.

She'd said: 'He likes Paddington Station.'

So to Paddington Lyl – no, wait, not Lyle, not tonight – Lin, Thomas and Tess now go. Because tonight, if nothing else, justice is walking hand in hand with vengeance.

Hyde Park: neat grass melting into neglected grass where lovers go in secret moonlight; young plane trees growing up between the old elms where the gallows used to stand and heretics suffered and where, now, bright electric lights are displayed among the branches to the amazement of all. Heading north, past high railings and grand terraces, proud in their white facades still fading to smudged coal-blackness. Even on the new, wide thoroughfares of Queensway and Bayswater there is no escaping the smoke of the city. Factories cluster to the north to be close to the goods trains into Paddington Station and its gleaming line into the west, an artery fed by the coal of Wales and the wealth of colonial ships coming into Bristol. Here, the bobbies are out tonight, swinging their rattles and challenging every loitering shadow on every half-finished building site, turning their eyes one way and their palms another for a few pieces of silver taken from the local area-sneak to look the other way, to ignore any shouts from number fifteen, where the maid was foolish enough to leave the silver visible in the kitchen window.

But tonight, none of this matters.

Now run!

Horatio Lyle dreams.

This is what:

Once upon a time . . .

(Deep breath, it could be important.)

Once upon a time there lived a young boy called . . . called . . . look, I'll get back to you on this point, and he had a mother called . . . and a father and they lived in the city of London. It was a big city, it was growing every day, black and beautiful and terrifying, a place of endless alleys and fog, of thick smoke and the smell of dung and hay and cheap gin. And this boy was lonely, but he never said so because it wasn't done, you didn't say such things in polite society. Boys were not supposed to say these things, because boys are boys and have to be Strong, just like Mrs Bontoft's Practical Advice *said, have to be strong like . . .*

Mrs Bontoft's Practical Advice?

Pay attention! Once upon a time in the city of London a child decided he never wanted to grow up . . .

Hold on a moment, hold on . . .

. . . never ever ever. He was going to play with his friends and never be lonely an—

Mrs Bontoft's Practical Advice?

Listen! You have to listen to the story! Horatio, you have to pay attention to the story! One day a circus came to the town and . . .

Mrs Bontoft doesn't approve of the circus.

Forget Mrs Bontoft's Practical Advice, *you don't need her, she's boring, a boring adult who does boring things and has forgotten how to play, and what it was to be young and alone.*

Stuff that, every damn child thinks it's alone. 'No one understands me', that's what they say, what would Mrs Bontoft do if—

Shut up shut up shut up!! Once upon a time . . .

Poisoned.

Don't you want to be a child for ever?!

And it seemed to Lyle, as he slept and dreamed, that this question being asked by – by what? By an uncomfortable taste on the lips? By a voice nudged in at the back of the head?

Once upon a time . . .

Hold on just a minute!

(Poisoned?)

Once upon a time there was a child who never wanted to grow up . . .

. . . who ran away to the circus . . .

. . . who laughed and played . . .

. . . who got poisoned and seriously messed around by a villain.

No, no, not right! Children don't get poisoned! Children don't suffer, they don't hurt, they mustn't. It's the rules! Adults can get hurt, adults can feel grief, but if you're a child you're not allowed! Not allowed, dammit!

(Not that it works like that. Only in stories do the children not get hurt. Only when you begin it, once upon a . . .)

Oh, shut up!

Well then, whispered a voice, a different voice, an older voice in the back of Lyle's wandering head, *isn't this a pickle?*

Yet for all this, through the haze of pain and sleep, he thought he could hear footsteps on dirty pantry stones.

There it is!

A great metal arch over the sky, against smoking chimneys, filthy canals, iron bridges, crumbling tenements, houses pressed right up to the railway line. Smoke, so much smoke, and steam, shooting upwards every time a railway locomotive passes under the end of the arch where the metal tracks wind towards the west.

Though it is late, the crowds in Paddington Station still pitch and heave within this town within a city. A thousand gaslit faces pursuing the night's last train. Engines belch great long burps of *chuff chuff chuff groan*, brakes squeak in metallic irritation at some fresh command, whistles scream, *hiiii-eeeeyyyy!*, while the stationmaster wonders if he should learn to wind his fob watch faster. The coal-stained engineers scurry to couple the carriages, the oil-soaked drivers rub their blackened hands across their overalls to make their fingers stick a little better to the valves and the levers and the pumps. Pressure gauges climb into the red, steam vents itself, scalding hot, seemingly from beneath and around every part of the train as if to say: 'Approach ye who dare.' The poor go to the third class, pressed in ten to every four seats, wooden seats, hard benches beneath scrawny knees. Or perhaps you are the clerk travelling into the city, top hat resting on your knees, little paper stub for second class handed to the guard in his black peaked hat. Only the few may sit in the plum-plush fat chairs of first class. Learn to knock with respect should you come here! Doors clatter in every carriage, be careful of your hat, don't lose your luggage, strap it to the roofs, shove it in the racks, last call, last call for the train to Bristol, mind your skirts as you climb the steps, welcome to Mr Isambard Kingdom Brunel's marvellous railway, the only way to travel, all the time, any time, anywhere! Calling, some of them, at all the stations down the line, starting with deepest elm-fringed Middlesex: the village of Ealing, not so humble since it's become the night-time destination of commuters, whatever they are; through the quiet countryside round the great house and parkland of Osterley; past the empty fields of Heathrow, the rural slum-row of cottages on the heath, where nothing stirs but rabbits and scrawny goats; and on to the once unimaginably distant market town of Reading, forty miles from London, and now little more than an hour away by express – and then on! At Bristol itself you need not stop, but can take ship to other continents.

Paddington Station: next stop, anywhere.

And here is the call for what may well be the last train, the guard standing astride the gap between the train and the platform, shrilling on his whistle and calling, 'Take her away!'

Footsteps on stone.

Thick swathes of fabric moving in the dark.

Smell of mince pies.

The sound of someone . . .

. . . tutting?

A voice.

Human.

Female.

Warm.

'Well,' it says, 'what a fine pickle this is.'

And it dawns on Tate, being the only conscious and arguably the most intelligent witness of the events that are occurring in Lyle's pantry, that something rather wonderful is about to happen.

In the crowded night-time streets between Marylebone and Paddington, three voices are raised over the sound of iron-shod hooves clanging on wet cobbles, of loud-mouthed drivers, of creaky old wagons with no way through and, over everything, the muffling of any sound from an almighty, fog-bound London traffic jam.

'Why ain't it movin'? Why ain't it bloody movin'!' demands Tess. Her frustration boiling over, she leans out of the cab window and shouts down the street, 'Oi! You up there! You move your great fat lazy arses!'

Only Lin is free from haste and frustration. Unlatching the cab door, she asks the others, 'Do you really plan to sit there like a pair of herons by a pond? To use a most excellent phrase — move your bottoms!'

So Thomas, Tess and Lin get out of the carriage, turn towards Paddington Station, and run.

They are not the only people running in London tonight.

In Wapping, a pickpocket caught by a crowd while lifting a bookseller's handkerchief flees through blackened alleys and broken riverside stairs, hearing behind him the hue and cry of the angry mob, half of whom don't know what it is they're running after, but run just for the sake of the chase.

In Westminster, a messenger boy runs the full length of the Colonial Office to deliver a warning fresh from India of more trouble brewing; nothing as bad as in '57, sir, not yet, sir, but johnny native is bound to kick up a ruckus if you let him.

In Drury Lane, the clown whose act went down like a Frog frigate at Trafalgar flees from the stage to the pelting of rotting cabbage, sold three a farthin' special by the enterprising young woman outside. In King's Cross, the Scotsman runs for the last train back to his civilised native land, where they damn well don't water down the drink and people will at least look you in the eye before they knife you.

And somewhere in the middle of London, between the black slums of Soho and the genteel manors of Mayfair, someone else is running. And as this shadow runs through the streets, this sound can be heard rising up between the tumbled-down chimney pots and twisted old washing lines. 'Buggery buggery buggery. Nitro-glycerin, check. Magnesium, check. Phosphorus, check. Capacitor – not bloody charged. Damn!'

There is the clattering of some piece of equipment being thrown aside, rolling limp and abandoned into the gutter with the thick black rats who cluster in the comfort of the darkening night, while its some-time owner, a long-eared dog at his side, runs on into the night.

Someone watches them go.

'Oh! Are we there?'

Tess had stopped so hard that Thomas nearly ran into her. Through the smoke and gouts of steam within the vast walls Thomas could see top hats bobbing, feet dawdling or running, trunks half upright on the porters' barrows, swerving through the crowd. He hastened into the station. Sweat prickling on his skin at the heat from the great smoke-blackened locomotives, each chugging sulkily in their lair between the long platforms.

'We'll never find Greybags in all this,' he breathed. 'Where do we begin?' He looked about him frantically, and saw . . .

Hundreds of people. He'd never imagined there'd still be so many, so late at night. A porter banged into Thomas from behind, mumbled an apology and staggered on, dragging a great bundle of suitcases strapped to a gurney; another man, all moustache and important side whiskers, accidentally stepped on his foot. Down the side of the hall, vendors competed to sell oranges, hot chestnuts, pieces of suspicious-looking meat, mushy peas boiled in great steel cauldrons, and all the snacks and feasts that you could dream of. A stall near the entrance proclaimed that here was the enterprise of one W. H. Smith Esq., ready to sell them a range of newspapers and magazines, including the latest satirical offering from *Punch*. At this hour, though, Mr Smith Esq.'s newsagent's was shutting up for the night, since most of the passengers thronging past had already reached their destination, and had no more use for his wares.

'He'll be looking to leave by the first train he can find,' said Lin. 'He'll go back west, head to the old country, where he came from.' Shoving their way through the crowd, they went towards a tall board where a man in the peaked cap and uniform jacket and trousers of the Great Western Railway was chalking up details of arrivals, along with those of the very last trains still due to leave.

'There!' Tess gestured towards the train mentioned at the top of the board, departing from platform nine for some remote junction called Didcot. Run, catch it while you can!

They ran. Tess ducked around trousered shins and vast crinoline hems. Thomas elbowed his way through with a chant of, 'Sorry, was that your foot? Sorry, sorry. Oh, I am dreadfully sorry, ma'am!' Lin needed no elbows: the crowd parted spontaneously, in fear and revulsion before a woman so foreign and in such uncouth attire.

Platform seven: empty, the last train long since departed. At platform eight the new service from Wales was depositing its hundreds of passengers, mingling the soot-specked common sort, conveyed here third class in grubby trucks, with the ranks of first-class travellers, who strode away from the train elegantly empty-handed while their servants attended to the luggage now being unloaded from the luggage car.

'Coming through!'

'What the devil is that woman wearing?'

'Sorry, sorry! Oh, I say, sorry about that. Was that your foot?'

'Come on, bigwig!'

Platform nine. It lay at the gloomy far end of the station, against the lofty far wall. A ticket inspector stood at the near end, but Tess had ducked past him and was running for the train before he had a chance to go, 'Oi!' Then Lin was there, grabbing him by the collar and snarling, 'A child! Have you seen a child, grey hair, grey skin, adult's clothes, heading for this train?'

'Well, I—'

'A child! Think!'

Then Tess's voice came down the platform. '*Miss Lin!*'

Lin let go of the unfortunate inspector and ran down the platform. Thomas was there already, standing by Tess's side, following her gaze.

Standing squarely in the middle of the platform, hair dishevelled and thumb wedged in his mouth was Mr Marvellous, the mighty strong man of the circus.

He wasn't alone. Next to him, on a low wooden trolley, was a large box, high as a man and covered in purple silk. A rhythmical sound came from it, low and steady, and with the sound, the silk gently stirred.

'You!' snapped Lin, pointing at Mr Marvellous. 'Out of my way!'

He removed the thumb from his mouth with a faint pop and said, 'I ain't s'posed to listen to you, miss!'

'You will do as I say!'

He giggled, and brought out his other hand from behind his back. Held between his stubby fingers was a curved piece of metal. It looked like the handle from an ancient cauldron, yanked off its hinges.

Lin's face fell. 'Oh.'

'I gotta keep hold of the metal an' then I get a prize!' said Mr Marvellous.

'Miss Lin!' shrilled Tess. 'Ensorcell him!'

'It's magnetic iron,' murmured Thomas. 'How . . .?'

'Greybags said I'll get a prize if I hold on to the iron!' Mr Marvellous happily explained. 'An' if I kill you. He said that,' he added, as an afterthought.

'Thomas, Tess,' breathed Lin, 'get on the train.'

They edged past her towards the nearest carriage door. 'You ain't allowed on the train!' wailed Mr Marvellous. 'It ain't part of the rules!'

'Rules are for children to break,' replied Lin, stretching her arms to their full length and turning her head this way and that to loosen her neck muscles. 'Now, seeing you didn't choose to be intoxicated, and possessed with the spirit of an infant, I will try not to hurt you.' Planting one foot before the other in a fighting stance never seen before on English soil, she added, 'So long as you don't hurt me.'

The guard blew the whistle, just as Tess and Thomas made a run for the train. In the same moment, Mr Marvellous, with a little giggle, raised the thick iron handle and ran straight for Lin's head.

CHAPTER 21

Thomas and Tess were still on the platform as the train started to pull out. With each distant 'chumpf!' from the engine, the boxy wooden carriages were yanked forwards, then paused in a noisily accelerating rhythm. Running alongside an open door in the last carriage, Thomas took a leap, which became a stumble, onto the train. He just managed to pull Tess up from the platform before the door slammed shut behind them by the train's stuttering increase in speed.

Inside, they met with the pale faces of a Presbyterian couple, who'd never seen anything more exciting than biblical tableaux at the chapel's annual temperance supper, and for whom, therefore, this particular incident would be conversation at dinner for months.

At the same moment, Mr Marvellous swung the iron bar down towards Lin's head with all his marvelled-at strength . . . to where Lin wasn't any more.

The bar thudded into the planks of the platform, and Mr Marvellous blinked in surprise. He looked up, to see Lin standing a short step to the side of where she had been, fists raised, bouncing on her toes. He mumbled, 'How'd you . . .?' and realised that no, she was only bouncing on one set of toes. The toes attached to her other foot were shooting towards his throat on the end of more leg than he'd ever imagined. He stepped back, and the kick bounced off his shoulder, knocking him backwards nonetheless. He mumbled, 'But yor a girl!'

'Yep,' replied Lin cheerfully. 'Do you know, some people think I should let that stand in my way.'

He swung the bar at her head again, and she dodged and swivelled so that she could grab his arm from behind as he turned. She turned with him, adding her momentum to his, to spin him round in an entire circle. He staggered as the bar slipped in his fingers. But he didn't let go. Instead, with a determined grunt, he regained his foothold and tensed his whole body like a rock. As he caught his balance and his breath, so Lin's fingers slipped from his arm.

He half turned to face her again, mouth agape in anger. 'Oh,' murmured Lin, 'it usually doesn't work like that.'

'You ain't no good to play with!' roared Mr Marvellous. With one hand he swung the metal handle, with the other, he aimed a punch.

Lin sprang back, but slipped onto one knee. 'Look,' she

bluffed, 'I really don't want to hurt you. It's bad form to leave too many prostrate bodies when all I'm attempting to do is to maintain some civilised norms of behaviour.'

He growled, lowered his head like a charging bull and ran straight at her. She rolled to one side, came up low and got a kick into the back of his knee. It was like punching a sandbag: it felt heavy, soft and utterly unresponsive. Mr Marvellous roared, 'Yor not nice!' and before Lin had time to move, his hand was round her throat. He lifted her up as if she was weightless, dangled her in the air and said, 'You ain't getting no prize!'

Lin's green eyes stood out from her face, her hair flopped dishevelled over her face. She clawed at his fingers in vain. As her face began to turn red, then white, then purple-blue, she lunged with two fingers at Mr Marvellous's throat, found the ridged hardness of his windpipe, pressed in and pressed down.

Mr Marvellous would have preferred to give a yell of pain, but for that, enough air would have had to make it past the sudden stab of Lin's hand. Instead he made a little, *nnnckkk*, *nnnckkk* noise, dropped Lin into an undignified heap, wheezed like a dying rattle snake and sagged to his knees.

Lin picked herself up, and dusted herself off, her eyes fixed on the now distant train. 'I wish I could inform you,' she said as Mr Marvellous gagged and heaved for breath, 'that that was a strike known as "lotus sings lullaby to crane" or some such pretentious nonsense. It's not. It's known as bloody nasty two fingers into the throat, and there's a reason we don't teach such things to children.'

Her eyes moved to where Mr Marvellous was now trying to pull himself up beside the big silk-covered box.

No . . .

. . . wait . . .

. . . not pull himself up. Release a *catch* on the side of the box itself.

The purple silk fell away.

The catch came free.

Now that Lin's mind had time to catch up with the rest of her, it occurred to her that she'd already recognised the sound coming from that box, as the thing inside slipped out onto the platform. It had been a purr. A lion's purr.

Lin looked at the lion.

The lion looked at her.

She felt the creature was likely to bring more to the encounter than she herself could muster, since her own reasoning wasn't getting much beyond: *Oh dear, it's a lion. Whoops, it's a lion. Um . . . it's a lion. It looks quite hungry. Oh well, it's a lion.*

Slowly, as slowly as she could, she eased a brass-bladed knife out of her sleeve. She said, 'I didn't realise Greybags poisoned *animals* too.'

'He made the circus pretty,' replied Mr Marvellous, staggering to his feet. He wore a broad grin – of satisfaction, Lin guessed – at the hopelessness of her situation. 'Greybags made everything right. Everyone at the circus likes the stories what he tells.'

'*Of course.*' Lin sighed. 'And in his stories, the lions at the circus always do what their tamers command. Lovely. Poignant. Nice lion,' she added with a squeak, as its great triangular shoulder blades rose and fell above the long curve of its spine.

'You mustn't hurt the children.' Mr Marvellous chuckled. 'You mustn't make them get old. It ain't nice to make them get old.'

The lion was still purring, but its jaws were ajar and she could see great spiked teeth and a soft pink tongue. She felt that to blink, to take her eyes for one second off that orange-yellow stare, was to die. Her fighting instructor had trained her in the art of causing damage to every form of human and its evolutionary neighbours, armed with any weapon from any corner of the earth. She'd never said anything about mystically possessed lions.

As she watched it drop its chin, raise its hind legs and saw its tail flatten behind it, she turned the knife, thinking: *Perhaps if I'm fast. Perhaps perhaps perhaps perhaps if it's an arthritic intoxicated old lion with only one good eye and a cramp problem, then perhaps . . .*

And a voice said, very gently behind her, 'Close your eyes.'

The words were soft, warm, kind and, for the most part, unconcerned by the giggling, thumb-sucking strong man and a menacing pet lion. In the face of so much reassurance, of such familiarity, Lin felt she had no choice, not even a moment to think and doubt. Without a word she obeyed.

She closed her eyes.

There was a fizz, a pop, a hiss, then a sudden and loud *snap-fuzz*! Even from behind her closed eyes she saw the flash of white light, bright and sharp enough to burn its image across her eyeballs, then seem to track back and forth to the edge of her vision as she moved her eyes in the darkness.

Immediately there was a human cry of distress, together with an animal mewl of pain. She heard a footstep move by, a jingling of metal, then the strange animal sound quickly subsided into an indignant, fading *mmmmmrrrrwwww*.

Lin half-opened one eye.

A man was kneeling over the lion, an empty syringe in one hand. Already the great beast lay docile at his feet. He straightened up and reached into a pocket for another vial of stuff. Nearby, Mr Marvellous was on his knees with his hands over his eyes, sobbing like a child. 'I can't see!' he wailed. 'I can't see nothin'!'

The man was dressed in a long beige coat stained with all sorts of chemical and culinary accidents, hatless above his sandy-red hair, and accompanied by a dog composed mostly of a big brown nose and trailing ears. He stepped round the stupefied lion, knelt by Mr Marvellous and took the strong man's hand in his own. 'It's all right,' he murmured. 'I'm here now. You don't have to be scared. I'll see that you're all right.'

'Who's there? I can't see nothin'!'

'It's all right,' repeated the other man, pulling out another syringe and uncorking the vial with his teeth. He spat the cork away, filled the syringe and touched it to the strong man's arm. 'I'm going to give you something to make you better. It'll sting for a little and then it'll all be all right.'

He pushed the syringe under the skin, injected the contents, and waited for the big man's breath to slow, for him to relax, and his hands to fall away from his face. At length, with a little sigh, Mr Marvellous fell asleep. The man with the syringe lowered Mr Marvellous's head carefully to the ground, straightened up, and turned.

'Lions?' he said with a shrug. 'Not to worry. I really feel I've understood the whole lion business and frankly, in retrospect, the whole situation was overblown.' He saw her startled expression. 'Um . . . Hello, Miss Lin,' he added.

'Hello, Mister Lyle,' she mumbled.

There was an uncomfortable silence.

Finally, they blurted together:

'How are you—'

'About the whole kissing business—'

And they fell silent again.

'If I find out that your not being dead was because you were merely pretending to be that ill,' Lin exclaimed, wagging a disapproving finger at Lyle, 'in order to win my sympathetic feminine favours, I will, so help me . . .'

'Miss Lin, which would you rather?' asked Lyle, grinning brightly. 'My having faked what I can only describe as one of the most frightening and agonising experiences of my rather exciting detective career, *or* a blow-by-blow account of the likely chemical, biological, bio-chemical, medical, existential, philosophical, spiritual and metabolic reasons why I'm standing here right now talking to you and not, in fact, singing lullabies to Newton.'

She thought about it a moment then said, 'You frame a difficult question, Mister Lyle.'

'Not as difficult as this one.' He put his head on one side, and though he was grinning, she could see the exhaustion in his eyes and weariness in his sagging shoulders. 'Where the bloody hell are the children?'

Lin looked to the far end of the platform and beyond, to where a single red rear light on the back of the train was vanishing into darkness.

'Oh dear,' she said. 'This is going to be a problem, isn't it?'

It was not the easiest thing in the world to explore the train.

For a start, working up through the carriages was a difficulty none too easy to solve. Certainly, in the third-class compartments where grey faces stained with dirt were pressed in shoulder to shoulder along hard wooden benches, the only real obstruction to observation was the shove and bump of swaying bodies obscuring sight. But with no joins between carriages, Tess and Thomas were left with no better means to move between second and third class than by waiting until the train lumbered into each slow station, hopping out of the end of the third-class carriages and running round into second class, where each compartment door was slammed tight on its own little world. In this way they peered through every compartment window and, where the curtains were drawn across the wooden doors of the compartments, they slid the doors rudely back and, seeing no one of any consequence within, Tess would bob her polite courtesy and say, 'Sorry, m'm, I were lookin' for my lost uncle see?' and so they would scurry on.

For nearly an hour the train rumbled through London and, as it did, the commuters slowly began to leave until those left in the carriages were the sunk-eyed weary of the long-distance travellers, men clutching leather cases or woven sacks, women holding sleeping children to them, who were now too tired to cry. The slow train to Bristol, five hours and a half by moonlight and the dull yellow glow of the driver's lamp. Tess had never left London before. Thomas had never left London in quite such an undignified way. As the city houses melted away, black countryside slipped by, real black, solid black, full of the chittering of cold insects after rain, the smell of mud and other things richer and less salubrious, and as far as the eye could see, stars. Ten thousand thousand thousand stars that only seemed to grow brighter the more you stared, looking down on the red bricks of

slumbering stations, freshly built in a place where one day a town
might spring up, candles going out in the station masters' windows.

Tess and Thomas had covered nearly the whole length of the
train in this manner, and both were beginning to lose patience
with the matter when they stumbled on the compartment. In fact,
both were so bored with their search that at first they hardly
noticed, but glanced inside with the brisk regularity of people
who had done this too many times already, moved on and only
by the next compartment door did the reality of the image they
had seen settle in.

Tess grabbed Thomas by the left sleeve, Thomas grabbed
Tess by the right, and then immediately let go lest he be considered inappropriate. 'It's him!' hissed Tess in an overly loud
whisper to be heard over the rumbling of the train.

'Erm . . . yes.'

'An' he's got *people* with him!'

'Yes!'

'The bigwig from the circus with his stick an' the man with
the dancin' monkey!'

'You mean Mr Majestic and the organ grinder?' echoed
Thomas meekly.

'An' they're *gigglin'!* Why do they always seem to be gigglin'?' demanded Tess.

'Um . . .'

'What do we do now?'

'I suppose . . . I suppose we follow them to wherever their
final destination is and inform the authorities.'

'Inform the authorities? What you gonna say? Oi, bigwig
beak, you need to arrest this child what has grey hair cos he ain't

a child really, an' then you gotta send him to clink cos he steals other children's dreams an' they never wake up never after?'

'Well, I thought I might dress it up a little.'

'Bigwig,' she said firmly, 'I see as how you're a nobbly bigwig an' all, with like – you know – aristo thin's an' all, but I don't really think as how this is your brightest idea.'

'I don't hear you coming up with a productive solution to our dilemma!'

'I didn't want to be sneakin' round 'ere like some two-farthin' chimney sweep what thinks he's gonna be the next big pinch-purse cos he's got little fingers!'

'What?'

'I said I didn't want to be sneakin' round 'ere like—'

'No, that wasn't the problem.'

' 'Sides, you're rubbish at bein' all inno— innoc— at bein' all not noticed like! You even stick out when you're with other big-wigs an' they're like all . . . all bigwigy like you!'

'Miss Teresa, I'll have you know that I am highly competent in the detective arts, including the sometimes base yet necessary skills of surveillance and—'

'You don't even talk like proper people!'

'I talk like a well-bred gentleman of society, versed and learned in oratorical, rhetorical and philosophical skills that have been nurtured within the bosom of polite civilisation since the time of Sophocles himself and . . .'

His voice drained away. A strange expression had come over Tess's face, and her eyes had drifted up to a point about a foot and a half above Thomas's head. He said, 'Tess?'

She said, 'Knife.'

'What?'

'Knife! Bloody knife!'

So, since her attention seemed so focused, Thomas half turned and looked at the object behind him.

Which object turned out to be a man.

Which man turned out to be wearing a large, rather overly ornate cloak, a little trimmed salt and pepper beard, and to be carrying an interesting, slightly bent, shiny and extremely sharp knife.

The knife-thrower said, 'Hello, children. Do you want to play?'

In the gutter where the tracks run, between platform seven and eight, where the arch of the station ends and silver-laced night begins, an argument is going on.

It goes like this:

'We'll go faster without the carriages . . . Whoops, watch your foot!'

'Are you sure this is a good idea, Mister Lyle?'

'Miss Lin, I find that desperate, dare I say, impossibly dangerous situations bring out in me a light of such brilliance that in retrospect, I am amazed at my own ingenuity, insanity and inspiration. So shut up, Miss Lin, with all respect, and do what I bloody say!'

'I still don't entirely believe you're not dead, Mister Lyle.'

There is the clinking of heavy chain being dislodged, the cranking of a gear being released, and a voice proclaims, 'We can discuss medical trivialities at another time.'

'But you were poisoned!'

'Indeed. By a drug intended to act speedily in inducing a narcotic state from which an altered consciousness would

297

emerge. But I didn't achieve an early narcotic state, did I? Indeed, by the time I actually lost consciousness the poison had been in my system for several hours, that part of it which I hadn't already, if you'll pardon the descent into crude, non-scientific jargon, puked-up all over the place. Over those several hours my body would, naturally, have been fighting it, not to mention the various chemicals Thomas plied me with, and while the body is not particularly good at targeting and destroying toxins, sooner or later a combination of acids in the stomach, cellular barriers, and sheer metabolic process was bound to wash the thing out of my system. So that when' – something loud and heavy went *clunk*, something else went *whoosh* in response – 'when I finally achieved the narcotic state into which the poison was meant to plunge me, it was a greatly weakened dosage that affected my higher cognitive functions resulting in' – a clank, a foot on a metal stair – 'a process that, while I would classify it as surreal, I would also regard as largely medically irrelevant.' Lyle let out a long breath in satisfaction at the profundity of his own analysis. 'See? Not complicated at all.'

Lin thought about this a moment. Then she said, 'So the fact that you didn't fall asleep in the initial few hours, saved your life?'

'Well, there is a little more to it than that.'

'And you didn't fall asleep, Mister Lyle, because I commanded you not to.'

'Again, who knows what interesting side-effects were taking place in my brain.'

'So, Mister Lyle, effectively I saved your life! Ha! You're never going to hear the end of this!'

'Miss Lin, while I concede you helped stave off the inevitable,' growled Lyle, his patience wearing thin as he struggled to decouple an engine from its carriages while avoiding the watchful eyes of the station guards, 'there is one factor you have failed to consider.'

'And what is that, Mister Lyle?'

'You have failed,' he grunted as metal came free from metal, 'to consider the fact that Mrs Hobbs upon immediately departing my company, went in search of the one other person in London whose grasp of organic chemistry is as rich and complex as mine.'

Lin waited. When Lyle seemed to offer no more she asked, 'Well go on then! Who?!'

There was a slightly embarrassed pause. Then, 'If you tell anyone this . . .'

'Me foreign lady-demon, you Caucasian male in a patriarchal society.' Lin sighed. 'Who would believe me?'

'Mrs Hobbs,' growled Lyle, crawling between the tracks, 'went to get my mother.'

There was a silence.

Then a long, slow, disbelieving, 'Your *mother*!'

'My ma has an excellent head on her shoulders!'

'Your *mother* saved your life?'

'My ma hasn't just spent the last thirty-five years making scones and cream teas you know.'

'Your *mother*—' Lin stopped dead in the middle of her sentence. 'Does this mean there's a cure?'

'I'm here, aren't I?'

'Your *mother* found a *cure* to the poison?'

'Yes, my mother!' snapped Lyle. 'Thank you for reminding

me, and may I say that while I'm grateful to her and grateful to you, the children are missing, Greybags is fleeing the city to God knows where, so will you please help me steal this train before someone notices?'

Thomas and Tess were pushed unceremoniously down onto the seat opposite Greybags, in the compartment containing Greybags, Mr Majestic the ringmaster, the organ grinder still turning the handle of his now very out of tune and clunky organ, and the knife-thrower, who twiddled the end of his blade nervously between his fingertips.

Greybags sat chewing his sleeve. He looked at Tess, looked at Thomas and curled his lip in distaste. 'I knows you,' he said, flapping one little arm in a great sleeve indignantly. 'You were at the circus!'

It had been less than a day since Tess and Thomas had seen Greybags last, but already, some of the youth he'd stolen from Effy Hall was beginning to fade, and his face had the thinner, more settled look of a teenage boy of Thomas's age, rather than the fresh glow of his stolen moments.

'This is your fault, bigwig,' hissed Tess, nudging Thomas in the ribs.

'My fault? If you hadn't been arguing all the time then we would have—'

'You can't talk like that to me, I'm a lady!'

'Miss Teresa, polite ladies don't argue back when the gentle-man of the house is offering a productive plan!'

'Well then, polite ladies are stupid an' rubbish, an', 'sides, you ain't no gentleman of no house, you is Thomas an' I is Tess an' that means you should do everythin' as I say!'

'That isn't how it works! I am the man and you are . . . well . . . you are . . .'

'Ah-ha! You're the man an' that means you can get blamed when it all goes wrong, see. Cos if you're s'posed to be in charge then when it goes poo-pooey like I said it would, then you is the one what must shovel the shi—'

'Hello?'

They both looked up at Greybags.

'Yes?' snapped Tess. 'What'd you want?'

'You're a clever girl, aren't you?' asked Greybags.

Tess's eyes immediately narrowed. 'Yes I am,' she said, 'but random blokes what goes round sayin' it in a dodgy way ain't none what I'd trust with the silver. You start by sayin' "You is a clever girl", see, an' then you say "You're beautiful" or summat an' then you propose marriage an' run away with my dowry!'

'You haven't got a dowry, Miss Teresa,' Thomas pointed out politely, feeling he ought to say something, if not in the lady's defence, then at least to show he was interested.

'I'd bloody go an' pinch one, so I'd *be* respectable! 'Sides, weren't I havin' a go at you for bein' a useless toff?'

'Yes, Miss Teresa, but I feel in the interest of factual accuracy—'

'I don't like you,' said Greybags, and there was nothing in his childish drawl but malice and distaste.

Thomas's eyes flew quickly up. 'What?' he barked, and then cringed at how much he'd sounded like his father.

'You're borin',' said Greybags. 'You're talkin' all posh like – like you were one of *them*. Like you were all grown-up. You wanna sound like one of them! You wanna sound like a borin' adult, as if you weren't just one of us! You want to be *old*!'

Thomas swallowed. 'Now look,' he began firmly, 'I'm sure we can settle this if we just discuss our mutual—'

'You scared of your pa?' asked Greybags suddenly.

'What? No!'

'I think you're scared,' he replied. 'I think you tries to talk like your papa so as how he will think more of you. You think as how he don't want a child, he just want a son, a thin' what will be just like him, what will talk like him an' walk like him, an' have a son of his own what will have the family name an' will have more sons an' more sons cos that's what the sons have to do. They have to be like their papas. I think you talk bigwig so as that's so. So as when you grow up you'll be just like your papa, not nothin' like *you*.'

There was stunned silence at this, except for the slow slither of the knife-thrower cleaning one of his nails with the point of his blade.

Then Tess nudged Thomas in the ribs and whispered, 'You know, he might 'ave a point an' all.'

'Teresa,' breathed Thomas, eyes wide and face red, 'not now.'

Greybags snorted. 'You're borin',' he repeated. 'I don't like you.' He looked up at the ringmaster. 'It'd be funny if we went an' threw him off the train, wouldn't it?'

'What?' barked Thomas.

'*Wha*?' shrilled Tess.

But the ringmaster just shrugged, grabbed Thomas by one arm, and reached for the door. Tess threw herself between him and it, put one hand in the air and snapped, 'Oi! You lay one finger on my bloody bigwig an' I'll scream so loud as how you'll be cryin' for two bloody weeks!'

The ringmaster hesitated and looked to Greybags for advice.

Greybags said, 'Why'd you want to play with someone so borin'? He's just a bigwig what don't know how to be fun.'

'He may be just a bigwig,' snapped Tess imperiously, 'but he's *my* bigwig, what I gotta look after cos he's too daft to go an' look after himself proper. An' if it's the last thin' I do – which it ain't gonna be, by the way, cos I've got all sorts of thin's to do with my life – I ain't gonna let some . . . some . . . some snotty child with bad hair go an' throw him out of the train!'

Greybags clapped his hands together happily. 'You are wonderful, little girl!' he said. 'You are so bright!'

'Don't you little me! You're just a child in a big coat!'

'Oh no! No no no no no!' Greybags laughed. 'I'm old. I'm so old as how I knew your mama an' your papa when they was just children themselves. I met the drummer boys what played at Waterloo. I saw them make tea in Boston Bay. I'm real old, see? I just don't like it that way. An' I ain't never goin' to die.'

Thomas raised his one free hand. 'Excuse me? About my being pushed out of a moving train?'

'What?' asked Greybags, seemingly having forgotten.

'Ignore my bigwig,' said Tess quickly, 'he has all these daft ideas 'bout duty an' justice an' responsibility an' all.'

'Ain't right for a boy,' sneered Greybags, reaching into his pocket, 'miss . . .'

'I'm Tess. Lady Tess,' she added with a little glare at Thomas, 'of . . . of . . . Wales.' Uncomprehending faces stared back at her. 'The *good* bit, course! Proper lady, me.'

Greybags's hand slid from his pocket. It held a small green bottle. 'Lady Tess, would you like summat to drink?' he asked.

Tess's face had turned the colour of freshly burnt ash. She

shook her head and mumbled, 'Um, no. Thanks a bundle but nah, I'm fine, really, honest, really, fine.'

'But you gotta 'ave summat to drink! Else you'll get all thirsty.' He waved the bottle closer. Tess backed away until she was up against the compartment door, the sound of the night whistling by outside, the rattling of the engine on the tracks ahead and . . .

. . . and behind?

'Drink, Miss Teresa! I wanna you to drink!'

'Don't you touch her!' snapped Thomas.

'Children what don't behave get a smack!' wailed Greybags.

'*Bigwig!* I ain't drinkin' nothin' of yours!'

'Ain't we friends?'

'No, we bloody ain't! Didn't you hear the part 'bout you bein' a snotty thin' with bad hair?'

'You gotta drink!'

'No!'

'You gotta drink! I *always* gets my way!'

'Well then you is just a spoilt little boy!'

'I ain't!'

'You is!'

'I ain't!'

'You is!'

'I ain't I ain't I ain't I ain't I—'

'Excuse me?' murmured Thomas feebly.

'I ain't I ain't I ain't—'

'Is is is is!' shrieked Tess.

'Ain't ain't ain't ain't—'

'Excuse me?' Thomas raised his voice.

'Is is is to infinity!'

'Wha's infinity!'

'It's like so big as how you can't never measure it cos it goes on for ever an' ever an' ever, an' that's how spoilt an' snotty you is!'

'*Excuse me!*'

Thomas's voice cut through the row. All eyes turned to him. He smiled meekly, and pointed out of the window behind Tess. 'Forgive the interruption,' he mumbled, 'but they seem to be wanting our attention.'

Every eye now turned from Thomas to the thing just outside the window. Running along the parallel track to their train was a great fat black locomotive, chuffing thick white smoke from its chimney stack, between which bursts could be faintly seen the unmistakeable form of Lin, covered in coal dust, standing on the ballast truck and waving merrily. Driving the train in the main compartment was Horatio Lyle.

He was waving with one hand, the other was locked on a lever of some sort, and from his gestures, Tess had the feeling he wanted her to open the door. She reached out for the handle, and as she depressed it, saw Lin crouch on her uneven platform of coal, ready to spring. 'My guv'nor's gonna be so mad at you,' Tess declared firmly and, with a shove, pushed the door open onto the whirling night.

They had stood on Paddington Station and watched the smoke of the slow train depart. And at some point shortly after, Lin had said, 'Can you even drive this?'

Lyle had said, 'Of course I can bloody drive a train! It is the pinnacle of modern technological achievement, a device whose impact on society itself we are only just beginning to comprehend, a tool of sublime craft, beauty and relative design simplicity. Of course I can bloody drive a train! It's – you know – just a question of working out which bit does what. Which I'm sure can't be too hard! Besides, that isn't the important question right now.'

'I don't know, it seems reasonably important from my technologically ignorant point of view,' murmured Lin, just loud and sarcastically enough for Lyle to hear.

He'd scowled. 'The question is,' he had said, 'how well can you jump?'

The door opened.

Cold rushing night air snapped and pulled at Tess, sucking her towards the darkness of the tracks between the two rattling trains.

Lin jumped.

She didn't know much about fighting lions; she didn't *like* being on trains, too much iron, far too much iron, just being near them gave her a headache; she didn't really understand machines or how they worked, didn't really understand the English and why they were so pleased with themselves, wondered sometimes at children, feared that she was losing her mind in liking humans at all, but through all this, all the doubt and confusion that she hid so well, Lin Zi knew one thing about herself that would never change.

She was bloody good at jumping.

Tess ducked as Lin leapt, which was what saved her from getting a pair of sensible, intricately laced black leather boots in the head. She had a vague impression of the foreign lady uncoiling like a striking snake, fingers first, so that it seemed for a moment that she still had feet in one train and arms in another, but that moment was fleeting and then Lin's fingers had caught the top of the train and her feet were pivoting up from under her and swinging straight inside the carriage. Greybags scrambled towards the corridor door, whimpering piteously and flapping at his protectors to do something, anything, as Lin landed on the compartment floor, straightened up and grinned.

'Ta-da! And I'm not even descended from monkeys!' she exclaimed cheerfully.

On the engine behind her, Lyle, after a certain amount of tentative fumbling, had found what he hoped was the valve which controlled his locomotive's speed, and was throwing fat shovels of coal into the hissing, spitting red furnace to put more speed into his train.

Thomas felt the knife-thrower draw a blade, ready to hurl at Lin and, without thinking, half turned his body and buried his teeth as hard as he could in the hand that still held his arm. The knife-thrower gave a yowl of pain and tried to drag himself free but Thomas had locked his jaws like a vice, and clung on for dear life as his teeth rattled in his skull. Thomas and the knife-thrower were in Greybags' way as he made for the corridor, and with the others rising to their feet, there was no room to move so he scrambled on all fours across the soft carriage seat. Lin's hand closed round his ankle and he whined, 'Never done nothin'!' as she dragged him back.

'Nasty little specimen,' she hissed, and then had to let go as Mr Majestic, resplendent in cheap silk and expensively curled moustache swung his cane as hard as he could towards Lin's face. She ducked then straightened up as the cane over-shot her, grabbed Mr Majestic's hand and gave it a short sharp twist.

At the front of the train, the driver was somewhat startled to see a locomotive, without any carriages and only one, inappropriately dressed, oil-stained driver, pull up level to him on the track beside his. The driver was waving and shouting something, but through the belch of the furnace and the great gouts of smoke and steam, he couldn't hear what, so he shrugged helplessly.

'Bloody brake!' shouted Lyle over the din. 'Bloody *brake!*'

The driver smiled a bewildered, helpless smile. Cursing, Lyle threw more coal into his furnace, heard the pipes squeak in overheated indignation, saw the pressure gauge mount another few frightened points towards the red, and his train accelerated.

In Greybags's compartment, Lin's predicament, which she had thought reasonably good, was becoming complicated by the organ grinder, who, with an expression of benign boredom on his face, had somehow managed to crawl onto the seat behind her and wrap one arm across her neck. While she knew a hundred exciting and only occasionally lethal ways to deal with the problem, her situation was further complicated by the ringmaster's constant treading on her feet and clawing at her arms which made manoeuvring in the tight, hot confines of the compartment next to impossible and she lost her grip on Greybags. Thomas was still locked tooth-to-hand with the knife-thrower, while Tess was crawling on her hands and knees away from the rush towards the corridor.

The noise was attracting attention, Tess could hear people stirring in other compartments, and prayed to all the gods that had never listened to her before for good manners to keep everyone appropriately disinterested in the events of the night. She saw Greybags, also on his hands and knees crawling for the door to the corridor and, worming through the legs of the over-occupied ringmaster grabbed Greybags' ankle with both hands, flopped to the floor and shouted, 'Oi! You ain't doin' nothin'!'

He kicked and twisted and mewled, but Tess's fingers were locked round his foot with no intention of letting go. She had that very special expression of utter wilfulness on her face usually reserved for baths and bedtime, and which brooked no argument at all. It was by no means a dignified struggle and, for a quick minute, all that could be heard was the impolite grunting and humphs of people too breathless to curse. For a moment Greybags's foot slipped free of Tess's fingers and he made a break for the corridor, but she was there again, flopping half in and out of the compartment to get hold of him and bring him with a great 'phwamph!' to the floor. The knife-thrower took a handful of Thomas's hair in his hand and tried to pry Thomas's teeth free by physically dragging his head away. He was as surprised as Thomas to discover that the young man's reaction to this was to stamp very hard, petulantly and repeatedly on the join between the elder man's foot and ankle until he howled in pain. The organ grinder and ringmaster were trying to drag Lin towards the open door and the roaring night outside, and for all that she kicked and punched and dug her elbows in, bared her teeth and swore in an exciting range of languages, inch by inch they were pushing her closer. Now her right foot dangled on the edge, now her right shoulder was being eased out into the blackness, now her right arm, now the side of her head. Just one more push and . . .

But what that might have been, no one ever found out as, with a scream of brakes tortured beyond endurance, the whole train lurched backwards like a frightened rabbit, slamming every passenger in every compartment against the furthest wall, shattering the glass of every other lantern from first to third class and plunging the train into mish-mashed darkness.

The reason for this sudden and desperate stop in the night that nearly burst the gears which controlled it, was standing in an oil-stained bulging beige coat about three inches from the front of the panting green engine, holding a bright ball of white light in his right hand and looking up at the belching metal face of the engine with a slightly bewildered expression. A few hundred yards further on, another locomotive, black and creaking in distress, sat on the opposite track going *chuga . . . chuga . . . chuga . . .*

'Bloody hell,' he muttered, as the driver stuck his head out of the train and started shouting abuse, 'I thought the brakes would be a little more efficient than that.'

He gave the slightly nervous laugh of a man who has seen the face of mathematics and discovered it has a leer, and ignoring every word of abuse coming from the driver above, Lyle tossed his bubble of light aside, and jumped on to the train.

Chaos had broken out among the gloom-soaked carriages.

The British travelling public, although usually tactful to the point of total apathy, needed only one small push to move from polite acceptance of the woes and dangers of regular travel, to a state of such furious, bitter, acrimonious and, for the most part, pointless complaint that all sense and reason fell by the wayside and no sternly worded letter of indignation could explain their wrath. It was as if a lifetime of excellent manners had merely contained a beast of fiery rudeness and, at the provocation of the railways, this creature was now unleashed.

So it was, as Lyle marched determinedly down the length of the train, that from every side he could hear the moaning and cursing of dislodged people. From first class came indignant shrills of, 'I say!' evolving into outbursts of, 'An outrage!'; in second little men with nasal drawls intoned, 'I shall complain, I shall! I shall complain!' while from third class – Lyle had heard some language in his time, but this was *creative* in a way he hadn't imagined possible.

A shout of, 'You little . . .!' from the end of a carriage grabbed and held his attention. He ran towards it, and saw the object of the cry was at the same time running towards him, jacket torn and trousers flapping. Behind him, emerging from the half-gloom of the splintered shadows, Lyle saw a man with a curved, oddly weighted steel knife, draw the blade back to throw and shouted instinctively, 'Thomas, get down!'

Thomas, the running boy, obeyed automatically, too battered and bewildered, his head bleeding from the knock he'd taken when the train had thrown him against the wall, to question the source of this voice that seemed to know his name. Behind him the knife-thrower's scowl darkened. His eyes were a pair of bright black plums in a pale face and he threw the blade even as Lyle ploughed head-first into a compartment of furiously bickering men, each competing as to who could be the more belligerent on the subject of the railways today. He heard the dull thump of the knife striking wood somewhere behind him, shouted, 'Thomas? You all right?' and heard in the distance a muffled, 'Mister Lyle?'

'Thomas, get out of the damn train! Run!'

He heard a door open somewhere, rushed to the end of the carriage and stuck his head out of the window to see Thomas half scrambling, half falling the some-foot drop from the compartment door to the ballast floor. Lyle fumbled in his pockets, searching for something that would serve as an appropriate projectile even as he shouted, 'Run, lad! Don't let the driver move this damn train!'

'Mister Lyle?' shouted Thomas, obeying even as he called, 'You're alive!'

'It's only a temporary condition,' Lyle snapped as footsteps thundered angry and fast in the corridor outside. 'You!' he added, grabbing one of the bewildered men by the collar. 'Get out of this compartment *now*!'

'Oi, you can't just—'

Lyle pulled something out of his coat pocket. It was a fat green bottle, corked and carefully labelled. 'You can get out,' he hissed, easing the cork back at arm's length, 'or you can pass out.'

There was something in Lyle's tone which suggested humour was not high on his list of priorities. It only took one man in the compartment to believe him, which he did, for the other three to follow his sudden and undignified break for the outside door. Lyle backed away from the corridor and, covering his mouth and nose with one sleeve, carefully dribbled liberal quantities of the clear thin liquid in the bottle across the floor round him. It hissed very quietly as it fell, giving off a thin low mist that shimmered into smelly nothingness in the air. Lyle pressed his back to the open window of the compartment, half turning his head to breathe fresher air as the knife-thrower stepped inside, blade already raised.

'Now, just wait a moment!' Lyle said as he saw the anger in the other man's face. 'Before you go throwing that knife of yours, can I offer you a whole series of excellent reasons – moral, philosophical, biological – why you shouldn't.'

The knife-thrower hesitated, and it seemed for a moment to Lyle that he was actually considering it. Then his eyebrows tightened and he exclaimed incredulously, 'No!'

'Wait, wait, wait!' Lyle raised his other hand to cover his face. 'Then can I ask you – Are you feeling sleepy?'

The knife-thrower hesitated, then his gaze slowly turned to the floor where for the first time he noticed the rapidly evaporating liquid spilt across the wood. 'Um . . .' he mumbled, and staggered a drunken step towards Lyle. 'It . . . smells funny.'

He staggered another pace, tried to throw the knife and fell face-forward onto the nearest seat. Lyle, still keeping his face turned to the open window, eased open the door behind him, and slipped out again into the fresh-aired night, to leave the man snoring in the dark.

Lin picked herself up carefully, looked round the compartment and swore.

She swore for two reasons. Firstly, because both the organ grinder and the ringmaster, both of whom had been knocked down by the shock of the braking train, were also picking themselves up, and had the look of men who both didn't know when to quit, and hadn't heard of chivalry to ladies. Secondly, because the jarring of the train had knocked the lantern which was the compartment's only illumination off its hook and sent it flying into the door frame, where the glass had broken, the oil had spilt and now the little flame had caught and was beginning to burn merrily. This was also annoying for two reasons. Firstly because the train was now on fire, and secondly because that burning door had been her main way out.

She said, 'Gentlemen—' and had to duck as a swipe of the ringmaster's cane nearly took her ear off.

Oh yes – one other problem. Of Tess, Thomas and Greybags, she could see no other sign.

'Gentlemen,' she began again, 'let me just say how sorry I am that we have come to—' She jumped a kick from the organ grinder's left foot, grabbed hold of the stiff lines of the luggage rack above as she did so, and, swinging like an acrobat, planted both feet very firmly in his chest. He didn't even have the breath to grunt but was spun backwards towards the open compartment door, clung onto the frame for a moment of slipping nothingness, and then with a little, '*Eiiii!*' fell out into the night.

Lin landed on her feet just in time for the ringmaster to try to wrap his hands round her throat. She staggered back and felt the sudden burning heat of the flames on the compartment door. 'Listen,' she tried again reasonably but, with a snarl, the ringmaster was on her, knocking her down onto the carriage seat and trying to press the life out of her with his cane across her chest. 'Really . . .' she wheezed as black and white sparks started to spin across her vision, 'I'm sure we can . . .' She wriggled her arms up just about high enough so her fingers were level with the ringmaster's temples. 'Please don't make me,' she added, but if there had been any capacity for understanding in the ringmaster's eyes, it had long since been wiped away, leaving nothing but petulant childish fury that would hear no reason.

'Damn,' she muttered as the world swam into blackness, and struck out at the ringmaster's temples.

Her left hand hit, fingers slicing deep into the soft tissue just behind his eyes, but her right hand was caught by another before it had time to strike, which was odd, she thought, because both the ringmaster's hands seemed to be occupied in throttling the life out of her.

There was a strange smell on the air and the pressure across her chest was suddenly relaxed. She half shook her head to try to clear it and blinked up at the ringmaster, whose eyes were already drifting shut. A single slim steel needle glimmered in the side of his thick neck and behind him, she saw the flame-flickering shape of Horatio Lyle easing the ringmaster to the ground.

'You and your . . .' Lyle made a strange series of drunken dance-like gestures that Lin guessed were supposed to represent some sort of martial combat, and then shook his head and tutted. 'Not sure if it's all it's cracked up to be?'

Lin straightened, smoothed herself down primly and announced in a voice husky with too little air, 'Mister Lyle, when *you* are trained to be a lethal killing machine more finely honed than any the Americans could invent for their petty civil war thingy, *you* will find how hard it is to incapacitate without actually maiming.'

'Right,' intoned Lyle with a slow nod. 'Of course. That's what it is. The train appears to be on fire.'

'Oh you *noticed*,' sarcasm dripped off Lin's voice. 'Insight!'

'Where's Tess?'

'She isn't with you?'

'No.'

Lin's face seemed to sink for a moment into something that might almost have been fear. 'Then . . .'

There came a voice from outside the train. It screamed, '*Bigwig! Bigwig bloody help me bloody now!*'

It was a child's voice.

CHAPTER 22

Greybags

The whole train was watching.

Greybags, seemingly a child barely older than Tess, was backing across the rough stone ballast of the tracks, one hand holding Tess by the hair, the other with a knife across her throat. This was attracting tuts of disapproval from the train's occupants but no attempt was made at rescue since, really, it was none of their business and what if they only made it worse?

Lin dropped down onto the tracks with Lyle behind her, and the two advanced slowly towards the retreating children, thus proving to the satisfaction of all onlookers that the situation was being handled and well done.

'Miss Lin!' shrilled Tess, 'some of your demon-lady magic please!'

'Shut up, shut up, shut up!' whined Greybags, dragging her head back further by a fistful of her hair. Tess's face was white, tears shimmering in her eyes, her lips curled in pain, but still she called, 'Miss Lin! Summat special now, please!'

Lyle stepped carefully past Lin, head on one side and face locked in an expression of disinterested curiosity.

'Mister Lyle!' If there hadn't been a blade at her neck, Tess would have bounced with glee. 'You ain't dead!'

'But – but you should . . .' whimpered Greybags as Lyle approached, 'you were . . . you should be . . .'

'For someone as old as you are, Greybags,' tutted Lyle, 'and in such an interesting biological predicament yourself, you're a right idiot when it comes to advanced bio-chemical metabolic interactions.'

'Don't come nearer! I've got the child an' . . . an' children can't get hurt, them's the rules. You never hurt children never an' . . . an' I'll hurt her, an' then that'll be the end of the story an' . . . an' . . .'

Lyle stopped a few paces away from the gibbering Greybags, head on one side, hands buried casually in his coat pockets. 'You'd hurt Tess?' he asked carefully.

Greybags gave a sound halfway between a giggle and a whine. 'Don't you come closer!'

'I'm not. Look, here I am, not coming any closer. I mean, obviously, you're going to have problems in the long term despite this, because if I do come closer and you *do* kill Tess, then I'm afraid I'm going to have to kill you and there'll be bugger-all you can do about it. And since you're *threatening* me with the prospect of killing her, and that's really the only thing you can threaten me with, I'm actually somewhat less than impressed, owing to the previous logic of she dies/you die herein discussed.' Out of his pocket he pulled a small bundle wrapped in red and white cloth. Greybags stiffened at the sight of it, but when unwrapped it turned out to be nothing more than a couple of thick, dark orange-coloured ginger biscuits. Lyle broke off a corner and took a bite, then another, then another, and, as if only finally aware at the last piece of all the eyes fixed in horrified fascination upon him added, 'Don't mind me. I'm waiting for you to come up with something resembling a good idea, Greybags. You *can* think of a good idea, can't you? I mean, someone as old as you, should have a smart thought now and then? Miss Lin? Would you like some biscuit?'

Lin didn't answer so, with a shrug, Lyle kept on eating. From every window of the train, every face and every eye, Tess and Lin and Greybags included, watched, hypnotised by the slow movement of Lyle's jaw.

'Not like my ma used to make,' he admitted conspiratorially, when the last bite had been taken and the crumbs wiped unconsciously away from the front of his coat. 'God, but she's a terrible cook. Did your ma make you biscuits, Greybags?' No answer. 'Miss Lin, Greybags did have a mother, didn't he? I mean, Tseiqin don't just hatch, right?'

'He had a mother, once,' replied Lin with a shrug. 'A long time ago.'

'Oh,' answered Lyle, looking disinterested. Behind him, the train's engine slowly went *chuga . . . chuga . . . chuga*. 'My pa was always the cook of the house,' he went on absently. 'He wasn't a very good cook either. But he did understand the importance of hot plum on a Thursday afternoon. Now, me? I'm not that good at cooking either. But it's partly the ingredients. You would not believe how many people are putting chalk in their bread these days, or boiling oranges to make them look fat. Disgusting. Not that food is anything other than fuel for the intellect, of course.'

He started on the second biscuit. The train went *chuga . . . chuga . . . chuga . . .* the ginger biscuit went *snap* between his fingers. They were the only sounds.

'Do you want some?' he asked finally, waving a piece towards Greybags. 'I mean, since we're stuck here waiting for you to make up your mind.'

'I just want to be with the children,' Greybags said.

'No, technically speaking, you want to *be* a child,' replied Lyle. 'But since you aren't, in fact, a child, merely a . . . curious biological adaptation . . . you have to steal the thoughts of children, the colours and the dreams and, I've got to tell you, the stupidity and the ignorance, because that's all part of the growing-up thing, and so, in conclusion,' he took another bite of biscuit, 'you aren't a child, you don't want to be *with* the children, you're just a parasite. A little stupid snotty parasite whose got himself into a ridiculous situation from which there is no really pleasant outcome.'

'I ain't!'

'Oh, that's so mature.' Lyle sighed, rolling his eyes. 'Fantastic deployment of logic. "I ain't a snotty parasite . . . cos I ain't!" Well reasoned. How sophisticated.'

'You can't hurt me!' whined Greybags. 'You can't!'

'Of course I can,' said Lyle, 'because at the end of the day, I'm big and you're little, I'm strong and you're weak, and I'm very,

very angry. Are you sure you don't want any of this biscuit? It's
the last one.'

'Mister Lyle,' whimpered Tess, 'do summat!'

'Nag nag nag. You know, that's all I ever really get? I'm sure
it was supposed to be the other way round, parents nagging children, and all that, but it doesn't seem to have worked out that
way.' His eyes were two bright blacknesses blinking in reflected
firelight. 'Did your mama nag you, Greybags? Do this? Wear
that? Say this? Not that? Probably more of the "not"s than the
"do"s. You mustn't run, mustn't talk loudly, mustn't say naughty
words, mustn't steal, mustn't cheat, mustn't lie . . . And then I
suppose the day came when you realised your ma did all these
things anyway, so why should you listen to her? Nothing to do
with her wanting to make you *better*, oh no. Because you're just
a child, too little to understand that. Did your mama read you
bedtime stories, Greybags?'

He twitched, fingers tightening round the knife. Lyle grinned,
half turned his head down to the ballast as if seeking some long-
lost secret in the chaos. 'My ma used to read me bedtime stories.
They'd always begin, "Once upon a time" that's how the best
stories go, isn't it? And in them the good would always be very
very good, and the bad would always be very very bad, and the
wicked would get their come-uppance and the good would live
happily ever after and the children would be happy and the
princes would marry the princesses and so on and so forth.
Codswallop, of course, but important, wonderful, hopeful
codswallop. A fairytale of how things *should* be, that's what the
stories were. Children should not be hurt. Parents should not die.
Perfectly well-meaning scientists should not get poisoned and so
on. What stories did your mama tell you, Greybags?'

'I . . . I . . . I don't . . . it was . . . I don't remember.'

'That's sad.' Lyle scrunched up his now empty red and white cloth wrapping and stuffed it back into his pocket. He fumbled in the bulging mass of his pockets until he found something else – a little silver flask – which he pulled out and started unscrewing. 'Not to remember the stories.'

'I . . . I take . . . I need . . . the stories are . . . the children who . . . I need . . .'

'You steal, actually,' said Lyle casually, pausing with the flask held carefully in the air. 'You steal other people's childhoods because, as I said earlier, you're not really a child, not any more. You're just an old, old man who likes to think of childish things that aren't his own. It's a bit twisted, really.'

'I . . . I . . . I ain't . . .'

'I don't imagine your pa told you stories, Greybags. Poor Mr Majestic, he was a father once, and you made him into a prancing clown. You turned the whole circus into your story, and it was horrible and twisted. Poisoned little boy. Did your pa punish you when you were naughty? Did he have a coal shed with a bolt on the outside? Did he tell you that things in the night came for naughty little boys?'

'Shut up shut up shut up!'

'You're old, Greybags. Lin told me. You're so, so old, an ancient mumbling toothless crone in a child's skin. Your thoughts are petty cruel nothings, your mind is an empty black and white shell that you have to fill with stolen dreams because you've lost all the dreams you ever had. You're old enough to wither, age, rot and die. Old enough to have seen your parents die, be buried and be skeletons together in the earth, old enough to . . .'

'Stop it!'

'. . . have thrown dust on their graves, seen the world and the things men do, to understand that life isn't like it is in the stories, the beautiful stories where the good end happily.'

'Stop it! *I hate you*!'

'Mister Lyle,' whispered Tess as the knife bit tighter to her throat.

'Quiet, Tess, the grown-ups are having a conversation,' he replied casually, 'you're too young to understand.'

'Stop it, stop it, stop it!' shrieked Greybags. 'I'll kill her!'

Lyle shrugged. 'Very well,' he said casually, 'you'll kill her and I'll kill you and it'll be a right bloody mess. But you know what? I probably won't care. Because at the end of the day,' he sighed and stretched, 'I am a grown-up who has seen people die and I have suffered and felt grief and loss and all that lot, so frankly, if Tess was to snuff it right now, I'd only really kill you because society expects it. It's not like a grown-up is really up to *feeling* anything any more, not like a child. But you understand that, don't you, Greybags? Being as you are, so very, very old.'

'Stop it!' he shrieked. 'Stop it!'

'I'm sorry, stop what? I was just having a polite discussion with a peer.'

'I'm a child a child a child. I'm a child. I'm a—'

'*Lambkin*,' breathed Lin softly, eyes glowing in the night.

'Mister Lyle!' wailed Tess, closing her eyes.

'You're a lonely grey old crone too scared to ever grow up,' concluded Lyle brightly. 'All the other children managed it but poor little Greybags was just too damn scared to grow up and now—'

'I hate you, you don't understand. I hate you. Always think you're right an' you don't understand nothin'. *I'll kill you!*'

Greybags's scream sliced through the night as, with a shove and a snarl of fury, he pushed Tess to one side and lunged, blade-first straight for Lyle's chest. Lin stepped forward but Lyle waved her back, raised his silver drinking flask to arm's length and gave a final twist of the cap. Inside the flask, something went *slosh* and Lyle threw it down hard in front of Greybags' feet. The flask clattered onto the loose ballast, something inside starting to go *sssss*. Greybags hesitated in his mad lunge and opened his mouth to say, 'But it ain't nothin'!'

'Well . . . *no*,' replied Lyle. 'Not really.'

And as Greybags looked up with horror in his eyes, eyes far, far too old and knowing to be in a child's face, Lyle smiled and said, 'Good night, children. Sweet dreams.'

The flask exploded.

It wasn't *exactly* an explosion, not in the traditional exothermic combustion sense of the term. Explosion implies flames, fire and much rending of garments. It was simply as if something very tight and loud was suddenly told, *Hello! Would you like to go for a walk?* and as if the wide world were not wide enough to accommodate it, it came bursting out of the flask in a tumble of tight pressure so fast and so loud and so enthusiastic that it seemed to shatter the air round it, pick up the ground and shake it, slam the breath out of every pair of lungs within reach, and the way it did this was with sound since, as Lyle would be the first to point out, sound was little more than a compression in the air. And both were a lot more than what they seemed.

The blast of noise shattered the windows in the train, picked Lyle off his feet and sent him sprawling backwards, slammed into Tess's ears and made them ring, echoed down the length of the train and sent people diving for cover. At the front of the train, where Thomas had been imposing, with all his aristocratic might, on the bewildered driver the need not to move the engine, the sound cracked the already bewildered pressure gauges and rolled like a billow of smoke onwards up the line.

And then it was gone, as quickly as it had come, leaving only a high-pitched *eeeeeee* in every bewildered ear that had heard it as the brain tried to work out what was real and what was not in the lingering, total silence.

Not quite total.

The *chuga . . . chuga . . . chuga . . .* of the train.

The slow rattle of Lin's footsteps over the loose ballast of the track.

The crackling of splintered glass.

The hissing of rising flames.

The slow tumbling of hot steam from the engine.

Tess, trying not to cry.

Lyle knelt down next to her, hesitated, then reached into his pocket and pulled out a suspiciously stained and unappetisingly smeared handkerchief, spat into it once, and carefully wiped away the tears from her face.

'Hello, Teresa,' he said.

'Hello, Mister Lyle. I weren't cryin'!'

'Of course not. You know, blasts of that nature can cause spontaneous weeping-like effects as the pressure on the eyeball releases tears from the tear duct to . . . Oh, you get the idea.'

A few feet away, Lin squatted by the side of another body.

A child in adult's clothes, lying still and silent on the track, chest rising and falling steadily, blood running out of one ear. She looked at it long and hard for a good moment, then bent down, picked the boy up with a great grunt, slung him over her shoulders and turned away from the tracks.

'Miss Lin?' Lyle called as she started to walk towards the shadows on the edge of the railway embankment. 'Where are you going?'

She paused, half turned, smiled. 'Why, Mister Lyle, I'm going to take this poor child home of course!' And with a half wave and a little smile, the sleeping Greybags slung across her back, Lin, the demon-lady Tseiqin, vanished into the night.

Lyle helped Tess carefully onto her feet. She blew her nose loudly in his handkerchief and then offered it unconsciously back to him. He flinched and said, 'Tell you what, Teresa, why don't you keep it for now?'

'I weren't cryin'!' she snapped.

'Of course you weren't,' he replied gently, eyes sweeping the silent gazing faces on the train, watching them, unmoving. 'Now, somewhere round here is a locomotive engine that I pinched from Paddington Station.'

'You went an' pinched a train?!'

'Borrowed under extremely trying circumstances.'

'You went an' *pinched* a bloody *train*!' Tess beamed through her puffy red eyes. 'Oh, Mister Lyle! I is so proud of you!'

He patted her absently on the head. 'That's what I was afraid of.' He sighed. 'Come on, Tess. Let's go home.'

And so, Tess already cheered at the prospect of larceny, Lyle's arm wrapped protectively round her shoulders in case anything else in the night should even *dare* think of harming her, never ever, ever again, they wandered on together, down the silent railway track.

CHAPTER 23

Time passes.

When it has passed, what it leaves behind is this . . .

'Miss Chaste? Miss Mercy Chaste?'

'Yes? Who are you?'

'I'm the chief inspector, Board of Health, Marylebone district. Do you mind if I ask you some questions about certain financial irregularities that have come to our attention?'

'I . . . um . . . no, I don't . . . I mean, I . . .'

'Most kind of you to cooperate, Miss Chaste. Perhaps if you will just step this way.'

'But the children, I can't leave the—'

'The children are sleeping peacefully, Miss Chaste. I'm sure you can leave them for just a little while.'

And here are the sleeping children.

Not dead, not alive, just . . . peaceful. Utter bland peaceful nothings, lying still beneath their crisp white sheets in the ward in Marylebone. They do not dream bright and wonderful dreams, they do not run from crawling spider-legged nightmares. They do not dream at all, not any more.

Except, perhaps . . .

Once upon a time . . .

. . . there was a child . . .

. . . who ran away to the circus . . .

But why would they run away to the circus?

. . . all alone so ran away to the circus . . .

. . . Mama and Papa will protect you, children, they'll keep you safe, so long as you don't run away to the circus . . .

. . . once upon a time . . .

. . . once upon a time . . .

And they stir in their sleep, the peaceful empty children and, for a moment, as the trains rattle by from Marylebone Station and the chimneys belch and the bells clang and the carts rattle and the donkeys bray and the horses stamp and the boats creek and the city rumbles and the people gossip and the lights flicker and the wind blows, just for a moment, they dream of. . .

. . . running away from the circus . . .

. . . a child called . . .

. . . a great big running away, running from, running to, a great big empty infinity just waiting to be filled . . .

. . . once upon a time . . .

. . . there was a child called Sissy Smith, who ran away from the circus . . .

Sissy Smith pulls the sheets higher above her shoulders and lets out a little sigh in her sleep. She can't help the feeling that she's still missing something, some gnawing little detail that is crawling round at the back of her mind, but for now, the dreams whisper on, slithering across silent sleep, and she dreams. . .

Once upon a time . . .

. . . there was a child called Sissy Smith . . .

. . . who ran away from the circus . . .

. . . and slept for a hundred years, never getting old until the prince could wake her with a kiss . . .

. . . and they all lived happily ever after . . .

. . . once upon a time . . . Two figures stand at the end of the bed.

They're having an argument.

One says, 'It's never a good idea to know what goes into the medicine, dearest.'

'Ma, I am quite old enough to know what goes into an organic compound of this nature.'

'You used to moan terribly when we gave you your medicine.'

'That's because you'd always begin by saying "It may taste like a spoonful of dog doings, Horatio, but that just means it's extra good for you," Ma—'

'May I remind you, dear, that I made the cure in the first place.'

'Yes, Ma.'

'And saved your life.'

'Yes, Ma.'

'After you were so careless as to endanger it recklessly!'

A sigh of infinite patience. 'Yes, Ma. Sorry, Ma.'

'Excellent! Now, let *me* give the children the medicine and *you* can look on admiringly as a son should in the face of the work of his good old mother.'

A deflation, a giving up of breath and arguments. 'Yes, Ma. Sorry, Ma. Thank you, Ma, for making a cure and all. You should use it on the children, seeing as how you made it, when I just went and got myself mortally endangered and beaten up and poisoned and chased and punched and all that for the sake of this moment,' intoned Lyle wearily. 'You just go ahead.'

The sound of liquid sloshing in a spoon.

The tinkle of glass.

A hand moves round the back of Sissy Smith's head.

A teaspoon is pressed to her lips.

All things considered, it could have tasted much, much worse.

Time passes.

Thomas Edward Elwick sits in the smaller parlour by the fading light of the setting sun, and reads.

The title of the book is *Mr Edgehill-Peart's Investigations Into and Conclusions on the Relationships Between Density, Pressure, Mass and Thermodynamics*. It is a weighty tome covering several weighty topics, and, though Thomas is trying, the tedium of the text is beginning to drag his eyelids down.

There is a sound at the parlour door, and looking up, he sees his father, who, finding his son reading, immediately clears his throat and says, 'Oh, excuse me, I will find another room.'

'You can sit here, sir,' says Thomas quickly.

'No, no, I wouldn't want to distract you from your studies.'

'Really, Father, I would . . . I mean, sir, it would . . . I've nearly finished.'

Lord Elwick stands uncomfortably in the doorway, scratching at his thinning grey whiskers. 'Well, I suppose,' he finally mumbles, 'if it's . . . if you're . . . you know . . . boy . . .' The 'boy' is added as an after-thought, a reminder as much to Lord Elwick as to his son who is still, theoretically, running this relationship.

Lord Elwick eases himself down onto the couch opposite Thomas, waits a few moments and then blurts out, 'So what are you reading, young man?'

'A study into dynamic mass relationships,' replies Thomas meekly.

'A what?'

'It's entitled *Mr Edgehill-Peart's Investigations Into and Conclusions on the Relationships Between Density, Pressure—*'

'Sounds like a load of balderdash to me. Boring stiff scientists, what?'

Thomas hesitates, feeling the urge to defend scientists and all their wonders rise up as it had so many times before from the pit of his soul. He looks down at the page in his lap, wrinkled with crabbed notes and crawling, unintelligible waffle and feels the pit shudder inside him.

He closes the book. He smiles. He straightens up, looks his father in the eye for the first time since . . . since . . . looks his father in the eye and says, 'Yes, sir. It is very dull, sir.'

Lord Elwick grunts his disapproval.

'You should read proper stories, lad. Read them while you're young, eh? When you're a little bit older you'll have to read that dreadful tedious Gaskell woman that your mother is always on about – the tedium! It will be your duty to attend plays in town which that wretched Bowdler man has gone out of his *way* to make dull! Read a good swashbuckling novel, that's the thing for a young man, none of this science stuff!'

Thomas hesitates, then says, 'Father?'

'Yes, boy?'

'When you were in the army, did you ever have to fight?'

'Fight! Of course I had to fight! I was in the damn army, what do you think, boy?'

'You never talk about it.'

'Well, no. Neither you nor your mother have ever seemed to be interested. Things that were important at the time are just stories now. Not really important in the grand scheme of things. Not important at all.'

Thomas leans a little closer. 'Tell me about it.'

'What?' barks the old man.

'Tell me . . . tell me . . .' Thomas's eyes glowed. 'Tell me a story.'

Time passes.

On the island of Holyrood, the sound of evening prayers mingles with the swish of the sea and the constant, unending baaing of the thick-furred sheep nipping at the thin green grass. The sun is setting, and soon the tide shall turn its course and rush out, cutting off the island from the land once again as the sandy causeway between one and the other vanishes beneath the sea.

On this not particularly special night, at an unremarkably unremarkable cottage there is a knock at the door.

A woman answers it.

She is old, stooped, with pinned-back stiff grey hair and a tight black dress wrapped modestly around her bent old frame. But her eyes are bright and green – emerald green.

Two people stand at the door. One has dark almond skin, straight black hair, bright green eyes and a smile that suggests it was made for laughing. One hand is resting on the arm of her companion. He is old, so old he cannot move without help, every part of him is bent like a gnarled old tree, his thin grey hair falling from his skull, his thick grey eyebrows overgrown above his sunken green eyes. He moves his lips in the little, toothless silent old sounds that the ancients make when they speak a language only they can understand, and keeps his eyes to the ground.

The woman on the cottage step says, 'Good evening. My name is Lin Zi. I think you were told we were coming?'

The lady inside the cottage nods. 'A pleasure to meet you, Miss Lin. Will you come inside?'

'No, thank you,' the other replies. 'I have to get back, and the tide is coming in. Is everything prepared?'

'A nice room upstairs. Do you have any luggage?'

She is addressing the old man, who, at the sound of the voice, half raises his head, turns it on one side like a curious bird and giggles, drool running down his bottom lip. He sticks a thumb into his mouth and mumbles, '*Wanna play.*'

Lin pushes him gently inside. 'He's very old now,' she murmurs to the woman inside the cottage. 'Very frail. He shouldn't give you any trouble.'

'I understand. Does he have a name?'

'Oh yes,' says Lin, 'his name is Greybags.'

*

Time passes.

A dozen new trains are launched onto a dozen new railway lines, spreading out across the countryside to make here closer to there. People gather and cheer politely, break a bottle of very cheap champagne against the side of each proud green engine, eat the free nibbles provided, and then, their jobs done, slink away. A once unusual event, is getting regular and old, and the trains *chuga-chug* away into the evening mist.

Time passes.

The tide sloshes the sewage of London out to sea, and on the turning carries the ships of the sea into London to off-load sailors and their prizes: tea from the colonies, silk and raw cotton threads, drugs and spices, precious metals and ores, news of rebellions risen and uprisings suppressed, tales of this war in such and such a place, and the glorious victory of the redcoat army. Whispers of foreign gods and Christian deeds, of an infinite world of possibility, secrets washed into the port of London.

In Lyle's house in Blackfriars, Tess was interested and pleased to discover that the prospect of imminent death barely averted had produced in Lyle a temporary caring streak that she rapidly learnt to exploit. This exploitation featured no less than three breakfasts in bed over three days, *five* mugs of hot milk provided over a similar time and, at occasionally ridiculous hours, a whole stack of penny dreadfuls to read, one new pair of shoes, two new sets of lockpicks of different calibres for different jobs, one trip to a new fangled thing that called itself a restaurant and seemed to serve some sort of foreign French food, as if any self-respecting Englishman would *choose* to eat foreign muck! Two trips to the music hall, three trips to the local bakery and its sausage roll shelf, and a grand total of *no* baths.

Of course, no good thing could last for ever, and on the fourth day of this indulgence, Lyle sat by Tess's bed as he had sat for many nights before to wish her good night and make sure she really *was* tucked up properly and not about to sneak out and commit larceny, when he declared, 'You know, Teresa, it occurs to me that I might have been indulging you a little bit—'

'Indulgin' me, Mister Lyle?' Tess endeavoured to flutter her eyelashes, which immediately roused Lyle's suspicions.

'Indulgin' – indulging, yes!' he proclaimed. '*Mrs Bontoft's Practical Advice* says that an indulged or spoilt child is a useless child, an unproductive child, a child who—'

'Why *do* you read that book, Mister Lyle?' asked Tess, as sweet as sugar on a rotten tooth. 'It seems a bit rubbish an' all. Seein' as how it's for parents.'

'Well, I – you know – I'm the patriarch of this household and it's my duty to . . . to . . . you know . . .' Lyle flapped uselessly.

Tess yawned.

'Ah-ha! Time to go to sleep!'

'I ain't sleepy!'

'You just yawned!'

'Only to make you feel stupid!'

'Don't give me that, that was a proper yawn. What do you mean make me feel stupid? Mrs Bontoft says that respect for the parent is—'

'Will you tell me a story, Mister Lyle?'

'What?' he asked, face freezing.

'A story? To send me to sleep.'

'Erm . . . what about?'

'Dunno. Pirates? Sieges? Ohohohoh, do you know anythin' 'bout that Napoleon bloke? With all the really *bloody* bits an' all the stuff 'bout legs being cut off an' bodies an' everythin'. *Urrrrgghhh!*' Tess stuck her tongue out and bounced happily between the sheets in obvious glee at this prospect.

'Teresa! Polite young ladies neither go "Urrgggghhh!" nor do they take gleeful joy in stories of violent military campaigns!'

Tess thought about this, face wrinkled in concentration. Then she said, 'You know, Mister Lyle, I been thinkin' 'bout this an' all, an' I think that perhaps I ain't a polite young lady after all.'

Lyle sighed, patted Tess absently on the head. 'No, you may be right there.'

The two sat together in silence a little while, not looking at each other, shadows stretched thin across their faces in the light of the dying fire. Then Lyle straightened up and said, 'Have I ever told you the story of Sir Isaac Newton's investigations into gravity and calculus?'

'Borin'!'

'No, really, it's got good bits.'

'Borin'!'

Lyle bit his lip, and brightened at a sudden thought. 'It's got Black Death in it.'

Tess's eyes lit up. 'Really? Is that a really horrid death?'

'Your armpits swell and turn black and little pustules appear on your skin in a rose-shaped pattern, and it's spread by the rats!'

'*Really*?! That's disgustin'!'

'I know!'

'Go on, Mister Lyle! Tell tell tell!'

So Horatio Lyle cleared his throat and, as Tess edged a little closer to the end of the bed to hear it, he licked his lips, stretched his neck and began.

'Once upon a time . . .'

But as Lyle would have pointed out, any story with Black Death, even when it's responsible for world-shattering insights into advanced geometry, mathematics and a re-assessment of mankind's role in the universe (as well as a vague explanation of why, if the world really is round, all the convicts in Australia don't fall off), is hardly a happy ending.

So it was, that as London slept — or at least that part which didn't value crowbars in its work — Horatio Lyle stood alone on Westminster Bridge, and listened to the sucking of the river against the new walls of the embankment, the bumping of the little wooden hulls of the ships, the distant jangling of bells caught in the wind, the slow smelly hiss of the gas lanterns, the rattle of a carriage lost somewhere to the night . . .

. . . not quite alone.

Not quite.

Lin said, 'Hello, Mister Lyle.'

'Hello, Miss Lin.'

'You know,' she said, leaning over the edge of the bridge to look down at the hint of dark river passing somewhere through the sickly green fog, 'In my native land, young men are still in the admirable habit of composing epic odes to sacred rivers in a classical vein.'

Lyle, not sure if this was a statement he was meant to react positively to, settled for a muted, 'Oh.'

Lin smiled sideways at him. 'It's very pompous.'

337

'Oh.'

'You should see the hats.'

'Ah.'

'And you'd be amazed what they can do with a snake's heart in Guangzhou.'

'I see.'

'Mister Lyle?'

'Yes, Miss Lin?'

'Does your natural and boundless curiosity about the world extend to foreign parts?'

Lyle thought about this a good long while. 'Yes,' he said at last, a note of caution in his voice, 'but unfortunately, the current fashion among my peers is to exhibit great curiosity about foreign parts, journey to them, discover that they're not like Taunton at all, not at all, you see, and immediately go about imposing civic order on said far-flung climes.'

'And you're not tempted by this cultural occupation?'

'Miss Lin,' sighed Lyle, 'I have discovered, to my great distress, that I can't impose order on my own household, let alone on the classical poets of your native land. I can, on the other hand, induce all sorts of elements to assume an excitingly stable crystalline form through the mere application of pressure at a fixed volume and through this begin to derive some concept of the—'

'Horatio?'

Lin's voice is gentle, quiet, old.

'Yes, Miss Lin?'

She spoke long and slow. 'In time,' she said carefully, 'my people will fade and die. I accept this. I understand this. I do not blame any one man, woman, toothless crone, drooling widow or fresh-faced child. I am not a creature of this time. The people you call your peers have spread across the face of this world and with them come machines: railways, great engines, chimneys, smoke, coal, iron, steel. An inevitable future, power in machines, and no one, especially not humans, can resist power, whatever face it wears. You spread knowledge, science, order – crystal order – created of nothing more than pressure and heat, and the volume of the world. We cannot change. We are compressed by your science into this ridged form.' A twinge of something more than sadness, a hint of playful resentment entered her voice. 'You spread *cricket*.'

'Well, yes.'

'Cricket, Mister Lyle! You spread *cricket*!'

'Miss Lin, I wish you to know that despite my cultural background, I still to this day don't know which end of the stick thing hits the ball or to what purpose, although I can probably give you a mathematical explanation of the ballistic properties that result.' Lyle half turned his head to stare at her direct and rude. Her face was turned down to the river, her hands folded together in front of her, her eyes half shut as if lost in some distant world. 'Lin. . .' he stammered. 'I . . . can't . . . it's not . . .'

'It is inevitable, Mister Lyle,' she replied, not looking up. 'The world will change. Everyone must change.'

Lyle sighed, turned back to the river, drooping over the balustrade, shoulders hunched, fingers tangled together in front of him. 'Very well,' he said at last. 'I understand. I imagine I'll see you the next time some mystic chaos walks the street. Good luck – until then.'

Silence.

He looked up.

Lin was still there.

She was smiling.

'Aren't you going to vanish mysteriously into the fog to go and perform acts of unspeakable, scientifically unexplained – for now! – acts of mystery?' he asked carefully.

'Why would I do that?'

'I don't know. It just seems the thing you do.'

'Horatio Lyle,' said Lin brightly, 'for a reasonably well-educated sample of your species, you sometimes manifest the intellectual properties of what Mr Gladstone would probably term a complete dolt.'

'I do?'

'Does it not occur to you, Mister Lyle, that if change is all this world will bring, the inevitable unpredictable destiny of everything, a certainty of chaos, that if this is so, it is my duty as a modern, highly educated, extremely capable, breathtakingly handsome, magnificently nimble, extraordinarily well—'

'I think I get the idea,' mumbled Lyle.

Lin threw her arms open, not missing a breath, as if she was embracing the whole world. 'Is it not the wisest thing for me to do to say, "Welcome, change, chaos, and a future in which cricket is the sport of islands yet untarnished by the advance of progress. My name is Lin Zi, and I am here to make this future mine!"'

Lyle stared, eyes agog, mouth hanging open, waiting to see if there was anything more.

'Well?' she demanded. 'Come on, think about it.'

'Yes?'

'Well then!'

'Uh . . . Well then, what?'

Lin almost stamped a foot in petulant frustration. 'There are civil servants in the rural provinces of Sichuan with more social graces than you, Horatio Lyle!'

Lyle scratched his chin uneasily, head on one side. Then, like a man solving a great and difficult problem, he said, 'You mean . . . that despite the fact that you are the product of a people who have been known more than once to scheme in a distinctly evil way . . .'

'Piffle!'

'. . . that you have a tendency to resort to violence as a problem-solver. . .'

'*Please.*'

'. . . that you take pride in your ability to ensorcell and ensnare . . .'

'Wouldn't you?'

'. . . and that you, Miss Lin, wouldn't know a linear Newtonian force if it kicked you smartly in a region that even the grave-robbing anatomist would not refer to in polite society . . .'

'See how I refrain from violence right now?' she sang sweetly.

'. . . are you perhaps suggesting, Miss Lin, that despite all these hindrances, against society, wisdom, politics and prudence, we might have something in common after all? Something more than something in common?'

Lin's eyes flashed the brilliant bright reflected green of a cat caught in the light. Her fingers slipped into Lyle's own. 'Me, Mister Lyle?' she asked. 'I am a polite gentlewoman. I would never suggest anything of the kind.'

. . . and perhaps here . . .

. . . on Westminster Bridge, with the river below and an infinite sky lost somewhere far, far above, spread over an infinite world of infinite change . . .

. . . perhaps just for a moment . . .

. . . until the sun came up and the fog parted and the tide turned and the strangers flooded back onto the streets, until the next time . . .

. . . just for tonight . . .

They all lived, happily ever after.